Quantum Heretic

Quantum Heretic

The Helix Signal
~Book One~

William Cross

ISBN-13: 978-1-970554-00-7

1 – Challenge 1

2 – Rundown 7

3 – Breathless 21

4 – Prismata 35

5 – Penance 43

6 – Purge 53

7 – Menageries 65

8 – Escapes 79

9 – Counsel 89

10 – Spirals 97

11 – Beasts 107

12 – Noodles 115

13 – Chemmers 127

14 – Cadaver 135

15 – FLIPP 147

16 – Jurisdiction 159

17 – Productivity 169

18 – Dances 185

19 – Voidskin 203

20 – Excursions 215

21 – Skeen 227

22 – Payback 243

23 – Chase 255

24 – Deputized 263

25 – Killer 271

26 – Flow 279

27 – Processional 287

28 – Husk 295

29 – Revelations 307

30 – Decisions 315

SKAFOS REACH

THE SPAN

NEPHRIL

CARCINIA

ORBITAL LENS
(OUTER)

MERATIS

ORBITAL LENS
(INNER)

URM

KAEL

VEXAR

AYU

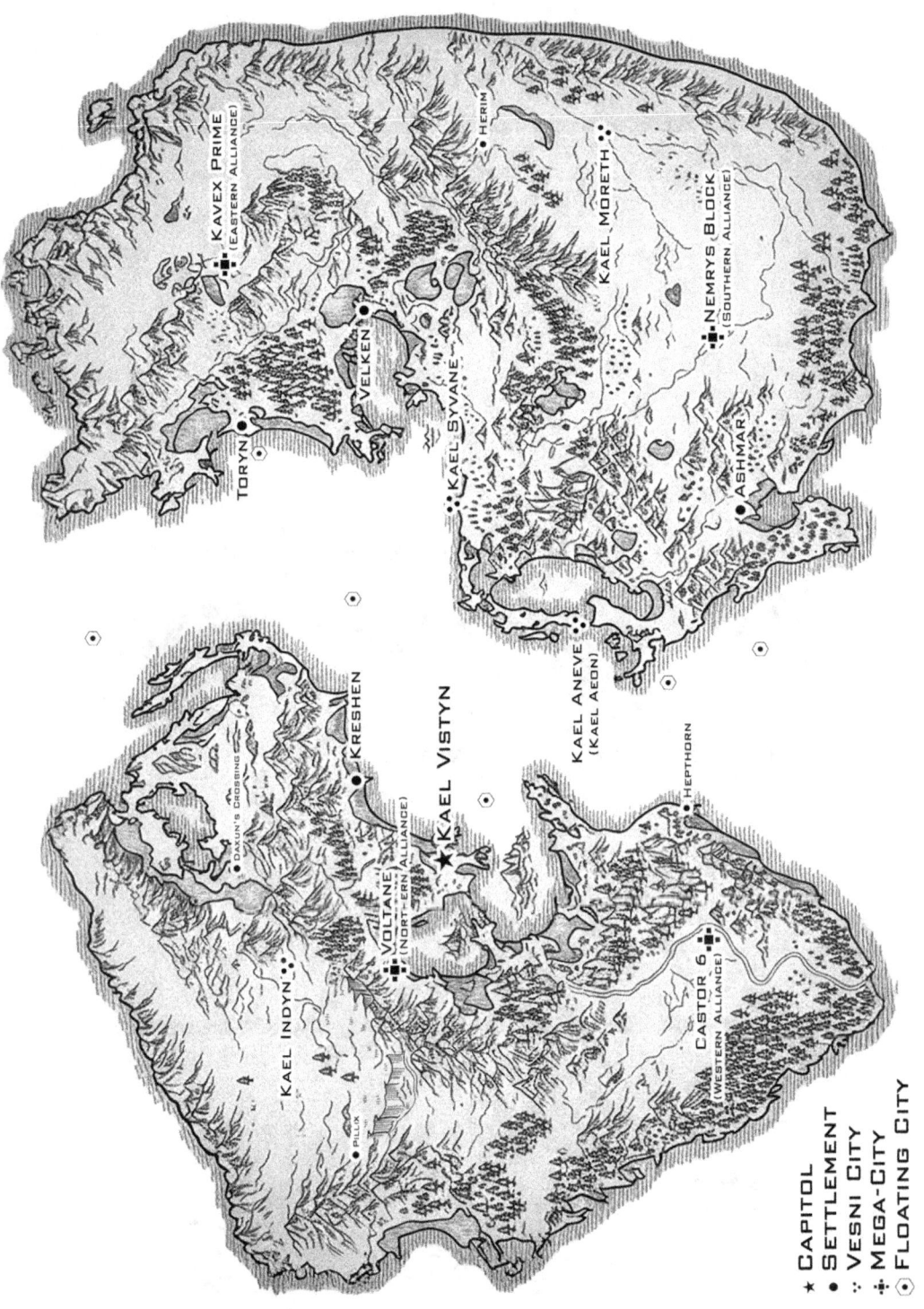

KAVEX PRIME
(EASTERN ALLIANCE)

HERIM

VELKEN

KAEL SYVANE

KAEL MORETH

TORYN

NEMRYS BLOCK
(SOUTHERN ALLIANCE)

ASHMAR

KAEL ANEVE
(KAEL AEON)

KAEL VISTYN

KRESHEN

DAXUN'S CROSSING

HEPTHORN

KAEL INDYN

VOLTANE
(NORTHERN ALLIANCE)

PILLIK

CASTOR 6
(WESTERN ALLIANCE)

★ CAPITOL
● SETTLEMENT
∴ VESNI CITY
✦ MEGA-CITY
◉ FLOATING CITY

vii

Vesni Hierarchy
(and male attendants)

The Mitera
(voithos-moro)

|

Earia
(voithos-ka)

|

Vys
(voithos-ka)

|

The Clans

Vaconix	Lauris	Eshota	Kharja

Sentinel	Sage	Visionary	Warden

(voithos)

|

Maiden	Maiden	Maiden	Maiden

(vikos)

|

Omyym Plainsfolk

The Heretics

Gharsa	Myrtu	Kosonor

1 — CHALLENGE

"It's pronounced Shard!"

Xard didn't bother to look up as he corrected the teacher. After all, he wasn't trying to make a scene. He had simply grown tired of being slighted at the mere mention of his name. For, although it was a good one, a solid one, it wasn't without controversy. In fact, it was the only thing he could remember his father actually giving him, so he tended to cleave to it more tightly than he should. In his mind, the least he should expect was to have some agency in what he was *called*.

Unfortunately, this world had other plans and rules—rules that had formed an ever-tightening cage around him. For it seemed that, through no fault of his own, Xard had inherited a name that could be pronounced using sounds that were considered sacred to the planet's ruling class—the Vesni Matriarchy. Yet, because he was male, the use of such sounds had inadvertently made his own name a curse word whenever he spoke it. So, he hurled it back at them as often as he could.

He hated everything about this planet—its azure skies, its fresh ocean air, its grand city-states of wood and stone and colorful mosaics. It all mocked him as a treasure for the observer, but not the participant. He'd heard there were other systems, better ones, but it took lifetimes to reach them. For better or worse, his forebears had chosen Ayu as the star they called home, and now Xard was left to trudge his way through the social morass they had built on top of it.

1

His new classes were almost always outdoors in full view of others. If the morning was crisp, they were in the orchard. If the afternoon was warm, they sat near one of the city's ornate fountains. Today, the tide was coming in, so he had the misfortune of being seated cross-legged under a crimson canopy on a high cliff overlooking Kael's massive ocean.

A sudden breeze gave him an opportunity to run his fingers through his hair. He cast a sideways glance out from under his long dark bangs towards the other preteens sitting around him to see if his comment had caused a stir. As the smallest member of his cohort, he often found himself trying to compensate by asserting this kind of surreptitious dominance whenever he could. If nothing else, he reasoned that it would be a good opportunity to test his standing in the group.

After all, they were expected to push the boundaries. Seizing an advantage was a skill that all good vikos would need to learn if they were to become voithos when they turned 13. Besides, Xard was growing bored with the training and the overly stoic nature of his cohorts.

"Cowards," he muttered when nothing more than a quick widening of their eyes was noted. The others simply stayed focused on the day's 'critical' training—how to peel a karob fruit.

Their instructor, Timeon, continued with the lesson. "Remember, vikos, there is always a deeper meaning to everything you do. Today, you must learn to perform complex calculations while simultaneously completing this seemingly mundane task. However, later lessons will require more complex diversions. For now, we'll keep it simple so that even the slow among you can keep up." It was an indirect dig, so Xard couldn't tell if it was aimed at him specifically.

Xard simply remained hunched over the small hairy fruit, fumbling with it out of frustration that no one had responded to his outburst.

His instructor was voidskin as well as being one of the few high-ranking males in the matriarchy—truly a rarity even on Kael. They were known for their keen intellect and physical strength, but their wit could be as black as their skin. He had hoped his instructor would appreciate his bit of brazen correction, but time continued to click by unfettered.

The moment didn't become uncomfortable until it became clear that the instructor didn't intend to respond to the incident at all. The boy next to him made a point to drop a scrap of fruit near his foot. As he leaned over to pick it up, he whispered under his breath.

"You are sooooo in for it, cupa."

Xard simply scowled back at him.

Sadly, his classmate wasn't exactly wrong. As a voithos-ka—a leader among the voithos—his instructor was *required* to administer corrections among his cohort of trainees. The fact that he hadn't posed a problem, and he knew it. It either meant he was calculating a particularly harsh response for later or he was saving the punishment for someone who was his superior. In either case, Xard felt a sudden surge of regret course through him.

Finally, his instructor broke the uneasy silence. "Very well then, present your karob fruits, please."

The cohort began holding out their fruits with both hands extended, elbows locked. It was the fashion all voithos would use to present items to their future Vesni matriarchs and was seen as an act of submission. Xard had barely even carved into his karob as Timeon moved around the group inspecting their work. He saved Xard for last.

"Alas, young *Zard*." He stressed the hardened pronunciation of his name so the class would hear it clearly. "It appears you're having some difficulty with today's lesson. Is it that your mind was

3

burdened by other unimportant matters, or were you just upset that the karob fruit is hairier than you?" Xard winced as the class all began to chuckle under their breath. "Don't worry, you won't be a Vesni consort until you are 13. You'll have hair there... one day."

The stifled laughter now began to erupt unchecked throughout the class. Rather than put an end to it, Timeon simply allowed it to continue and turned to sit down at a small wooden gaming table under one corner of the canopy. Xard was already struggling to make a name for himself, and his teacher's words had now pushed him even further down the pecking order. He sat bewildered with embarrassment for a moment before noticing that his teacher was beckoning him toward the table.

As the rest of the class chuckled amongst themselves and worked at cleaning up their karob scraps, Timeon leaned over the small game table and whispered to Xard quietly.

"I'm going to teach you a new game that is not well known on Kael. It's a voidskin game, and I will only teach it to you once. If you can learn it and ignore the social pain and distraction, you will be one of the only people who is not a voidskin to know it. Shall we begin?"

Xard immediately brightened at the opportunity to have an edge over his peers. He watched intently as Timeon's dark hands rolled several white dice and then placed several numbered bones on the intricate board.

"It's called kavarti, and no one can tell you how to play. You have to learn it by watching and uncovering the meaning of different moves."

Xard quickly became frustrated with the teacher's methods because not only could he not win, he couldn't even understand what the rules for losing were. The continued comments and laughter from his cohort made for painfully distracted learning, but he forced himself to block it out.

Timeon restarted the game. "Think. Today's lessons were about fruit. What is the fruit of each move that I make in the game? Learn what actions produce fruit and ignore the others."

Then he saw it. When Timeon made a move that didn't reach a certain space on the board, he abandoned it and chose another path to reach the center. When Timeon recognized that Xard had caught on to his pattern, he ended the game and spoke to him again very softly.

"When you discover a path that isn't working for you, you will need to do the same in order to reach *your* center."

Xard looked up at Timeon and grinned from ear-to-ear. His respect for him grew in that moment despite the present social aggravation he'd just caused. Mostly he marveled at how Timeon had been able to publicly upbraid him and still get him to learn the day's lesson, all while giving him what he was really seeking, an edge over his peers.

"Will we get to play again?" Xard asked.

"As in life, there is much more to the game than a single lesson."

"That sounds like something my mother would say," Xard replied glumly.

"Yes. Shayameen's had a life full of lessons, many of them hard and terrible. Sadly, I doubt she would consider your training much of a game. You would do well to remember that." As he spoke, Timeon pulled a spare bone from his sleeve that he had been using to cheat with during their game and held it up casually. "It's always the move you don't see coming that can alter your path forever."

Xard smirked again at this new revelation and went back to his space under the crimson canopy and sat dutifully cross-legged waiting for the next lesson to begin.

2 — Rundown

"We're just about to our descent point. Switching to lower atmospheric controls in 3... 2... 1... engaging."

There was an immediate hush as Shayameen's fighter retracted its array of static panels. All at once, the white noise from the electrical discharges which powered it fell silent. Shayameen looked up into the rear-view mirror at her co-pilot behind her. Her mellowed whiskey-voice broke the prolonged silence. "Well done, Drasha, barely even a lurch coming out of the static belt."

Drasha was stunningly beautiful, like all Vesni women of any significant rank. A stray lock of golden hair dangled down in front of her face, having broken free from the confines of her helmet. She looked up at it momentarily and let out a puff of air to blow it away. Drasha looked up into Shay's rear-view mirror.

"Well, my hair is out of place, so I think you're going to have to let me have the controls a while longer. Perfection *is* the Vesni goal after all." She could only see her eyes, but she scanned them eagerly to see if Shay had caught the joke, but she had already looked away. "I realize it's your name on the side of this stormblade, Shay, but if you want to take over, you'll have to fight me for the controls."

This time there was an audible laugh from the front seat. Drasha dropped her guard a bit in response.

"You're going to go places among the Vesni, Drasha. Count on it. You've already bested most of your peers in combat, theology, academics, the feminine, I could go on."

She stopped speaking for a moment and peered back at Drasha through the mirror again to stare at her intently this time. "The thing you lack is force of will. You have the confidence, but you need to be ready to exploit it. Despite what the locals say, the Vesni aren't thieves; they simply take what's already theirs. That's why you're still flying, and I haven't ejected you out of the top hatch." Shay chuckled wryly.

She turned her attention toward the ocean below. "The stormblade's yours for now. Just keep us on an unpowered glide until we're within 10 distance markers. I rather enjoy the silence before an engagement."

As Drasha turned the fighter down closer to the planet's surface, the sound of the winds over Kael's massive oceans were all that could be heard rushing over the canopy. A glint of sunlight against the badge-rank on Shay's right breast made her pause and stare for a moment. It was a raised star chiseled from one of the sacred rock-faces of Kael Aeon. It was made up of five individual triangles of differing colors of rock which fused together as a symbol of her rank of office. She studied it intently, thinking about how much it had cost her to attain. Two tan, two brown, and a single black triangle—she'd given her whole damned life to get that little bit of black, and she felt every bit of its cost.

Shay was in her mid-30s now; a raven-haired woman with pale blue eyes. Everyone told her that her facial features were the stuff of Vesni legend—an undeniable beauty, but she couldn't see it. All she could see were the changes that pain had brought to her countenance. Of course, in her mind she didn't deny that she had all the qualities necessary to become a future Vesni-earia, or even the Mitera herself, but for the first time in her life she had started to wonder whether or not it was worth it.

The sudden sound of the propulsion engines starting up jarred Shay from her thoughts. Adjusting herself in the seat, she scanned the approaching landing marker. "Take us in low. If we can catch the perp in the act, we'll have a better chance of ensuring he stays under our jurisdiction." Shay watched as the ocean gave way to the stark white cliffs and arid landscape beyond. "The location checks out. Easy to run a smuggling operation this close to the tidal areas. Target's just ahead in that rocky outcropping."

Drasha's response was clean and clipped. "Small enclosure. Single entry point. Covering the exit. Touchdown in 3. Stand by, we've got runners."

"Discharge the static on anyone leaving the field radius! I want to put eyes on all of them." Shay shouted.

Drasha began discharging the collected static from the stormblade toward the people scrambling to escape. Lightning danced from small protrusions on either side of the ship in short cracks and pops as it hovered in front of the compound's entrance. Several men on the ground wearing face coverings chose to take their chances and run for the exit only to end up falling rigidly before escaping the dusty enclosure. The rest simply sat down where they were and put their hands on top of their headwraps to await interrogation.

"It looks like we have a few folks here that know the drill, Drasha. Let's see what they know."

Drasha popped the locking mechanism as she gracefully set the stormblade down on the dusty surface. Shayameen pulled off her helmet and let her dark mid-length hair tumble out over her left shoulder, being careful to leave her badge exposed. She poured herself out of the cockpit in a single fluid movement and strode past the handful of twitching masses on the ground toward one of the men who sat cowering with his face to the ground. Her polished boots were all he dared look at.

"You there, you're the one in charge of this facility, are you not? Stand up," she commanded.

The man was ragged and in his late 50s with a poorly-shaven face and a large mole near one eye. He struggled to stand and shook nervously. "H-h-how did you know I was in charge?"

She stared at him for a moment, having sized him up by his response. "Your face. It's the only one that's not covered, that tells me everyone else is doing all the hard labor. The only reason I haven't broken it yet is because you asked *how* I knew you were in charge instead of denying it."

She paused for a moment to let him ponder what she had said before looking around at the natural rock compound. It was an open-air octagonal venue with high, natural walls and a single exit which Drasha was busy guarding. Within were several tents covering boxes of empty crates and a pre-fab outbuilding that seemed hastily created. Shay noted that despite its shabby appearance, the building's door had been recently reinforced, but it was otherwise nondescript.

The man finally ventured a word to her through his stuttering. "Why would the Vesni bother to come all of the way out here? Is there something wrong? We have nothing against the Vesni. We are just omyym. We follow all of the Vesni customs here." He began to wring his hands as he tried to convey his devotion to her religious principles, but she continued to scan the area as she talked.

"We're well aware that you are all omyym, but it's unusual for omyym to stray so far from the central plateau. When you migrate this close to the tide wall, it makes people ask questions."

"Questions?" he asked nervously.

"Yes, questions. Like why you would build a business this far from any natural resources or commercial traffic lanes." She turned her gaze back toward him and stepped closer. "It all creates a great many questions, ones which all point to one answer. If there is no commercial traffic, then whatever commerce you are doing here is probably illicit. If you had produce or livestock here of any kind, I'd write it off as simple nomadic bartering, but that's not the case, is it?"

She reached out with a snap and grabbed the man's arm and slid up his sleeve. "You have a dermal credit tag, but it's been dormant for..." She paused momentarily to scan his arm for his personal information, "six months." She turned to look at him condescendingly. "That's an awfully long time to not be buying or selling anything, isn't it Mr. Agarai? How do you even eat? Unless, of course, you have some other means of making payment, so why don't you just help us understand what it is you're doing out here."

Drasha couldn't hear the conversation from her position, but she knew the routine quite well. Fly in, assess the situation to make sure heretical or indecent material wasn't being peddled and then return. She'd done this a hundred times now, but watching the perps sweat never got old. Occasionally they would catch an actual criminal involved in something illicit that didn't involve the religious hierarchy, and it made them both crave the excitement a solid investigation might bring. Unfortunately, the locals got to handle all the grubby secular work. After all, the only thing that truly mattered in life was the Vesni Order, and she was well on her way up the ladder, hot on Shay's heels.

By this point, Drasha had nearly finished securing the other suspects. As she glanced over at her partner, she could see that the leader had begun flapping his arms wildly in protest, as if his private nest had somehow been invaded. It was an unusual display considering the fear most had for a Vesni-sentinel like Shay. Drasha reasoned that Shay must be playing good cop, so she put on the most intense face she could muster and walked toward them with her hand by her sidearm.

"You can't go in there! Please! It's not safe for you... or my children... Yes, my children! You would contaminate the growing environment!" he protested.

Drasha strode up to him intending to be the bad cop, but the man instead turned his pleading to her. Shay stopped him.

"Mr. Agarai, if it's toxic for your children, why are they inside? Your story doesn't wash. All I have to do is look at the door of this facility to know that you have some kind of techno-farm inside, so what is it? A grow-farm? Hallucinogenics? What?!"

The man's shoulders slumped as he realized there was no way out of his predicament without at least letting them see his operation. "Please, if you must, but put on a mask please because I don't want contaminants in the inner room. Then you will see, we have nothing of heresy here, no bad things, only good things for omyym."

Drasha whispered to Shay as the man fumbled with his access card to enter the building. "That dialect. It sounds tribal. He's probably just an old migrant who couldn't make the leap from farming to city life and ended up a smuggler. The poor guy probably fell in with the wrong crowd and just needed to support his family."

Shay didn't even bother to look back at Drasha but kept her eyes squarely on the man in the head wrap before them. "The problem is that the law trumps intention. His heart is irrelevant. If he's a lawbreaker, he'll eat what lawbreakers eat, and his children will eat from the same table."

As Mr. Agarai breached the intricate seals of the security door, Shay and Drasha could immediately smell the pungent wet interior as it began to waft from the entrance. Shay found the scent welcoming, in that it reminded her of the moist forest floors near her childhood home, but braced herself at the juxtaposition of being on an arid coastline. She kept her eyes trained on the interior of the room as she

12

fitted her breathing mask over her face. Drasha kept her eyes on the perp.

As their eyes adjusted to the dim light, they could see rows upon rows of thigh-high grey orbs lining the room. Instinctively, Shay reached out to touch them even as he pleaded with her not to. "I'm well aware of what these are Mr. Agarai. They're birthing pods. Although I can't say I've seen any quite like this." She continued speaking as she ran her hands along the moist leathery surface of the one nearest to her. "Are these the children you were referring to?"

He nodded nervously in the affirmative. "Please, there is nothing here against the rules. We just want to offer the tidal people a way to reproduce. Nothing more."

Drasha began taking a closer look at the tech panels next to one of the orbs. "No dermal credit inputs here. It's only fitted to accept K-rings. If there is nothing against the rules, why go out of your way to conceal the transactions with K-rings instead of using dermal credits?"

He turned and looked at her nervously and began gesturing more with his hands until Drasha put her hand back on her pistol. "Tidal families almost never have dermal credits. They live on the ocean cities. They migrate. Please. We only do this to help, not hide."

"As you are probably aware, reproduction requires a license and approval by a Vesni signatory. While I am not convinced you even have licenses for this activity, something else concerns me more. These pods you are using are quite large; possibly large enough to spawn ivos. You aren't planning to spawn fully grown adults here are you Mr. Agarai?"

He became incensed at the suggestion and spit at the ground. "What ivos? We don't have any of that here! Adult pod-born would kill us as well. Please. We're poor, not stupid." Mr. Agarai continued

13

mumbling as he tried to brazenly insert himself between Shay and the pods at every turn.

"See?" he continued. "We only grow children here. They grow normally. No crazy spawn! No killers! Only baby children. If anything, we make children that have higher intelligence and thinking, ones with strength of character... a-a-and will!"

Drasha's eyes widened as she checked the K-ring logs. She spoke quietly to Shay, "He has enough K-credits here to fund thousands of these birthing pods. And did he say they make *willful* spawn? It sounds like they want to breed an army of your son, Shay." It was a deliciously snide remark, and one that was not lost on Shay who simply turned her gaze back to Mr. Agarai.

Shay's wording was direct and almost mechanical. "While such birthing methods are morally repugnant in Vesni society, there's nothing here that violates theocratic law if you have an appropriate license to do so. Still, we are going to need to report what's happening here to the omyym authorities, so they can investigate your licensure. We'll also need to collect these empty K-rings. You can keep the funding you currently have, but since K-rings are often used for black market currency when moving Vesni relics, we will need to have them logged. You can collect the empty K-rings from the nearest omyym constabulary in 30 days."

Shay officiously read the man a required statement and picked up the large bag of K-rings. Then, without any further comment, she turned abruptly and left the building. Drasha wasn't certain what had precipitated the sudden exit, but she knew better than to ask in front of the perp. Mr. Agarai just stood there, mouth agape among his embryos as Shay and Drasha let the door close briskly behind them.

Shay returned to the stormblade with some measure of determination. She quickly stowed the contraband K-rings in the side storage panel and climbed inside. Normally Shay liked to drag out these kinds of encounters, but Drasha noticed a subtle change in

Shay's demeanor this time. She was skilled enough to pick up on it, but also smart enough not to inquire right away.

"You can bring us back to the station," said Shay. It was all the invitation Drasha needed to mind her own business for a while. They had a good relationship, almost like sisters, which was something not easily acquired in the Order. It worked because they knew each other's limits, but more importantly they each had a certain measure of respect for one another. Drasha gave another quick glance toward the front-seat mirror as the canopy closed. She was trying to catch another glimpse of Shay's eyes to see what they might reveal, but she had already secured her helmet in place and brought down the visor.

The initial ascent was uneventful and quiet. Shay remained lost in her thoughts for a time until Drasha tried to break the silence. "Damned things are so artificial—everything the feminine is not."

Shay half-smiled back at her. "Indeed. It would take some foolish desperation to try using those filthy things today." More awkward silence ensued.

Drasha waited a few more moments and then continued probing Shay somewhat timidly. "Have you ever seen an operation that large before?"

Shay drew in a long breath and exhaled her answer almost as a sigh. "Not that large, but yes. I've seen one once before." Shay suddenly looked back up at Drasha in the rear-view mirror and smirked. "Is my demeanor so changed that you feel the need to use a de-tangling protocol on me?"

Drasha tried to cover her fumbled attempt at reading Shay by looking away, but Shay mercifully began to chuckle. "There's no need. It's just that I haven't seen one in a very long time, and it was under much darker circumstances. Back when I still made decisions based on emotion rather than the Great Mother's wisdom, my consort had nearly convinced me to use one myself."

Drasha looked back into her eyes again. "I had no idea. Is Zard...?"

"No. No. He is my natural child, Goddess help us. I decided to wait on her leading instead of taking matters into my own hands. In the end we conceived. Faith was essential, of course. We all have momentary lapses in judgment, but the Great Mother always delivers us. Remember that.

It's just that sometimes the effects of those decisions take some time to completely efface. You get good marks for your perception, Drasha. Unfortunately, the pain of poor decisions is often carried alone. Don't worry, I'll do some cleansing meditation and get this all cleared out while you take us back to base."

Drasha simply nodded as Shay turned to stare back down at the ocean expanse below. The hypnotic waves easily lulled her back into her thoughts about him even as she tried to purge them from her mind. It frustrated her that they had returned now after all this time. She paused to focus on her cleansing rituals: Springs, Statues, Chasms, Rivers, but all she could see were his vivid details despite her best efforts to forget.

She closed her eyes and began to meditate on the wispy steam from the hot springs of Herim, but the steam simply merged into his long dark waves that mingled with his beard. She turned her attention onto the great sculptures of ancient Kael, but they only led her back across his chiseled lips and his swarthy broad shoulders. Meditating on the great chasm of the highlands was an empty void that was known to bring about a deep 'nothing', but today it only reminded her of the deep and consuming recesses of his dark eyes.

But the river? It was a sound of great rushing water, and it called to her now just like he did. The deep resonance of his voice always seemed to stay with her. The images she could put out of her mind, but his voice was a thousand men all speaking at once, and she cursed under her breath that his words were still alive in her head.

As she watched the oceans fall away below her, she finally gave herself to the memory of a moment they had shared staring out at the same sea many years ago:

***

"So, tell me more about your life before me," Shay prodded coyly.

Taigan smiled at her as he wound a large piece of rope around his forearm. "Wouldn't you prefer for my actions to speak for who I am?"

Shay guffawed. "I'm serious! How were you not snatched up at 13? Were you sickly? Deformed? It's a good thing I was wrapped up in training, or I would have been assigned a consort long ago. When they told me I would be assigned to an older consort, I thought it was a punishment at first." Shay paused to laugh to herself and drink in his smile.

He simply smiled back at her as he tossed the other end of the rope back into the small floating platform and motioned for her to step aboard. She sauntered toward him and leaned back against the sturdy railing all the while assaulting him with a barrage of queries. As she continued to prod him for more information, he steered the free-floating aerial lift to an ascent just above the tree-height and out of the range of any casual observers. Shay continued her monologue as it echoed over the descending tree line.

"You know, I could have renamed you when I took you, but I like the name Tai. I think it suits you. Did your parents choose your name at random, or was there some deeper meaning behind it? Parentage is important among younger consorts after all. It's how we assess their potential vigor and acumen. But when they told me about all of the things you'd already accomplished for the Order, well, quite honestly, I didn't believe them." Shay stopped mid-thought as Tai put his finger to her lips and slowly turned her around by her shoulders. She had been so insistent on him answering her questions

17

that she had almost missed the grand spectacle he was preparing for her.

She hadn't noticed, but Tai had led her to an incredible view of the Kaelian sunset over the city. The soothing golden hue of the waning sun now formed a warming blanket over her skin as the gentle ocean breeze began to rise. Gone were the sounds of the city and forests; only their breath and the wind remained. She inhaled sharply as she took in the sight. "I've lived here my whole life, but I've never seen it like this."

"Sometimes, the best gifts were there the whole time," he replied softly, as he turned her back around. "You want to know history and peerage, but that's how voithos and Vesni see each other. They look for points and status. But if you truly want to know everything about *me*, you need only look here," he said tapping his chest gently.

Shay looked into his eyes intently. She was warming to him, but she couldn't help but chide him gently. "Will I find your parents in there as well?"

He looked intently into her eyes and replied "I have no parents."

Suddenly, everything around her seemed to stand still. She took its meaning immediately as a sign of his absolute commitment to her. He didn't say they were passed on, or that they had abandoned him. Instead, he had used the ancient Vesni greeting in which a consort indicates that the woman is now his life rather than his own parents. She was amazed that he had learned such a nuanced sentiment and had found such an opportune moment to speak it.

She felt unguarded and yet completely safe in his presence for the first time in their union. He continued moving closer to her until her breasts began to gently graze his skin through her silken wraps. He moved intentionally, letting his hands glide from her shoulders to her cheeks until he held her face gently in his hands. He began to

18

whisper to her emphatically, almost desperately, in his signature resonance.

"Don't you know by now that you are all that I live for? I have no hopes, no ambitions, no dreams of my own other than to watch you in complete wonder." He let his gaze fall all around her face, studying her as his hands dropped back to her bare shoulders. His eyes feasted on her with every gaze; every inhalation lapped up her presence. She felt consumed by him, and yet she relished the consumption. The Vesni had trained her from her youth how to use her body to control her consort, but loving Tai had become effortless.

He placed one hand firmly into the small of her back and began to speak softly into her ear. "I may not always be here, or here, or here," he whispered as his lips slowly moved down her neck and shoulders, adding a new 'here' with every kiss. As the trail of intimacy finally made its way between her breasts, he paused to admire the strength of her heartbeat. As he held her there, with his lips barely grazing her supple flesh, her heart suddenly ached to pound louder, if only to close the slender distance between them.

His words continued to pour over her skin like a warm oil. "But here?" he continued, "here I will always be. In a hundred thousand worlds I've found no one like you. And if this world ever separates us, just know I'll always find a way to return to you."

Always find a way. The words soured her face as they tumbled back into her memory again. She had tried to carve those words from her mind a hundred times in the years since, but the scars of his eventual leaving never seemed to fade.

***

Suddenly, the notification panel began to chime. Shay was abruptly shaken from her thoughts as Drasha patched through a message from one of the voithos at her son's training grounds. It wasn't good news—another embarrassment.

19

"Something else to handle. We'll have to make a short detour before we're back," Shay muttered. "Bring us to the canopied training areas."

Drasha simply corrected the course without asking any questions. The stormblade careened up into the higher atmosphere until the planetary static enveloped the ship in white noise again. For Shay, the change in sound mirrored her change in mood. She had gone from wistful and longing to angry and incensed.

The reality of her present situation now hung over her like a cloud. Tai had abandoned her. After all that he had spoken and all that they'd shared, he had ultimately left her—alone. Instead, he went off to chase the one thing that was the complete opposite of her and the life she had built for them.

Now it enraged her even more to know that their only son was following in that same contrarian vein. Her sisters in the Order had all told her it needed to be stomped out years ago when Tai left, but she was still too wounded to do anything about it then. Now five more years had passed, and it had gone on long enough.

Timeon strode to the front of the small group of seated vikos and twirled around to face them. He was wearing his usual lightly colored, bloused pants and ankle boots, but the gold filigree in his over-vestments caught the day's sunlight in a spectacular way as he turned. He studied each student's eyes as they perched on their colorful silken pillows. "Life!" he shouted to grab their attention.

"Once confined to a small corner of the galaxy, now flourishes anew here in Ayu. Our ancient forebears, emboldened by the prospect of finding an advanced civilization, set sail across the stars with no hope of ever personally seeing the prize they sought. What then was their motivation?"

"Faith," said one of the vikos dutifully. Xard simply rolled his eyes under his bangs.

Timeon twisted his face in thought. "An accurate answer, if somewhat uninspired. Anyone else?"

Befuddled by not having given the *best* answer, the same viko blurted out, "curiosity then?"

Timeon gave the suggestion an equally flat response. "Yes, but how would curiosity sustain them if they themselves would not survive the trip? Remember, there was no way to regenerate at the time, so only their offspring many generations distant would have that curiosity sated. Anyone else? *Zard*?"

Xard let out an exasperated sigh at being singled out again with the unfriendly form of his name, but he responded with the first thought that came to mind. "Boredom." A subtle murmuring began to rise within the class at the audacity of the response, but Timeon chose to engage this time.

"Explain," he asked expectantly, placing a single finger to his lips as if processing an extraordinary amount of data about Xard's demeanor, the question itself, and the meaning of life, all at once.

"Well," Xard began, "maybe they already solved the mysteries of their home world and needed a challenge."

A look of obvious disappointment flashed across Timeon's face. "You think our forebears traveled across the galaxy because they'd solved all their own mysteries? Remember, the original travelers that brought us to Ayu came in response to an advanced helix-shaped signal, one that clearly suggested superior intellect. So, suggesting their motivation was to condescend to something more advanced seems a poorly drawn conclusion."

"No," Xard interrupted. "I didn't mean they'd solved *every* question. I meant that maybe they'd solved every question they *could* on their own. If the first travelers were the ones who discovered the signal coming from Ayu, maybe they thought there were more answers waiting for them here than if they stayed home and just studied it from afar."

Timeon kept his eyes locked on Xard as he spoke aloud to the rest of the class. "While *Zard's* answer is incomplete, it's not incorrect. The correct answer is that each first traveler vessel had its own motivations for coming to Ayu. The discovery of the helix signal simply meant they were aware of the *possibility* of advanced civilizations, but their motivations were as diverse as any human today.

"Some hoped the new worlds would afford some kind of genetic resurrection after generations of travel. Others sought comfort in simply knowing their offspring would inherit a better world. But some," Timeon paused as his gaze telegraphed his deepening introspection. "Some, indeed saw Ayu as a chance at one of the galaxy's great puzzles. It was an itch that could not be scratched with only an eye. It needed to be touched, manipulated, dissected, broken down into its smallest pieces and understood."

He broke his gaze with Xard and spoke directly with the rest of the vikos again. "We don't know exactly how many ancient traveler ships came to Ayu. Some likely never survived. Some were dismantled after arriving. But what we do know, is that at least one of those vessels contained voidskin." He gestured to his own dark flesh with a laugh to lighten the mood and return the students to an appropriate level of learning cortisol.

"Because of this, we can be certain that at least for them, Zard's suggestion of boredom may hold some weight. Ultimately, the first travelers to our star were likely disappointed. The civilization they came to see was apparently long gone, having left only relics in their wake. So, while their reasons for coming here varied, they all stayed for what was left behind.

"Now Gallamar mines cyptum and uses it to develop new technologies. They power our great cities and enhance our bodies. Sentia's life sciences study the system's unique biomes. They improve our biological functions and streamline our harvests. Meanwhile, our blessed Vesni mothers scour the ruins to recover and understand the relics of a lost era. Some have scoffed at these efforts, calling them wasteful. But what their science and technology have been unable to bring, the Vesni now can. Do you know what that is?"

Timeon paced back and forth a moment before trumpeting the word "Life!" again, startling a drowsy-eyed viko near the back. Then he drew their attention to his hand as he held it out before them. Rubbing his fingers together, a tendril of smoke briefly appeared and dissipated. "Once a wisp, a vapor, nothing more. Now, through everyone's cooperative effort, we live in a world where diseases and illness live only in our history. And while that has improved the *quality* of life lived, the one barrier has always remained—death.

"That is, until now. Some of you may be wondering why I chose this place for our class today. It's because this location is one where the original travelers were known to have once camped. Alone in a new world, around a distant star, with all their hopes of finding an advanced civilization shattered, they must have looked out on this same view and wondered what form of death would soon overtake them.

But it's not the dream of death that finds us here today. It is my great privilege to reveal to you that because of the efforts made by the Vesni Order, the Goddess has finally revealed to us the secrets of extended life through our own study of the ancient relics." The vikos began to stir, one by one as the weight of the announcement began to dawn on them.

"Are you saying none of us will ever die?" one of them asked.

"I'm saying that in accordance with prophecy, the first of two revelations has occurred. The long-awaited life extension will soon be available to all for as much as 200 years. The second, immortality, is yet to be revealed, and it will likely fall to *you* to uncover it. And this, my young vikos, is why you should feel proud to be future members of the Vesni Order. As voithos in the Order, some of you may have the opportunity to conduct first-hand research on the relics themselves. Who knows what lost secrets one of you may unlock next."

The class began to thrum with excitement at the news. 200 years. A discovery by one of their own had practically doubled the lives of everyone in the system. Xard sat abnormally still given the magnitude of the news. A strained look flashed across his face as he considered it carefully, but nothing escaped Timeon's notice. Seeing the unusual display, and not wanting to let a teachable moment go to waste, he silenced the class and motioned for Xard to speak.

"Teacher," Xard asked, "will everyone get access to extended life, or just *some* people? You said everyone benefits from our cooperative efforts. But, if that's true, why don't the kosonor get access to immunity foods? If they get sick, we just let them die. I mean, I don't think we even allow them medical care, do we? Since they also study relics, shouldn't they also benefit?"

Timeon's eyes began to close at the extremely poor timing of Xard's question. He'd been aware of their visitor skulking through the billowing silken walls for some time—it was his job to notice such things. However, he was unable to prepare or protect Xard in any way from what was about to be a very unpleasant confrontation. Timeon simply braced as he felt their unseen guest enter from between the sheer panels behind him.

A look of terror suddenly came over Xard as he saw his mother appear like some dark specter from behind Timeon. He realized that she must have heard his question, but it was too late to take it back. She closed the distance between them like a viper and struck him in the sternum with a heavy kick before most of the other vikos were even aware of her presence. Xard began gasping desperately for air, writhing on the ground as his mother held him there under her boot. The rest of the class immediately stood and followed Timeon's lead as he bowed and simply said, "bless her coming."

"Bless her coming," the startled class said after him.

"I hope you don't mind that I dropped in," she said through clenched teeth as she watched Xard writhe beneath her. "You're quite a good teacher, Timeon. I respect you greatly for that, but you seem to have at least one student who still seems confused. So, let me explain it to this one.

"The Vesni *create* life, immunity foods from Meratis *purify* it. The law provides that all who *contribute* should reap the benefit of a purified and extended life, although I am seriously contemplating whether yours should continue at the moment." Shay paused to look up at the class of startled vikos whose expressions ranged from stoic to fully terrified. She spoke to the one she thought best represented the idea of 'stability' in her mind. "The kosonor do not contribute, therefore they do not receive the benefits afforded to others."

Shay removed her foot from his chest and began to stand more formally. Xard's heaving gasps for air continued as he rolled over onto the pillows beneath him. He was seething with rage and embarrassment as he struggled to regain control of his own breathing. The light coming through the sheer panels around him only served to further illuminate his suffering to his classmates, but they didn't dare look at him.

Shay continued speaking to the class of young vikos with her hands gently clasped in front of herself now like a demure maiden. "Women bring life. It is the way of the Vesni. Those who fall ill too soon, the Great Mother can purify with the gift of food.

But she cannot be expected to sustain those who mean to destroy her any more than your own bodies could be expected to survive by sustaining viruses lurking inside of them. That's what kosonor theology is—a virus. We don't revive it; we eradicate it." Shay turned toward Timeon and smiled as if nothing out of the ordinary had transpired, and he turned to meet her gaze and bowed. The rest of the class bowed in response.

"I trust you'll see that your confused pupil will find his way to the local sanctuary when classes complete? He's likely to be scheduled for penance," she said flatly.

"As you say," was all Timeon replied as he held his bow. Then as swiftly as she had arrived, Shayameen departed, leaving the cohort to continue its training in eerie silence, punctuated only by Xard's muffled gasps. As the sun passed its sixth mark in the sky, the vikos rose from their pillows and were dismissed to return to their homes. Xard already knew he wasn't free to go, so he remained cross-legged on his pillow until all the others had left. He fumbled with a small nectar-fruit from the basket next to him as he sat there waiting for the inevitable chastisement.

Timeon pulled up a pile of pillows and rather uncharacteristically flopped down in front of Xard. His tall dark frame loomed like a shadow over him even when seated. He folded his hands in front of himself and let out a short, sharp breath as a preface to what would be a carefully-worded speech.

"As vikos, you are learners. You will make mistakes. If you're not making mistakes, you're not learning. As a voithos, you'll be so much more. To become voithos is to become the very reflection of the divine by being the bearer of both cups and seeds. Your service to the feminine as a voithos is an astounding honor. You know it, and your fellow vikos know it. All of them felt and shared your pain today. You are part of a brotherhood now."

Xard interrupted him and tossed the nectar-fruit aside as he spoke. "It's a brotherhood of losers bound to peeling fruit and dusting antiques."

Timeon stayed focused as he changed his approach. "You realize that all of them envy you, don't you?" Xard had been trying to avoid Timeon's gaze, but his statement forced him to look back at him quizzically.

"What do you think is the greatest fear of your fellow vikos, hmm? Do you think it's fear that they'll have an abusive matriarch? Do you believe they fear not being able to perform their duties properly? Perhaps you think they fear being assigned to someone with low status. The truth is, like you, they fear becoming forgotten, a nothing in a world that already has everything."

Timeon suddenly stood and reached out his dark hand to Xard. "As I said before, this is your time to learn, and you have asked a question today that's not been fully answered. Come." Xard reached out his hand tentatively as Timeon's dark grip pulled him up with one swift movement.

"I have something to show you. When you become voithos, the brotherhood extends to all voithos, including elder voithos-ka such as myself." Timeon made his way through the sheer panels of the classroom and continued walking with his hands behind his back. Ahead stood an ornate outbuilding overlooking the city that served as his off-day domicile. Once inside, he could see that it descended underground several levels as well. It was furnished in much the same style as other natural stone buildings on Kael, earthy with hints of understated opulence.

He led Xard to a small sitting area before continuing. "As my brother in the Order, you will be privy to certain things that might be considered 'sensitive' in nature. As you already know, your father and I were good friends for a very long time. It's not appropriate to speak about him or the kosonor teachings in a public forum like the classroom, but here?"

Timeon poured some steaming iluma tea into a small red earthenware cup and handed it to Xard. "Here, we can discuss all manner of things. I know you see your role in society as some kind of handmaiden or relic duster, but your father never saw it that way." Xard began to feel uneasy under Timeon's direct gaze. He calmed himself by sipping the tea and studying the exquisite décor that cluttered the earthen shelves.

Timeon simply leaned back in his chair and continued his uncomfortable stare, studying Xard's every expression. "You're a lot like him, but I know you feel alone. Powerless." Xard stayed focused on the bottom of his cup as he tried to keep Timeon from reading his expressions. "You believe your life will be about serving others and preserving old books and baubles, but it's much more than this. I believe that with time, you will find that some relics may hold your interest better than others."

As Xard continued to sit quietly taking in his surroundings, Timeon stood from his chair. He walked across the small room to a pale wooden cabinet carved with a relief on its face that Xard didn't recognize and inlaid with black onyx. He carefully removed a forearm-sized black pyramid from within the case and set it gently on top of a leather footstool in front of Xard. Timeon continued speaking, more softly this time, as he kneeled in front of the black pyramid and motioned for Xard to lean in closely.

"Although the kosonor are largely known for their insistence that the matriarchy is a perversion of reliquary scripture, they have other, lesser-known beliefs. The most problematic one for the Vesni is the belief that these ancient relics were put here for our practical use, not solely to tell us stories. Ever since the first relics started appearing, the Vesni have been racing to collect them all to prevent groups like the kosonor from using them improperly. In truth, your father lived the life of a servant to perfection, but he never followed the Vesni mold when it came to interpreting the scriptures found within so many of the relics."

Timeon gently brushed what appeared to be several sticky filaments at the top of the pyramid. "This is why we teach you to take great care with tender things such as the nectar-fruit. To pry this apart would destroy it, but a gentle hand will allow it to reveal its true nature." As he rubbed his fingers across the filaments again, the pyramid popped open with a sticky *snap*, and more small filaments appeared along each length. "Go ahead and run your fingers along each of its sides gently."

Xard momentarily forgot about his impending punishment and quickly became engaged in what was unfolding before him. As instructed, he ran his index finger along each side. He felt the sticky tendrils vibrate under his touch, allowing the pyramid to flower open before him. Inside was a ball of crumbled black material that seemed to be connected to the triangular plates on the pyramid itself.

Timeon continued speaking as Xard put down his tea to reach inside. "This item is one your own father was working on." Xard paused to look at Timeon momentarily but then returned to slowly examining the pyramid's contents. As he hoisted the ball of material out of the pyramid, it shook out into a kind of sleeveless black jacket with the triangular plates shaking out into soft fabric when properly held.

Xard looked at Timeon and risked a chuckle. "My dad took a priceless alien relic and turned it into a shirt? No wonder everyone hates me."

Timeon closed his eyes again and raised a finger in front of Xard as if to have him hold his speech. "Knowingly *damaging* proto-relics from the previous age is a great crime. It's one of many your father was accused of. However, he also had the uncanny ability of being able to find the perfect use for every relic he ever uncovered. There was much the Vesni learned from him in this regard, however, his interpretation of reliquary literature was considered beyond heretical. It threatened the very fabric of society."

Timeon took the jacket from Xard's hands and stood up in front of him, shaking it out as if to invite him to try it on. Xard stood up and turned his back to Timeon with his arms out. As Timeon slid the material over Xard's small shoulders, he could feel the sticky tendrils from the seams pressing through his thin shirt and sticking to his spine from the base of his neck to his lower back.

"Eww, gross," was all he could manage to say as the tendrils sucked onto his skin. Still, the vest was slightly more comfortable than it looked. It had a bit of heft to it, but still seemed to flow freely like a normal garment. Timeon guided him back around to face him and looked him in the eye.

"Do not hold your mother's abrupt demonstration today against her. She has lost much because of your father's unsanctioned actions, and the jacket is one they're not even aware of yet. What's amazing to me is that your mother even still holds her rank as a sentinel enforcer. By all accounts, she should have been a far lower rank than she currently is. You must understand that there are many among the Vesni who would like nothing more than to see her brought back down. If it were not for the Mitera—"

"Bless her coming," Xard interrupted instinctively.

"Yes, bless her coming," Timeon continued. "If it were not for the Mitera, many of your father's supposed 'indiscretions' would not have been overlooked. Your mother's usefulness and friendship to Her Holiness has been a valuable shield to you all, but it's not impenetrable. Your own failure to walk a steady path now could easily tip the balance against her, and she could lose everything—as could I. If you must be rebellious, do so surreptitiously.

Take this jacket and wear it right in front of them if you must. Take your satisfaction from knowing something they do not. Just make sure that if its true nature is ever discovered, you do me the favor of forgetting where you got it. It's an unregistered relic, but your word could trace it back to me."

Xard smirked at the notion of sticking it to the Order by wearing contraband right under their noses and nodded his agreement with Timeon's terms. He looked down again at the sleeveless black vest and ran his hands over the material again and again, curious about how or why his father might have handled it. As he gripped the ornate collar on either side of his neck, he drew in a deep breath hoping to catch some faint remembrance of his father, but there was nothing. It was just one more discovery about his father that seemed to bring more questions than answers.

"I... I appreciate what you are trying to do, but this will probably only make my situation worse. I think you've forgotten how much of a brutal skika my mother is."

Now it was Timeon's turn to wince as the profanity fell from Xard's lips. "Are my efforts to assuage your angst that feeble?" Timeon laughed to himself. "You really don't understand how fortunate you are, do you?"

"No, I mean, I realize that there are hundreds, maybe thousands, of omyym from the plains who would have fought to have my spot as a voithos in the Order. I get that. The problem is that I had no choice in the matter. I *have* to be here by virtue of my mother's rank. That hasn't exactly turned out to be a benefit."

Timeon cast an understanding smile back at Xard. As he lifted his hands from Xard's shoulders, he turned to grab a large gnarled walking stick. "I understand your situation better than you know. Now, I am afraid you have an appointment at the sanctuary. I'll send word ahead that I have released you to go, so my advice would be that you don't delay."

Timeon raised his heavy walking staff in front of Xard as he spoke and drew it back in a combative stance. "But just so you don't leave here thinking your father never did anything good for you..." Timeon let loose with a powerful blow to Xard's sternum with his staff, knocking him backwards onto the ground.

Xard yelped instinctively as he reached for his chest where he had been struck, but there was no pain. There wasn't even a wound other than the one his mother had left earlier. Timeon held the staff at the ready again as he spoke. "Put your hands on the jacket and keep them there while I hit you again."

Xard struggled to keep his hands down knowing another blow was coming, but he complied nervously. Timeon held back on his second swing, forcing the boy to flinch. This time, Xard could feel the

32

material harden like a shell in anticipation of the strike. As Xard began to understand what was happening, Timeon brought his staff back down without striking him again.

"When your father made this item, I believe he made it for you. It's a little big for you now, but it also would have been much too small for him. He most likely planned to give this to you when you were a little older, but it seems right that you should have it now. It's made from a reliquary material that responds to neurological impulses. It will harden like armor every time you can anticipate an attack, but be careful; it won't work if you are caught flatfooted.

Since you seem to have a penchant for earning physical discipline on a regular basis, I would suggest that you keep this item handy, and keep your wits about you more often." Timeon chuckled and pulled Xard off the ground with another swift tug at his left arm and escorted him to the door. "Now off with you! You definitely do not want to be late to sanctuary."

"You seem remarkably calm given the circumstances. How do you do it? You realize the Mitera herself will want to visit with you when she hears of this." Drasha continued probing her stoic companion as they returned to the station and checked out for the day.

Shayameen finally offered a nod back at Drasha once they left their local precinct. "No news travels faster in the Order than bad news. I'm sure she already knows, that's why I am headed there now."

"I swear, it seems that child would be the end of you if he could. I realize what he did was probably minor, but your enemies in the sisterhood will use anything they can to damage you."

Shay cast a sideways glance back at Drasha. "Are you sure it's me you're worried for, or your own reputation?"

"I meant no disrespect."

Shay laughed to herself as she refocused her gaze toward the tram home. "Not to worry. The sisterhood is predictable if nothing else. I've been at this game a long time. When you've been playing it as long as I have, you start to see that every move is a repeat of a past one. There's no maneuver here that can be used against me, Drash; at least not if I strike first." She smiled back at her companion as the tram doors closed between them, but the weight of her situation dragged her countenance firmly down once she was out of sight.

When she arrived home, she stowed the K-rings from her earlier encounter in the secure lockup she kept in her room. She simply didn't have time to log it at work if she had any hope of intercepting the Mitera before word of Xard's behavior spun out of control. She was becoming far too efficient at changing from her flight suit into her audience wraps of late—a skill which she had hoped to avoid improving. The armored pauldron, which was an indicator of her status in the warrior sentinel class, shimmered atop a long, silver silken sash across her indigo wrap-robes.

She left home and made good time in arriving to meet the Mitera, she just hoped it didn't seem too preemptive. It was a delicate balance to address issues in their proper timing. She adjusted herself once more as she stood before the great wooden doors of the Prismata, the Mitera's grand audience chamber. She then turned to one of the two voithos on either side and nodded to indicate she was ready to enter.

As the doors slowly swung open, light filled the room. Floors of rare and colorful woods gave way to a vast colonnade of white and caramel marble pillars and arches. The etched glass domes above and walls surrounding them diffused and refracted the light in such a way that the entire room was filled with shimmering color. At the end of the airy chamber, surrounded by attendants, was the Mitera herself. Shay approached uneasily despite the unusually close relationship they had.

She had no throne. Rather, she stood on a small dais as she met with members of the Order as a symbol of her strength. She was curvaceous, plump even, but she held herself regally. Even so, she was a beautiful woman, youthful even in the face of a decade on the dais. Her typical flowing white brocade robes were accented by the day's hairpiece, a large half-moon-shaped golden fan. The flow of the fabric over her skin decorated and celebrated each curve as if it was its own monument—a solitary orchid in a vast greenhouse.

"Shayameen, I greet you in the name of the One who comes," she stated as she held out her hand.

"Bless her coming," Shay replied as she held out a hand in reply and bowed slightly.

The Mitera wasted no time and turned to the handful of attendants around her. "Leave us." The immediate sense of isolation in such a vast room was palpable for Shay. As the room cleared, the Mitera removed the golden fan from her hair and closed it, letting her long, loosely-curled brown hair tumble down around her. It was her way of letting Shay know they were speaking as sisters now rather than in their formal capacities.

The Mitera walked down the handful of steps toward Shay and began to lead her toward a nook on one side of the large chamber with a white velvet chaise and three, more formal chairs opposite. "So." She decided to start with something simple to further ease Shay's obviously strained visage. "Am I to understand that you have uncovered an illicit birthing effort today?"

Shay simply nodded.

"Well, the omyym have always been slow to accept Vesni laws. Regardless of what many of my advisors may think, you and I both know they are not indispensable. If it were not for them, a great many of our own Order would be put to work managing the more mundane aspects of daily life." The Mitera continued with a sigh, "They commit these little indiscretions from time to time, but they'll come around. We cannot force a theocracy on them, they have to want it, as do the tidal cities."

Shay finally broke her uncomfortable silence. "If they want to live long, they will. When the omyym in the plains and the people of the tides figure out they can be practically immortal, they'll probably submit to any law we proffer. It's as simple as that."

The Mitera smiled and proceeded to recline sideways on the chaise so that her white robes poured down along the front. "You're always so pragmatic. I want them to *want* to serve the Order, not to feel obliged to. Still, the more we can ply them with benefits from the Order, the more likely they will be to come around.

Once they see serving the Order as a means to wealth, prosperity, and longevity, I think you'll find that they'll legislate morality *for* us. We won't have to push it on them at all. The real risk is in weakening relations with Sentia I'm afraid. If they think they can get a better offer from those wealth-hoards on Carcinia we might soon see a social apocalypse.

"Control is a delicate balance, Shay. Sentia thinks flesh is the answer while Gallamar focuses on the technology. The voidskin? Any combination of biotech is a valid means to advancement. And though they all seek cyptum to fuel their advances, none of them understands the ethereal nature of the crystal itself. All of them think the 'spiritual' will fall by the wayside as they advance, but I know better. When the blessed one comes, she will balance all three.

But, let's talk about why you think you are *really* here," she said matter-of-factly as Shay sat down in the formal chair opposite her. "I'm sure you are aware that news of your son's behavior comes to me constantly from all the little birds who want to clear a space in the nest for themselves. They envy what you and I have. In truth, there is no one else in the Order I would trust as a sister besides you. But there are limits to what I can do."

Shay just sat silently for a moment before tightening her lips and muttering under her breath "He's just like his father."

"You forget, I know Taigan well, and I know that you loved him. The two of you had something not often found among consort relationships. You actually cared deeply for one another." The Mitera paused for a moment to let the thoughts of him simmer in Shay's mind and then began again in a whisper.

"Taigan was a brilliant man, a true rarity among any voithos I've ever met. He could have easily become a voithos-ka consort and you a

Vesni-earia were it not for his leanings toward kosonor heresies. I put myself at great personal risk by making the decision that these leanings came about *after* your relations with him began, although you and I both know that not to be the case."

"There's still one thing that's always bothered me about that whole decision process," Shay replied. "Even though he wandered into heresy apart from me, I still should have been sanctioned. I don't understand why the council allowed me to retain my position."

The Mitera smiled knowingly. "Do you think I became Mitera because everyone loved me? Power belongs to those who can wield words better than swords. I convinced the council that it was the influence of the omyym people in the high-plains.

When they realized the story of Taigan's fall could be re-worked into a story about the evils of omyym life without the constant structure of the Vesni teachings, they accepted it and used it. The truth of it didn't matter to them as long as there was a parable they could use on their clans. As for you, when Taigan disappeared, I worked it for you politically among the three largest clans by framing you as the one who held firm to the Vesni faith in spite of your consort's abandonment."

The Mitera reached for a small flute of deep-red dorberry wine on the table next to her and raised it in Shay's direction. "To the love of a woman! The highest of all forms of love! And to you, dear Shayameen, who offered it unconditionally!"

The Mitera chuckled between sips and continued. "By the time we were finished, the council was singing your praises as the epitome of feminine resilience. It only made sense that they would allow someone who was the sovereign of womanly strength to remain in the warrior caste."

Shay finally broke out with a chuckle. "Sovereign of womanly strength? You didn't really say that, did you?"

The Mitera simply raised an eyebrow and sipped gently from her glass. "In truth I needed you. As a sentinel, you had access to the audience chamber. If you'd been demoted, our much-needed friendship would have died. I couldn't allow that, not while it was within my power to prevent it. Besides, as fellow 'sovereigns' we can discuss these delicate topics more discreetly."

Both let out a laugh that echoed around the chamber before the Mitera returned to a more serious tone. "Speaking of delicate, I want you to know that I have and will do everything in my power to remain your friend. But my powers are not limitless. Your son continues to press the edges of this rather small niche I've carved out for your family's security. Using the sacred sounds in his own name; discussing kosonor in front of a class of impressionable vikos?"

The Mitera let out an exasperated sigh. "Next, he will be tearing apart priceless relics just to see what's inside. In order for me to retain some semblance of impartiality on this issue, he must be assigned to penance."

Shay interrupted with a nod. "I assumed as much, which is why I already sent him to the sanctuary."

"Excellent. News of that will travel as well and show your devotion to the Order above all else, including your offspring. However, in light of the consistency of his behaviors, I have asked that the voithos-moro at the sanctuary personally see to his retraining."

A sudden look of surprise came over Shay's face. She wanted to object, but she didn't dare. Xard had brought this on himself, but her maternal instincts were straining inside of her. She tried to pass off her surprise as a joke. "Well, just make sure he makes it back to me in one piece. He has other work to do when he returns home tonight."

The Mitera laughed over the small mouth of her glass before taking another sip. "Of course. He'll be gentle with him. Just some mild retraining. He's only an inquisitor despite his reputation, but your son won't know that. Still, I thought having someone more skilled in torture than teaching would remind him of the seriousness of his offenses."

"As you say." Shay nodded in agreement, though she couldn't shake the feeling that penance with the moro was overkill. She'd replaced her own affections for her son with raw discipline years ago. After all, pressing him toward duty to the Order was the only logical safeguard against turning out like his father. The boy certainly had the same stubborn streak. Yet, as much as she fought against it, it was the only memento of Taigan she had left, and she secretly grieved that she may lose it altogether if the moro was too aggressive.

5 – PENANCE

Xard had taken the long way down the rocky classroom escarpment toward the sanctuary below. He knew that if he delayed too long it would go poorly for him, but he felt the need to ponder the reliquary jacket a bit more. The anxiety of the day's events had clouded his thoughts about it earlier, but now the long path down offered him a few brief moments to dwell on it more deeply. He could still feel the sticky tendrils clinging to his neck and spine as he brushed his hands gently over the soft fabric.

He kept his eyes fixed on it as he walked, wondering what the original relic might have looked like. He had very little recollection of his father; yet *here* was something of his very own making. He wanted to hate the tardiness of the gift, but he couldn't—pausing momentarily to imagine his father putting it on him. But his face turned sour again as he realized there was no father there, nor had there been for many years.

He sighed at how everything in his life seemed to be some kind of religious ordeal he was expected to suffer. It couldn't just be that his father had left, it had to be turned into a lesson about the waywardness of men. He wasn't just a child experiencing loss, but a young servant whose void could now be filled with the Vesni teachings. He'd grown up under the smothering weight of it all, but now his training had exposed him to other ways of life.

The worlds around Ayu's star had become a hotbed for their religious activity, but escaping their grip wasn't impossible. Every city-state on Kael felt the heavy hand of their presence, yet neither the omyym living in the plains nor the people of the floating ocean

43

cities typically saw their kind. Neither of these were good options for a boy of no means, but the notion of poverty with freedom was growing on him. As he pondered his situation, the sounds of distant drumbeats and twanging sitars suddenly rousted him from his daydreaming as he picked up the pace. It was almost time for vespers, and he had an appointment to keep.

Kael Vistyn's sanctuary was impressive. Although all Vesni cities had one, theirs was most well-known for its imposing atmospherics. Xard had never been here at this hour. So, by the time he arrived, the waning daylight had already begun casting its deep crimson light through the tarramen fronds that decorated its outer courts. Long shadows now mingled with the red and green hues to create a sickly setting against the opulent white stone, causing a slight queasiness to wash over him.

As he swung open the heavy metal outer gate into the sanctuary, he was mindful to keep a lookout for things he might be able to do as a penance. It wasn't uncommon for him to be asked what he thought was an appropriate punishment, so it helped to have a few things in mind. Inside was an enormous deciduous tree that soared upward a full six floors into the circular apse adjacent to the main sanctuary. Having been designed as a call-back to the theme of creation, its towering heights now formed a vertical menagerie for all manner of birds and tree-dwelling creatures that now perched among its branches. So, cleaning up after the animals was always going to be an option.

The thick humidity that permeated the inside air held the incense firmly in place while creating a thick layer of cloud-like mists atop the sanctuary's heights. Normally, the room would be full of voithos tending to animals and visitors from across the city. Today, there were none. Even his own footsteps could be heard over the distant chirping above. As he pressed further inside, he turned the corner toward the office of the voithos-ka that managed the sanctuary, but it was empty. Indeed, the whole sanctuary seemed abandoned save for the small enclave of musicians playing in the main hall.

44

Xard wandered around for a few more moments before venturing inside the inner court. As he cracked open the doors and peered inside, there at the center of the room stood the voithos-moro, waiting. He was a dour-looking man, tall and gaunt. His long grey robes did nothing to add any color to his deathly pallor. Xard's eyes widened at the sight of him. He knew him by reputation, but had never met him personally. He stood there as if he'd been expecting Xard for some time.

"Ah! At last, the little bird has arrived. Hmmm, to a nest or a cage, I wonder." His voice was clipped and dry, but he made no movement toward Xard. It was clear he intended that Xard should come to him and that every second of delay from here would be a problem. Xard quickened his steps and approached with the words: "I greet you in the name of the one who comes."

The voithos-moro reached out his hand as Xard approached and placed it on his head, stroking his black hair. "Yes," he paused. "Bless her coming." He continued to move his bony fingers through Xard's hair momentarily. "Hair like a raven. Ravens are loud. They speak when you don't want them to and fascinate themselves with baubles and trinkets." He continued, being sure to succinctly speak each consonant. "But. They are also free birds that typically repay kindnesses given to them. But first a test. Follow me."

The voithos-moro led Xard through a large red door in the rear of the inner court. It led down a long dark corridor and finally up a stony spiral staircase. Xard kept his mouth closed, taking it all in as he walked. Finally, the voithos-moro stopped and turned to Xard directly as he stood in front of another large red wooden door.

"This is an area not open to the general public. Normally, the place I am about to show you is one you would only see as a voithos who has completed their training."

Without further delay, the voithos-moro opened the large wooden door and motioned with his weathered palm for Xard to go in ahead of him. Xard's eyes widened. Inside the room was a large floating orrery with each of the planets in the system moving slowly around the central star of Ayu. Each planet floated in precise sequence around the light at the center with the help of gravity balancers suspended from the ceiling: Vexar, Kael and Urm, Meratis, Carcinia, Nephril, the Span, even the icy reach was represented.

The voithos-moro walked quickly to the point in the orrery where Kael and its binary planet Urm floated in a tandem orbit around each other. His speech became more officious now, as if he was teaching a whole class of students rather than just Xard. "This is an example of what you will see when you arrive on Urm for your advanced voithos training. It is there that your ranking exams will take place, and your future in the Order will be determined.

"Today, however, I want to find out what kind of voithos you might *possibly* be." The voithos-moro turned to focus his attention closely on the porous black rock floating in polar orbit with Kael. "It is a lightless place. You will be tested. You will be scourged. You will be... *enlightened*. In truth, the voithos are typically the only light the people of Urm ever see." He shifted his steely gaze back to Xard. "I want to know if you're ready."

He clasped his hands together as he began to speak, an indicator to Xard that this was now an academic session. "As a voithos you will become a living repository of reliquary information. Tell me, what do you know of the ships scattered about the edge of the system?"

Xard cleared his throat. "It was thought they were the original generation ships that brought humans to Ayu. Most omyym still hold to this view, but the Vesni teach that they were constructed more recently."

"Precisely. How do we know this?"

"None of the ships have the capacity for interstellar travel. They're all built for in-system flight."

The moro's lips pursed in tepid approval. "Correct. We know almost nothing of the original travelers, but logic suggests they would have dismantled their vessels for parts when they arrived. Instead, we believe these were built by their descendants. Look here."

He passed his hand through a small beam of light within the orrery and triggered a series of holographic markers strewn about the edge of the system. "This is the location of every known reliquary vessel in Ayu. Relics were discovered in some of the ships, and so the Vesni seek them out whenever a new one is found. Though they vary in form and size, their interiors hold a single commonality."

Xard hazarded a guess. "Technology?"

The voithos-moro scowled. "Ucgh. A raven's answer. Yes, but you oversimplify. Each held enough renewable life-support to sustain large numbers of people indefinitely. That the vessels remained as new, with nothing more than empty beds, suggests swift calamity—a disaster they prepared for, but couldn't outrun.

"Knowledge was lost. The exact nature of the cataclysm and why the ships were built, but never used, remain a mystery. So, tell me, why do the voithos study and internalize reliquary knowledge?"

Xard smiled because this was an answer he knew. "Because a living, oral history becomes part of the civilization and can't be lost unless all men are lost."

"Correct, and what do we call those who hold no reliquary knowledge?" The voithos-moro eyed him closely out of a single eye waiting for a quick response. Xard knew the answer, but he held back because he didn't like repeating it. The voithos-moro continued his gaze relentlessly.

Xard mumbled back, "They are the unwashed—tools with no higher purpose."

"Correct. This is why the omyym can only inhabit the great waste plains and highland plateaus. Those who do not learn to internalize the knowledge have no part in reaping its benefits." He stopped to analyze Xard's body language again. "You have a different opinion? Defend your position."

Xard's face twisted as he tried to fumble the right words out to avoid a sharp response, but the hardening scowl on the moro's face only emboldened him. He saw it as a very one-sided caste system and indicative of Vesni hypocrisy. "I understand that they are considered lower than us, but the omyym make almost everything on the planet work. They fix the soil, they manage all the banks, they collect static from the wastes to power our cities.

They withhold nothing from us. They don't ask us to do anything except pay for their services. Why do we expect them to follow our rules? We shun them like they are diseased or something when they do more work than we do."

The voithos-moro scoffed. "Quite the contrary! We do not view them as wretches; they are merely unenlightened. Even if a tool can turn itself, it has no purpose without someone to guide it. It's still just a tool.

Without us, they lack purpose. Without us, they lack a sense of place in the universe. We provide meaning. Don't you understand? All the goods and services they provide could be gone tomorrow if we fail to figure out what triggered the first cataclysm.

The ancients were fully prepared for it. They built a vast armada of arks on the edges of the system to shield and protect themselves from the coming disaster. And yet, when the cataclysm drew near, no one climbed aboard. Learning the reasons why remains our sole priority and the only mystery in our world today worth solving. Look here."

The voithos-moro pointed to several large lenses floating in orbit around the star. "These orbital lenses are the largest of all the artifacts left behind, yet we know less about them than any of the others. They focus the light of Ayu upon Meratis and Carcinia and float in a mathematically perfect orbit with them, turning them into habitable worlds. Their creation would have been a colossal undertaking, but all knowledge of it is lost because its builders were lost. We must discover why lest we share their fate."

He paused for a moment and then began to look up into the ceiling with his hands raised over his head. "The Goddess who comes speaks through the Mitera herself, providing direction and guidance for all those who listen." His hands dropped to his sides as he stared intently back at Xard. "...in order that they may not die as their ancestors did. Do you not recall this saying from your training?"

Xard had a question but didn't want to make it sound like he was doubting, so he tried to think of a way to rephrase what he was thinking. "Teacher, how should we respond to those who doubt that the Mitera actually hears from the Goddess? How do we convince them?"

The voithos-moro smiled a broad but knowing smile. He answered as if Xard had asked it himself anyway. "I myself once doubted until I saw her enveloped in light. I could hear the words being spoken to her with my own ears, though I could not understand what was said. Have faith, little raven. The Goddess is guiding us into all understanding so that we can interpret the signs in time to save ourselves."

Xard interrupted. "But how do you know, uhm, I mean, *we* know, that the lights and sounds were the Goddess herself?"

The voithos-moro quickly retreated into moral superiority to shame Xard with his knowledge. "I said I didn't understand what was said, not that the sounds weren't language. It was clearly a pre-cataclysmic language, the likes of which few have heard even in academic settings. It was a language your father was studying out in the highlands among the standing stones." He squinted at Xard. "For someone

49

who seems to want everyone to know about his father, you seem to know surprisingly little."

"I didn't say I wanted people to know about my father," he shot back.

"And yet you act as if you do." The voithos-moro's countenance now turned distinctly darker. "Did you know that he was once a hero of the Order? How do you think we unlocked so many of the secrets we now know? How else would we have developed freedom from disease?

He made more progress in a handful of years than had been done in all the centuries before. And yet, all you want to highlight about him is his dalliance with the kosonor. If you want to be angry that the Vesni withhold such boons from heretics, who do you think is to blame? It was your own father who uncovered the technology and gave it to the Vesni, not the kosonor.

We then proffered that reliquary understanding of Kael's biomes to Sentia so they could create the actual immunity foods. Naturally, it fell to us to decide how to distribute it. Your father would have known that." The voithos-moro seethed at Xard for a moment on account of the day's insolence. "He would be so ashamed of you if he could see you now."

The voithos-moro paused for a moment, delighting in the damage his words had done to Xard. He could see the pain on his face. It was a delicate tactic, but it needed to be followed up quickly with a salve lest it fester into a rage. His goal was to wound Xard into seeing the Vesni as the light-bearers of the world, so he watched Xard closely for any kind of physical expression that he had internalized the wound. Then he pressed on toward his grand finale.

"Nevertheless, redemption for ignorance is always possible. When the time is right, you will be sent for your advanced voithos training on Urm. There, you will bear witness to the miraculous power of our Goddess firsthand. The light speaks, the dead come to life, power

50

and knowledge appear from nothing. It will be an experience you will dwell on the rest of your life.

Have you never wondered why the voithos don't just rise up and overthrow the Matriarchy? It's because when they go to Urm, they learn the truth of the Goddess. They become brothers in service and in unraveling great mysteries. Yet, you seem content with questioning things that *already* have answers. Meanwhile there is an entire civilization's worth of information out there needing to be restored."

The voithos-moro bent down and placed his skeletal face close to Xard's. "You are inquisitive, but your efforts are mis-spent. That's why I'm going to show you something no one of your stature has ever seen. When this day is over, you will know more than many voithos twice your age and far more than your peers. Consider it a gesture of good faith that some view your rebelliousness as mere eagerness to discover greater truths. This will be enlightening for you, but sadly there is no enlightenment without pain. Come."

6 – PURGE

The voithos-moro led Xard from the orrery into an adjacent chamber. "You will need to disrobe here. Beyond this chamber is the purging walk. To gain entrance to the vault beyond, it's necessary to be free of any micro toxins or bacteria which might damage the delicate relics inside. When the door in front of you unlocks, you will pass down the hallway to the right holding the railing on your left. Do not open your eyes for any reason. The nanite gas is designed to exfoliate the upper layer of human skin, but it has been known to burn and scar the eyes as well."

Xard returned a horrified look to the voithos-moro, but his gaunt face gave no indication that he cared. He continued. "When you reach the chamber at the end of the corridor you will find a robe that you can wear while inside the vault. I will meet you at the other end when you are dressed." Without any further word, the voithos-moro left him there, presumably to follow his own separate purging walk.

Xard hung his belongings on a small hook on the wall and heard the door in front of him unlatch. The corridor was completely out-of-place among the sanctuary's rough-hewn wood and marble. It was made of a smooth white enamel which was accessible via a small set of metal stairs. It was completely unlit except for the layer of fluorescent blue light about three steps down where the nanites undoubtedly began.

A voice emanated from an unseen intercom. "The darkness is necessary to prevent cyptum from entering the chamber; the nanites will take care of the rest. There is a railing on the opposite wall. Hold the railing as you were instructed and proceed to the right." Xard

53

stepped down the first few stairs until his foot broke the nanite plane. It felt warm on his skin, and he began to step forward into the tingling corridor. As the door closed behind him, he fumbled toward the handrail and gripped it tightly with his left hand before turning and walking forward into the darkness.

The walk seemed endless.

The longer he walked, the more the nanites began to burn. He clenched his eyes tightly, but the rest of him began to feel like it was on fire. Everywhere on his exposed skin, he began to itch and then burn.

The intercom crackled again "Don't stop. Keep walking."

Xard was scared now; something was wrong. He could feel a wetness on his legs and arms. Was he bleeding? He couldn't stop to look. The burning was becoming so intense he started crying. He hurried along the corridor as fast as he could shuffle, but the handrail just continued.

The intercom crackled again. "Just a bit further."

Xard was frantic now. His crying had inadvertently allowed some of the nanite gas into his mouth. His tongue began to itch and then peel as the nanites worked to strip away the upper layer of cells.

"Stop!" came the voice from the intercom. "Reach to your right. There's a handle. Pull it to purge the corridor." Xard stumbled to the handle and pulled it as many times as he could until the gas began to recede. He slumped to the smooth floor and curled up into a ball, his cries echoing audibly down the darkened hallway. He lay there in the dark for several moments until a hatch next to him opened, and light began to fill the now-empty corridor.

As he wiped away the tears and regained his composure, he glanced at his body to see the damage, but other than some minor redness, he was physically fine. He was still shaking from the pain on his skin and his tongue when he noticed that the corridor he had just traveled was simply a large circle. The notion that he must have passed this hatch three or four times in his walk through the darkness only made him angrier and more confused. He stumbled to his feet and darted into the adjacent room to cover himself with the oversized black robe he found and winced as it touched his raw skin.

The voithos-moro emerged from the adjoining chamber in the same clothes he had worn at the entrance. The slightly upturned corners of his mouth belied his normally stoic expression. "It was necessary. Come." Xard wiped the remaining tears from his eyes and put on the most serious face he could muster. He knew this was a game now. They all played it, and he wasn't about to give the voithos-moro the satisfaction of winning.

Xard choked out the most pathetic sounding, "as you say" from between his raw red lips and tongue, but inside he hurled them with venom. He would destroy them for this. The whole Order was an abusive sham, and he was going to make a mockery of them to the whole stellar system. He held no affection for his mother, but he held even less for the Vesni and their Goddess-worshiping brutality. The pain gave him focus, and he followed the smirking moro into the adjoining room.

The gaunt figure continued to walk very uprightly in front of Xard into yet another dark room without looking back. Xard winced at the thought of entering yet another lightless place, but the moro was in complete control. His every movement a clockwork of precise discipline. His rigid gait ticked mechanically as he stepped up onto a small platform in the center of the room and clasped his hands together in a specific tempo five times.

Xard already felt hobbled and small next to him, but as the lights began to illuminate the room, he felt even smaller. It was a vast chamber; probably the size of an entire level of the sanctuary and twice as high. His mouth fell agape as the light began to reflect off the white enamel walls and illuminate scores of large and unique relics from a lost age. Each one was a magnificent artifact suspended in place.

"There are no maps or building schematics that show the place you are now standing. There are no lifts or doors, save the one you entered and my own access door. This room is entirely unknown to the people of Kael." The voithos-moro impatiently beckoned to the shambling Xard as he strode toward a long black cloth. It was a tapestry of sorts, suspended at eye-level and running almost the full length of the chamber.

"This room is also unknown to the Mitera herself. In fact, *none* of the Vesni matriarchy are even aware of its existence. The cloth you see before you was found rolled up on the high plateau, the place your father once worked. You asked me earlier how I knew that the Mitera hears from the Goddess. This is how I know."

The voithos-moro gently brushed his fingers along the long black cloth until images began to appear on its surface. It reacted to his physical touch by revealing a story along its length. He caressed it almost sensually, explaining each mystery that he had unlocked as his bony fingers fumbled across its surface. "This is the story of all of us. Though it makes no mention of the original inhabitants, it speaks of our arrival in Ayu, and how in our hubris, we expanded across the system in search of cyptum. The result was nothing short of cataclysmic.

As we expanded onto Urm and began to mine its surface, we unwittingly created a planet-sized bomb right over our heads. No one knew then that cyptum required the star's continuous light to remain stable when uncompressed. So, the voidskin flocked there in great numbers, harvesting the bright red ore from its subsurface. Here you can see the great migration to Urm led by these black figures. They became rich and powerful, but riches belong to the Goddess."

The voithos-moro snapped his fingers at Xard. "Look here. This symbol is one we believe means 'judgment.' Place your fingers here and explain what you see." Xard wasn't sure how willing he was to touch anything marked 'judgment,' but he did as he was told.

As he anticipated, it responded to him and illuminated an image of the planetary system on the fabric. Xard's mind, however, suddenly became overwhelmed with a surreal flood of images and sensations he did *not* expect. In his mind, he could even see and feel the distance between the planets and the fragility of each one as they danced around their star. He was suddenly one with the scene. When the planets came into alignment, however, time began to slow as he watched Urm's scarred and over-mined, red side plunge into darkness. It exploded with such force that part of Kael's atmosphere was stripped away in the resulting blast. With it, came the screams of millions of voidskin men and women.

Xard immediately screamed and lurched back away from the tapestry. His emotions, already overwhelmed from what he had just been through, suddenly became charged again by the emotional pain of millions of people who no longer existed. It was so personal—so raw. The voithos-moro was unimpressed.

"Stop being ridiculous! I just wanted you to read the fabric because you will be doing a lot of similar work when you become a voithos! Do you not understand that this could have been a very painful day for you? Instead, I have offered you leniency and preferential treatment in the hopes that one day you will bring me some other artifact for my personal reliquary. Because of your mother's relationship with the Mitera, you will undoubtedly be afforded your choice of relic sites, fool!"

It became immediately clear to Xard that the voithos-moro had not understood what he had just experienced. Rather than explain it, Xard stood back up quickly and apologized. "The tapestry, it shows that the planets aligned and blocked the sunlight. Then Urm exploded." Xard tried to hide his shaking as he spoke.

"Yes. Yes, that's good. Perhaps we'll make a reliquary historian of you yet," he replied. "Now that I have explained what I hope to receive from you one day in exchange for my graciousness, I want to explain to you the reason for such a request. Look here. Do you see this point on the tapestry? Beyond this point are all future events. The things written on this tapestry are known by only me. It has been an essential element in helping to unlock other key relics."

He paused to look back at Xard directly. "The things that the Mitera reports she has heard from the Goddess are identical to what is written along this fabric. No one has even seen this fabric but you and me. It is my safeguard against heresy. So long as I can confirm what she says aligns with what I have seen in this tapestry, I have complete faith in her as an emissary of the Goddess. This is also why I publicly rejected your father's heretical leanings. However, I believe there may be more relics such as this hiding among the high plains, and they belong in here with *me*."

Xard suddenly began to realize that he had more of a position to play than he originally thought. Still, he pressed on as the ignorant student for the time being. He was afraid to touch the fabric and possibly lose his composure again, but he had to know more. "What does the fabric say about the future? May I see?"

"Inquisitive now?" The voithos-moro let out a guttural bellow. "Follow me toward the furthest end." Xard resisted the urge to touch the fabric as they walked along its length knowing that his reaction might give away the fact that the tapestry offered more than he was letting on. "Here is the prophecy of the dragons of Kael and the return of the Goddess."

The voithos-moro ran his hands along the surface revealing a series of images which showed dragons breaking forth all over Kael. "Here we see a future in which Kael is overwhelmed by beasts from the sea. I suspect it's symbolic of the death cult who worship such things. But here we see another symbol which comes to save the people of Kael.

You of all people should recognize it. It's the symbol for your mother's house."

Xard leaned in close to see the symbol of a two-headed dragon. "It's a vaconis."

The voithos-moro scowled again but refrained from striking Xard. "It's a vaco*nix*, the female of the species. See here, it's giving birth to an egg which holds Kael's salvation in it. Most likely it's an indicator of the constellation Vaconix.

This is why we keep our observatory focused on that segment of the sky. I believe the original inhabitants who survived whatever cataclysm took place here left for those distant stars. Perhaps one day our Goddess will return from there. When she does, she will bring everlasting life, represented by this egg."

He pointed to another small section of the tapestry. "Here you see the final montage; the end of the story. You can see the two twins here, Kael and Urm, locked together with this white figure establishing her throne on Kael. The script is ancient, but it reads: THE MONARCH WILL ESTABLISH THE THRONE at... but the remaining word hasn't been deciphered yet. Based on the flow and structure of the sentence, the word is a place marker of some kind, but it's not clear from the tapestry. All that is known is that the Goddess will establish her throne—somewhere."

Xard could no longer resist reaching out again to touch the tapestry. As the fabric ignited the story along its threads, Xard's mind flooded again with sights and emotions as he saw the twins not as planets, but as two humans dressed in white, locked in a physical conflict. THE MONARCH WILL ESTABLISH THE THRONE at...

Something didn't sit right as the words danced across his eyes. Touch seemed to convey more than mere letters did. The word 'monarch' written in the script was communicating more than just majesty. It communicated masculinity as well. This wasn't a prophecy about a Goddess. It was about the end of a tyrant and the reign of a king!

Even the threads of the tapestry were woven differently at this end, suggesting a divergence of time lines which merged again at the end. Planes of existence collapsed in on one another and cascaded across his mind as future-memory. The words themselves now carried more than ideas, they also carried a signal across every time line—a signal that was searching for something or someone.

Time seemed to stand still as his mind continued to explode with understanding. Xard didn't know how to pronounce the last word either, but he knew intuitively from the vision what it meant. It *did* infer a 'place' as was suggested, but it was merely a reference to the back of the fabric. The mysterious word the voithos-moro could not discern was simply telling him to look on the back for more!

He couldn't discern much more without seeing the reverse, but one thing was immediately certain—the entire Vesni theology had been built on a *lie*. His mind absorbed it. Internalized it. Consuming meaning from the images in a sliver of time. Yet, before he could even fully form his thoughts into a statement, the voithos-moro struck him on his raw hand.

"Do not mistake my familiarity as permissiveness. You are still a viko, and I am the voithos-moro of this city. You will move and do what I say and when I say it and not before. I only invited you to touch the artifact once because I wanted to give you a taste of the divine, not let you feast on it. If you want more, then complete your training and find a way to get assigned to the high plateau like your father. Now that you understand what I'm looking for, if you bring it to me, you may be afforded another chance to look at the artifacts here a few years from now."

Xard became suddenly very irritated again that his newfound interest in ancient relics was being immediately quashed. It had become a drug to him, and he was instantly addicted. The voithos-moro needed him because he knew he would have access to assignments not normally afforded to the average voithos. He wasn't sure yet if the voithos-moro was simply trying to consolidate personal power for himself or if he was genuinely a student of Vesni lore. In either case, he considered him a fool for sharing this huge piece of leverage with him.

The fact that there was a piece of reliquary history being withheld from the Mitera was already very valuable information. He couldn't expose him outright, because the moro had a reputation for making problems disappear. What bothered him most was that the Vesni religion he already despised was being foisted on the entire planet by people who didn't even understand what the relics meant. Yet, in a single touch, he understood and internalized the most surprising and profound element of the entire message of the tapestry—there was no Goddess.

Xard seethed inside at this new revelation. He had always assumed the religion was just a lie they told to justify their control. Now he knew there was a genuinely bigger truth behind the brutality, but they still had it all wrong. He had suspected as much before, but his brief experience with the relic sealed it for him. In truth, he wasn't as good at hiding his feelings as he supposed, but the voithos-moro just mistook it for frustration at not being able to see more of the relic. Xard, however, was already scheming.

Whatever it was, his interaction with the fabric had not only given him knowledge, but zeal as well. There was no way he was going to spend his life in service to a false god now. He needed to be free of the pervasive Vesni presence in his life and find a way to bring it all crashing down. He felt trapped and controlled. There was no way out so long as he remained in any of the city-states; he probably needed to leave Kael altogether. Still, his mind felt invigorated by his brush with the truth.

The voithos-moro suddenly turned the conversation back to penance. "Now, as to your behavior. What has been done and shown to you here can never be known. So, we must deliver a penance that *can* be known to your peers."

Xard interrupted him almost without thinking. "The Goddess! You've shown me so many things to help me understand the truth of her. I've been so stupid talking about kosonor and all the things that they believe that I feel I should make it up to her personally."

Xard stumbled over his words for a moment as his mouth tried to catch up to his brain. "If only there was some reserve of aurum available for me to create a new ceremonial headpiece for the Mitera, I'm sure my mother could have it presented to her personally. At least then I could show sorrow for my thoughts with the works of my hands... or something."

Xard knew the voithos-moro would not be able to resist the possibility of his name being dropped in front of the Mitera as the one who commissioned such an extravagant item. Quoting the Vesni scriptures about the 'works of his hands' was just an afterthought he would congratulate himself for later. They were all the same, Vesni and voithos alike. Everyone wanted to improve their position, even the ones who were already at the top. He simply needed him to take the bait.

"And what will you use as the model for this headpiece, hmm?"

Xard felt the tug on the line. "Since she obviously recommended me to you personally, it only makes sense that we use one of the animals from the menagerie as a model. Perhaps one of the ones in the aviary would work well to remind her that it was my experience here with you that changed my mind."

"Changed your mind about what?" he inquired.

"Everything. I mean, before I doubted everything, but this, this experience with the tapestry, I... I no longer doubt the truth about the Goddess. Bless her coming."

"Bless her coming," the voithos-moro replied flatly. He studied Xard for a moment as he processed the possibilities the offer could afford him. "Your artistry is already well known by the voithos-ka of your cohort, but I must insist that you work with a master craftsman on the actual construction. The design, however, can be yours, and we will proclaim it as your act of penance to your peers."

Xard's face brightened as he reeled in his catch. His exuberance in fooling the voithos-moro was now being mistaken for true repentance. Pride and self-promotion had blinded the voithos-moro, and Xard was going to make him pay. "I will do the best work I can... with whatever aurum I am provided, of course!"

The voithos-moro smiled again with only the corners of his mouth. Xard had begun to wonder if he was even capable of more. "I will have one of the menagerie's voithos meet you in the great aviary with the aurum you require for something befitting the Mitera. Just keep me apprised of your progress."

Xard's thoughts now raced with possibility. Despite his cluttered mind, he returned to the main foyer with haste and went straight to work. He hurriedly grabbed a large piece of fine parchment from the sanctuary's storeroom and stared up into the mist that formed near the sanctuary's roof. A large spiral staircase and several terraces encircled the great tree in the center to allow it to be seen from every side.

Circling slowly, he searched for an appropriate model for his design and finally found one three levels up—a wild-plumed coronet. It was a beautiful bird by any measure, but the wild version had a singular long tail feather with a unique design. He positioned himself on a stone bench in front of it and began to sketch a possible headpiece from the colorful plumage.

It was all just a pretense. Drawing was effortless for him, so it allowed him to focus his thoughts on more important matters. As he began to sketch the large feather, he became lost in his experience with the tapestry. It had affected him in a way he didn't expect. He could still feel the movement of the planets around the star. He intuitively knew their distances, their speed, everything. He desperately wanted to touch it again and see what was on the reverse side, but there was little chance of him ever getting back into that room anytime soon. He didn't know everything yet, but he knew enough to feel dangerous.

His sketch was nearly complete when the coronet suddenly flew to a different part of the tree. One of the Vesni from the kharja clan had scared it off by her presence. It was Shafiti, a middling woman by

Vesni standards, whose only redeeming features were the bright blue-green streaks that adorned her dark hair. She sauntered up to Xard playfully, locks aflame with strange fire, and sat down next to him. "Beautiful work. I hear you're working on something for the Mitera."

Xard shot her a surprised look. "Word travels quickly."

"We don't get too many penitents in the menagerie. I make it my business to know. Besides, my voithos is the one collecting all of the aurum required for your work." She paused to observe his drawing again coyly. "It's a good thing you're doing. You know, for the Mitera. Sadly, it doesn't improve your position much."

All Vesni were a little cutthroat when it came to maneuvering for power, but kharja clan members were notorious for it. It was probably because they were the clan that oversaw animal husbandry. Their symbol—the black kharja—was an apex predator in the wild, but their caste had been relegated to little more than zookeeping and agriculture in modern times. Xard played along, but he knew there was a pitch coming somewhere within all her word-dancing.

She placed her hand on Xard's shoulder now as she spoke, not realizing how condescending she already was *before* the gesture. "You see, your issue is trust. People don't trust you. Making this headpiece is lovely, but it won't repair the trust you've broken from your mother. Instead, why not show her that you can be trusted again in some meaningful way?"

"How do you mean?" Xard feigned his interest to lead her along. He didn't know what she was getting at yet, but he suspected it would humor him to think about later.

Shafiti began to speak in hushed tones even though no one was around. "I'm going to share with you a little-known secret about the Vesni. Do you see this insignia I'm wearing?" She pulled it off her chest and showed the reverse side to Xard. "As you can see, there's nothing on the reverse side. Your mother, however, is a sentinel.

66

When a sentinel finishes her training on Urm, she receives a small box along with her badge-rank. Hers has a small mechanical device on the reverse side which acts as a key."

Xard became more and more uncomfortable with her increasing closeness. The Vesni were trained to manipulate with their words and their bodies, but Shafiti's efforts had the opposite effect. She was more pecking bird than slithering snake, and he imagined it was probably why she was still a nobody among the Vesni.

"Here is some free advice for you, young one, find the box your mother received and use her badge-rank to open it and see what's inside. I suspect that since she no longer carries her selasin weapon, she probably keeps it in there. If it is, just leave it there, you don't want to touch it. Then wait a few days and talk to her about it. It will show her that you're trustworthy with both her valuable things and very closely held Vesni secrets. She would have no choice but to recognize that."

Xard thought that was the dumbest idea he had ever heard. He saw right through her ham-fisted play. If he even got caught with his mother's badge-rank, he would be subject to more penance. But to put his hands on a selasin weapon? It would be treasonous for a voithos, let alone a viko. His mother would certainly report him and suffer additional embarrassment. However, even if she didn't, it created a window for Shafiti to bring up charges against her for concealing a security breach. Either path worked for Shafiti in terms of improving her standing.

Xard continued playing the game. "Thank you. You've given me a lot to think about."

"Well, just remember I'm here for you if you need to talk. My voithos and I were your age once; we know how tough it can be. When you're ready, I'm sure he's down in receiving with your aurum. Good luck with your project." Shafiti ended the conversation with a flat smile and then turned and gimped away.

Xard exhaled deeply as if he had been holding his breath during their entire encounter. He had to get away from the whole lot of them. The resources were waiting for him in the form of aurum, but he had no plan. He couldn't run off with the aurum directly, it would be too difficult to spend. He just continued going through the motions, hoping for an opportunity to present itself.

He paused for a moment to admire his own artistry. Then, he rolled up his sketch and meandered down the spiral stairs past the tree's base and into the receiving area for the animals. It was common for the menagerie stock to be rotated, but the area doubled as an agricultural shipping area as well. Shafiti's voithos consort was in the middle of a holo-call with a client but waved Xard in as he spoke. He was a heavyset man, already balding even though he was probably only in his early 30s.

"If you cancel the order now, you still have to pay the shipping fees on three crates. We don't control the shipping. You ordered three Sark beasts, now you wish to change it back to two. That's fine, more milk for us, but three crates have already been paid for and assigned. We assign shipping containers weeks in advance to match the tides. We work according to the floating cities' schedules, we don't control the tides, sir." Then the holo-call ended abruptly.

The balding voithos simply turned and looked at Xard with an exasperated sigh. "You see what we deal with down here? I hope you're a good artist because if your project flops, you'll probably end up like me!" The voithos laughed and slapped Xard on the back causing him to wince. "Now, let's get you that aurum."

Xard was a little more at ease with the balding man. It was the first moment of peace he had had since he left Timeon's shelter. What Timeon said was true, in part. The voithos *were* a kind of brotherhood, but only because of shared trauma.

"You're actually in luck. We had one of the tidal cities come in last week with a big crate of aurum. We hadn't been able to move it yet

68

because no one in the city takes it. It's just been stockpiling here. You're going to need a lev-sled to move it though. Stuff's heavy. You have a place to secure it at your residence?"

Xard nodded. "My mother's a sentinel, so we have secure storage."

"Well then, I just need a dermal imprint for the release, and you can be on your way." The balding man held out a small gel pad for Xard to place his hand on. "Just place your hand on the pad for dermal verification."

Xard's face turned sour again. His skin was already raw from his visit with the voithos-moro. So, he was genuinely worried that he might start bleeding if he lost any more. It was one more insult he would have to endure if he was going to get access to the aurum, and it bothered him to know that the voithos-moro probably foresaw this encounter. Nevertheless, his drive to escape pushed him to lay his left hand down firmly on the pad as it singed off another layer of his epidermis.

Xard yelped loudly enough that he saw the balding man jump, but he tried to avoid eye contact. Without saying any further word, he grabbed the handle on the lev-sled with his opposite hand and hurried out of the room. He walked determinedly out through the grand hall and out of the sanctuary. The days were long now, and the lowering sun still shone a golden color along the caramel and white alabaster buildings.

As he passed a small flower vendor's cart, he noticed a beautiful grouping of flowers that nearly matched the colors in the coronet he had seen earlier in the menagerie: deep purple, bright green, and metallic gold. He was mesmerized by them for a moment. Perhaps he could use them to open the conversation about penance with his mother in some way. Heavens knew he needed a way to cut through the anger. He bought all three and carried them gently with him on his way.

He was almost home now, and his heart was still full of dread at having to see her again. Each step closer made him shudder until he was finally shaking uncontrollably at the bottom veranda of his own home. It scared him that he had so little control over his body. In his mind, there wasn't a single place he could go and not be beaten or mistreated on Kael. There was no respite anywhere. His plan wasn't perfect, but none of that mattered. If his evening didn't go well, he would be forced to do something drastic.

As he stepped inside, the silence told him she wasn't home yet. It was a welcome relief for as long as it would last. Xard used the opportunity to find his way inside her private suite, which also held a security lockup. The storage lockers inside would certainly be the most secure area to store the aurum. They were almost always empty anyway. It was common for the sentinels to have such storage spaces for evidence because local policing stations were so small within the city-state enclaves. Only the omyym had such formal administration centers.

On occasion, however, some relic would end up in there that she would collect from a smuggler or heretic. Today was one such occasion. It surprised him to see one of the storage bins loaded with what looked like a nomad's pack. Although he would normally avoid disrupting her things, his brush with the tapestry had kindled his hunger for mystery.

Filled with craving for whatever she might have stored in there, he fumbled with the latch. It was open. "*Careless,*" he whispered under his breath with a smirk. He quickly opened the pack to see hundreds of luminous white ceramic circles—K-rings. Originally known as Kelty rings, their use had fallen out of fashion after some scandal involving the wallet's namesake, but none of that mattered to Xard.

To him, it looked like the motherlode. Each pristine ring clinked softly as he pawed through the massive cache, their smooth ceramic surfaces cool to the touch. When activated, these rings would project shimmering holographic displays just above their surfaces—

translucent azure interfaces showing credit balances, transaction histories, and authentication patterns unique to their owners. He picked up a handful, watching as a few accidentally activated, their dead projectors flickering weakly with **UNREGISTERED ACCOUNT** warnings hovering in the air before fading out.

He scurried to the scanner, anticipation building. His racing mind became quickly deflated, however, when he confirmed they were no more than empty wallets now—their holographic displays showing zero balances or complete disconnection from the financial network. Still, he might be able to use the situation to his advantage. He quickly stuffed a handful of K-rings into his pocket and secured the pack back in the storage unit. Perhaps he could use the fact that he had secured something for her as a means for gaining her trust after all. The white ceramic circles might be worthless as currency, but their hardware still held value to the right buyer.

Waiting for her to return was interminable. The long days made the sunsets last for several hours. Soon the massive tide would be in, and the arid cliff-side city would become a sea-side resort again. Urm was already fully visible in the sky above. Its deep red areas of cyptum glistened within the amorphous black abyss that was Urm. It was a horror of a planet, but in that moment, he could only think of how much better his life would be if he was up there instead.

He hated the waiting, but he used the time to place his flowers for her in a tall earthenware glass in the kitchen. The sitars from the sanctuary had finally stopped now, giving him some indication of the passage of time. Now the silence bothered him. He decided to sit down with his hand pan near the window and begin to play. A haunting tune began to emerge from the resonant sounds. As he played, his mind started to click together a plan for getting out of his current situation should things turn sour again.

The whisk of a briskly-opening door caused his stomach to drop as Shay finally strode in. She was still in her brocade robes from her visit with the Mitera, struggling to remove an earring as she walked past

71

him. Xard jumped at the sight of her, but her demeanor was focused, almost pensive. She had almost forgotten that Xard was an unsettled matter waiting for her at home.

"You know I love when you play the hand pan. Smart move," Shay blurted out. She continued past him and into the earthy, open-walled kitchen. The makeshift flower vase being the most convenient glass, she hurled the bright trio of watered flowers out of the window and hurriedly poured herself a generous portion of wine into the now-empty cup. She had little time for games. Life had become about efficiency.

She returned to the living area and leaned against a large wooden post that served as the door frame to the kitchen. She took a slow long sip from the tall glass to make sure Xard saw her drinking from it. "Who taught you that song?"

Xard began to feel ill as he looked up at her. "We learned it in class. Timeon taught us."

"Hmmm. I should have guessed that. Your father used to play that song as well. They probably learned it together."

Xard wasn't sure what to do at this point. Bringing up his father's past was what got him into trouble in the first place. He couldn't redirect to the flowers; she had already eliminated that as a conversation exit. He simply stopped playing for a moment, but she coaxed him into continuing the song with her free hand.

Shay finally sat down across from him on a bright red hassock. To Xard, the sight of her indigo robes on the bright red leather hurt his eyes and only served to make him feel more uncomfortable. As she put down the wine, she turned to look at him more directly before speaking. Her opening line told Xard all he needed to know about how this was going to go.

"You were never my first choice for a child," Shay began. "Nevertheless, you're the only one I have. So, here we are. If you're going to survive long enough to finish your training, I guess we're going to need to answer some of these questions you seem to have about your father." She paused to sigh. "When we're finished, you agree to never bring up your father or the kosonor ever again. Agreed?"

Xard simply nodded at her. His eyes were locked tightly on to hers, but her words had already lit the fuse of his escape. It didn't seem to matter anyway. His mother had already decided this would be a one-sided answer session. She simply leaned into her tall glass and tried to keep it as impersonal as possible. It was clear from the slight tremble in her voice, however, that she couldn't broach the subject without emotion. He knew her well enough to know that losing control of herself made her even more angry.

"I'll be the first to admit that your father was one of the most sought-after voithos in every city on Kael. He was strong. He was virile. He seemed to know everything about Vesni culture, the Order, the relics. Quite honestly, if he had stayed you would have had an impossible set of shoes to fill."

She paused a moment before becoming more reflective. "In truth son, he was an almost superhuman find among the voithos, and he ended up assigned to *me*. Can you imagine? We might have been the one Vesni couple in a hundred years that were actually in love with each other. We were destined to ascend to the heights of society." Shay raised her glass to emphasize her point only to bring it back down and stare into it with disappointment.

"But there was one problem. I was unable to have children. He proposed a pod birth like many of the omyym do, but that's not our way. The womb is what makes the Vesni who they are, and all of who I was had been left desolate. Using such a thing removes the woman from the birthing process. I hated the idea, but there were so few choices at the time."

73

Shay took a generous swig of her wine as she continued to become more and more introspective. "I loved your father so damned much, I finally agreed to the indignity of it all. What I *wouldn't* accept was how cold and impersonal the process was. Insert genetic data A. Insert genetic data B. Wait for embryo. I refused to give him something as inane as a 'sample.' It had to *mean* something.

So instead, I had one of my own eggs fully harvested and placed inside a small holographic capsule, so he could physically see the egg with his own eyes. Then I had it mounted on a chain and gave it to him. Do you know what that means, Xard? For a Vesni woman to give you one of her eggs?"

Xard just kept staring back at her, wide-eyed.

"No, of course you don't. How could you?" Shay sighed. "It was a dark time for me because my womb is what kept the embryos from being viable. Giving him an entire egg was a profound token of my affection. And the best part is... he *knew* that it was. He understood my every gesture of affection to him. Unlike you, my efforts with him were never wasted.

Fortunately, the child never happened. Seeing how much it pained me to submit to such a humiliating gesture, he relented. I did it because I loved him, but now I think he just wanted to see me follow his lead, to see if I would do as *he* said. The perverse kosonor were already working him over even then and filling his head with their patriarchal ideologies and rubbish mantras." Shay was becoming more irritated as she spoke.

"In the end, I just told myself that he never really loved me. He just wanted to control me. When he realized he couldn't, he left. The reality of it all is that it was a blessing from the Great Mother herself that we never conceived in that way. Not long after that, the Mitera's own sages found a cure for my infertility. That was six years before your father disappeared into the highlands."

Shay looked back into her drink again as she pondered the moment; a brief smile crossed her lips and then spirited away. "That moment. When there was nothing but ocean breeze between us. I'd never felt so *alive*. I felt your conception, son. I know it sounds ridiculous, but I felt the moment you came into existence with my whole being."

Xard looked away for the first moment in their conversation.

Shay noticed him wince at the thought of her intimacy with his father and took it as a challenge. "Do you know that I carried you in fear and pain for 7 months? Not a day went by that carrying you did not cause me misery, but I loved your father and, in fairness, I also loved the status it brought." Shay stopped and mused for a moment.

"And now? You *still* bring me misery. I now have neither the love your father promised nor the status I should have because of your behaviors." Her expression began to change from wistful to pained as she lashed out at him through her clenched teeth. "You *shame* me, child. You and your father both bring me terrible shame with your kosonor talk. Just let it die."

Xard had gotten lost in the story. His heart had even gone out to her in some ways as he tried to connect with her pain. He had no love for his father either, but her insistence on linking them in her memory put Xard on the defensive. Still, he knew better than to engage her when she'd had too much wine. He decided on subtlety.

"Kosonor? Hrmmpf." Xard interjected. "As far as I'm concerned, my father left me a long time ago as well. What he left me for is irrelevant. Timeon is as much a father to me as anyone else."

The answer startled Shay who had become used to the silence from her audience. She regained her composure and set down her wine again. "As it should be, Zard, as it should be. You'll be 13 soon and ready to become a man. Then your trials will come. You'll have an opportunity to regain significant status in the community if you can excel in the mind trials."

She paused for a moment to ponder whether Xard might make something of himself before continuing. He recognized the thought process in her. He'd seen it before. The fact that she continued speaking indicated that Xard had at least passed *this* mental hurdle in her wine-addled mind. "By the time you reach your 16th year for the martial trials on Urm, this kosonor incident will be long forgotten."

"Now, as to the other issue from today. I realize that the architecture of your name can be pronounced with the sacred feminine sounds, but they are reserved for the Vesni." She paused and closed her eyes in disbelief that she was having this conversation.

"I don't understand why this has become something you feel the need to explain and challenge among your viko cohorts. Are you just trying to embarrass me further, or do you genuinely wish to identify as a Vesni woman now? Because if that's the case, I'll be happy to fetch a knife and speed along your transition." She stared at him expectantly.

The look on Xard's face indicated that he was perfectly content to be addressed in a hard consonant if it meant he could keep all his members. It was just a name. His father had picked it. It wasn't even until that moment that he realized the spelling of his name might have been a *kosonor* move to undermine some sacred Vesni teaching.

He simply bowed his head at her, hoping she would leave. He couldn't stand having to constantly walk so tentatively around her; he could never predict where the conversation was going. Somehow it had to end.

"No" was the only answer Xard could muster. It was the briefest moment of self-awareness, but he realized he was no longer shaking. He wasn't afraid anymore. He just felt nothing. It was time to go.

Shay wondered if she was making any headway at all with her wayward child. She had already lost a husband to heretical thinking; she wasn't about to lose her son as well. But as she saw him there with his head down, she was satisfied that her words had made some kind of impact. The sun was finally setting now, and the wafting scents of ocean breeze signaled that she should probably retire for the evening. She squinted at the glass she was holding for a moment and set it down on the table beside her before standing again.

"Honestly, son, between you and this bitter wine I've had a very challenging day. You do realize why I'm hard on you, don't you? It's because I see in you the same spark of creativity and genius your father once had. It scares me to think it might be leading you down his same path. You could do extraordinary things for the Vesni one day, but not if you let your creativity run without borders."

It was all she could think of to soften the blows she had given him. Between the Mitera's wine, the stress of reliving her experiences with Taigan, and Xard's embarrassments, it was the best she could do. It was a backward compliment at best. She just needed him 'handled' so she could get on with her life. Soon, she reasoned, he would be a full voithos and become someone else's problem.

Without any response from Xard, she strode into her personal quarters and let her silken wraps fall away. Standing between a pair of posts in the far corner of the room, her body began to be showered in a fragrant, anti-microbial mist. Looking in the mirror, her body seemed as immaculate and toned as it had been a decade earlier. *Wasted* was all she could think as she looked at it now. It was a beautiful form, but it no longer had an admirer. Loneliness had become the ugliness she wore rather than time, and it soured her soul. As she emerged from between the misting posts, she passed through the set of tapestry-laden door panels into her inner bedroom and went to sleep. She would leave it to Xard to clean up before morning.

The process of escaping the trap of Vesni life was always going to require him to gnaw off his emotions; he just didn't expect her to do it for him. It made the decision to leave an easy one. If he left now, he reasoned that she could at least be rid of him. She would certainly find a clever way to handle the social fallout. He cared nothing about that. All that mattered to him in the moment was that she had recognized something he had suspected for some time—he was a genius. He smiled with delight that he had gotten her to admit at least *something* good about him.

A plan finally began to form in his mind. Her condescending acknowledgment of his mental prowess had become fuel for his escape. It was the first time in weeks he felt good about something. He was far too used to feeling helpless and suicidal. He needed space, but the Vesni life refused to offer it.

He sat down on his bed and reflected for a moment about how he had considered killing himself after their last argument. That just wasn't going to be a good escape anymore. The new Vesni 'blessing' meant they were close to having the ability to just "bring him back" if he tried. The one who died almost always got labeled as 'weak.' Their memories were disregarded almost immediately in society. He'd have none of that.

No, Xard wanted to make a statement. Killing himself would only weaken his position. He wanted to survive without them somehow and make a mockery of their beliefs in the process. The religious regimen on Kael was too polished to afford any opportunities to expose the lie at home. Urm's training academy was a different matter entirely. It would give him the space he needed to avoid the Order while allowing him to work on exposing them from the shadows. Hopefully, he could find something *there* among the trainees to further his plan.

He winced as he brushed against the door post. His skin had been weeping for hours from the nanite gas causing his shirt to cling to him. Peeling it off was painful but somehow therapeutic. He wanted to be rid of this life, to molt and become something else entirely. He stripped off the remainder of his clothes and laid there on his bed for a moment trying to calm himself, but it was no use. His mind was racing, and his raw skin made his bedding feel like sandpaper. Instead, he got up and leaned his shoulder into the pair of weighty wooden doors that led out onto his personal balcony overlooking the flagstone terrazzo streets below.

It was evening now, and the sky was lit in that deep brilliant blue that it seemed only Kael could bloom. While there was still some scant activity in the streets down below, he had the view mostly to himself. Naked as he was, he couldn't help but be somewhat lost in the moment. The warm breeze was filled with the scent of spiced trees and fruit blossoms. It held him there, wrapping its poultice around his skin and reminding him of the safety this world could sometimes offer. He closed his eyes for a moment, savoring the momentary solitude. But it was a breeze that held his skin only.

The gentle rustle of the trees, the spectral blue skies, the warm sweet air—all of them beckoned him back into their womb, but his mind just wouldn't allow it. It rejected that world as a lie now. His body embraced the bliss, but his heart had already shaken off its gilded shackles. His face flashed from pleasure to sadness to determination and back again, a tiny storm under a tranquil sky. And with that, he opened his eyes to Kael one more time, heaved a heavy breath of its fragrant aroma, and squinted back at it in anger that he had to leave it.

He kept the lights off as he strode back into his room and gently slid into the softest pair of pants he could find. The light was fading now, and he didn't know when another opportunity like this might present itself. He walked quietly into the antechamber where his mother's flight suit had been haphazardly thrown. Clearly, she had been in a hurry to have her audience with the Mitera.

It was all or nothing now. He carefully unclipped the badge from the front of it and saw the mechanical locking mechanisms on its reverse. It was just as Shafiti had said. All he needed now was to find the box. He had never seen it directly, but he had a good idea of where it was.

He walked back to the living area near an old whitestone obelisk. It was an ancient fertility relic his father had found that shimmered like an opal. Though it was supposed to symbolize 'life,' his mother kept it as a memento mori of his father. He'd seen her crying at it several times when his father first went missing, lighting candles around it, and muttering strange prayers. So, he reasoned that it might be home to other long-forgotten offerings.

As he walked around and studied it, one of the stone panels beneath his feet clicked, and he smiled. A small pneumatic lift let out a brief *hiss* of air as the floor panel raised up to reveal a storage container with the mysterious wooden box inside. Xard winced for a moment hoping the sound hadn't woken his mother. Without any sign of her stirring, he continued attempting to explore its contents.

There was an obvious depression in the box's surface, and Xard quickly oriented the badge-rank into it. It locked into place with a brief hum, and a small series of holographic numbers appeared on the surface which changed as the badge-rank moved. He cursed under his breath at Shafiti. She had given him just enough information to get into trouble but hadn't explained that he would need a code of some kind as well. Too late now—it was locked into place.

"Come on, Xard, think," he whispered to himself. He tried several numbers and dates relating to specific Vesni prophecies he had learned—even ones that were particularly obscure that he'd heard her mention before. Nothing. He tried to get inside her head about why she would have hidden the box in the first place, but he had no idea. His heart was pounding as he began to recognize the very deep trouble he was about to be in if he couldn't get her badge-rank back on her flight suit without her knowing. Out of sheer desperation, he entered his own birth date only to find it open with a satisfying *snap*.

He'd expected her to use something more logical. Instead, it was clearly an emotional choice, and one that could have been too easily uncovered by most anyone who found it. A twinge of regret washed over him knowing that she was thinking of *him* as she locked this away. Nevertheless, he pushed it out of his mind by reminding himself that whoever it was that locked this away wasn't the same person he lived with now.

As he opened the lid he saw it—her selasin weapon. As dark as the room had now become, the scant light that remained glistened from it. He smirked to himself about how careless she had been to leave it so accessible and mused at the great confluence of events that had dropped it into his care. *They were all to blame, the whole society of them*, he thought to himself.

"Bet the damned thing's never even been fired," he muttered. It was daintier than he had expected, but heavy. It was a simple, yet heavily ornamented, fingerless glove with a slender metal clamshell affixed to its back. Its intricate etchings and jeweled fabric seemed to announce its presence with great fanfare even in the dimmest of light. Yet, despite its delicate appearance, the true pearl was the quantum weapon core it held within.

Seeing one in person was a true rarity. Only 100 were ever made, and only the best sentinels were ever in possession of one. He reached in and tried it on. It seemed enormous on his small hand, but he was all-in now. He hurriedly closed the box, retrieved the badge-rank, and secured it back in its place on his mother's flight suit.

He returned to his room as silently as possible and threw together a few clothes in a pack. He decided to dress casually because he knew the tidal cities were not the place to look like you had deep resources. Still, he wore no shirt, only the reliquary field vest Timeon had given him.

In part, it was because he thought it made him look tough, but he also knew that the heavy air of Kael would seep into his pores on the way. He didn't know how long it might take to get totally off-world, but he gathered that the trip might be a long one. On some level he knew that he would still be able to gather the scents of home from his arms along the way even though he would never, ever admit that to himself.

If he could make it to the menagerie docks with the aurum, he might be able to catch one of the floating cities to another port and find a way off-world before anyone was aware he was even gone. But he needed to get moving. As he grabbed his pack and donned the ill-fitting selasin glove, he caught a glimpse of himself in one of the tall metal mirrors in his room.

He stopped for a moment to pose with his newfound gear and weaponry, taking aim at himself first, then cycling through a half dozen heroic stances. He didn't even notice how frail he looked beneath all that equipment. All he saw was the hero, and it made him more determined than ever to succeed in a life far from this place. Then, without another glance, he was gone.

Xard's adrenaline kept his mind moving quickly as he scurried out of the residence and back across the city toward the cliffs. Kael was relatively safe at night owing to its predominantly religious population and the severe consequences for even the smallest of infractions. Still, he took the side roads to avoid being seen. The smells of the incoming ocean tide had already begun to overpower the scent of the orchards. It only served to remind him that his opportunity to make his move was quickly fading.

When he arrived at the city-linkage point, he was surprised to find it already docked and transferring cargo. The tide was quickly overtaking his plans. He scurried with his lev-sled down to the sanctuary loading platform and found that the three menagerie crates bound for Urm had already been loaded. He knew one would be empty; he just needed to find it. He only had a few hours before the city would have to detach to follow the polar tides.

The streets of the largest floating cities lined up perfectly with whatever city-state they were currently docked with. They were almost an extension of whatever city they visited, rotating their mass of floating streets and businesses until the appropriate side linked up perfectly with that day's host. Today it was *Marwei*, a larger city that only docked every few tidal cycles.

Even though the streets were contiguous from Kael Vistyn onto the floating city, it quickly became obvious that he was in unfamiliar territory. The foreign smells and subtle differences in clothing and facial features created an uncanny valley for him. Although the Vesni lumped them in with the omyym commoners, he had learned that each city had its own governance and culture. Xard suspected that this city was probably a boon for him because people from *Marwei* normally asked very few questions.

He followed the streets of the floating city until they became too narrow for animal crates and doubled back the way he came. The tangled mass of ropes and cables hanging from storefronts were already casting eerie shadows along the darkened streets as the city's floating edge bounced and swayed subtly under him. He became more and more uneasy as he struggled to find the crates from the sanctuary. If he couldn't find them, he would have scant time to put everything back the way he found it.

Xard ran his hand through his dark mop of hair in the front in a futile effort to keep it from impairing his vision. He had almost given up when he caught the distinctive whiff of manure in the air. It was the most glorious smell he could have asked for—the smell of freedom. He hurried after it as fast as his legs and his gear would allow.

Smells led to sounds. Sounds led to animals. Animals led him directly to the three menagerie crates bound for Urm. Xard listened closely at each of the sealed metal crates until he found one that sounded empty. Xard held his breath and gave the grimy access panel a hard *thud* with the side of his hand. Empty.

He exhaled loudly and scrambled inside the barren container with his pack and his lev-sled. He would camp there for the night and forage around the floating city at daybreak to resupply and hopefully find a way to convert his aurum into more useful currency. Until then, Xard curled up into a corner of the crate and attempted to sleep.

***

Shay's own sleep was filled with a restlessness that not even the wine could abate. The ocean breeze filled her senses as she clung to the thin veil between arousal and rest. Her memories pressed against her even here in the night hours. She felt trapped by them. Mistakes from long ago now echoed again in her relationship with her son.

As the night thickened, the briny air washed ashore a memory Shay had once hoped to bury in its depths. She tensed in her sleep as she pleaded endlessly in her mind for her consort to just let go. She needed a consort. She wanted it to be him, but he had to come around to her way of thinking for it to move forward. Her efforts felt futile. He was committed to something he perceived as 'truth' and refused to let it go.

85

Shay pressed him. "You are destroying everything that we are a part of. Centuries, maybe even millennia of tradition are in danger at that dig site. The site was declared heretical. It's over. It's done. You made your case and it was rejected. It's time to let it go!"

Taigan snapped back at her with equal passion. "When did searching for truth become heresy? If the Vesni scriptures are true, then they will stand the test of scrutiny, will they not?"

"Tai, you can keep your career. Stay in the archaeological caste if you must, but let this site go. I can't protect you if you keep going down this path. If you have any love for me at all, for us, just let it go." Shay let her hand fall gently to her swollen belly as she dragged out her words for emphasis.

"It's *because* I love you that I won't. Everything about us is buried in that site. The past, who we were, what we tried to be and failed at; it's all sitting there in the ground. Our future is buried under the wreckage of the old worlds. We need to uncover it."

Shay felt profoundly inept at arguing with him. Every angle had an answer, and it frustrated her to no end. "How do you expect to find and decipher ancient messages when you can't even see the one I'm sending you right now in plain language. This path will forever damage our name, our standing, and the standing of our son. Every Vesni knows that parents tainted by kosonor will have children who chase the patriarchy. Our son will be rejected at every turn if you continue like this. Is this what you want?"

Shay studied his reactions closely. His eyes and ears were open to her, drawing in what she was saying. On some level she could tell that he understood the cost, and even grieved over it. Yet, it didn't seem to matter to him. "Tai, please. These kosonor leanings are a cancer, and the Vesni treat them as such for a reason. That's why they are cut out at the root, and all their branches are burned. If you keep following this path, you are better off dead to us, because if you stay with the kosonor it will end in our deaths anyway."

86

Shay woke clutching at her abdomen. It took a moment for her to realize she was no longer pregnant nor in a dream. The salty fullness in the air had passed and taken her child's memory with it. As she stumbled into the bright morning light coming through the open kitchen walls, she realized she must have slept in quite a long time. She had meant to wake earlier to give Xard his work assignments for the afternoon, but he had already gone, presumably to go be with his training cohort.

The dream had ended, but the emotions of it lingered. The previous loss of her consort now mingled with the present loss of not having been able to find any closure with Xard before he ran to class. Her emotions were playing havoc with her, and she needed to clear her head. She knew the work would do it. It's all she had now to keep her going through the day. With any luck, she and Drasha would find some new perp to hassle and Xard would finally have a day without incident.

9 – COUNSEL

The animal crate stank of disinfectant and salt. Xard's back ached from another night spent on the metal floor, his only comfort a thin blanket that did little against the cold that seeped through the container's walls. Dawn's light filtered through the ventilation slats, casting lined shadows across his face. Another day on *Marwei*—the floating city that would carry him closer to Urm.

Outside, the floating metropolis groaned as massive hydraulic stabilizers adjusted to the morning tide. Xard unlocked his crate and stepped into the salt-heavy air. The hexagonal platforms of *Marwei* stretched before him like a mechanical lily pad, buildings rising from its center while the edges undulated with each passing wave.

From this vantage on the outer ring, he could see how the city's sixteen interlocking sections formed a perfect snowflake pattern. The central hub rose highest, its gleaming spires reaching toward the sky, while below the waterline, enormous ballast chambers extended deep into the ocean. The outer rings—where he'd found refuge—moved visibly with each swell, the corrugated metal walkways flexing by design.

His stomach growled. His meager rations had done little to sate him, so he made his way toward the city center to find something more filling. As he walked, Xard felt the gentle roll of the platform beneath his feet—a sensation that residents seemed oblivious to but that left him slightly nauseated.

Unlike the stationary cities of Kael Vistyn, floating cities like *Marwei* followed Urm's gravitational pull across the planet's vast oceans. It made them perfect for trade—and perfect for someone looking to disappear.

Xard paused at a railing, staring at Urm's crimson sphere hanging in the morning sky. His new home, if he survived the journey. The dark planet's pull was already dragging *Marwei* northward toward the polar regions. In two days, they would dock at Kreshen before his container would be shuttled to Urm. Just two more days of hiding.

His hand instinctively touched his chest, wincing at the tenderness where his mother's "parting gift" had left its mark. The embarrassment still burned fresher than the wound itself. The Vesni matriarchy, the Good Mother, the whole religious system—lies built upon lies. And he would expose them all, once he reached Urm.

But first, he needed to survive. And to survive, he needed currency.

The inner rings of *Marwei* buzzed with morning commerce. Maintenance workers calibrated the massive hydraulic pistons that kept the sections level despite the ocean's undulation. Food vendors called out their breakfast offerings, the smell of fried fish and freshly baked bread cutting through the omnipresent brine.

Xard slipped between the crowds, keeping his head down. He carried a few of his finger-length aurum bars—technically illegal as tender under Vesni law but potentially valuable to the right buyer. He needed information on where to exchange them once he reached Urm.

A rickety diner caught his eye, its windows fogged with condensation. TIDAL EATS, proclaimed a flickering sign. Inside, the regulars appeared to be primarily dock workers and maintenance crews—exactly the sort who might know the black markets of Urm.

He slid into a booth, carefully observing the other patrons. Two older men occupied a corner table, their weathered faces marked by decades at sea. One wore a faded maintenance uniform with a *Marwei* insignia, while the other's clothing suggested off-world travel.

A server approached, her expression bored. "Order?"

"Whatever's hot," Xard replied, keeping his voice low.

Minutes later, she returned with a bowl of steaming porridge, its surface dotted with unidentifiable marine protein. Xard ate mechanically, his attention fixed on the two men.

"...seventh time the eastern stabilizers have failed this month," the uniformed man was saying. "Central Authority keeps pushing back inspection cycles."

His companion grunted as he nodded toward the sky. "Same everywhere. Urm doesn't even bother with inspections unless the product's at risk. No one cares about the workers. Last time I was there, the entire band of cities along 64 was running on auxiliary power."

Xard's ears perked up at the mention of Urm. He finished his meal quickly and, gathering his courage, approached their table.

"Sorry to interrupt," he said, feigning casualness, "but I overheard you mention Urm. I'm headed there for the first time. Any advice?"

The older men studied him suspiciously. The one in uniform snorted. "Runaway, are you? Don't worry, boy. We see plenty passing through *Marwei*. Usually headed the other direction, though."

"I'm not running away," Xard lied. "Just... seeking opportunities."

The other man laughed, a harsh sound like grinding metal. "Opportunities on Urm? That's a new one." But his eyes softened. "Sit down, boy. You're going to need help if you're serious."

Hesitantly, Xard joined them. The uniformed man—Trell, he called himself—signaled for more stim-drinks.

"First thing you need to know," Trell said, "is that Urm runs on different rules. The Vesni still claim authority, but their grip is looser there. More factions, more danger."

"And more opportunity," added his companion, who introduced himself as Marko. "If you know where to look."

The conversation flowed more easily after that. Xard carefully steered it toward currency exchange, mentioning that he had "items of value" he might need to convert.

Marko's eyes narrowed. "What kind of items?"

Xard glanced around before discreetly showing the edge of an aurum bar beneath the table.

Trell inhaled sharply. "Where'd a boy like you get something like that?"

"Family heirloom," Xard lied again. "I just need to know where I can exchange it safely."

The men exchanged knowing looks. Marko leaned forward, lowering his voice. "There's a noodle shop in the eastern district of Urm's landing port. Owner's name is Attrus. Skinny fellow, quiet. Sells the best rum noodles in the habitable zones."

"And he buys aurum?" Xard pressed.

"He doesn't," Trell said. "But his back-room contacts might. Tell him Marko sent you, and he'll give you a fair rate. Just don't chug the broth in front of him—he takes his cooking seriously."

Both men chuckled at this apparent inside joke. Xard committed the information to memory, thanking them. As he rose to leave, Marko caught his arm.

"Word of advice, boy. Urm isn't kind to outsiders. Find yourself allies quickly, or you won't last a week."

The words lingered with Xard as he left the diner. *Allies*. There wasn't anyone he trusted among the Vesni. Would Urm be any different?

***

The gentle chirp came over Shay's comms before she had even had a chance to arrive at her patrol site. At first, she refused to answer it. Drasha finally prodded her gently from the back seat.

"Would you prefer I answer?" There was only a steely silence from the front seat where Shay was seated. She wasn't ignoring her, she only sought to buy a few moments to center herself and purge any emotional responses that might suddenly go unchecked.

"No, I have it." The news was grim. She'd been summoned to an impromptu meeting of the lesser council for Kael Vistyn. "I don't know what he's done this time, but I think we can assume with certainty my son is somehow involved. Contact Patrol Delta to handle our follow-up on Mr. Agarai. I need time to dig up the details on whatever it is he's done. I don't want to walk into this thing blindly."

"On it," Drasha replied. She paused for a moment to read the response. "Patrol Delta is asking if re-tasking them is urgent. They are in the middle of prepping a sting operation on a smuggling ring near Kreshen. Something about smugglers using animal shipments as mules to get reliquary objects off-world."

Shay pulled hard into the turn, shoving them both solidly into their seats. For Shay, the maneuver was a stress reliever, but Drasha understood that this was the answer to her question. She immediately contacted Patrol Delta and ordered them to drop their current activities and redirect to their patrol route. Shay leveled the stormblade back around toward Kael Vistyn. She was sure to stay just below the static belt this time to ensure low-band comms worked well. She didn't want to use an open frequency for something personal.

If it was something Xard had done, she assumed Timeon would know. By the time she reached out to him, he'd already put the cohort to work on a self-directed project and was awaiting her call. It was a bad sign.

"Give it to me straight" was all she said.

Timeon explained the details as best he could. "The voithos-moro has brought a complaint against Xard. Apparently, he was given a large amount of aurum for a project which never arrived at the metalworker's guild. I was contacted about Xard's status, but he never actually arrived at his cohort today. When I heard the voithos-moro was handling his penance personally, well, let's just say he was not expected here today to begin with. Now it appears he cannot be found at all."

Shay sighed on the other end of the comms. "How much aurum are we talking?"

"Over 200 half-ingots."

"Goddess! What was he supposed to be doing with it? Building a house?"

"Apparently it was for a headdress of some kind for the Mitera."

94

Shay immediately smelled a set-up. The amount of aurum Xard had been given far exceeded what would be necessary for even the most ostentatious headwear. "Okay, thank you Timeon. I appreciate your assistance as always."

"Bless her coming," he said on the other end, but Shay switched off the comms without a response.

"Okay," Shay mumbled under her breath. "Which one of you skikas is running the snare this time? Drasha, who else might be affiliated with this 'penance project' for the Mitera?"

"I'll run some names. You think someone's moving in for a kill shot?"

"It's possible. Xard is no fool, but he *can* be manipulated. Someone has a hook in him. I suspect whoever it is won't be far from this meeting. Keep your eyes on the galleries when we arrive. Whoever it is won't be able to resist gawking at my failure. In the meantime, I've got an idea that might work."

10 – SPIRALS

Xard spent the remainder of the day exploring *Marwei*, studying its structure with newfound attention. Unlike the static cities of his home, these tidal metropolises were engineering marvels—designed to flex without breaking, to move with the ocean rather than resist it.

The central hub housed administrative buildings and expensive residences, their foundations extending deep below the waterline for stability. Middle rings contained markets, educational facilities, and public spaces, all constructed from lightweight composites that could withstand the constant movement. The outer rings—where "temporary visitors" like himself stayed—were essentially glorified docking areas, their modular construction allowing sections to be reconfigured based on shipping needs.

By late afternoon, the wind had picked up considerably. *Marwei* was entering northern waters, the platforms now rising and falling visibly with each wave. Most residents seemed unaffected, but Xard felt increasingly nauseated. He decided to return to his crate before he embarrassed himself.

The route back took him through a deserted maintenance corridor. Hurricane lamps swung from chains overhead, casting shifting shadows across the metal walkway. The isolation felt oppressive after a day surrounded by people, yet somehow safer. At least alone, he couldn't be betrayed again.

A voice came from nowhere: "Wondering about your future, young voithos?"

Xard spun around. An elderly woman sat in a recessed doorway he could have sworn was empty moments ago. Her spine was bent at such an impossible angle that her head seemed to emerge from her chest rather than her shoulders.

"I'm not a voithos," he said automatically. The religious title felt bitter on his tongue.

"No," she agreed, her eyes unnervingly bright in her wrinkled face. "You wear the face of a voithos, but I see the heart of a heretic."

Fear spiked through him. Had she somehow recognized him? Was she Vesni?

"Come suckle at the Good Mother's breast a while. She'll tell you what you need."

Every instinct told him to walk away, yet curiosity held him in place. She couldn't possibly know who he was or what he carried. And if he'd been discovered, better to know now than later.

She hobbled over to a small table on her portico as if she already knew he would come sit with her—her gnarled hands fumbling with a lantern. "You don't need to sit. Just come closer so I can see you." The point-light from the lantern began to cast harsh shadows across Xard's face and shoulders, creating eerie forms against the wall behind him. "Many paths for you I see. Well, let's see which one you are on now."

She reached out and snatched up both of his hands with a quickness that belied her age. Then she began to marvel audibly as she examined his hands more closely. Her stiff flesh pressing and probing them, impatiently twisting and adjusting them to get them positioned correctly. Her skin felt paper-thin, yet her grip was surprisingly strong.

"I see two people who are strangers; yet they are not. This is your line, but another double line... no... a hollow line intersects it here.

Yes. Very unusual. Fragmented lines of all kinds are entering into your path. But this... this is not normal at all. You have a line here as well coming from... wait... there should not even *be* a line in this place."

Xard wasn't a believer in her superstitious palmistry. He scarcely believed in anything anymore, but he was intrigued by what she thought was different about him. "Go on then. What is it?"

"This mount in your hand is called 'the ether.' It sometimes hides small marks which show any gifts the Goddess has bestowed on a person. Very few people even have marks here. But you have a strong line that runs from your ether mount directly into your path. Such a thing is unheard of." She paused her reading to turn her small, glassy eyes up at him before speaking again.

"I would tell you what this means, but I would only be guessing." Her face began to contort as she fumbled with the mystery she couldn't explain. "You are an enigma, child. I would think it a good omen, but no one has ever seen such a thing before. This is like an ally from the netherworld—a quantum, ethereal ally. Perhaps it's even the Goddess herself!"

Xard began to let a smile cross his lips. He knew exactly what this meant, if it meant anything at all. The selasin weapon he lifted from his mother's box was, in fact, a quantum energy weapon. He prodded her for more details. "Is it a weapon of some kind maybe?"

She dove back into interpreting the small lines and marks on his palms. "Yes, it could be. This could be a key or a door or yes, even a weapon. But context is important—this mount never has a line! Please, you must tell me your name, so when your future unfolds, I can understand this symbol's meaning." She began to grasp hold of his forearms tightly, imploring him to tell her who he was.

But Xard had heard enough. He controlled his own destiny, not a bunch of lines even *she* didn't understand. He tugged his hands away and looked at her as he began to back away. "My name is Xard," he said, being sure to carefully enunciate the sacred '*sh*' sounds in his name again. Then he turned without waiting for a response from her and disappeared around the corner.

By the time he reached his crate, night had fallen completely. Urm's massive silhouette now dominated the sky, bathing the platform in rusty light. The wind howled between containers, and the platform's edge rose and fell dramatically with each wave. Definitely northern waters now.

Inside his metal sanctuary, Xard secured the door and huddled under his blanket. Despite the discomfort, exhaustion quickly pulled him toward sleep. His last conscious thought was of the noodle shop owner. Attrus. Just two more days.

Dreams came swiftly.

Xard found himself a child again, perhaps six or seven, lying beside his father in their home. No anger, no betrayal—just the peaceful sound of Taigan's breathing beside him. His father rolled away, sitting up on the edge of the bed to stare out the window at Urm's light filtering through.

"*It's time to wake up now,*" his father said, looking back over his shoulder. "*The things that move away always come back around.*"

Xard pretended to be asleep, slowly reaching for a pillow before flinging it at his father with all his childish might. The impact seemed to echo, happening again and again though he'd only thrown it once. Each time, his father laughed.

Taigan finally caught him, pinning him playfully and giving him noogies until Xard screamed with laughter. He became tangled in the sheets, wrapped tight in their warmth, feeling safer than he had in years.

"*It's time to wake up now,*" his father repeated. "*The things that move away always come back around.*"

The dream shifted. His father stood on a golden path that spiraled upward into white clouds, walking away from him. Xard ran after him, his small legs pumping furiously, but he never gained ground. When he paused to catch his breath, he realized his father was now directly above him on the spiral's next level.

The pattern repeated—Xard running, tiring, seeing his father just overhead—until finally, Taigan disappeared into golden light, leaving one final echo: "*The things that move away always come back around.*"

Xard jerked awake in the darkness of his crate, tears streaming down his face. The warm safety of the dream vanished, replaced by cold metal and loneliness. He pressed a hand to his bruised chest, trying to summon anger instead of grief. Anger was safer. Anger would carry him to Urm and through whatever waited there.

But in his exhaustion, even anger failed him. Silent sobs wracked his body, muffled by the howling wind and crashing waves outside. He curled into himself, wrapping the blanket tightly around his shoulders. It was a poor substitute for human contact, but it was all he had.

When morning light finally filtered through the crate's vents, Xard blinked awake with salt-crusted eyes. Outside, he could hear the sounds of docking procedures—mechanical groans as *Marwei* secured itself to whatever northern port they'd reached.

One day closer to Urm. One day closer to the truth.

Xard closed his eyes again briefly, his father's words lingering in his mind like a prophecy or a warning. *The things that move away always come back around.*

Whether it meant salvation or doom, he would soon find out.

***

The sun had already slipped below the horizon by the time they reached the Great Council Hall. Lacking any time to formally prepare, they arrived still clad in their form-fitting flight suits. Shay knew this was going to be a gritty encounter. Although the voithos-moro was a man, he still held considerable sway in the day-to-day happenings in Kael Vistyn. He needed to be handled carefully.

Shay and Drasha walked confidently past the main doors and descended a large, wide spiral staircase. The Council Hall was a subterranean room whose ceiling was held aloft by dozens of white marble pillars which extended into the darkness in all directions. Around the base of each pillar grew bundles of luminescent white fungi that cast a gentle light throughout the room.

Although the chamber was not extraordinarily large, the edges of the room were completely unlit, which gave it a haunting and cavernous feel. Directly at the base of the stairs was a single hexagonal table with two chairs on each side. Two seats were for each of the four clans: Lauris, Kharja, Vaconix, and Eshota. Two seats were at the head of the table for the Mitera and the most prominent voithos in the room. This left two seats for the supplicants; in this case Shay and Drasha. Many of the members were already seated as Shay and Drasha made their descent.

Shay whispered back to Drasha, "Remember, your entrance sets the tone for the meeting, not the mood of the room. You control a room with presence first, words second." Shay continued down the stairs, ensuring every *click* of her boots echoed throughout the chamber like a metronome until every eye was on her descent. She wanted them to know she was coming. She wanted them to stop talking and bring all their attention to her. Each click of her boots echoed rhythmically around the room, lulling them into a pace of her choosing.

The Mitera had abandoned her usual formal gowns as well in favor of a loosely-corseted blouse with a simple golden armband. Her gentle brown curls flowed down her shoulders, nearly covering the expensive ornamentation the blouse had to offer. As she approached the candlelit table, she could see the Mitera had a small smile forming in the corners of her mouth as she approached. Apparently, the grand entrance had made an impression.

"I greet you in the name of the one who comes!"

Shay and Drasha bowed as they approached. "Bless her coming."

"Please, sit. I'm afraid there is some business that has been brought to my attention concerning your son. Voithos-moro, would you please elaborate?"

The voithos-moro was already a gaunt man, but the flickering of torch-light in the darkened room made him look positively skeletal. When he spoke, she was almost certain she could see dust being disturbed with every wheezing puff. It was distracting, but she focused on him out of respect for his position and reputation.

"Shayameen, it appears that your son may have absconded with a large quantity of aurum and has left the viko training. As of this moment, we do not know where either he or the aurum may have gone, and we were hoping you could explain where he might possibly be."

Shay looked at him directly. "I have no idea where he may have gone."

He was taken aback by her directness. "So, you admit that your child is in open rebellion? That he is a thief? That he was just yesterday in penance for using the sacred sounds and discussing kosonor with other students, and has now left the faith?"

None of the other clan members at the table spoke, but Drasha's eyes roamed around the table at every new accusation, looking for tells

103

and indicators among the meeting's participants. When the voithos-moro finished his charge, every member looked surprised at the strength of the accusations being made against the young viko and his mother. Then she saw it. The blue-haired Vesni from Kharja clan gently bit her lip and then let it slip away.

She could barely conceal her growing delight as the charges were laid out in totality. Drasha continued to scan the blue-haired Vesni's body for clues as she waited for Shay to respond to the voithos-moro. Shay maintained her composure as she chose her next words carefully.

"No. I suspect this is more miscommunication than malice."

Shay leaned into the gold-leafed table as she spoke. "When you sent him home with the project for the Mitera, I already knew he was planning to run. I had all but led him to that conclusion deliberately. He'd been planning it for quite some time, but he always lacked the resources to do it. My goal all along had been to lead him into a position where he had to choose between the love and protection of the Vesni faith and his own limited wit and reason.

Perhaps if we had coordinated better, I could have alerted you to this, but since penance is a private matter, I understand your discretion. Still, you can understand my surprise when a penance with the voithos-moro himself leads to my son hauling a treasure trove of precious metals around the city rather than something more punitive." Shay paused for a moment to let her words filter around the room and leaned back into her chair. "Fortunately, I think our collective lack of oversight has created a window of opportunity.

He'd be hard-pressed to spend the aurum anywhere apart from the floating cities. When he runs out of resources or simply finds he has no way to spend them, he'll come simpering back. When he does, he'll be humiliated and mocked into a more genuine submission and will have chosen the Vesni of his own free will. I know him. It's his pride that fuels his arrogance, especially in these recent episodes."

The voithos-moro looked even more grave at her response. "...and if he doesn't return?"

"Then the problem solves itself. I will repay the aurum personally from Taigan's former holdings, and we'll have all rid ourselves of another stubborn heretic."

The council members all marveled in astonishment at this new information until the Mitera finally spoke. "Shay, I know that I am speaking for the sentiment of the entire group when I say that your attitude in this matter highlights a level of commitment to the divine principles rarely seen among Vesni women of any clan. You have created an environment where your own flesh and blood will have to come to the truth about the scripture if he is to survive. You've committed yourself fully and have withheld nothing from the Goddess, even the fruit of your womb."

Drasha's gaze continued to catch every tic, every subtlety around the table. She'd been trained by the best. There it was again. This time a slight shifting of weight in the seat as Shay was being showered with effusive praise from the Mitera for her foresight. It was the blue-hair again, she was certain this time.

Drasha had little time to celebrate her discovery, however. Patrol Delta was chiming in with an important update across the comms on her wrist. "My apologies for interrupting, Mitera. It appears that a larger issue has just emerged. The birthing pods have been moved overnight and the merchant has committed suicide."

Shay struggled to pull herself away from her performance at the table, but she had to admit, it was news that needed attention. "It would have taken a very large crew to move all of those pods. It had to be a tidal city crew. Where is the merchant's body now, did they say?"

"At the base of the cliffs, probably hoping the tide would carry him off. I realize it's not really our jurisdiction, but the omyym have asked

105

for our cooperation personally since we have firsthand knowledge of the operation from when it was active."

The Mitera smiled at them both. "Well then, it looks like you both have some work to do. If all goes as planned, such suicides could be eliminated entirely by next month's synod with the omyym people. Do keep me informed when Xard returns, will you? This is just the kind of tough redemption story the people need to hear."

"As you say, Mitera."

11 - BEASTS

Xard's transfer off the *Marwei* and into the omyym city of Kreshen was thankfully uneventful. He needed to stay out of sight now if he didn't want to blow his cover and get tossed out of the crate. A carrier sled picked up the three menagerie crates and deposited them, with him inside, onto a large off-world shuttle bound for Urm. He was disappointed that he wouldn't get to watch the trip through a viewport, but he had enough other details to worry about. He flopped into the corner of the container once it had stopped jostling and began to take an inventory of his current resources.

He studied his plan again out of habit. 220 aurum half-ingots, 5 days' rations (7 if he stretched them), three blank K-rings to transfer his money to once he met with his contact, a handful of Urmian currency to handle small exchanges. And, of course, he had the selasin weapon to handle any hostile variations to the plan. He dozed off for a moment then awoke still reciting his plans to himself in his head: *Meet Attrus at the noodle house under the sixth mining sluice between 27:00 and 27:15 local time, transfer the aurum to the K-rings evenly under 3 separate accounts.*

He paused from his mental planning for a moment to re-read the instructions from the men in the eatery and adjust his blanket there in the dark container. He'd appreciated this level of specificity when he was developing the plan, but now, he wasn't certain if he could meet his own deadline. A lot would depend on his next connection and whether he successfully slipped the Vesni's attention getting off-world. He began to lose track of time as he pondered all the complications that might arise.

The sudden introduction of animal urine smells interrupted his thoughts as some new variety of beast got loaded in next to him. He held his nose in his blanket for a time hoping to filter out the acrid smells, but the lack of proper ventilation made the scents impossible to ignore. This new distraction made the ride to Urm even less comfortable than his previous foray to *Marwei*, but there was nothing he could do without revealing his presence there. He had to resign himself to the imposition and cover himself in his blanket as best he could. He was as prepared now as he could possibly be.

Several times on the journey he was jolted from his thoughts by a loud *bang* or a shambling crew member, hoping it was a signal that they had entered Urm's atmosphere. Instead, he would find that only a few moments had passed. He drew up his legs and held them as he put his head down in his arms to keep warm. Even the faint smells of Kaelian spices that once lingered on his skin were of no consolation against the emanation from the neighboring crates.

He fought desperately against homesickness now, and he wasn't even fully at his destination. Even the silence seemed to shout at him. For all his planning and determination, the open wound of leaving still cut deeply. His mind was his ally, but his heart was still alone.

***

Shay sighed and stared at the ceiling in her bedroom as the golden dawn broke on the following day. Her demure repose belied the anxiety that was churning within her as she woke. A gentle electronic *whirr* broke her early morning trance. It was Drasha.

"Sorry to rouse you so early, but I wanted to know if you needed me to follow-up with the investigative team on my own or if you would be joining me today."

Shay's half-awakened voice cracked as she instinctively snapped into mission-mode. "I'll be there. We need to close the birthing pod investigation quickly. Besides, if the others have been watching the tidal cities, they should be able to help us narrow down where our own little escapee is."

Drasha's voice seemed to smile through the intercom. "See you in 20."

Shay lay in her bed for what seemed like a wasteful six or seven additional minutes before tucking her anxiety away and bounding out of bed. Quickly grabbing her flight jacket on her way out of the door, she paused to adjust her badge-rank which had somehow become slightly askew. She thought nothing of it as she hurried to meet her partner at the hangar deck several train-stops away.

Drasha shouted to her from the open cockpit. "They're just finishing up their sting operation from yesterday. I told them we'd be happy to assist with their clean up since they were good enough to allow us to leave them short-handed yesterday."

"Proactive. I like it," Shay said as she scrambled up the ladder. She kept to herself the rest of the run-up. She spoke only as much as necessary to cycle up the stormblade's static engines and get underway. For Drasha, it was another interminable stretch of time filled with awkward silence and she wasn't willing to let it slide this time. She tried to cut the stagnant conversation with something light-hearted. "We're almost to Kreshen, I'm pretty sure I can smell the sun-spoiled fish and cut bait from here."

Her attempt at levity worked. Shay smirked back at her. "Well, that's going to make it a lot easier for my little rat to blend in now, isn't it?"

Drasha let out an obvious gasp of surprise from the back seat. It quickly turned into a chuckle of relief. "I don't understand how you do it. I was honestly worried personal circumstances were going to get in the way today. How do you compartmentalize your life so well?"

"Sadly, practice. Besides, I probably need to joke about it regardless of what my actual emotions are. People are always prone to trigger some unwelcome emotion in you when you least expect it. It's human nature. With Xard it's a combination of rage, exasperation, disappointment, and worry."

Shay paused for a moment and looked up from the controls to stare directly into Drasha's eyes. "I choose which one I wish to amplify. It gives me focus. You'll learn to do it in time. Besides, with a known Vesni effort to try and upend my position at the moment, I need to present myself as indifferent about Xard as possible." Shay paused again and looked at Drasha in an unusual display of vulnerability. "How am I doing?"

Drasha laughed. "Damned good, sister. Damned good."

Shay finally brought the stormblade down gracefully near Patrol Delta and popped the hatch. The pungent smell of overripe fruit and seafood filled the air around them. "Goddess!" It was all either of them could say as they laughed at each other climbing out of their seats into the putrid air. After the two had regained their composure from the overpowering smells, they followed a short dockside path to the cargo staging area.

A confrontation was already underway between the animal containers. The two of them approached cautiously as they came upon Delta's team-lead berating a short middle-aged man. Shay announced herself by hailing the leader from behind, "Ashonia!"

Ashonia was one of the tallest Vesni-sentinels in the Order. She was also one of the most voluptuous. Her tight form-fitting leather flight suit was unfastened to mid-cleavage, causing her breasts to heave out of the tight crevasse with every breath. Shay suspected this had more to do with her desire to put her sexuality front and center than her inability to zip it up. Still, Shay had to admire the sheer terror her enormous frame had to be projecting onto the poor man who was now face-to-face with the heaving masses.

"I greet you in the name of the one who comes," Shay announced.

"Bless her coming, sister! You are just in time. We caught this one just before he had a chance to load up these containers for Urm. We've been tracking these shipments for some time. I'm just glad we caught one of the leaders before they had a chance to move all of the artifacts."

The small man began to protest. "As I said before, these are simply Sark beasts. Urm orders them all the time. We have regular shipments because they have regular orders. It's no mystery."

Ashonia simply scoffed at the man and began to fumble with the metal clam shell on the back of her fingerless glove. "I don't believe you sir." She paused a moment to stare into his eyes until he looked away. Then without any further word, she raised her arm toward the beast's midsection and fired the selasin on the back of her hand.

A quick flash of light emanated from within as a fan of blue-green energy emerged striking the Sark beast at its midpoint. A cloud of disintegrated molecules, about the width of a small finger, glittered momentarily in the light and then simply vanished as the beast groaned and fell to the ground in two pieces. As the vaporized molecules began to settle and disperse, the familiar oily smell of carbon residue began to permeate the inside of the animal container.

From inside the broken beast's digestive pouch rolled two small spheres. Ashonia's partner reached down to pick one up and present it to Shay. She recognized it immediately. "It's definitely a data storage device. It looks like it's of highlands origin. You were right. Local operation for sure."

Ashonia turned back to her partner. "Okay, let's open up the rest of them."

The small man suddenly began to protest by standing in front of one of the larger beasts. "There's no need for this! Please, I can give them a regurgitant. You don't have to destroy them. This one belongs to my son. He has worked most of his life raising this one to sell. It will ruin him!"

A sudden cry erupted from behind the sentinels. A boy of about ten came running between them and into the container throwing himself around the neck of the prized animal. Ashonia rolled her eyes. "Hysteria! We don't have time for this." She nodded to her partner.

Ashonia's partner drew back her arm and released it with a quick snap. Her palm struck the boy's father squarely along the bridge of his nose causing him to fall backward onto the ground. The small man began to twitch and writhe on the ground as the boy looked on in horror. Ashonia turned to the boy. "There, cry over something important." The young lad let go of the beast and threw himself onto his twitching father until the twitching finally stopped and he lay there dead.

Ashonia proceeded to cut the prized beast apart next, revealing more of the spherical relics. Her tight leather suit creaked and strained as she bent down to pick one up from the now broken beast. She held it up and spoke directly to the sobbing boy. "Your father was a law-breaker. *He* brought this moment on you. No one else." The boy simply wept over his father's corpse, nudging him endlessly in the vain hope that he would wake.

Shay was used to the brutality of the Vesni. She relished their penchant for law and order. However, the sight of the boy's dark mop of hair weeping over his lost father pierced Shay. It was too close to her own reality with Xard's paternal loss, but she walled it off and turned to Drasha. "Tragic, but at least that one has closure."

Drasha quickly changed the subject to help get Shay back on task. "Ashonia, when you investigated our illegal birthing site, was there any indication which way they might have been headed next? We want to see if we can track down the shipment in both directions."

Ashonia laughed. "To be honest, I don't think they took them anywhere. We found plenty of biomarkers in the sand all along the cliffs. The things must have been leaking like crazy. If I was going to guess, I'd say they were dumped into the ocean. The perps probably just didn't want to leave any evidence behind since they knew they were busted. I suppose it's possible they still moved the pods, but it wouldn't have been on a tidal city of any significant size given the jagged waterline in that area. They would have had to use small floaters, a lot of them based on the size of the operation they had going."

Shay pressed her for more. "Would you happen to have the tracking information of the lesser tidal cities that were in our area that week? I think I'd like to follow up to see who might have been requesting them. If we can uncover the destination, we may be able to trace it back to its origins."

Ashonia smiled back at them as she cleanly slit another beast in front of them. "Not a problem at all, I'll have them uploaded to your stormblade as soon as I finish here."

Shay and Drasha thanked the team for their help and made the short walk along the dock back toward their stormblade. The sounds of the harbor birds along the city dock at high tide had finally drowned out the shrieking child. It was a welcome distraction. Drasha's face grew more concerned. It was obvious that the scene that had just played out was still deeply wounding for her partner.

Shay broke the silence again once they were out of hearing range from Patrol Delta. "Once the tidal data is uploaded, we should also be able to narrow down Zard's possible exit routes. The tidal city that left Kael Vistyn could have docked with any number of unregistered barges before arriving at Kreshen. If we can narrow it down, we should be able to monitor his movements and intercept him."

Drasha looked at her with concern that she could be so stoic. Shay reassured her that she was fine by gently nudging her as they walked along Kreshen's bustling harbor. Drasha encouraged the new playfulness with more jokes at Xard's expense. "It will probably be a bit before they finish up. If Zard did somehow manage to make it this far he's probably starving by now. I suspect that if he's ashore here, he's probably hovering around some back-alley restaurant digging for scraps."

Shay laughed. "These omyym cities are so dull. Can you believe this is what passes for 'trendy' in the North? Bunch of brown domes covered in bird ska. If he ended up here, he's probably already on his way back. Come on, let's see if we can find anything to eat that doesn't make us retch."

12 – Noodles

Xard waited until the animal container he was in had remained motionless for some time and light no longer eked its way through the small breathing holes. Silence soon followed. When he was certain the coast was clear, he grabbed his gear along with the lev-sled of aurum and released the hatch to see what awaited him. It was a planet-side warehouse of some kind. He'd expected to see more workers on Urm, but for now it would work to his advantage.

As he eased past the handful of dock workers, he found an old utility exit and scampered out onto a rocky ledge outside. The first breath of Urm's sour air immediately seized his lungs. He quickly covered his nose and mouth with a shirt to filter the smells, but it was the view that made him feel most ill. Squinting toward the city for the first time, his heart sank as he discovered its entirety was wedged into the sideways gash of one of Urm's massive, blown-out caves.

Jagged spears of rock and metal jutted out toward the opening as reminders of just how dangerous life on Urm could be. Flickers of orange and yellow lights, more embers than signs of life, dotted the cavern's barren expanse. Yet within this spear-laden hellscape, spindly towers ascended and descended from both floor and ceiling. The dark commercial towers from above reached down toward the up-stretched habitation towers below—an illusion of arms desperately straining to touch one another, but forever out of reach.

Xard became gripped with a sudden and overwhelming sense of hopelessness. Even the jagged outcropping that he now found himself on seemed to stab at the settlement's structures. Xard's trembling hands told him that fear was already overwhelming him, but he tried to stay focused. *Okay. Okay, Xard. Think. Mining sluice. Noodle house. Where would you be from here?*

The cities of Urm had no names, only numbers. He'd learned that this was due, in part, to the fact that no one knew when a city on Urm might suddenly vaporize with another explosion. When a numbered city was destroyed, they simply built a new one further along the same longitude and gave it a different number. For Xard, city 87 was still in place, and for now it would have to be his home. Xard looked at his timepiece. 26:00. He had time if he didn't squander it.

He stared out from his rocky vantage point toward the city sprawl below. Natural light barely existed in the tight fissure that housed City 87. Even so, the mining sluices were easy enough to identify. There were about ten in this city; each glowing with an iridescent blue light to keep their prized ore from exploding before reaching its transport. Xard reasoned it would be wise to hide his selasin weapon before he went too much further, so he wrapped another cloth around his hand.

He struggled with his gear but managed to make his way down the rocky escarpment and into the street below. It was moist and humid at the cavern floor, not at all what he expected. Still, he kept the shirt tied around his face so that only his eyes peered out from beneath his dark mop of hair. Despite the taste, the air on Urm was entirely breathable, so it surprised him that almost everyone was wearing breathing gear. Much of it was even high-end. Yet the further he traveled from the shuttle port, the less fashion-friendly the wearables became.

By the time he reached the noodle vendor, he only had minutes to spare. It was a cheap, grimy cart with a half dozen stools welded to its exterior for customers. Behind the counter was a single, slender man with intricate tattoos covering the back of his bald head. He had his back to Xard as he approached and worked busily clanging pans together and stuffing ingredients into cabinets.

116

"I'm closing up now, all I have is what's left on the counter," he said flatly.

Xard waited somewhat impatiently for the man to turn around and look at him, but he didn't. So, Xard fished one of the small ceramic K-rings from his pocket and gently started tapping it against the counter. The noodle man kept his back to Xard, but paused for a moment to indicate that he had heard and understood the noise.

"It's a bit late in the evening for that, don't you think?"

Xard's muffled voice tried to answer through his makeshift mask. "One of your friends from the *Marwei* sent me." The sound of Xard's prepubescent squeaking made the noodle man finally turn around as he licked the last bits of leftover sauce from his coarse fingers. To Xard he looked decidedly unfriendly. His face was ruffled with a trim white beard and two metal pins piercing the bridge and septum of his profoundly hooked nose. What remained of the tattoos that originated on the back of his scalp now came to a point in the middle of his forehead between a pair of owlish brows.

The man poured a bowl of rum noodles for Xard. "Talk. Eat." It was all the man would say as he stared coldly into his eyes. Xard pulled the shirt down from around his face.

"I need to load up these K-rings. Your friend said you were a guy who could get it done."

"What are you loading them with?"

Xard looked down and kicked the small box of aurum ingots he had next to his feet on the lev sled. "220 half ingots." Xard slid one of the ingots across the counter to the noodle man, but his eyes never strayed from Xard's face.

"Eat. I need to make a call." The noodle man pressed a small button under his ear and his eyes rolled back into his head. The sounds of static began to bellow up from the man's throat as his face began to twitch and contort.

Xard yelped at the unexpected sight and fell from his stool, but the noodle man didn't budge. He wanted to run and run fast, but he had no way forward. This was the only path he knew of to make his currency usable. Cautiously, Xard crawled his way back up onto the stool and began waving his hand in front of the noodle man's face. No response. Xard's only comfort was the fact that this section of the city was almost completely devoid of human traffic now. It was just him and the presently-immobile noodle man.

He didn't know how long this 'call' would take, but he decided that he might as well eat while he waited. The bowl arrived steaming, not with ordinary vapor but with tendrils of iridescent mist that clung to the air above it. The noodles themselves were translucent, seemingly harvested from some deep-sea creature imported from Kael rather than made from grain—each strand refracting light like living glass. They floated in a broth that shifted colors with the ambient temperature, now amber-gold in the heat of the stall.

The first bite revealed unexpected complexity—not sickly sweet as most tourist fare, but layered with fermented umami and crystallized fruits that dissolved on contact with his tongue. The rum didn't merely saturate the dish but seemed integrated at a molecular level, releasing in micro-bursts with each bite rather than overwhelming his palate all at once. A subtle euphoria began to wash over him as his body became sated with the delicacy, nerve endings tingling as if the food were somehow tasting him back.

Time seemed to pass slowly, but he decided that he'd had enough of the rum noodles. The last few strands at the bottom had begun to pulse rhythmically, synchronizing with his heartbeat—a feature he found disturbing.

Xard slid the mostly empty bowl back across the counter, but the gentle euphoria now strengthened into dizziness. He wanted it to stop, but it only grew stronger. He was feeling sick now and could barely stay seated. He needed the noodle man to wake up. Out of desperation, he reached out to the man's contorted face and touched his cheek with his hand.

Immediately the man's eyes snapped back and stared relentlessly into Xard's face. The corners of his mouth now twisted up into a wicked grin. Xard tried to steady himself by holding on to the counter, but it was no use. He slid off the stool and onto the moist Urmian soil with a *thump*. Night was falling now, if only just for him.

***

Xard quickly found himself dreaming of past events. He was a small child again waking from a dream within a dream to the sound of arguing and distress. As he floated around the door post of his bedroom, he could see his mother in tears as she spoke with Timeon.

"We're still searching for him, but I doubt we'll find anything," he said.

Shay was desperately trying to regain her composure. "That site had been overrun with kosonor believers for months! That should have been reason enough for him to abandon the dig. But no, he couldn't let it go even when they uncovered the heretical inscriptions. Bahk! Tell me I'm dreaming, Timeon. Tell me it's all a bad dream."

Timeon sighed. "I wish that were so. As of right now, all we know is that Taigan was last seen heading toward the standing stones on the high plains. Moments later, he was gone. Some witnesses reported sensing a vibration, others reported blinding light. None of them has the same story or experience from the event. It's like they all experienced totally different events."

"Or they're all just covering for him." Shay began to clench her teeth in anger and frustration. "He just couldn't let it go. I offered him the world, but he went off chasing heresy instead. Don't pretend that's

119

not what this was about. I swear if he's not already dead, I'll kill him myself."

Shay's despair finally closed in on her, and she collapsed into a chair. "He's actually done it. He left me, and for what... some damned baubles? Damn those kosonor heretics. I knew they were whispering in his ears this whole time."

Shay buried her head in her hands. "I told him. I told him I knew how to navigate the Vesni world, but he wanted to remake it to fit us instead. He was *never* satisfied. Now he's ruined himself... and me."

Suddenly the dream changed and Xard was standing in front of them. A feeling of dread came over him as all her anger towards his father suddenly turned onto him. Shay spoke at him directly:

"Do I not offer safety? Am I not a good provider? And yet he ran off chasing something that is everything I am not. Now your father is dead. This is what happens when you go your own way. Life away from Vesni teachings is death. If you ever leave what I have built for you, boy, you will only find the same thing—loneliness and death."

***

Xard awoke with a start, staring upward into the matted nest of dark pipes and drains above him. His vision seemed to blur the harder he tried to focus. The gentle clinking sounds of the rocky slurry being carried away told him he was still near the sluice, but beyond that he wasn't sure. His head was pounding now, and he gripped his head with a moan.

He sat up and scratched his ear as he looked around for some sense of where he was or what had happened but became overwhelmed with an acute sense of nausea. He rolled over onto his hands and knees and began to retch. As the pain continued, he started to cry in between bouts of vomiting. He hated being sick, even more than he hated the Vesni.

As he started to regain his senses, it occurred to him that his sled of aurum was now missing. He frantically began to search the area for it before finally checking his own pockets. As he patted himself down, he discovered that he still had the three K-rings in his front cargo pocket. Inside was also a note. His eyes strained to see in the dim light, but he couldn't make it out.

Xard scrambled down from what could only be described as a trash heap and into the adjoining street. He began cursing under his breath, holding his head and stomach as he stumbled toward a street light. Against a nearby building, and within easy reach of Xard, a disheveled man lay slumped in the shadows. His deep, purple eye sockets and skeletal build gave Xard pause to consider whether the man might already be dead.

Still, he didn't have time to be afraid of anything but poverty. He needed to know where his money was—quickly. The hollow-eyed man never moved. He only stared into space, periodically twitching his bottom jaw. He was in the way of the direct light coming from a fixture on the wall above, and it irritated him now to have this lump of unresponsive flesh in his way. With a grunt, he put the heel of his boot on the hollow-man's shoulder and kicked him over.

He quickly unfurled the note from his pocket, trying to make sense of what was scrawled on it in the dim street light. It was some kind of verse that he didn't recognize. It wasn't Vesni, but it was clearly written as sacred text, but sacred to whom, and why was it here? It read:

116 Do not take all from your enemies but leave them something sour.

Do not slay them all outright but leave them one more hour.

117 For better to taste this bitter life and all it cannot offer,

Than to writhe in pain from wealth and bliss that glitters in the coffer.

121

118 For if he lives, he'll find the truth amidst his brothers-fair,

But if he dies, he dies in lies, forever in despair.

119 Yet if he comes around again with anger or aloof,

Be not afraid to end him then, for he does not take reproof.

Xard fished out one of his K-rings and held it up in the light. He rubbed the side of its ceramic surface until a small light appeared. Xard breathed a sigh of relief. There was currency on his K-rings; all of them. He just didn't know how much without assigning it to himself on a K-reader.

A vent suddenly lifted in the side of the building next to him just above the light. A small mechanical hand was holding it open as a greasy tuft of spiky hair emerged from the opening. It was a boy, a few years younger than Xard, sporting a pair of dark round goggles set into his dirty face. He smiled as he looked down at the hollow-eyed man.

"Hey! You saved me the trouble. Thanks for knocking him over for me. They're easier to land on that way."

As he emerged from the wall vent, he dangled down and unceremoniously dropped himself onto the hollow-eyed man's immobile frame. Then he grabbed the man with his mechanical arm and pulled him over so the back of his head was exposed. A small metal port was leaking a deep purple goo.

"Blech! He's a leaker. Damned brain jelly goo freaks are always here. I think they like the light. Anyway. My name's Kharik. What's yours?"

The young boy jutted out his mechanical hand and then realized that it was inappropriate to do so. "Oh sorry." He flipped a small switch in the side of his child-sized exo-arm until it retracted revealing his withered fingers beneath. Then he stuck out his hand again proudly.

Xard smirked and tepidly reached out his hand in response. The young boy still smelled like the oily vent he had just crawled out from, but he was relieved to have found someone that at least *seemed* friendly. "Xard," he said, being certain to use the sacred sounds. "You always this friendly with strangers? Seems a bit dangerous considering the area."

The young boy laughed in response as he fished a couple of cigarettes from his front pocket. "Clearly, you've never seen the crushing power of a Gallamar e-series exo-claw. No one hassles me around here. I'll probably replace the whole arm in a few years, but for now it works great. Besides, I just watched you roll off that trash pile. I'm betting you're pretty harmless." As he spoke, he lit the two different colored cigarettes and began to puff vigorously.

Xard crossed his arms. "Aren't you too young to smoke?"

Kharik laughed again. "You aren't from Urm, are you? No one inhales them, we just like the smell of it."

"Well, I guess it makes sense given the stench, but why two?" Xard began to fan the small plumes of smoke toward himself out of curiosity.

Kharik laughed. "It's mixing smoke, silly. You can't just smell trees and imagine you are on Kael. You have to have ocean and trees and air and all sorts of things. These are my last two I have on me, but we can share if you want. Come on, we can sit over here on this ledge where these goo freaks aren't stinking up the place." Kharik gave the hollow-eyed man a swift kick as he left but the man simply lay there.

Xard suspiciously followed his short companion to a ledge that overlooked part of a junk yard. It was a spectacular panorama of the city as the great mining haulers danced through the sky like incandescent insects. Kharik took a couple of puffs on the mixing cigs and wafted the smoke toward Xard.

"You're right, it does kind of smell like Kael," Xard said. "So, how old are you anyway?"

"Old enough." Kharik quickly changed the subject and pointed at the K-ring Xard was fumbling with in his other hand. "What's that?"

"It's a K-ring."

Kharik tilted his head. "What's it for?"

"Well, it's supposed to have my money on it, but I don't have any way to check to see if it's all there. I need to activate the account with a K-reader." Xard sulked.

"Ooh! I know a place you can find one. There's an old chem lab in Edge Tower. I'm actually supposed to scout it every week, but there's too many squatters to go there alone anymore. Hey! Maybe we can help each other! Wanna go eat first? I like fish. I know a great fish place a couple rows over if you want."

It was quickly becoming clear that his new companion was going to be difficult to keep on task. Still, if he had access to a reader, it would put his mind at ease. "Okay, sure, but the sooner I know how much money I have the sooner I can start spending it."

"Sure thing!" Kharik hopped and skipped and jumped in front of Xard all the way to the fishmongers. His hair was completely immobile from the oil and grease caked into it, and it formed a sort of tall hat on his head as he pranced from side to side down the empty street. It was a kind of parade for the boy, with Xard as its only participant or observer.

Xard's training at reading people was kicking in and he knew Kharik was trying too hard. Every few seconds the boy would turn around to make sure he hadn't run off into the shadows. He didn't seem to be a threat, but he had no reason to fully trust him outright. In any case, he kept some distance between himself and the boy's exo-arm for now.

As they emerged into a more populated area, Kharik bounded up to the fishmonger's stand and slapped the counter. "Two fish please!" He slid two small meal chits to the fishmonger who politely smiled and delivered up two steaming fish on sticks. Kharik passed one to Xard smiling but he didn't wait for Xard to eat before tearing into his own.

"Can you even eat fish from Urm?" Xard took a tentative bite from the belly of the cooked fish but couldn't quite determine its origin by taste.

"Nah. It comes from Kael. We're lucky. It's from yesterday's shipment so it's like only a week old." Kharik mumbled with his mouth full. "I get a bunch of food chits for my work at the mines and I can spend them in a bunch of different food places. This one's my favorite."

Xard gulped down the salty bite. He just hoped that his stomach would hold it down after his most recent noodle encounter.

As Kharik scraped the remaining flesh from the stick with his teeth, he tossed it to the ground. "Okay. Come help me finish my scout report and let's go see how much money you have."

13 – CHEMMERS

Xard followed the boy to one of the nearby towers that soared high into the heights of the cavern. He jumped onto a seemingly disused, open-air lift that clung to the outside of one of the spires and motioned for Xard to hop on.

"Keep your wits here, friend," he said, eyes darting excitedly. "It should be empty, but sometimes it's not. They use these empty rooms for all kinds of things. Even security avoids it." He made an exaggerated sneaking motion, his mechanical arm *whirring* softly. "But the chemmers are the real problem. They go crazy for the leftover meds."

"Chemmers?" Xard asked.

"You know, chem-heads, jelly freaks, sniffers. They'll cut your throat for a single vial of anything that makes them feel good." Kharik drew his finger across his throat with a dramatic sound effect, then immediately bounced back to his playful demeanor. "But don't worry! I know how to avoid 'em."

Xard instinctively reached for the selasin under the cloth wraps on his hand, reassuring himself it was still there.

As the lift ascended, the city's tall towers faded into dark silhouettes under the smoggy twilight air. It was cooler and drier the higher they went. Noises and sounds from the city below began to fade away until only the drone of heavy machinery could be heard in the distance. Halfway up, the lift shuddered to a stop.

"What's happening?" Xard whispered urgently.

Kharik's eyes widened with momentary fear before he forced a grin.
"Happens all the time. Watch this!" He kicked the side panel twice
with his boot, and the lift groaned back to life.

From below, a shrill voice called up. "Who's up there? You stealing
my spot again, you little grub?"

"Go, go, go," Kharik whispered, suddenly serious. "That's Nylka.
She's the worst. Burned half her face off trying to cook chems
herself."

When the lift finally stopped, they heard shuffling from the corridor
ahead—the unmistakable dragging gait of someone too far gone on
synthetic drugs. Kharik pulled Xard against the wall, his playfulness
momentarily suspended as they waited for the footsteps to fade.

"That was close!" Kharik whispered, excitement returning to his
voice as he tumbled from one side of the platform to the other in
what he clearly thought was a tactical maneuver. Xard rolled his eyes
but followed, crouching low just to humor him. As they passed a
room where a chemmer lay sprawled out, eyes open but unseeing,
Kharik put a finger to his lips and tiptoed past, making exaggerated
steps. Despite the show, Xard noticed how carefully the boy
moved—his antics masking what was clearly hard-earned survival
instinct.

Every few steps, a small, dirty, glowing panel would appear, casting
sickly green light across their faces. Kharik counted them in a
whisper as he moved deeper into the vacant structure, occasionally
making weapon noises under his breath when they passed dark
doorways, but stopping immediately whenever actual sounds echoed
through the halls.

A crash from nearby made them both flatten against the wall.
Through an open doorway, they glimpsed three chemmers fighting

over a small vial, their skin covered in weeping sores, movements jerky and unpredictable. One slashed at another with a piece of jagged metal. Kharik grabbed Xard's hand with his non-mechanical one and pulled him quietly past the opening.

"That's why I don't use the front entrance anymore," he whispered. "Too many of them there now." A few moments later, he finally stopped and turned with a triumphant grin. "This should be it."

Kharik rubbed off the gummy magnetic resin that was stuck to the biometric panel and slapped his bare hand down onto it. Nothing happened. He tried again, this time making a show of pressing harder, his tongue sticking out in concentration. The sound of breaking glass echoed from nearby, followed by angry shouts. Kharik's playfulness momentarily gave way to genuine panic as he slapped the panel harder.

"Come on, come on," he muttered. On the third attempt, the pneumatic door began to click as locking mechanisms inside began to release. The door finally slid open with a loud flatulent sound.

Despite the danger, both boys burst into uncontrollable giggles, shoving each other as they stumbled inside. Xard quickly closed the door behind them, engaging the manual lock. It was the first time he had genuinely laughed at anything since his problems began. For the briefest of moments, he was no longer a runaway viko on a dangerous planet—he was just a 12-year-old boy snickering at a rude noise with a new friend.

"Shh! They'll hear us!" Kharik whispered through his giggles, which only made them laugh harder before they finally managed to compose themselves.

Kharik moved around the darkened room with the confidence of someone who'd been there before, flipping switches and pressing buttons until he found the light panel. When the illumination sputtered to life, they squinted against the sudden brightness. It was a chem lab alright, but signs of intrusion were everywhere—broken containers, ransacked cabinets, and a dried pool of something that looked suspiciously like blood in one corner.

"This was supposed to be the clinic for this housing cluster," Kharik explained, stepping carefully around the stain. "I used to come here to transport meds and stuff, so my biodata still triggers the doors. I was always worried about getting one of those diseases you can get from the mines, you know?"

"You mean Obsidian Lung?" Xard asked, keeping his voice low as footsteps passed by outside.

"Yeah, that!" Kharik's eyes widened with dramatic horror. "And those little colored cysts under your skin that have all the spider webs and stuff that come out of them." He wiggled his fingers like creeping spiders across his own arm.

A loud *bang* from the corridor made him jump, but he quickly resumed his explanation, though his voice trembled slightly. "I absolutely refuse to get sick. Uh-uh. Nope." He shook his head vigorously, sending his spiky hair swinging. "The chemist here used to give me pills to keep me from getting anything bad like that."

The sound of something heavy being dragged across the floor came from just outside their lab.

"That'll be Malk," Kharik whispered, genuine fear flashing across his face. "He drags that metal pipe everywhere. Says it keeps the ghosts away." He tapped his head, indicating Malk's mental state. "Don't worry, he can't get in unless he has hand access like me."

As if on cue, the door panel beeped as someone tried to gain entry.

"Anyway," Kharik continued, "I remember he had a reader thing, kind of like you're talking about, somewhere in the back room. Check it out and see if it works." He pretended to hold a weapon, scanning the lab dramatically despite his obvious nervousness. "I'll stand guard!"

Xard worked his way around the maze of equipment. The smells of leftover chems still permeated the air. As he pushed open the door to the back room, the hinges squeaked, and he heard Kharik make a theatrical "shhh!" sound from the main room, followed by panicked whispering: "Someone's coming! Hurry!"

There, in the corner, half-hidden under a fallen shelf, was an antique K-reader. Its surface was dusty but the power indicator still pulsed with weak light. Xard quickly fished out his K-rings and placed them on the scanner. The machine hummed to life, its display flickering as it read the data.

The numbers that appeared made his stomach drop. Out of his 220 half ingots, only 109 had been transferred to his rings. He scanned them again, willing the numbers to change—they didn't.

The sound of angry voices grew closer outside. Through the cracked door, Xard could see Kharik pressed against the wall, his earlier bravado replaced by genuine fear as he stared at the lab's entrance. The door panel beeped again as someone tried to access it, followed by frustrated pounding.

"Is it bad? Did you get your money?" Kharik whispered as Xard returned to the main room, genuine concern momentarily overriding his fear of the chemmers outside.

"No!" Xard snapped, then immediately regretted his tone when he saw Kharik flinch. "It's not okay. He stole half my money!"

"Who?" Kharik asked, eyes wide, dividing his attention between Xard and the door that was now shuddering under repeated impacts.

"That stupid... *noodle* man over by sluice six."

Kharik began to back away from Xard slowly. "What did he look like? Did he have tattoos on his head?" He traced lines across his temples with his fingers, his playfulness completely gone now.

Xard stopped and turned to Kharik. "Wait, you know him?"

"I know that you shouldn't be friends with anyone like that." Kharik's voice was suddenly serious in a way that seemed too adult for his age. "He's one of them. He's gharsa. The death cult."

The door suddenly dented as something heavy crashed against it from outside. "You shouldn't even be alive. Did he say anything to you?" Kharik whispered, tugging on Xard's sleeve.

Xard pulled the small piece of paper he found in his pocket and showed it to Kharik. "He just gave me this."

Kharik recognized it immediately and thrust it back toward Xard. "Promise me you won't go back there. This is bad. Please say you won't go back!" His pleading was that of a frightened child now, all pretense of bravery gone.

"Fine, fine. Relax. I'll leave it for now, but no long-term promises. I don't like cheats unless it's *me* doing the cheating."

Xard tried to reassure his frightened guide by reaching out to muss up Kharik's hair but immediately regretted the gesture when he felt the thick layers of grime it contained. "Ugh!" He wiped his hand on his pants, making a face that got a small smile from Kharik despite his fear.

Another *crash* against the door, this time accompanied by the sound of failing electronics. "We need to go. Right now!" Kharik hissed, his momentary smile vanishing. He darted to the back of the lab, pushing aside an equipment cabinet to reveal a maintenance hatch. "I always have a backup plan," he winked.

Xard smirked as he quickly followed the boy into the narrow passage. "When we get out of here, I'm gonna need to set up a base somewhere for a little while till I figure out my next move. There's still enough money to live someplace nice, but I don't want to attract too much attention. And before you get any ideas, the K-rings are now coded to *me*. No chance of stealing them."

Kharik feigned a look of shock, dramatically clutching his chest despite their precarious situation. "I'm a scrounge, not a thief!"

"Well, if you can scrounge me up a place near the Vesni academy, it would help," Xard said as they navigated the dark service tunnel. Sounds of the chemmers finally breaching the lab began echoing behind them. "I just need someplace low-key, but safe."

"You want to be east of here," Kharik insisted. "Come on, I can show you a good place. We just have to avoid the Sentia outpost nearby, and we'll be fine." When they finally emerged, they found themselves on a different part of the tower's exterior. Kharik pointed to another lift nearby. "That one still works... most of the time!"

The sound of a sudden high-pitched scream erupted from somewhere down one of the hallways behind them—likely one of the chemmers finding their escape route—and the two of them quickened their steps to get away. As they slammed the grate closed on the exterior lift and began their descent to the moist floor below, they both let out an audible sigh of relief.

"Did you see their faces when they couldn't find us?" Kharik giggled, pantomiming confusion. "Stupid chemmers!" The lift creaked downward through the hazy air. Three days ago, Xard would have been horrified by all of this—the danger, the filth, the strange child with a mechanical arm. Now he found himself chuckling alongside Kharik, his hand still resting on the K-rings in his pocket. Sure, he'd lost half his money already, but somehow, watching the city unfold below them, that didn't seem like the disaster it would have been yesterday.

Despite the disappointment and the danger, he still felt he was in a good position. He glanced over at the dirty-faced boy beside him. To him, it had been a grand adventure. To Xard, it had been a harsh lesson about Urm—both the danger that lurked in every corner and the unexpected allies you might find there. In either case, at least he wasn't facing it alone anymore.

14 — Cadaver

Shay and Drasha had already sealed themselves away in their stormblade to escape the overpowering smells of rot from the city around them when Ashonia's tidal data finally clicked across the screen. The news wasn't good. Shay clenched her lips tightly as the tidal schedules came across the screen. "Dammit."

Drasha perked up in response. "What's up?"

"There weren't any smaller tidal cities on the coast this cycle because of the rough seas. Two were scheduled, but they canceled and stayed in deep ocean. The *Marwei* was the only city linkage, and that was a direct transit from Kael Vistyn and Kreshen."

"Could they still have moved the pods over land?"

"Possibly, but I think Ashonia is probably right on this one. It doesn't make sense to haul them over land when the heat was already on to them. Our best approach is to just check in with the Sentia outpost. Maybe they can shed some light on who's developing these gray birthing pods. We can check for overland marks if we do a flyby on the way, but I suspect they were probably just pushed into the sea like she suggested. It does give us one bit of good news though."

"What's that?"

"It means my little rat must have come this way. Put a notice out for Kreshen authorities to pick him up if he's spotted. Alert Kael Aeon as well. If he stayed on the *Marwei*, he's not going anywhere except under a blanket. They will be deep into polar tides for days. Kael Aeon can pick him up when he thaws out." Shay smiled a quick half-smile that signaled she was feeling slightly more in control of the situation now.

"Solid logic. I'll put out the electronic bulletins on the way." Drasha paused for a moment as the engines cycled up. "Do you mind if I ask? How long has it been?" It had suddenly dawned on Drasha that they were headed for an area near to the kosonor home lands.

"Hmm?" Shay feigned ignorance. "Oh. You mean the high plains. Drash, if I had a breakdown every time I ran across some place that traumatized me, I'd have to leave Kael entirely. Besides, we're here to catch perps, that's all the fuel I need to stay focused." She shot a reassuring smile back at Drasha. "We're doing the Goddess' work here, sister."

Shay spun up the static engines again as they lifted off from Kreshen and headed further west into the high plains. Far from the ancient coastal cities, and past the modern inner city-states, the nomadic omyym people clustered in small, dome-like, dwellings. Hidden away from the conformity of urban life, these rural villages were becoming a hotbed for heretical thinking. They were a necessary evil, but she took a deep satisfaction in bringing them correction when needed. "Let's make sure the worker bees are awake, shall we?" Shay didn't wait for a response but simply dropped in low over one of the small clusters of settlements that had linked their domes together as a small tribe.

Drasha steadied herself in the rear seat as Shay unexpectedly threw the stormblade down toward the ground in a 45-degree dive. "You're serious? Shay, history aside, you're making us a mountain of paperwork."

Shay stayed focused as she leveled out the dive at low altitude and increased the speed. "Not this time. See? Their collective is flying red banners. Only kosonor followers would be bold enough to fly

136

banners of patriarchy on a Vesni flight path. Sometimes, omyym need to be reminded that power comes from the Mother."

Shay blew over the complex at such a low altitude she could see the fast-approaching heads of the complex residents as distinct entities from their bodies. It was reckless, but she didn't care. She needed a clear head for their next engagement and petty revenge always offered her the afterglow of clarity. As she careened over the small domiciles at high speed, she heard a faint, low-pitch *blurp* below. Shay checked the rear ground cam and saw everyone scrambling for their homes.

"What did you do?" Shay continued to look back in her rear-view mirror at Drasha as she pulled the stormblade back up into a steady climb again.

"I blew them a kiss for you," Drasha smirked. "Just a bit of static discharge as we passed over. Nothing damaging, just enough to make their hair stand up and scramble any transmissions for about an hour."

Shay looked back at her companion in awe. "Great improvisation! Well-played, but damned if I shouldn't have thought of that." The two of them laughed and joked about the incident for the remainder of their flight.

In the westernmost corner of the plain was a somewhat larger cluster of settlements known as Pillix. There, in the center of the cluster, was their destination—a large, off-white building which lay rather unceremoniously across the middle of the swath of tiny shelters. Its bulbous architectural arrays and elongated, fetal footprint reminded Shay of some fallen god that couldn't stand back up on its own surrounded by hundreds of small blister-shaped followers mourning over its death.

Shay's smile turned sour as they got closer to the main structure. She let out an obvious sigh of disgust as they set down on the landing pad nearest the fallen god's 'ribs.' "For a place concerned with extending life you'd think they'd have chosen a design that wasn't so grotesque."

"What'd you expect from engineers trying to be artistic?" Drasha replied.

Shay's attention was suddenly arrested when she noted a group of three personnel coming out to greet them on the landing pad. "Did you tell them we were coming?"

"No. This was supposed to be a no-notice inquest."

Shay popped the hatch and climbed down from the cockpit with Drasha close at her heels. "This must be one of the engineers and a security team. I'll do the talking."

"Bioengineers to be more precise." The ruddy man flanked by two security personnel clasped his hands together as he began to lead the discussion. "I was wondering when the Mitera might send someone this way. I can't say it's a surprise, what with all the murmuring among the omyym about black market birthing and such. Oh, but excuse my manners. I'm Mehd Arkin, chief science officer here at the Western Highland Station. If you please, come with me and we can discuss your concerns away from the dust."

"I'm Agent Shayameen and this is Agent Drasha. What ever became of the previous administrator here? He hadn't been here very long."

Mehd Arkin continued walking inside as he answered their questions. It annoyed Shay that he was trying to lead them along by directing his voice in front of them as he walked to get them to pick up the pace. She'd seen his kind before. All these Sentia worms were the same condescending prick, just with a different face and name.

Mehd Arkin continued. "Well then. The administrator before me suffered an unfortunate exposure to a polycycline inhibitor. It seems he had been remiss in some of the more basic safety protocols and died when he contracted one of the tidal city infections. Dreadful really. Still, I'm grateful that Sentia Corp felt I was the right person to get the project running again."

He led them to a small, non-descript conference room and nodded to the security personnel that they could wait outside. The room was uninspired and barren, almost antiseptic except for a single projection system in the middle of the polished steel conference table. He motioned for them both to be seated as he took his seat at the head of the table.

Shay wasn't about to play this game with a man. Shay grabbed the back of one of the chairs and pulled it right next to Mehd Arkin so that there was no table to act as a barrier between them. "So then. It's clear you've had some time to consider that someone would be by to inquire about illegal birthing. I can appreciate that. That should save us the trouble of the initial denials and redirects Sentia usually throws up at the first few meetings."

Mehd Arkin smiled patronizingly at Shay. "But of course. Our contract with the Mitera is our top priority. Any kind of illegal birthing operation would be a threat to us as well. Surely you could understand that. We control the means of reproduction for the omyym at her behest. If some other agency is working behind the scenes to undercut that, it only serves to weaken our position."

Shay leaned back in her chair and ejected a small black cylinder from the bracer on her wrist. "Here's the holo from our encounter with the perp. I need you to look at the pods and see if you can identify anything unusual about them, where they might have originated, their usage, anything."

Mehd Arkin slid the cylinder to a small groove in the table and brought up the holo of the encounter. He let out a sarcastic gasp as he fast forwarded past the initial encounter with Mr. Agarai. "*Brutish,*" he muttered under his breath as he scrolled forward. As the scene went internal to the building, he leaned in closer to the images. "See this? There in the background. A class-IV generator. It alternates the power based on individual pod requirements. It's definitely a birthing operation."

"We're well aware it was a birthing operation. Does it give you any indication where the operation might have been launched from? What about the pods themselves? We've never seen anything like these. Could it be stolen hardware?"

Mehd Arkin continued to stare at the operation intensely, ignoring Shay's probing. "Fascinating. The brown hue on the pods themselves, very unusual. The white pods we use at Sentia are rich in calcium. The child inside draws calcium directly from the pod for bone development. These seem to be completely devoid of it.

"Although, it's possible that they are infusing calcium in some other way. As you're aware, full-sized pods like this pose a risk of psychopathy if used for gestating a full-sized adult. If I have any good word to offer you, it's that your Mitera was wise to have us develop the smaller versions, even if it isn't entirely profitable for us."

Shay squinted. "You have exclusive rights to birthing pods. How is that not profitable?"

"People are patient to wait for a child, but they're desperate to regain one they've lost," he sighed. "Our people had factored in regenerative cloning into our pricing model, but demand quickly died off. With cloning, there's no memory transfer, so it fell out of favor once people realized they weren't actually getting back the loved one they'd lost."

Mehd Arkin nodded toward the holo again as he continued. "These men you accosted, they're either birthing new children, or building an army. In either case, it's a new player in the game. Someone with resources by the look of these cooling units. How unfortunate for them that they have you to look forward to."

140

"Hardly," Shay retorted. "In another month this issue will solve itself. Once people learn that extended life is a perk of obedience to the Order, I think even the omyym would wait their turn to bear children. Their legal birthing window is two years. I suspect the law will double that with the new life-extension cyrums coming to market."

"Yesssss. About that. There might actually be some delay in our original estimation of when that can be delivered."

Now it was Shay's turn with a sarcastic sigh. "You can't be serious?" Shay leaned back in her chair and crossed her arms as she passed a glance to Drasha and back. "Is the Mitera aware of this?"

"She is not. However, I should say that the delay is only temporary. In fact, it's conceivable that we may still be able to deliver by the deadline she requested, but there is no guarantee." He stood defiantly as they pressed him with their silence. "You seem to think life extension research is something that just occurs naturally as a result of funding. It is not. It also takes resources.

Need I remind you that you are all about to be the beneficiaries of our finest work? The missing link, the bridge between life and death, the very essence of man can now be etched into the ether and drawn back out again. What pod-births failed to do, our new genomats will finally accomplish. The days of back-alley birthing are almost at an end, and I can assure you that if your Mitera is getting all the glory, we're getting all the profit."

Mehd Arkin paused to call up an image of a roughly human-sized packet of cellular slurry. "Stem cell genomic matrix. It acts as a biogenetic clone scaffold from a fixed-in-time cyrum imprint. Trigger the genomat with any remaining genetic material and the person is reformed fully intact. They can be recalled endlessly for 200 years and cloned again. With the right *resources*, that imprint could last indefinitely."

Mehd Arkin stood up and walked around the side of the room and stood again where the table was between them again before bringing up a hologram that marked each planet's productivity. "Our main facility on Meratis, as you know, is primarily concerned with terraforming that planet for further research. Our other outposts however on Urm and Carcinia are all overflowing with funds and resources. Great strides have been made in service to our contract with the Mitera *there*. Kael on the other hand, has only funds."

"Explain," Shay said stoically.

"Kael's tidal cities are petri dishes of microbial soup, as it were. They are sick, infectious. Each one gestates its own diseases in isolation and then suddenly spreads them to the next point of contact. We spend what resources we have simply countering the diseases on Kael. It's why *we* are suddenly without an administrator and why *you* are suddenly behind schedule."

Shay leaned forward in her chair, holding him in her stern gaze. "You mistake me for someone you can casually ascribe the blame to. I'm well aware of what kind of 'resources' this outpost has at its disposal. All I have to do is look at how quickly all the ghettos around the highlands have emptied to know exactly what kind of resources are being consumed for your research. The Mitera turns a blind eye to your methods because you produce results. Do not expect that arrangement to remain intact if the deliverables don't appear."

Mehd Arkin stood upright and looked directly down his nose at Shay. "Perhaps then, the answer is to increase the birthrate. We are restricting the use of birthing pods at her behest, but it is the Vesni that license the natural births. Pod-born are largely sterile and entirely inadequate for human research as you are also aware.

"If the rate of natural births were increased, we would have an ample supply for our research. While our methods might be questionable, we are not inhumane. Survivors are always returned to their communities. No harm done. However, if population growth is the

Order's concern, I'm sure we could come to some arrangement in which such overages could be quietly disposed of."

Shay threw a disgusted smile at him. "Oh, you're good. Slippery but good. Our arrangement exists only because it's mutually beneficial. If it ever ceases to be so, I suspect you would find that 'lack of resources' would be the least of your concerns. The Mitera's requirement for licensing is largely ceremonial anyway. It's merely a way to assert influence. Something you probably already understand. I can respect that, but as to increasing the birthrate, that's something you would need to take up with the Mitera herself next month."

Mehd Arkin smiled back at her officiously. "Well then, it would be in my best interest to press the issue with Sentia Meratis to accelerate the research as best they can."

"Indeed."

Mehd Arkin put his hands behind his back and began to pace in front of the table as he spoke. "In the meantime, I'll have one of our own agents look into this renegade pod issue for you. Who knows, perhaps if we can uncover the pods you are speaking of, we could find a way to use them for our own experimentation purposes. It's a win-win."

Shay stopped him before he got too far. "Wait. Sentia has *agents* now? What kind of agents? I thought you were using local omyym officials."

He looked at Shay as if she'd asked the dumbest question he'd ever heard. "Well, let's see. The Vesni handle all the religious business. The constables handle the city-states. The local omyym handle pretty much everything else out here in the wilds.

"But, you see, there's still one glaring problem. We can't exactly have the locals snooping around on this issue if their own people could be behind it. Predators guarding the livestock and all that. Besides, they're mired in bureaucracy as you well know. They might be dim, but they are fiercely protective of their own interests. But, not to worry. I have just the right agent in mind for the job."

Drasha finally spoke from her forgotten corner of the room. "Is he loyal?"

"To the money at least, yes... and to the enhancement drugs. He's omyym himself, but he's been slowly improved since childhood. Strapping young man, not a single cybernetic enhancement, it's all biological. A wonder really. We plan to market the finished process to the Gallamar where the living conditions are much more extreme. In any case, he goes by the name Fasaan. I'll be sure to send a communique with his details, so your people don't accidentally try to kill him. Now, if there's nothing else, I really should get to work on the Mitera's research."

Shay and Drasha both stood in unison. It was clear to Shay that Sentia had a play in this evolving mess, but she didn't know what it was yet. For now, she was content to know she had followed this trail to its end. As they walked to their stormblade, they could feel the heat of Mehd Arkin's stare ensuring they made it completely off the property.

As the hatch closed and the engines cycled up, Shay looked up into the rear-view mirror at Drasha. "I know you were observing his mannerisms; what was your take?"

"He's over-confident. They either already have the research completed and are lying about it, or they are completely oblivious to how strongly the Mitera will react to this news. It's difficult to think that stupidity is the reality here."

"I agree. He's hedging, which means he has some other stake in the game. And agents? I didn't buy that whole discretion argument. He's lying. I've come to expect it from men when they get a little taste of power. They all unravel the same way. Let's get back to Kael Vistyn and report in. We have one more loose-end to follow up before we can worry about apprehending my son."

15 — FLIPP

Xard and Kharik traveled quickly across the dimly lit streets being careful to avoid any unwanted attention. The younger boy had pulled out a small respirator from his cargo pocket and offered Xard a few quick breaths. "You look like you're gonna pass out."

Xard waved him off. "Nah, I'm fine. We have training for all these kinds of locations. This shirt works perfectly well."

"What kind of training? Where are you from anyway?" Kharik continued to talk as he walked backwards looking at Xard through his darkened goggles.

Xard hedged. "Well, I'm actually on a special program right now with the Order. It's a test, to uhm... see if I can bypass the security at the Vesni academy."

Kharik continued to look at Xard as he walked backward, but he didn't speak. His goggle-covered eyes gave no immediate indication as to whether he was buying his story or not. Xard continued to elaborate in bits and pieces as ideas came to him, becoming more confident in his lies with every turn. "You know, I really shouldn't be telling you any of this. You could be one of their spies. I mean, you knew exactly where the academy was when I mentioned it."

Kharik stopped in his tracks and pulled down his respirator until it revealed his filthy grin. "No, no, no. I wanna help! What do we have to do? I know where everything is here. I have to. I run errands for FLIPP, and they send me all over. What's your secret mission? Do you get to kill anybody? Do you have to sneak around and stuff?"

"Woah. Slow down." Xard looked around as if spies could be listening and began to whisper more of his half-truths to the boy. He didn't like lying to him, but he was good at it. Besides, the boy had what he needed at the moment, and his impromptu guidance was proving useful.

"We can't talk about this out in the open. If the Vesni academy is alerted, the project will fail, and they'll just continue training the new voithos the same way they always did. But if it works, well then, there could be a whole new program to train the new recruits. That's why it's so important. I have to infiltrate the academy and find their secrets."

"What secret? Is it a super weapon? A new cure or something? Do they have a bunch of cyptum in there? Oh, I know. Is it a super weapon?"

Xard cut him off. "You already said super weapon."

"So, it *is* a super weapon!" Kharik bounced on his tip-toes.

"No, I didn't say that, but I mean, it could be. I just don't know. Whatever it is, it's hidden in there and I have to find it."

"I wanna help. Are you allowed to have helpers? I can be a helper. I can be like your general or something. Ooh, I know. We can be like stalkers and sneak around and kill people and stuff." Kharik continued alternating between martial arts and shooting sounds as he bounded down the darkened street.

"First off, there's no such thing as a stalker. The only things even close to that are Vesni agents. Second, you can't be a general. What would that make me?"

Kharik brushed off Xard's rebuttal. "Wrong. Wrong. Wrong. Wrong." Kharik emphasized each step with a new pronouncement of "Wrong."

Xard stopped and crossed his arms until Kharik turned around and noticed he had gotten too far ahead of his new friend and ran back. Xard looked down at him and persisted. "No stalkers. No, you can't be a general. I've traveled all over Kael and now Urm and I assure you the Vesni are the only true human weapons out there anymore."

Kharik crossed his arms right back at him. "I've seen one. Right here on Urm. Hiding in the shadows. The next day, one of the FLIPP vendors was dead."

He paused for a moment as he held his ground and then broke into a smile again. "Can I be a captain? How about a captain? You can be a general if you want and I'll be a captain. Captain Kharik. Captain K for short." Kharik didn't wait for Xard's approval. He simply turned around and began bounding down the street again until they reached the outskirts of the city's Sentia outpost.

***

Kharik's pupils dilated as they approached the oxidized pipes and corroded metal troughs that formed the informal barrier to the medical grounds. His breath quickened, fogging his respirator with each shallow gasp. "Wait," he hissed, grabbing Xard's sleeve with trembling fingers. "Look at it. Too clean. Too white."

The Sentia outpost gleamed like a polished tooth in the mouth of a decaying beast. Unlike the rust-bitten structures of Urm, its surfaces were sealed with antimicrobial enamel that repelled the omnipresent grime of the mining cavern.

"It looks okay," Xard whispered. "We just—"

"No!" Kharik's voice cracked. "It's never okay. We stick to the pipes. Any tech spots us, they'll tag us as specimens." His eyes darted toward the outpost's iris-like entrance ports. "That's what happened to Mev's older brother. Said he was going in for a lung flush after the Sector 8 collapse. Never came back out. Next time Mev saw him, he

149

was wandering the chem dens, eyes all milky, tubes growing out of his arms like they were part of him."

"Like the chemmers back at the tower?" Xard asked.

Kharik nodded frantically. "Where do you think they get the chems? Sentia makes them. Tests them. The chemmers are just... leftovers. Failed experiments that can still walk." He pointed to faint blue lights pulsing along the perimeter of the outpost. "See those? Scanner arrays. They can read your biopatterns from fifty spans away. They're always looking for new baselines.

I usually crawl through the pipes to get back, but there's no way you would fit." Kharik paused, his gaze locking with Xard's. A sheen of sweat glistened on his forehead despite the chill air. "Just promise me you won't leave me if they spot us, okay? They separate you first. That's how it starts." True terror flashed across his face—not the false bravado of a child, but the raw fear of someone who'd seen something no one his age should ever witness.

Xard nodded silently, an uncomfortable knot forming in his stomach. He pulled his shirt back up over his face and followed Kharik into the twisted labyrinth of metal.

The outpost stretched broader than it stood tall, its sterile white exterior an unnatural intrusion against Urm's rusted, decaying skeleton. As they reached the furthest edge of the complex, a piercing klaxon split the air. It wasn't the dull warning of a mine collapse— this was a high, almost surgical sound that seemed to slice through their skulls.

Kharik shrieked, his eyes wild with recognition. "Specimen alert! They've scanned us!" He bolted through the maze of pipes and metal, movements frantic and primal.

Xard lunged after him, grabbing the scruff of Kharik's shirt as the boy stumbled on a metal ledge. "Come on, captain! No time for napping." Xard took the lead now, though he had no idea where they were going. He only knew he never wanted to discover what made the small boy so terrified.

As they fled, Xard glimpsed something through a gap in the twisted metal—a figure in white being escorted from the facility. Its movements were mechanical, almost puppeted, with tubes snaking from beneath its sterile coveralls. Two techs in blue masks guided it toward a transport pod, their gloved hands never actually touching their charge.

The klaxon faded behind them, replaced by their labored breathing. Xard doubled over, lungs burning, while Kharik collapsed against an abandoned hab unit, head buried in his hands. When he finally looked up, the tearstains had carved clean tracks through the grime on his cheeks.

"Can we find a new base for you tomorrow? I want to go home now." His voice quavered, all pretense of adventure stripped away. "They'll scan this whole sector now. Looking for anomalies. Looking for us."

Xard put his arm around Kharik and patted him on the shoulder as he caught his breath. "Sure thing, captain. Sure thing." When they had rested a moment, Xard finally stood up and reached out his hand to Kharik to hoist him back up. "So. You're the scout. Which way should I go? Should we just meet here tomorrow?"

Kharik brushed himself off, still trembling from their recent brush with discovery. "You can try to come stay with me at FLIPP if you want. You just can't tell anyone that you have a mission. They only take people that have no job or are lost. You have to say you're lost or something. Maybe you can say you lost your memory and don't know where you came from. They like it better if they think no one will come looking for you."

"Sounds charming. You live there? I thought you just worked for them."

"Yeah, a bunch of us do. You just have to not make the guards angry because the matron always sides with them. She's the boss. If she likes you, you'll get a lot of work."

"Hmm. If they let me stay there, I may not need my own base at all. I could just use FLIPP as my base. Could that work?"

Kharik smiled again from under his respirator and nodded. "You can stay in my bunk pod. They have an empty one you could have. Come on. Let's go home."

***

Xard and Kharik made the shortened trek across the dark expanse of dilapidated buildings until they came to another somewhat urban area. Such was his experience across all of Urm so far; areas teeming with life nestled between areas of urban rot. They were nearer to the cave opening now, and nearer still to the Vesni academy. Xard's mind quickened as he started to get a better sense of the scale of City 87. This decision to follow his young companion was paying off and things finally seemed to be moving in his favor.

When they reached the urban area near sluice two, Kharik moved quickly between the growing volume of local denizens on the street, dodging between legs and carts as he worked his way toward some unseen destination. Xard struggled to keep up, excusing Kharik's rudeness to passers-by out of habit. They finally reached a solitary black spire that stretched up into the core of the cave. It seemed monstrously tall to Xard, owing to its lack of exterior light against the dark.

Along its base wrapped its only illumination, a dim holo-marquee which announced its somewhat pretentious name: Foundation for Lost Indigents' Protection and Productivity. The words cast an impersonal green hue onto the surrounding structures, but Kharik seemed at home in the blighted building and darted ahead before turning to wave Xard closer. "Come on! I'll let you meet the matron."

All around the foyer, lightly-fed children of various ages scrambled in and out of the utilitarian structure. The oldest one couldn't have been more than 15 by Xard's reckoning, but they all moved with purpose. He followed Kharik through the main foyer toward a door on the far side guarded by two fully-armed and armored men. He wasn't sure at first if they were real or merely statues owing to their rigid stance and highly-polished obsidian face shields.

It wasn't until Kharik provoked them that they even bothered to look his way. Kharik bounded up to the door, pulled down his breather and shouted directly toward the black-masked guards. "Hey! Let the matron know I have a new FLIPPr for her."

One of the guards slowly turned his polished head down to meet Kharik's face. He put his hand on Kharik's chest and slowly pushed him back away from the door. "Stop showing off for your new friend." Then the guard turned to Xard.

"New FLIPPr, huh? Meh, new meat for the grinder. Don't let this little cupa convince you that you can disrespect us. You'll learn that quickly enough." The other guard piped up from behind his mask. "Gods! I hate foyer duty." He reached up until his wrist was at his ear. "Matron? New arrival if you are interested... Okay, in you go."

Kharik stuck out his tongue at the guard as he walked past him and led Xard inside the matron's office. It was opulent by Urmian standards, but the peeling metal coatings gave way to flashes of rust even within her well-appointed room. At the center was a small bureau with an even smaller woman whose head was obscured by an expansive holo-sheet of expenses. As she collapsed the image between them, she forced a toothy smile from a pronounced jaw. Her pointed features lacked any kind of softness in spite of her efforts to appear friendly, and it made Xard immediately uncomfortable.

"Ahh! Young man, what have you brought for me today?" The matron stood as she spoke but gained little in the way of height as she did so. She walked deliberately toward Xard and clasped her hands as she waited expectantly for Kharik to respond.

"Well matron, I was scouting the far sluices like you requested and I found him on one of the junk heaps."

The matron snapped her eyes back to Kharik. "Did you finish the report? Have you turned it in? We don't get paid for late scouting reports."

Kharik's body went rigid with her gaze. "I have it ready. We even got the chem station. I just have to drop it off at the counter."

"Well done. See that you do. Now, as for you, young man." The matron began to walk in circles around Xard occasionally grabbing his arm or poking his sides. "Hmm. Not mal-nourished. Reasonably strong. Good stock. Where did you come from?"

Xard's training kicked in. "I just remember being on the heap. All I know is that my father abandoned me, and my mother beat me. I've been on my own ever since." He tried to keep it as close to the truth as he could without giving too much away.

"Who is the father? Anyone I should be worried about changing their mind and coming back for you?"

"Last I heard he was dead," Xard replied.

The matron nodded. "Very well then. You should know that FLIPP is not an orphanage, and I am not your care-taker. Although we do provide for housing and other essentials, FLIPP is a business and it makes me a great deal of money. You make me money; I give you purpose. The harder the task, the greater the privileges. As our name states, we provide protection, you provide productivity. Does this seem amenable to you?"

154

Xard nodded.

"Very well then. Welcome to FLIPP. I'll have Amnon escort you up to your quarters with Kharik." The matron simply turned away from Xard and went to sit back behind her desk.

Xard leaned over and whispered to Kharik, "Is that it? She didn't even ask my name?"

Before Kharik could answer, a large dark hand rested on Xard's shoulder from behind. "Gentlemen, I'll be escorting you to your room now." Xard turned in surprise to see a very young, dark-skinned man standing behind him out of nowhere. "My name is Amnon. Follow me, please."

Xard was astounded. "Woah! You have a voidskin here on Urm? That's amazing! The matron must really be rich!" Xard grinned from ear to ear as the three of them left the office and walked back into the bustling foyer.

Amnon simply rolled his eyes. "There are two of us here. You'll learn who we both are in time." Amnon walked deliberately toward the lift near the opposite side of the foyer and waited patiently while Kharik dropped off his scouting reports.

Xard began to study the man closely. "Wow, I mean, I didn't think they let two voidskin males work in the same city let alone the same building."

Amnon turned and smiled condescendingly at Xard. "Yes. We're special. You know something of the voidskin culture, do you? That's a surprise for someone so covered in filth." He plucked at Xard's shirt and let it snap back until puffs of Urmian dust filled the space they were standing in.

Xard realized he was probably giving too much away, but it suddenly didn't make sense the more he thought about it. The voidskin were extraordinarily rare and highly respected. It was improbable that one would even be on Urm let alone be living there, but two? Amnon stared impatiently across the foyer at Kharik as Xard's gaze began to peel away at the man's persona. One thing was certain, there was never a voidskin that was intimidated by Xard, and this man was uncharacteristically perturbed.

Xard tried to unbalance him. "So, will you be teaching us things? What are your favorite subjects? Do you do complex mining calculations? What kind of weapons are you skilled in?"

Amnon scoffed and paused his distant stare across the foyer to silence Xard's pestering. "How old are you, 12? I've got about 10 years more experience on Urm than you by the sounds of it, so just focus on learning what the matron has in your learning queue. You won't be doing any quantum physics here."

It was working. Xard respected the voidskin to a fault and it was becoming clear to him that Amnon was some kind of charlatan. He tried to resist the urge to call him out on it. It wasn't a prudent move given his precarious situation, but he respected the voidskin too much to let some hack claim to be one. Xard tried to allay his fears by sticking out his hand as a peace offering. "Well, if I'm a new FLIPPr then I guess I should introduce myself. I'm Xard."

Amnon reluctantly stuck out his hand in response.

Xard's visage suddenly darkened. He held on to Amnon's hand and looked back into his eyes with deep disdain. His sense of pride in what the voidskin were to the system, and to him personally, swelled inside of him. "The voidskin don't shake hands. It's against their culture because it exposes the serial number on their wrists."

Amnon returned Xard's gaze and tightened his grip. "Perhaps I've simply adapted to local culture?"

Xard winced as the grip got tighter but turned his gaze momentarily to the number on the man's wrist. "The voidskin don't even get their dermal numbers until they're 25. You're not even old enough. Besides, the last three numbers are the intelligence score. Your numbers would mean you were a vegetable.

So how did you darken your skin? Dermal stains? Gene therapy?" Xard yelped as the grip got tighter but held his gaze.

Amnon suddenly relaxed his grip not wanting to draw attention to the situation. He smirked at Xard and whispered to him. "What's your play here, kid?"

"I don't know yet, but I know how to keep a secret. Maybe one day I'll ask a favor in exchange for keeping that secret to myself."

"Pssh. You'd only be hurting yourself. Where do you think all of the money for this building comes from? Scavengers running errands? Child-sized miners? No, kid. It comes from us—two voidskin men teaching the lost rabble of Urm how to have a better life.

It's why wealthy philanthropists from Carcinia to Kael send us credits by the transport-full. But... if someone were to call our authenticity into question? Well, I expect you, your friend, and just about everyone else here would end up back out on the street."

Amnon pointed toward the two guards across the foyer. "See those two? They are two of hundreds that work here. They've paid their dues and worked all of the different roles here. The foyer is the last station before they leave. The pay here is miserable, but they put up with it because a glowing review from the matron opens doors into the big mining security jobs. It's very dangerous and very lucrative work."

Amnon turned his gaze back to Xard. "I imagine that if hundreds of skilled security personnel suddenly lost their big payday after babysitting here for years, there wouldn't be anywhere the responsible party could hide. So, tell me again. What's your play here kid?"

Xard suddenly realized that he'd lost his immediate edge, but it was still valuable information nonetheless. Whatever his move, it would have to wait until he no longer needed FLIPP and was safely away from Urm. Kharik bounded up to them before he had a chance to respond. "Mission complete! What did I miss?"

"Amnon was just telling me the virtues of minding my own business... and being nice to the guards."

"Ha!" Kharik slapped him on the back as he laughed, sending another plume of dust into the air. "So true! Except for the foyer guards. You can pretty much do anything to them. They're all mad because they have to play nice or they won't get picked for any good jobs on Kael. Come on, let's go meet the pod mates!"

16 – Jurisdiction

Day had worn into deep night for Shay by the time she'd returned to Kael Vistyn. As she walked the cobblestone streets toward her home her mind was awash with thoughts. She liked her work. It kept her personal life at bay. Now that it was over, she had to face the silence again.

She avoided going home right away, instead opting for cloistering in the streets around her home again and again until she had forgotten where she was. It wasn't until she saw the wilted remains of the three flowers across her path that Xard once again intruded into her consciousness. As she looked up, she noted her kitchen portico and realized she was home.

At first, she wanted to leave the dreary flower remains there. It had become a familial crime scene of sorts. She needed to look at it—to catalog it. She needed it to remind her of what she had done so that she could validate her actions with a bit of self-talk.

Instead, Shay let out a resigned sigh and squatted down by the frail stems, gently picking them up in her hands in the pale city lights. "*I guess you deserve a proper burial after all,*" she whispered to herself. She walked into her home and drew a small book out from a dresser beside her bed. It was an archaic piece of memorabilia stuffed with fragments of things she once associated with Tai. She paused and poured herself a glass of wine first, taking a generous swig before opening its pages.

As she flipped through the tiny book, she found a section which held a poem Tai had once written her about their son. It had made her laugh when he read it to her all those years ago because he had so accurately captured his persona within its verses.

Heart of fire; head of flint.

Fear not its lighting; heaven sent.

It was a hollow echo to her now. She laid the remains of Xard's three colorful flowers inside its pages as a memorial and pressed them closed. It had been days now with no report of Xard's sighting. She hated him... and she needed him. He was all that was left of Tai, and she needed him to somehow answer for all of the questions his father had left unanswered.

"Where the hell are you, boy?" Shay muttered to herself as she blinked away a stillborn tear from her eye and walked back toward his room. It was a disheveled mess. She hadn't noticed it on the day he'd gone missing. Clothes and cabinets were all laid bare owing to his hasty packing. It was a good sign. It probably meant his departure was spurious, unplanned. Perhaps he would be back sooner than expected.

Shay lay down on his bed and pulled his pillow close into her arms as she pondered his possible moves. She inhaled it deeply, grasping for his scent but only found Tai's. It was unmistakable. The scent had consumed her throughout their marriage.

Now in her moment of isolation, it had become a ghost, haunting her every decision. The sudden, unexpected fragrance of her consort became an aerial assault against her carefully constructed defenses. They were her shield against the pain of his betrayal, but with every new breath, memories and emotions still roiled to the surface. Before long, the emptiness of his absence had begun to consume her in the dark.

When she could resist his memory no longer, she surrendered to the pain and began to sob into the pillow. Between her cries she lashed out in desperation at Tai, blaming and pleading in equal portions. "Why did you leave me here alone? Why didn't you take me with you? You didn't even ask. Even if you knew I'd refuse you, you should have let me choose. Why did you leave me with nothing?" But the night offered no response.

***

The gentle *whirr* of Xard's alarm woke her the following morning. She sat up trying to reorient herself in her unusual surroundings. She had fallen asleep in his room but roused herself out of bed and attempted to refocus for the day. With any luck she would get a definitive lead on the illegal birthing case and close it out quickly.

She grabbed the sack of K-rings she had seized from the operation out of her personal lockup and headed out the door. The sooner she could get to work, the sooner she could be focused on something other than her own personal issues. Drasha was already there and waiting as Shay tossed the sack into the side storage compartment on her stormblade.

"You look like hell, Shay. Are you ill?" Drasha chided her gently. "It was the dorberry wine again, wasn't it?"

It hadn't occurred to Shay to check her own personal appearance before darting back to work. "I'm fine, it's just that the wine didn't mix well with that mess we ate in Kreshen." Shay checked her face and hair in the rear-view mirror as she hopped into her seat before giving up and covering it all with her helmet. "Let's check these serial numbers on the K-rings from the perp. Hopefully it's not going to be another dead end. It's all we've got at the moment."

"Got it, Shay. Voltane central cluster then? I'll alert the city municipality we're incoming."

Shay nodded, and they were on their way. Time passed almost imperceptibly before they were out of the static belt again and screeching over one of the larger city-states within the central plateau. "Goddess, I hope we don't have to deal with one of those overly-bureaucratic imbeciles today. I hate getting involved in local affairs."

Drasha teased her playfully. "What's the matter, Shay? Longing for the days when Xard's cohort called every few hours? This is the most interesting case we've had since the traveling cult evangelist we arrested a few years back. You remember, the one that tried to use the 'power of the 12' or something? Or was it 10? I can't remember. One's as crazy as the next."

Her comment elicited a small chuckle from Shay. "True enough statement when it's just us. But collaborating with the slag here is predictably frustrating—every time. Don't let the urban view and fancy walls here fool you. They're still omyym. You'll see that once you have to start working with them for any length of time. Come on, let's go check in with whatever they are calling 'authorities' these days."

As they touched down on the station's hexagonal roof, Shay didn't waste any time. It was clear that the place made her uncomfortable, but she knew how to play the game. She swung open the translucent door to the local omyym precinct amidst a cacophony of arguing and struggle as the local authorities took turns handling a swarm of domestic issues. Arms and hands flailed in wild protest as suspects buzzed about their innocence. There, in the center of the hive, was a singular station chief. His expression changed from frustration to defeat as Shay and Drasha entered the building.

The metronome of Shay's boots clicked into a hypnotic rhythm across the stone floors and slowly silenced the rabble inside. By the time they had finished their impromptu processional to the chief's central office the noise of the building had dulled into a gentle murmur. Shay dropped the sack of ceramic K-rings down onto the bureau in front of him. She looked him up and down before speaking, sizing him up before apprising him of their situation.

162

"It seems there was an illegal birthing syndicate operating on the central coast not long ago. The perps apparently scuttled the operation after we discovered them. All that's left are the empty K-rings they were using for the op. Any idea where they might have originated?"

The central chief was a disheveled looking man, overweight and leathery. His mouth drew in a breath of air through his pursed lips until it made an involuntary whistling noise. "Well, will you look at that. More work. Just leave it on the counter and if we find anything out, we'll let you know as soon as possible." He ducked his head back down into a tablet as if to say the matter was concluded.

Shay scoffed. "Oh, my apologies. Am I inconveniencing you? I forget how difficult it is for omyym to manage mundane tasks. I mean, you would probably have to lift the sack all by yourself and dump it into that sorting batcher that's directly next to you. Goddess, it might even require some low-tier intellect to read the near-instant results to me. What were we thinking Drasha? Forgive me, I sometimes forget that the omyym can be a bit disabled in these matters."

Drasha began to join in by making an announcement to the crowded precinct. "Excuse me, good citizens! Is there anyone here that might possibly have an intellect score higher than tier one? We seem to need someone with a skill level that might be high enough to possibly turn a wrench or maybe even recite what is written in front of them. Anyone?"

The station chief sighed and slid the sack towards himself and dumped its contents into the currency batcher. He drummed his finger on the counter looking at them for a few moments as he waited for the batcher to finish processing. A sudden screech from one of the resisting detainees drew his attention back to another corner of the room as two pale and misshapen officers ran to assist in the restraint.

Shay casually glanced back at them and then back to the station chief to chide him some more. "How do you even manage to maintain order with this group? Those two with 'screech' over there look oxygen-starved. Your city gets a double allotment of immunity foods; you shouldn't have such unfit officers."

The station chief paused and looked back at her as the K-ring report began to generate on the screen in front of them. "Some people like that look," he chuckled. "You don't think the Vesni are the sole arbiters of what constitutes beauty, do you?"

Shay cocked an eyebrow at him. "I'm a cop. More than that I'm a woman. I'm unfortunately well-aware of the diversity in what men find desirable."

The station chief shot her a subtle smile before a sudden alert broke the silence. "This batch you brought in? Looks like it's been linked to a series of K-rings involved in a serial death cult case we've been working. We've actually been hitting dead ends with it for some time."

Drasha moved closer to the counter. "That's religious jurisdiction. Since when did the omyym start working death cult cases?"

"When the death cult started operating here in Voltane." The station chief started to stand a little more upright as he began to realize that the two Vesni in front of him were decidedly out of the loop. "I'm surprised you aren't aware. As religious and misogynistic as the death cult is, I'd have thought you'd have had them cornered and disintegrated by now."

"Why are the omyym working the case then? We are supposed to be notified the moment any heretical activity occurs in the plains." Shay replied.

"Murder is murder here. Unless they come out and say they are killing for some heretical reason we can't make assumptions based on background alone. You know how dangerous assumptions can get when they're made by people with tier one intelligence," he retorted.

"But now that we can connect them to your illegal birthing operation it makes more sense. Ever since the Vesni cracked down on unlicensed reproduction, death cult ideology has started to infest local thinking here on Kael. If they could get their hands on illegal birthing systems, it would make them very popular."

Shay turned to Drasha with a concerned look. "What if our perps weren't just trying to make some fast, black-market currency? If this is part of more organized death cult campaign to undermine the Mitera's reproduction monopoly, it could be far more serious than we thought. We need to find out how pervasive this is."

"Look, if you want to officially take over the case, you'd be doing me a favor. As far as I'm concerned it's officially a heretical event, and I'm transferring it to the Order."

Shay and Drasha stared at each other for a fast moment. "The Mitera is going to want to know about this immediately," Shay replied.

"Hold on a second," the station chief muttered to himself as he finished scanning the k-ring report. "There are three K-rings missing from the series. They would've been empty like the others. You don't happen to know their whereabouts, do you?"

Shay's face turned pale. Drasha offered up a plausible explanation to cover for her partner's sudden pensive silence. "It's possible the death cult siphoned a few before we arrived thinking they wouldn't be noticed. We'll have our people do an accounting trace on it to see if we can track it down. If they're still using them, they probably don't realize they've exposed themselves. We'll scoop them up."

"As you say. We'll be here if you need anything else." The station chief motioned his hand with a flourish to indicate his part was complete and then turned back to other matters. Shay and Drasha made a quick exit with their report but kept silent until they were back in their stormblade.

"What are the odds Xard has the missing K-rings and not the death cult? Investigating this further could be part of the trap this blue-hair is laying." Shay's voice was filled with genuine concern now.

"You think she convinced Xard to swipe them from your lock-up? Oh, that's brazen. What would he have to gain from that? He's a lot of things, Shay, but stupid is not one of them, he'd have to have a reason. They're no good to him empty unless he could..." Drasha paused as she considered the possibility that Xard had actually succeeded in filling the K-rings.

Shay laid out the options. "We need to solve this before the Mitera is even aware of the risks at play or she'll have no choice but to overreact by redirecting resources to Urm. It could push our culprit back into the shadows. We need to move cautiously from here on out, Drash. I can't ask you to go any further with me on this. If we follow the trail and it leads to the death cult, we may get the credit for the take down, but we could face sanction for concealing such an event from the Mitera. If the trail leads to Xard instead, you could be culpable in the possible cover up. It's a lose-lose for status."

Drasha laughed. "Appreciate the sentiment, but uh, if you think I'm gonna miss out on watching you spring the blue-hair's own trap back on her, you've seriously misjudged me. Besides, status is nothing if I can't outwit some upstart's ham-fisted swipe at my career."

"Anyone can teach you that," Shay smirked as she started up the engines.

"True, but your technique is far more nuanced. You can make an opponent fail without them even realizing you're onto them. Leaving them all twisted up in constant frustration—it's an art really."

166

Shay found her commitment reassuring. "Well then," she smiled wryly, "be sure to take good notes."

17 – PRODUCTIVITY

"Okay, you pod of miscreants, you have a new bunk mate." Amnon gave Xard a gentle push into the room as Kharik bounded in and flopped onto the lower bunk he presumed would be for Xard. "Your new duty schedule is posted. Be sure to get your reports in on time this week. Productivity is protection."

The group of kids in the pod all shouted back in varied levels of volume and enthusiasm "Productivity is protection!" Amnon shook his head at them and simply turned to leave the way he had come in. Xard scanned the room's inhabitants. There were probably 10 boys in the pod, all a bit younger than himself.

It was a good setup since it would mean very few interpersonal conflicts. Most of them were sickly looking anyway and most wore pants or other clothing on their heads to cover their baldness. They scrambled to the scheduling panel to see what their new assignments were, fighting for space to see what new danger they were about to be thrown into.

Kharik patted the bunk. "I already know what ours are gonna be. You don't have to look."

Xard plopped down next to him and whispered, "Please tell me that it's taking messages to the Vesni academy. I'm on a mission remember."

"Nope. Mining. Don't worry though, there's someone down there that can help you get in over there. One of the operators is a hacker named Ygger. Spies on all the mining accounts and then sells the info

169

to the matron. If anyone can get you in, he can." Kharik smiled at him, obviously awaiting some kind of praise for his forethought.

Xard smiled back and said, "You did good, captain. You did good. Just one question. Why are you the only person with hair in here?"

He beamed at the lavish praise and started bouncing on the bunk giggling. "They shave their heads in case cyptum dust gets in there. It would catch fire except my hair doesn't burn."

One of the bald pod mates overheard Kharik's comment and turned to laugh at another boy. "Yeah, you don't want to end up like this one. His hair actually burned off like a torch when that dust lit up!" He pulled the pair of pants off of the boy's head to reveal his scarred scalp. The group of them laughed as the scarred boy snatched his pants back and put them back over his scalp.

"What do you mean it doesn't burn?" Xard asked as he squinted at Kharik's hair.

Kharik shrugged. "Remember the chemist I told you about? He told me it's a genetic disorder. Don't worry though, it's not contagious."

One of the other boys piped in. "I keep telling him he needs to shave that mop off anyway, so the stalkers don't have anything to grab onto."

Xard rolled his eyes incredulously. "You guys believe in stalkers too?"

The boys all responded affirmatively in their own ways. Some raised their hands, a few shivered, while others nodded with wide eyes. "Amnon told us all about them."

Xard scoffed, but he didn't want to give away what he knew about him. "They probably just tell you that so you don't cause trouble." The entire pod began to talk over each other to disagree with him all at once.

"No way. Stalkers are elite killers."

"This one time I heard the guard on D-Pod saying he was going to skip foyer duty and go straight into stalker training."

"Yeah, they can grow claws and stuff."

"And they have wicked weapons!"

"Yeah, if I ever become one, I'm gonna go by the name Slash!"

"You can't, stupid. They all have names that match stars and stuff. You can't just make one up."

"Yes, you can!"

"No... You CAN'T!"

A small scuffle began to break out among the pod about whose stalker mythology was most accurate.

"Just ask Kharik; he's seen one."

"Yeah! Show him the fire trick!"

Xard looked back at Kharik as he smiled and hopped off of the bunk and bent down in front of the group of boys. One of them pulled out a small welding torch and held it up to the tips of Kharik's hand-length tufts of hair. Nothing. Kharik turned back to Xard and smiled again.

Xard looked perplexed. "Okay, so how does that mean you've met a stalker in real life?"

"I think they blasted him with one of their energy weapons!"

"No, they didn't. He would be dead! They got him with the goop gun. Tell him, Kharik."

Kharik became a little more pensive as the group began to probe him for more details. "They said it's just biofiber contamination. Self-lettucing or something. They don't know if I was born with it or if I got it from the stalkers. Either way it should have killed me, but it just messed up my hair. That's why I can't seem to comb it either."

"You mean self-*latticing*?" Xard inquired skeptically.

Kharik nodded. "Yeah, that's it. Self-latticing. Amnon told me the fibers were probably a stalker weapon that releases over time. He thinks they might be tracking me with it. As long as I stay here in the mines, they can't get to me."

"Ha! They can totally get you in here. We *really* shave our heads so they won't mistake us for you."

Kharik crossed his arms and scowled in protest while the rest laughed at him jokingly. "Heyyyyyyy. You guys are mean."

"Don't worry, captain, I've got your back. I still have a few surprises if we ever run into a real stalker." Xard smiled at him and plopped back onto his bunk with his arms behind his head. Kharik grabbed onto the bunk above and pulled himself up onto it but hung his head over the ledge to watch his new friend until he fell asleep. Xard didn't realize how exhausted he'd become until he was finally someplace reasonably safe.

It was the first time he genuinely felt like he could let his guard down in a very long time. Even with the utilitarian living conditions he now found himself in, it was better than the constant tension he had when he was living at home or the uncertainty of the tidal city. He never knew who he would find when he came home. Here, everything seemed more predictable—safer even.

A small chime indicated that it was time for lights-out as the boys scrambled for their bunks. "Goodnight, captain," Xard whispered.

"Goodnight, general," came the response.

Then the lights dimmed, and Xard drifted into the first dreamless sleep he'd had in years.

***

Another small chime indicated it was time to wake up. Xard instinctively reached for his gear and checked his pockets for his K-rings. Everything was still there. *Productivity is protection,* he thought to himself. As the boys scrambled around getting their gear together Kharik jumped down from the top bunk and patted Xard on the back. "Ready? We get to go to sluice 10 today. Hope you aren't scared of the dark... or heights... or fire. The entrance is outside the cavern. I like it out there though. Less people. Come on, we have to get geared up. You have to wear more gear out on the surface because of the chance for cyptum blowing around."

Xard hopped up, grabbed a meal bar, and followed Kharik to the ready-room. Older boys and girls were already gearing up with heavy mining lasers and jumping on the transport carts. Kharik nodded in their direction. "They're apprentices. If you do good here, you get to be one of the mining apprentices and get paid. It's a juicy deal. I'd probably do it as long as I didn't end up in the same mine these guards end up in. That would be the worst."

Kharik grabbed a duffle from one of the rows of racks and tossed it to Xard while he grabbed one for himself and started donning the padded gear. His respiration mask now merged with a complex headpiece that more or less resembled dreadlocks made from various filters and re-breathing hoses. It was obscenely big on him and he began trying to roll up the sleeves and cuffs around his boots. Xard simply put the gear on over his field vest and slung the oxygen tank over his back. It wasn't very stealthy, but it did disguise his face quite well on the off-chance someone recognized him here. "Okay. Where to, captain?"

Kharik flopped and clanked under all of his over-sized gear as he hopped on one of the transport sleds in the hangar that led to the edge of the city. Xard followed close behind and took his place next to him as the hangar door opened. The transport began to hum and then suddenly sped out into the central air of the cavernous city. Xard wasn't prepared for the height. He had assumed the hangar was closer to ground level but gripped the railing tightly as the transport flew out into the open air of the cavern with the city lights below.

He could see all of the sluices clearly now. Their bright blue ultraviolet glow forming the arteries of some long-dead beast. It was beautiful in a strange way, the life blood of the entire system pumping furiously out of its cold and lifeless body. It also afforded him a view of the Vesni academy that he couldn't have gained from the ground. It was darker than he had expected, pentagonal in shape at the base, but it formed its own spire into the center of the cavern.

Around its edges were several outbuildings, probably training centers. Xard hoped one of them would provide him with a means of access inside, but there was nothing he could do about that at the moment. Still, it served to remind him of his purpose for being here—to find a way to expose their lies once and for all.

As the academy passed swiftly beneath them and they came in for a landing on the outskirts of the cavern, Xard refocused on the day's task. "So, are we actually mining today?"

Kharik turned back to him as the transport came down with a clunk. "Nah. Just errands today. Mama will give us our assignments when we get down there. Today is just orientation. Come on. Lots of people to meet." Kharik and Xard jumped off the transport and watched it lift off with the remaining passengers and fly back toward some other part of the cavern. They were alone now, in a dimly lit area of the city that nearly spilled out onto the planet's surface.

Xard looked at the errand sheet briefly before they started on their way, "Okay, first stop is sluice 10. Is this where our hacker is?"

Kharik nodded excitedly and started bounding down the path until Xard called out to him.

"Woah! Hold on." Xard got close to him and began to whisper-shout at him. "People could be watching, captain. Don't you know anything about spying? You don't want to get snagged by another stalker out here, do you? You can't just go running down the street like that! Come on, I'll teach you some of the secret voithos skills. If you want to be a secret agent like me, you have to learn this kind of stuff."

Kharik bounced on his tip-toes and clasped his hands together with excitement. "Yes! Okay you lead, and I'll follow you. It's just over the next rise. Just head for the big open sky."

Xard relished the chance to show off for his new friend. He liked being the biggest in the group for once. Besides, it helped reinforce his cover as being on some kind of Vesni mission. With any luck, this hacker could be the connection he needed. His mind churned as he moved toward the cavern's opening ahead of Kharik.

He slinked through the darkness toward the destination listed on the matron's daily list. It was his nature to move in long, smooth strides, closely hugging the corners and moving from cover to cover. Avoiding open exposure was a core tenet of his training even as a child, and he moved this way mostly out of habit. Kharik tried to emulate his movements as they passed through the edges of the Urmian city limits.

Normally he would have been annoyed at this plagiarism of his technique, but Kharik's bumbling approach and his oversized respiration gear made it somewhat comical. Xard tried desperately to hide his smile in the growing darkness of the city's edge. Once they were finally outside of the City 87 cavern, the spectacle of stars above began to mingle with the blackness of the Urmian dust below. The further they walked, the fewer formal structures they encountered.

Kharik's floppy respiration vents, still dangling like long ears or tentacles from the top of his head, narrowly missed being snagged on a bit of overhanging metal as he worked to keep up. It occurred to Xard that Kharik's short stature gave him an advantage in these small spaces. With the right training he could possibly take advantage of openings and crouch points that escaped even Xard's ability. The idea that someone or something could be better than him momentarily changed the expression on Xard's face, but he pushed it aside by considering how he might ultimately put his short companion to use.

Kharik began to talk again about something inane his FLIPP brothers shared with him. Xard simply nodded and talked back to him absently, offering up as limited a response as the question could afford. He was good like that, mentally sorting multiple things at once and navigating the dark dust and dim light of the path with relative ease. Still, he wasn't flawless. As Xard continued his skulking through the now lightless structures just outside the city's entrance, Kharik's unmistakable sound of flopping rubber hoses ran to him directly.

"Did you hear what I said?" Kharik demanded, somewhat exasperated.

Xard retorted, "Of course! I hear everything. I just chose not to respond."

Kharik cocked his head slightly through his mass of tubes and hoses dangling from the crown of his head. Xard didn't have to be able to see his eyes through the goggles to know that the boy was wordlessly calling his statement into question.

Xard ignored his gaze and stared off into the surroundings. He wasn't actually looking for anything, but he acted as if it was part of his cover. In truth, he was lost, but he held up a hand to Kharik and shushed him quietly through his own respirator. They were just outside of the furthest man-made structures on this part of Urm.

Here, only the reflected light of Kael provided any meaningful light. It surprised him that FLIPP even sent its kids this far, but then again it didn't. Xard scouted the area and whispered back to Kharik without looking at him, "How many entrances?"

Kharik seemed surprised by this question. "One. It's right over there that's what I was telling you."

Xard, finally knowing the context of the question he missed, turned back to Kharik with a grin and said in a hushed yell, "Of course it is! But we have to always be on the lookout, don't we? I've already scouted six possible exit routes if we run into trouble. Now, you go ahead and lead the way from here and I'll take up a position behind to cover you."

Kharik seemed to buy Xard's attempt at covering for his ambivalence. "Woah! Six? I didn't know they trained the boys to do all this. I thought you were all like slaves or something."

"Who told you that? FLIPP?" Xard crossed his arms momentarily as he awaited a response.

Kharik just shrugged under his enormous gear. "That's just what everyone says."

"Hmm. Good. Then the trick is working. We keep our skills a secret, so no one expects it when we have to take someone down." Xard continued embellishing as they walked, but his story had at least some element of truth to it. They *were* all trained at 16 for combat, but mostly for sport and competition. Still, Xard didn't think Kharik needed to know that, so he pressed on with his stories.

In short order, Xard and Kharik finally reached the opening of mining sluice 10. It was a large, vehicle-wide, gaping hole in the dirt that descended down a dark ramp. Above the ground, a large, red, half-moon shaped awning was the only way to distinguish it from its bleak surroundings. Well, at least he *thought* it was red; it was difficult to tell in the dim lights that adorned the opening of the ramp.

The initial descent inside the sluice's gaping maw made Xard very uncomfortable. He used to use the phrase 'the dark side of Urm' as a superlative to describe things that were exceedingly black. Now he noted that it wasn't nearly descriptive enough. He was now *inside* the dark side of Urm.

As Kharik strode deeper into the darkness, Xard abandoned his slinking. There simply wasn't enough light to play games, and he couldn't risk losing sight of Kharik. It wasn't long before dark metal beams began to toothily jut out from the walls in random patterns, making the path even more precarious. Reinforcements perhaps, but he didn't bother to ask. He just fixed his gaze firmly on Kharik down the ever-darkening path until the sounds of scraping and grinding became more obvious around them. Although he could no longer determine how far or fast they were moving, the slowly enveloping sounds of machinery sputtering in the darkness gave him a sense of being slowly digested.

Finally, Kharik stopped and turned to Xard. "This is it."

Xard saw nothing but expanding blackness, but apparently, there was a door or a hatch of some kind right in front of him. He cursed to himself that he couldn't see it and cursed twice at the thought that his mother probably could have. As they entered the creaking doorway and clamped the hatch shut behind them, there was a sudden change in pressure and a small vibration in the walls and floor beneath them. Then, very gently, the room's walls began to slowly give off an increasing amount of light, and the sounds of the mine simply faded from notice.

Kharik pulled off his FLIPP gear and slid his goggles up to his forehead; the two clean circles on his face now revealed his bright green eyes. They seemed much brighter than he remembered on the surface and had a strange refraction to them. Xard ventured a comment as the lights and pressure continued to stabilize. "Your eyes, they implants like your arm?"

Kharik looked up at him briefly and then away as he realized the changing light made his differences more noticeable. "No," he replied quietly. "Rod enhancement. Helps me see in the dark. Color's cosmetic. I didn't pick it."

"Okay," Xard responded incredulously. "How does a FLIPP orphan afford that, because I know FLIPP didn't pay for it."

Kharik remained silent and simply went about removing the rest of his dust gear and hanging it on the wall. Now it had become a challenge for Xard, so he stopped removing his own gear and simply crossed his arms and stood with his weight on his back foot as if expecting an answer before the mission would be continued. Kharik could sense the expectancy, even though he had his back to him, so he finally just let his shoulders drop in defeat.

"Medical experiments when I was little. It happens to a lot of kids on Urm. You don't want your baby? You just give it to the mehdisticians. They do experiments to it and when they are done with it, they usually bury it."

Kharik began to forcefully stuff his remaining gear into a large duffle bag as he spoke. It was clear to Xard now that this was a conversation best left for another time, but it was too late. Kharik's cracking voice continued. "Sometimes... the babies don't die. Sometimes they survive the experiments and escape.

That's the way things happen on Urm. Everything is allowed here as long as the cyptum keeps coming out of the ground." As the lights finally reached full brightness there was a faint *ding*, and Kharik pressed a small recessed panel on the wall, triggering a door to open opposite them. He took a breath of the heavily filtered air and turned back to Xard, forcing a smile as he did so. "Okay. This is the easy part." And he darted off around the corner.

179

Xard held his tongue and followed him into the still-dim hallway. The air was cold, but clean, and Xard thought it had a kind of sterile aftertaste. As they wandered through the passage, rocks gave way to racks of computer equipment. It wasn't the bright, shiny equipment he was used to seeing in his Kaelian classrooms. It was weathered from years of use—possibly even scavenged—with only the sounds of gentle clicking under the hulls to indicate that any of it was operational.

The sounds of grinding were gone now, replaced with the incessant chirping of the computer equipment around them. Ahead, Xard heard the distinct sounds of arguing, and he momentarily hesitated out of habit before reminding himself that he wasn't at home anymore. A faint yellow light grew ahead of them, glowing and flickering through the tall forest of machinery.

As they drew closer, the conversation became more intelligible. Kharik announced their presence by suddenly banging on one of the metal computer housings with a small pipe. "What have you guys done to my hangout?" Kharik shouted out ahead of himself. "I leave you guys for a day and all the power is out again!" Kharik turned back to Xard with a smile to reassure him that he was just playing with them before rounding the corner into a small working area.

"Not now, you little rat. I almost have it," came a complaint from under a large bank of machinery. Xard wasn't sure what exactly was happening at this point, but he stayed to the shadows until whatever it was worked itself out. He knew there were all kinds of people scrambling in the dark around them, but he had it in his mind to just stay out of the growing chaos. Kharik, on the other hand, charged right up to the pair of legs jutting out from under the panel and kicked one foot.

"If I was a stalker, you'd be dead now!" Kharik chided. The legs simply ignored him as Kharik turned his attention to a heavyset teenage girl who was bending over the legs with a small torchiere, shouting at them. Xard noticed her right away.

The singular point of light in the room revealed her as a bulbous mass amid the sea of hard edges around it. Even though the darkness managed to obscure much of her form, he distractedly wondered where her flesh ended. He was pretty sure she was an enormous girl; he just didn't know how enormous quite yet. In any case, he was convinced that he could probably draw her using only circles.

Kharik simply bounced up and down on his toes trying to get her attention. "Mama Shyne! Mama Shyne! Let me hold the lamp!" Without missing a beat, she handed him the torchiere to hold as she resumed berating the pair of legs tinkering under the panel. As she continued to belt out her commands to the legs, all manner of workers, mostly children, zoomed around in the background darkness. Occasionally, one would run up with a tablet for her to sign and she would give the young boy or girl an order to do something else.

To Xard, even her voice seemed fat, popping out a thick, staccato diatribe of guttural frustration in between her more direct complaints. "This is de third time you have crashed my life support systems this cycle Ygger!" She paused to wheeze before continuing. "I will never finish de work in time!" Shyne paused a moment between heavy breaths to look up at Xard and then gestured to him with one hand while she went back to shouting.

"See? We have a new visitor here I need to introduce to de programs but I can barely see with no lights, oncha!" The legs simply ignored the protests from above and continued working while Shyne threw up her hands in surrender and then slapped them down against her sides with a loud *flap* before turning to Xard more directly and holding out her hand to him. "Shelby Shyne Shigoon, but you may call me Shyne, or Mama Shyne, if prefer. Sorry, my common tongue is not natural, but we make best of it."

He reached out his hand to hers and shook it as he tried to take it all in. "Xard," he replied simply.

181

"Now, on de normal days I would give welcomes to de mining operations with a cup of Urmian tea, but since I have no air systems now, you will accept my apologies, yes? I am always happy to see new childrens from FLIPP because they are always working so hard." As she turned to praise Kharik, she gave him a big squeeze, pressing him into her fleshy bosom as she gave him a peck on the head. Kharik eagerly returned the hug in a way that demonstrated a profound need for maternal affection until the legs beneath the panel started complaining about the missing torch light.

Shyne seemed quite young to Xard, probably only a few years older than him, yet triple his size. He knew that the people of Urm started working in their assigned professions at an early age, but he wasn't aware that they held positions of any responsibility so young. There was nothing about her demeanor which might suggest any kind of formal authority. She had no uniform, no badge of office, no weapon (other than her voice), and yet she was clearly the one running everything. He wondered to himself who would be silly enough to entrust a mining operation to a teenager, and a cyptum mine at that! It seemed foolish to Xard, but he kept quiet as he continued to assess the surroundings.

Finally, a *click*. Lights and fans began to *whirr*. Shyne threw her hands up in dramatic fashion to express her joy at being back in business. Her short forearms barely broke the plane of her shoulders as she laughed a sigh of relief.

In the light, she looked even worse. A pasty-skinned girl with long, nondescript brown hair, Xard had to catch himself from laughing out loud when he realized that she reminded him of a grub worm in this light. It was at that moment he realized she didn't even have any kind of feminine mystique from which to command favor from the workers around her. Having been trained in the Vesni culture since birth, it never even occurred to him that the FLIPP kids actually *loved* her or that she had earned the respect of the adults around her in some other way. To Xard, she was an enigma.

Finally, the legs emerged from under the control panel to reveal a swarthy and handsome young man of about 16. He quickly ran his fingers through his jet-black, shoulder-length hair letting it fall back into a disheveled mess that somehow made him look mysterious. His first impression to Xard was almost the complete opposite of what he saw in Shyne. Ygger was intense, with dark, deep-set eyes and an air of style he hadn't seen anywhere else in the whole of Urm.

Shyne threw her stubby arms around his neck as he sat up on the ground and she gave him a big fat kiss. "Thank you oncha!" Shyne squealed and she quickly shuffled off to attend to business matters.

Ygger sighed as he sat there and looked up at Xard and Kharik. Without standing, he jutted out his hand to Xard. "The name's Ygger." Working carefully to correct Shyne's mispronunciation, he was deliberate in his alliteration of the heavy 'E' sound at the beginning of his name. "And I'm assuming you met my half-sister Shyne. She's the muscle around here. I just fix stuff. Come on Kharik, I'll get you moving on today's orders. You too, clean-shirt. I'll show you the ropes."

18 – Dances

The mid-day sun hissed over Shay and Drasha as new data came pouring over the stormblade's systems. "The financial trace just came back negative," Shay said darkly. "It traces back to Urm as we suspected, but no direct location or user. Goddess.

It's been two days, and we're not any closer to closing this case. It's going to be a monumental task to track the culprit down without giving away our efforts if we use the AI systems. Primitive methods are still our safest option." Shay paused for a moment before glancing at Drasha again through the rear-view mirror. "If we don't turn anything up in the next day or two, I will need to use the AI. At that point, I can't have you affiliated with any of this—for your own safety."

Drasha stared back deliberately, indicating her commitment without words. "You realize if you use the AI it will tip off the blue-hair that her plan is fully in motion, right? Without knowing how her plan will play out, we won't know how much time we have, even if the AI leads us right to the culprit's door."

"Exactly why I can't have you implicated. Xard is *my* issue. The death cult is *everyone's* issue. If the Order becomes aware of death cult involvement before I track down Xard, they'll know about the missing K-rings. And if they know about the K-rings..."

Drasha finished her sentence. "...then they know about Xard's involvement, and your attempt at covering it all up, yes I know."

Shay stared out of the stormblade canopy momentarily before pounding her fists on it. "Damn that skika! There's no way her ridiculous swing at me would have worked without this death cult involvement. Goddess! What are the odds?"

Drasha changed the tone by slipping seamlessly into her most professional demeanor. "What's our next move then? We still have a day or two, that's more than the two of us need. If we're to be primitive detectives, then we need to start working the beat. If you're going to be outmaneuvered, it's not going to be by the likes of her, is it?"

Shay scoffed. "If my end comes by *her* hand, I deserve it. No, you're right. Maybe we're putting too much stock into the death cult's motive here. Let's strip this down to what we actually know and forget about what the omyym believe for a moment.

All we really know is that some death cult financier's K-rings were used to fund a small birthing pod effort. We don't even know if the death cult is really involved or whether the K-rings were simply stolen from the death cult. For all we know, there's no connection at all and we're stressing over nothing. We need someone who can distill all of this information for us logically."

Drasha was already following her train of thought. "Eastern shore, then?"

Shay nodded. "Kael Vistyn, but not the landing pads. Take us to the training ground cliffs. I've got one more potential partner to enjoin in this little dance."

***

Xard followed the two of them at a distance as he took it all in. It wasn't out of mistrust. Rather, it had to do with the fact that he was simply more cautious than Kharik. The rocky passageways still held their sharpened edges from some past catastrophe, and he didn't want Kharik—who had developed a bad habit of bounding pretty much everywhere—causing him some unnecessary injury. Still, he listened closely as Ygger explained the operations.

Ygger fascinated Xard. He was normally apprehensive around other voithos who were older than him, but Ygger was no voithos. He was a common-born Urmian but somehow carried himself with an unusual sense of ease. Though he dressed like a miner, he lacked the hands of someone who'd done any hard labor. In place of a pickaxe, he carried a small playing card that he flipped as he walked.

His black scarf. His long, industrial-blue jacket. His disheveled hair. His gait. It was clear he didn't belong here, or at least carried himself like he wished he was doing something else.

When the narrow corridor finally spilled onto the ledge of the cavernous mine, Xard instinctively clung to the wall. He could hear Ygger's voice up ahead telling him to watch his step, almost as an afterthought. "We're actually not very deep here even though it descends quite a ways," Ygger explained.

"From up here you can see how we start to quarry out the cyptum well below the surface rather than coming in from the top. Keeping a lid on the stuff increases the pressure and helps keep it more manageable. Lose pressure or lose light? Big boom. Easy, right? Your part is pretty straightforward—keep the lights on. See these sluices running below?"

Xard carefully peered over the makeshift railing into the massive quarry beneath them. Fissures within the rock glowed with artificial UV light to keep the exposed cyptum stable. He knew all about cyptum from his classes on Kael, but he'd never been this close to such obvious danger. Xard fumbled for words as he returned to hugging the wall. "Yes. I see them."

"Well, the sluices carry the freed ore to that central collection point over there. Sometimes a rubble cat or one of the other pieces of machinery will knock one of the reflectors loose. It's only a problem if several go out at once. So really, it's just nuisance work. But you guys are used to that. We just need you to make sure they stay aligned. Make sense?"

Xard nodded nervously as they continued around the narrow ledge that rimmed the quarry. It was peppered with tiny outbuildings that served as control rooms for the expansive digging below. Upon closer inspection, it was clear that the equipment and scaffolding were quite outdated. As they passed through several of the pillboxes toward their destination, a few even seemed to shudder under their own weight.

It was starting to be more than he bargained for. He wasn't averse to the risk, but he didn't like what he considered to be *unnecessary* foolishness. His cover was starting to be more of a burden than an asset. He needed to secure the hacker's assistance quickly and move on.

As they rounded the precipice, they reached a small portable equipment building. Ygger paused and motioned for them to go inside. "Okay, clean-shirt, this is your training room. Over on that wall you'll see mining helmets if you should need one. Over here we have a few of the grapple guns if you end up doing any mining. You get a few extra credits if you decide to mine, so most FLIPPr kids usually do it."

Ygger picked up one of the hand-held grapplers and switched it on. "Hmm!" He made a face that seemed to indicate he was surprised that it worked before continuing. "This barrel on top emits UV light, and the grappler on the bottom can pull you out of a tight spot if you happen to fall into someplace you shouldn't. Now, it won't stop any chain reactions, but it will stabilize any loose dust or granules around you and keep you from bursting into flames. Any questions before you begin?"

"Wait. Was that the training?" Xard's face scrunched up in confusion.

Ygger leaned back against the panel with his casual air and crossed his arms before taking a good look at Xard. "The daily routine is pretty straightforward clean-shirt. All you need to do is follow Kharik and make sure the debris shields stay aligned. Kharik, of course, will show you most of what needs to be done. It's pretty simple unless you're careless. Careless gets you dead, clean-shirt. So, nothing crazy."

"Yeah, nothing crazy" Kharik parroted and smiled at Xard.

Xard merely nodded as he looked around at the ramshackle surroundings. It was depressing. He didn't want to get stuck in a routine, especially this one. He needed to keep his plan moving forward.

Ygger continued discussing procedures for several more minutes, but Xard's itch to get on with his own priorities was starting to make him agitated. If Ygger was a good hacker like Kharik suggested, he needed to know quickly, or else this whole mining gig was just another waste of time. Finally, Ygger provided him an opening.

"So, any questions?"

Xard took a chance. "So, Kharik says you're a good hacker. Is that true?"

Ygger smiled as he turned away waving his hand. "I'm not hacking any more adult sims for you FLIPPrs. It'll rot your brain. Besides, you need to stay focused while you're at work here."

Xard interrupted his rant. "Actually, I was thinking something more... religious."

Ygger spun around on his heel and crossed his arms in front of himself again before flopping his weight against the wall. "Most

189

religious groups don't require hacking. If anything, they give their sacred texts out for free."

"Still, can you do it?"

Ygger shrugged off the suggestion. "Probably. I've just never tried because there's no money in it. Religious stuff just isn't a big commodity on Urm. Besides, playing around with relics brings a lot of unwanted attention. What's in it for you?"

Ygger's sudden interest and nonchalance about hacking a Vesni site put Xard somewhat at ease. Although, he remained concerned about sharing too much. Kharik put the issue to rest by just blurting it out.

"He's on a spy mission for the Vesni academy! He's gonna be an agent and break in and see if they can stop him."

Xard winced. "Well, something like that. But it's supposed to be *covert*." Xard swatted Kharik playfully as he clenched his teeth. "We're not doing damage. I'm just supposed to find out if they are as secure as they claim to be."

"Intrusion detection, eh? I wonder if they're running a simple simian codex or if they have something more elaborate. The Sentia facility? Now *they* have security. But the Vesni? Why would they need it? No one is going to be stealing ancient texts."

"But you could do it, right?" Xard persisted.

"Tell you what, I'll give you the same deal I give every new FLIPPr kid that strolls in. If you work hard for us and don't get lazy, I'll try to find some time to look into your project for you. Deal?"

"Well. How long are we talking?"

"Meh. Shouldn't take more than a few Urmian months to figure out whether or not you are a good fit and don't cause problems."

"A few months?" The disheartened words had barely fallen from Xard's lips before a strong rumble emerged under their feet and klaxons began to sound.

Ygger wasted no time and dashed out of the other side of their portable room where they were standing. He ran along the rim to a much larger central structure that was lodged deep into the wall of the quarry itself. Kharik and Xard just stood there looking at each other momentarily until another rumble made them start running after him. When they reached the large control room, they found Ygger scanning the control panel, muttering under his breath. With his dark hair covering his eyes, it was difficult to know whether he was working or praying.

He finally looked up and out through the large window toward the quarry below. Another rumble. Veins of bright blue light which held the cyptum slurries started to temporarily dim before returning to their original brightness. "No. No. No!" Ygger's cool composure suddenly took flight in a ten-fingered sprint across the console's controls. "The power is dropping! We need to call up the backup generators, fast! Kharik, throw the release panel on the door!"

Kharik scurried to the control room door and slammed his grimy palm down on the switch, slamming it shut. A sudden change in pressure made everyone's ears pop as the room sealed around them. Ygger scrambled at the controls. His fingers continued to whirl around the flattened interface, pirouetting and leaping from one end to the other in an endless dance. Then he stopped. The look on his face quickly changed from cocksure composer to wall-flowered loner as the warning lights continued to blink on his panel.

"Last call." Ygger closed his eyes and primed a lever on the wall next to him three times. The power to the UV lights below suddenly surged but then began to dim again. It became immediately clear that whatever Ygger was doing wasn't enough. As the first lights began to dim again on the far end of the quarry, a lone cyptum bin, no bigger than a backpack, finally ignited.

191

The sound and power of that singular blast erupted with such force that it ripped a large opening in the rocky ceiling above, flinging men and metal through the makeshift opening into space. Xard clenched his teeth as the shock wave rolled through, knocking them all to the floor. It all moved slowly now. Xard struggled to his feet and stared in horror at the enormous boulders of burning rock and embers that were steadily flying through the newly formed opening above them. Remnants of what were once FLIPPr kids, miners, and equipment roared into the flung-out space before them until ultimately being extinguished.

The remaining miners began to scramble for the exits as the realization of what was happening washed over them. Ygger climbed up to the control panel again and continued to stare out into the gash that had formed in the mine's ceiling. "You picked a hell of a first day, clean-shirt. You're probably going to die here. I just called in our last energy reserves. I don't have any idea how long it will last."

Ygger ran the fingers from both hands through his mass of hair as he tried to find a solution. Xard and Kharik followed Ygger out onto the precipice as he scanned the exterior of the bunker for a conduit access. "I could hack the power from the neighboring tower, but there's no way to access it remotely. Bahk! We could have hard-wired it, but the exterior ladder is blown."

Another large blast hurled three more segments of the mine into the sky above them, forcing the trio to retreat back inside what remained of the control room. From the rear of the room, another door opened. It was Shyne, running at full speed to get to Ygger. Her body continued to move under its own momentum for a moment even after her feet had stopped. Her eyes were wide at the sight of Ygger scrambling to pull up more power. A short scream emerged from her as she noticed the ejecta of burning miners flinging like sparks into the darkened space outside the quarry.

Shyne grabbed Ygger by the shoulders from behind. "Oncha!"

"Quit it!" he shouted as he rolled his shoulders out from under her grasp. "I'm trying to keep the whole mine from ejecting! I don't have any way to snatch auxiliary energy without a direct line. The nearest one is across the quarry."

Shyne shook her head and implored him excitedly. "No. No. There is another access cable in de fascia above de control room. There must be! I approved de designs myself."

Ygger looked up at the access hatch and climbed up the automated ladder in haste. It led into a honeycomb-like protective barrier that surrounded their entire capsule. It had been designed as a crush guard to shield the control room from sudden shocks and quakes, but it had already sustained significant damage. "It's too small. Blast already destabilized the rock. No one's squeezing in there without being crushed. We need to evacuate. Now!"

Xard suddenly realized that the stress of the ongoing events had hardened his reliquary vest, and his mind suddenly awakened with new possibility. "Wait. I can do it. I can do it! I just need to know where it is! What do I do?" Xard didn't wait for approval. Instead, he ran to the ladder and started climbing up into the bright orange crush-barrier above.

Ygger shouted back at him as he grabbed the ladder. "No time for heroics, clean-shirt. You'll be smashed from the pressure up there the second we have another blast. We have to go. Now!" Xard shot Ygger an annoyed look. He had spent enough time playing the part of helpless street urchin. He had an advantage, and he wasn't about to die without having used it. He just didn't have time to explain it.

Shyne studied Xard's face for the briefest of moments before passing him a fist-sized conduit adapter. "Take dis! There is a cable along de far wall above us. Just clamp it on at any point, and we can direct access de power!"

Xard scrambled up into the darkness without hesitation. After all, his own life was also on the line now, and he needed to preserve it. The honeycomb crush barrier—designed to flex and absorb seismic pressure—had already begun to compress. The waxy polymer structure, normally rigid enough to withstand fifty times standard atmospheric pressure, had softened from the heat of nearby cyptum reactions.

Three lengths in, he encountered the first collapse point.

The passage narrowed to a gap barely wider than his shoulders. He exhaled completely, compressing his ribcage, and pushed through. His vest scraped against the polymer like fingernails on metal. Behind him, another low-frequency rumble began building—the unmistakable harmonic signature of cyptum reaching critical instability.

Eight seconds, maybe ten before the next reaction.

He couldn't hear anything or anyone now except the rumbling of imminent death by cyptum. This scurrying was taking too long. Where was he going? Were they even still there below him? For all he knew, Ygger had convinced them to evacuate already, leaving him up there to die.

He changed direction, moving laterally along a secondary passage. Sweat dripped into his eyes, momentarily blinding him. The air here was thirty degrees hotter than in the control room, and oxygen-depleted. Each breath delivered less than he needed.

"Come on, Xard. What are you doing here?" Xard grew more and more annoyed as he made his way through the tangled mass of metal and wax. He cursed under his breath at the situation his efforts had wedged him into. *"Cable should be just right of this center axis,"* he muttered to himself, orienting by the phosphorescent guide markers embedded in the honeycomb structure.

The next rumble came sooner than expected. The entire passage compressed by twenty percent in an instant. Xard felt rather than heard the strange popping noise of the molecular structure rearranging itself around him. His reliquary vest hardened instantly, preventing his chest from being crushed, but his exposed limbs screamed with pressure.

Three jagged shards of rock punctured the floor beneath him. One missed his thigh by less than a finger's width. Not rock—superheated metal slag from the sluice, still glowing with potential energy. Then he saw it—five lengths ahead—the cable. Thick as his wrist, it carried enough power to sustain the UV containment field for the entire eastern quadrant.

Xard pushed forward, ignoring the burning sensation in his lungs. The passage narrowed again, forcing him to slither on his belly. His fingers touched something wet. Hydraulic fluid, leaking from a ruptured line. Highly conductive. If the next cyptum reaction sent a power surge through the system...

No time to consider the implications.

The cable was just beyond his reach now. Another tremor began— this one different. Higher pitched. The harmonic precursor to a chain reaction.

Thirty seconds at most before catastrophic failure.

Twenty.

The adapter felt impossibly heavy in his hand. His fingers, slick with sweat and hydraulic fluid, struggled to maintain their grip.

Fifteen seconds.

He stretched forward, extending his arm fully, exposing his unprotected side to the jagged edges of collapsed honeycomb.

Ten seconds.

His fingers closed around the cable. The adapter's jaws needed to align perfectly with the conductive elements. One attempt. No margin for error.

Five seconds.

He twisted the adapter, feeling for the magnetic lock. Nothing.

Three seconds.

He rotated it ninety degrees. Still nothing.

Two.

One final rotation and—*click*. The adapter locked into place. Instantly, the status indicators on the device flashed from amber to green.

Below, the UV containment field stabilized, its intensity doubling as power flowed from the adjacent facility. The harmonic tremor faded.

Xard lay motionless for a few more seconds, his heart pounding so violently he could feel his pulse in his fingertips. Then, pushing against exhaustion, he began the dangerous journey back. He yelled back to Shyne to give her the news but the shape of the honeycombed materials around him acted as a baffle, muffling his report. He would have to crawl backwards through the mass of waxy strands to even know if the effort was a success. The rumbles had stopped, but it didn't prevent him from mistaking his pounding heart for another imminent collapse. He had to move quickly.

When he reached the hatch into the control room, he didn't even bother using the ladder. He flopped himself down into the hole and dropped unceremoniously onto the floor with a *thud*. "I got it!"

Ygger stayed glued to the control panel assessing the damage but looked back over his shoulder at Xard as he heard the sound. "We know, clean-shirt, we know. As soon as you had it clamped, I was able to draw power from the neighboring mine. They won't be happy about it but, meh. They'll get over it."

Shyne scrambled over to Xard and picked him up, pressing his face into her bosom. She laughed and cried while simultaneously forcing the remaining air out of Xard's lungs. "You've saved us all, young one! Oh, sweet, sweet boy! And a new boy too! You have done something very wonderfuls!"

Ygger sighed to himself and then turned to look at Xard more fully. "She's right. The numbers aren't all in yet, but it looks like you probably just saved this entire mining quarry. Not bad for a first day." Ygger turned to look at Shyne before turning back to the analysis running across the monitors. "Could have lost 20% of our cyptum. Would have blown right out of that new hole we just made. At least some of us can appreciate that, right Shyne?"

Ygger turned his head back toward the control panel and began mindlessly strumming the controls for a moment, his dark locks obscuring his eyes again. Shyne sidled up next to him for a moment and gently placed her bulbous hand along the middle of his back as she stared out through the portal. Miners of all sizes still scurried like insects through the tangled webbing of metal and rock below, but there was nothing either of them could do directly to ease their suffering. It was now just a waiting game to see how bad the damage was.

Shyne broke the awkward silence with more gasping. Xard wasn't sure if she was at a loss for words or simply couldn't find a way to get enough air through her heaving mass until she finally whispered. "We have work now. Assessments to be made oncha, ya?" She rubbed Ygger's back gently as she spoke.

Ygger forced out a sarcastic "ya" in response. "Another lucky day for me, eh Shyne? As if I needed another reason for your father to hate me right now. And quit calling me 'oncha'. I don't know how much longer I will even be able to live in the quarry when he hears about this."

Shyne withdrew her hand and looked at him scornfully. "Ygger! You could have just prevented the second ablation and papa would not have given credit where it is due. But I still love you, brother. We will make it work. You worry about de mine. I will worry about him and de credits needed to get de mine working again."

"Psh. It's not just the bottom line with him, Shyne. See this?" Ygger turned toward her and drew circles around his face with his free hand as he talked. "This is the problem Shyne. Nothing has to be wrong in the mine. He just needs an excuse to come after me. Stop playing like you think this will be okay. There're gonna be real problems between him and me over this."

"No! I will take care of him. You did a great thing here Ygger, and he must know about it. He will listen to reason."

"Ha! Reason? You can't be serious Shyne. The moment he sees my face, he sees my father's face. You and I both know how *that* usually ends."

"He doesn't even need to see you. I will handle it. When was de last time he was even down here? Hmm? Exactly. Now. No more worry about this. We have work."

Shyne flapped her hand at him to indicate that she was done with the conversation and tuned to look directly at Xard. "And you as well, young sir! I don't know if you realize how much you have saved us. That was very, very brave of you!"

Xard absorbed the momentary praise as his adrenaline continued to wind down in his system. He liked being recognized for his efforts, but the risk to his life deserved more in his eyes. He ran his fingers through his hair out of habit and scanned all of their faces before asking the obvious question. "So, what happens now?"

"Now, we all find a way to double the work load on everyone to make up for the mining losses." Ygger continued to shake his head as he talked. "This will set us back another three months at least. But not to worry. You FLIPPrs will have plenty to do in the meantime."

Xard bristled at Ygger's remarks. It wasn't enough that he was already getting overly-entangled with the mining cover, now an apparent family drama was proving to be an additional obstacle. Xard grew irritated that his plans were being inadvertently blocked at every turn. He had to shift the flow of the situation before he was forced to abandon it completely.

Xard's frustration and waning adrenaline pushed him outside of his normal manipulative skills into something clumsier. "So, since I pretty much just saved everyone, do you think you can help me hack the Vesni academy now?" It was abrupt, but Xard was wasting time. He simply had no idea when a Vesni matriarch might show up unannounced and end his little venture for good. Everyone stopped what they were doing momentarily to stare at him. Xard doubled-down on his comment. "What? It's only fair."

Ygger returned to his control panel and talked over his shoulder at Xard. "Sure, kid. As soon as we finish sweeping up what's left of the miners in the quarry. Psh."

Xard didn't like delays, but he liked being brushed off even less. "Look. There's nothing to even sweep. They're all atmospheric dust by now. You're just trying to make excuses."

"Okay. I'll humor you. Notwithstanding the cleanup, we are now *months* behind schedule. Even if I *wanted* to help you I couldn't. There are too many financial obstacles now to even process something like that."

Shyne let out a deflated sigh and looked back at Xard again. "Even if Ygger had de time, his mind would not be in it. He needs his mind to do these hackings. But now he only thinks of my papa. He will be demanding we make up de lost monies. I'm sorry little one."

"Okay. First, I'm not little. Second, I can fix your credit problem, but I need to know you can help me... and not three months from now. *Now*."

Xard didn't wait for their reaction. He fished out one of the three K-rings from his pocket and slammed it down on the console's reader. Xard slid his finger around the small ceramic ring, dialing up the number of credits for transfer on the screen in front of everyone. He'd almost forgotten Kharik was in the room until he heard a small gasp followed by his familiar giggle.

Xard turned to look at Ygger as the confirmation button blinked in front of them. "Half now. The rest when you finish hacking the academy systems... assuming you can actually do it."

An unsteady mixture of shock and relief washed over Ygger's face as he stared at the vast number of credits ready to be transferred into the mining operation. Finally, a smile emerged as he turned to look directly at Xard. This time, the swagger was back. "Who *are* you?"

Xard smiled back at him. "Just someone trying to do something besides get blown up today."

"See? I told you he was a spy." Kharik interjected with a laugh.

Ygger laughed nervously under his breath. "Okay, clean-shirt. Deal."

With that, Xard reached out and punched the transfer button on the console, draining away a large quantity of credits. It was far more than he wanted to spend, but at this point he had no other way forward. "It's done then. When can we start?"

Shyne's face slowly changed from a sickly pale to bright pink as her massive heart worked to push blood back into her brain. "Is dis real?" The experience of nearly losing everything and suddenly having it all back again simply piled shock upon shock for Shyne. She quickly reverted back into business mode to keep her composure. "De mining ops will be down tomorrow to assess all de damages. If you are looking for time to do dis, Ygger, that is your vindow."

Ygger nodded back to Shyne. "Okay, clean-shirt. Tomorrow it is. But first, do you like heavy bass, or are you more of a treble guy?"

19 — Voidskin

Ygger threw on his high-collared, industrial blue overcoat and headed for the door. "Come on, what moves you? Heavy rhythms? Ethereal vocals? Neural synths?"

Xard's brow furrowed. "A mix, I guess. Why?"

Ygger clapped him on the shoulder. "Perfect. I know just the place."

"A club? Now?" Xard stared incredulously. "I mean, I get that you're grateful I saved the mine, but didn't we just lose a bunch of miners?"

Ygger tapped his temple. "Right. You're a clean-shirt." He nodded to Kharik. "Tell him the truth of the depths."

Kharik stopped mid-stride, drew himself up, and intoned the words like they'd been branded into his memory:

"Dig deep, die quick, no mourning.
Cyptum flows, wealth is dawning.
Every shift could be your last.
Drink tonight, tomorrow's blast.
No grave waits for those who fall.
Only cyptum claims us all."

Xard felt a chill despite the warmth of the corridor.

"Every mining clan knows those words." Ygger gestured broadly. "The Vex-Tharr Collective, the Quorax Dynasty, even the ZySec Conglomerate. Death's just another extraction cost here. They mourn by drinking the departed's share." He laughed darkly. "I'd bet my next cycle's pay that half the casualties' shift-mates are already three glasses deep. It's the miners' way. Everyone falls to the depths eventually—trick is getting your fortune topside before you join them."

He spun on one heel and held the outer door open. "Coming?"

Xard glanced at Kharik. "And what do you get out of this? I know FLIPP doesn't pay you."

Kharik's face lit up. "Productivity is protection, remember? When I'm twelve, they'll sponsor any training I want."

Xard shook his head. "Let me guess. Training to be a miner?"

Kharik bounded through the door past Ygger, laughing. "Nah. Already decided I'm gonna be a spy. Like you."

Ygger guided them back to the surface and into a more crowded sector of City 87. As they fitted their re-breathers, Xard noticed how Ygger's somehow complemented his stylish appearance rather than detracted from it—one more sign this man had adapted fully to life on Urm.

Pulsing electromagnetic beats grew stronger as they navigated the dusty streets. They rounded an alley where corners glowed with rhythmic neural-tech lighting. Ygger paused, turning to Xard.

"I asked about your music to read your character, not to pick our location." His eyes narrowed, evaluating. "It's been my experience that rhythm-chasers are too brutish to trust, while treble-hunters are dangerously optimistic. Either extreme is bad business. But you— balanced tastes suggest a balanced mind. I can work with that."

They slid into a sound-dampened booth, the music reduced to a tactical shroud around their conversation. Ygger flicked two fingers upward, and moments later, amber-colored drinks materialized before them.

"You saved more than just my operation back there," Ygger said after a long swallow. "I don't know who you are or where those credits came from, and I don't want to know. But the fact is, you might've stopped us all from becoming the next generation of voidskin if that cyptum chain had cascaded before the power was restored." He leaned forward. "And for that, I owe you one. Maybe more than one."

"How so?" Xard perked up at the mention of voidskin, unsure of the connection.

Ygger's voice dropped to barely audible. "Any more surface rock loss in that blast would've destabilized the entire pressure system. It could've ignited the ore vein itself." His fingers began to trace the potential connections on the table in front of him.

"We don't know how deep the network runs on Urm. A spontaneous ignition? Could just take out the quarry. Could take the whole complex. Or..." His eyes darkened. "Could light every cyptum vein on the planet simultaneously. Last ablation was a long time ago, but the veins are still there, still waiting."

"Ablation?" Kharik managed between gulps of his drink.

"The event that nearly ended the voidskin species," Xard said quietly, the vivid memory of his mental connection with the tapestry still raw. He didn't just know the story. He'd experienced it with his mind.

Xard steadied himself as he tried to explain it to Kharik. "The original voidskin came here from Kael by the millions, mining surface cyptum before understanding its properties. Then Kael and Urm aligned with the inner planet, Vexar, partially blocking solar radiation..."

He paused, sweat beading on his forehead. "The resulting chain reaction killed tens of millions instantly. The blast stripped away part of Kael's atmosphere, flash-freezing much of the region. Those few who survived became the foundation for a near-extinct species."

"It's also why they're so damned brilliant now!" Ygger slapped the table, startling both companions. "Centuries of selective breeding created minds and bodies built to survive. One voidskin could replace a hundred of my best techs, even part-time."

Realization dawned on Kharik's face. "Like the ones at FLIPP headquarters?"

Ygger and Xard locked eyes and simultaneously said, "Not exactly." The shared moment cracked their tension, drawing unexpected laughter.

Ygger drained his glass and fixed Xard with a penetrating stare. "Let's just say not all voidskin are created equal." He tapped the table twice. "Now. About this hack-job you need..."

***

Dusk had fallen by the time Drasha swooped in for a scouting pass over the canopied training areas. "Looks like class is out for today. We got lucky."

"Take us in low again and set us down next to the rocky outcropping. I don't want the stormblade visible from the city," Shay replied, mind fixated on the mission.

Drasha maneuvered in close to the solitary structure and set the craft down in a near-dustless landing before popping the hatch open. A lone dark-skinned figure, dressed in simple pale linens, walked out to meet them even before they had fully powered down.

"I greet you in the name of the one who comes." The gentle words flowed like oil over Shay as she walked toward her voidskin host.

206

"Bless her coming." Shay smiled as she reached out her hand to gently touch his arm. Timeon understood the gesture. This wasn't to be an official visit, but something more personal.

"Come. Take your rest." Timeon led them inside his well-appointed domicile and offered them tea before sitting down and dispensing with the pleasantries. Timeon set himself to lighting some incense as he spoke. "So. What brings the lovely Shayameen and Drasha into my home at such a late hour?"

"We're here for your counsel as a voidskin. There's a possibility we may have uncovered a death cult link in a case we are working on."

"Gharsa? Fascinating."

"Well, we don't know for certain. If it *is* gharsa, we need to inform the Mitera. If it's not, we'd prefer to keep it close. The issue is that one of our sisters is actively working to subvert me at the moment."

"Ah, I see. So, what you require is a bit of delicacy. Well then, share only the facts. No assumptions, if you please." Timeon continued to move around the room lighting incense as Shay and Drasha began to relay what they had learned up until that point. The K-rings, the birthing operation, the efforts by the blue-hair, and Xard's disappearance with the aurum until the room was rich with the scent of rare woods and smoke.

Timeon slowly sat down in front of them as he unfolded the details, plucking away the petals until only the core filaments remained. He heaved another whiff of the heavy smoke that clung to the air before speaking. "Rather than simply proffering advice and guidance to you, let me simply tell you what I know of the gharsa. Then, based on what I share, I have no doubt you'll come to your own conclusions and take the appropriate course of action."

Drasha scoffed. "If even the *voidskin* won't advise us, our mess must be worse than we thought."

Timeon smiled at her. "On the contrary, I just wouldn't presume to tell a Vesni what to do. It's important that their decisions are their own. But this was not always the case.

As you may recall, the voidskin of Urm aided the Vesni in liberating Kael from the Omai patriarchy ages ago. Before then, no woman had a say in anything, much less her own mind. As much as it pains me to say it, the voidskin men of that time were largely part of the gharsa belief-system."

Drasha interrupted him again. "Perhaps that's why the Goddess wiped them all out." Shay glanced at her with a look that let her know she was out of line but refused to correct her on the spot. Drasha had very little experience with the voidskin, but Shay had no doubt that Timeon knew how to handle himself in such situations.

Timeon parsed his next words carefully. "Every theocracy has its flaws in that they are managed by human hands in the absence of the deity. When the voidskin helped the Vesni gain control of Kael, it was with the understanding that a very structured, but shared, system of governance would follow. But as the Vesni ascended, they embraced the voidskin, but rejected their gharsa beliefs.

Those among the voidskin who followed gharsa traditions quickly discovered that they had simply traded one theocratic overlord for another. Only the dogma beneath it had changed. The face had softened, but the teeth were just as sharp. One flawed theocracy had simply been replaced with another."

Drasha's eyes widened. "This is heresy! I can't believe this is coming from a voidskin of all people!"

Timeon raised his voice to meet her challenge. "Yes! Hold that feeling! Imagine the righteous indignation you'd have if someone stole the very kingdom you built out from under you. *That* is the emotion that fuels the gharsa under the Vesni rule. So now I must ask: does the slow, methodical planning it takes to undermine the

Vesni through birthing pods seem like the approach of a firebrand cult?"

Drasha sank slowly back into her chair and drew a small smile to her lips as she understood what Timeon was attempting to do. "Well played. He's right, Shay. This doesn't seem aggressive enough to be a death cult action."

Timeon stood up and walked to one of his inlaid cabinets to retrieve a small bauble. "This is one of the many relics that exist from ages past. No one even knows what it does or what it's for. Even the brilliant Taigan couldn't seem to tell me how to use it.

I keep it here as an example of what the relics really are—simple, physical objects. No deity has proclaimed them divine, yet all people practically worship them. This one in particular has no intrinsic value. I can't eat it, or fly with it, or teleport with it. It gives me no special power or knowledge, yet by its very provenance as a relic it becomes priceless to the Vesni.

The difference between all religions can be found in their means to order. The gharsa view 'conquest' as the means to order. So, for them, scriptures and other relics without power are just symbols of a failed civilization—unworthy to be revered. The Vesni, however, revere all of these scriptures and relics, building 'laws' around them as the means to order. They vigorously chase down new ones all over the system in an unending quest to legislate morality and obedience to the Goddess."

Drasha interrupted his monologue. "And the kosonor? Where do they fit in? Could they possibly have a part in what's happening?" Shay bristled at the question.

"Strange as it may seem, kosonor philosophy *also* reveres both scriptures and relics. They simply refuse the Vesni interpretation of them. Since their doctrine is Omai in origin, obviously it holds to a more masculine view. But there are other differences. The kosonor of today believe that no one can forcibly live under the requirements laid out in any of our scriptures. In their view, 'laws' cannot be used as a means to control. Instead, the individual must 'submit' to them willingly."

Timeon held up three fingers. "Conquest. Law. Submission. Those are the three. Strangely, whoever is behind your mystery seems to be attempting to use the law while also subverting it. It's going to be the work of someone slow; methodical."

Shay and Drasha turned to look at each other. "The blue-hair."

"Perhaps," Timeon continued "but your situation has many moving parts. Just because you can identify the cog doesn't mean you've uncovered who is turning the crank. The larger gear turns the smaller one. It's possible your blue-haired nemesis doesn't even realize she's being used."

A sudden look of horror crossed Drasha's face. "Shay, have you considered that it's not *you* that's the target, but your *relationship* with the Mitera? What if they have a bigger target in mind? Who stands to gain if the Mitera steps down? The death cult or one of our own?"

Timeon responded for her. "You are asking the right questions, but the Mitera is far too shrewd to put herself at unnecessary risk, even for Shayameen. The death cult lacks genuine leadership anymore. It's made up of lone adherents now. Most are scattered about the system.

But you should use caution. The gharsa still have their fingerprints somewhere in whatever you're involved in, but they don't seem to be the primary player. I suspect that you won't find the answers you are looking for on Kael. Find the source of the K-rings and you'll uncover the next gear in the machine."

A look of excitement crossed Drasha's face. "He's on to something here, Shay. Whatever we are dealing with here on Kael is going to be low-threat. The immediate risk to the Mitera is negligible. We know the assets trace back to Urm where the cultists originate. If there is another cog in this machine, then it's most likely there."

Shay nodded. "Go spin up the stormblade. Whisper mode. We'll leave out of the port at Kreshen at daybreak to avoid too many questions. If we use the library at the Vesni academy on Urm we may still be able to do some research without tipping off the players on Kael."

Drasha nodded back succinctly and headed out to cycle the stormblade's engines. Timeon and Shay's eyes followed her to the door before turning back towards each other. "Now, why don't you tell me why you're really here?" Timeon insisted warmly.

His eyes pierced her as she spoke. "I have so much happening right now; I just needed a clearer head to help me sort these things out. I've always admired your commitment to Vesni teachings in spite of the fact that you could have been anything. Instead, you chose the Vesni way of life. That kind of sacrifice is rare."

"It's not sacrifice—it's submission. I don't submit to a Vesni mistress, but to the scriptures that tell me I *should.* Submission is strength. So, in truth, I've still chosen the path that brings me to strength and power. Not very altruistic of me, is it?"

Timeon smiled reticently to himself and stepped back. He crossed the small room where they stood and locked the entrance door. His hand pressed firmly into the gilded wooden frame around it as he slowly bowed his head. He spoke without looking her way but continued to face the locked door.

"I know why you're really here. You think you came here to ask me questions about a case, but it's fate that brings you back here again and again. You have questions with no answers, and they keep drawing you back here to find them. The irony is that the answers *are* here, but you won't hear them."

211

Shay's polished composure melted as her mouth fell agape with surprise. "How *dare* you. How dare you try and attack me about Taigan now, with everything else I'm dealing with at the moment!" Her body tensed as she stood alone in the center of the room. She had presumed he locked the door to prevent Drasha from coming in, but now she wasn't so sure.

Timeon turned to look at her directly. "I dare to do so because not only is he the answer to the question you asked, he is also the answer to the one you *didn't* ask. You and I both know Taigan was no heretic. He held firmly to the scriptures even if his understanding of them was often in question.

He believed that if the scriptures were true, they didn't need blind faith to support them. That the worlds around us could validate the truth within them, but it meant we had to *question*. Yet, what the kosonor did in loosely questioning the scriptures, the Vesni undid by forcing their rigid dogma onto society."

She stopped him—her volume escalating with each syllable. "Kosonor was just an excuse to profane our most sacred beliefs. We all remember the crazed misogyny that came about from the kosonor years ago. Masculine communes popping up all over the plains. All it did was make the whole of Kael into a cesspool of unmitigated brutality—men who, when unchecked, couldn't move beyond the basest of desires."

"That's humanism, not what your consort lived, and you know it. What you are describing is some kind of hedonistic lifestyle under the guise of being kosonor. But you're uncovering the very point I am getting at. Whoever is behind your mystery would have counted on the Vesni being prone to such black and white judgement—that they refuse to *question* too deeply.

You're meant to see the gharsa in the shadows. I wouldn't even be surprised if you find an actual gharsa being scapegoated along the way. But the pattern of movement in your case suggests a certain...

212

elegance. So be cautious about using the same rigid assessment you used on Taigan with your latest culprit. Their actions seem more nuanced, intuitive, and above-all patient."

Shay sighed and lowered her voice although the tension remained squarely on her shoulders. "You don't have to bring up my personal tragedies to make your points. I'm not one of your students. Still, I get the reference. Sometimes I forget that he was... different. It's so far past now that I've re-imagined him as who they said he was. It makes the leaving less painful."

Sensing her momentary vulnerability, Timeon moved closer to her. "Except that he didn't *leave* you."

She waved off his suggestion with one hand while she kept the other securely around her chest. "He chose the work over me and ended up dead. To me that's leaving."

He drew even closer. "Except that he didn't *die*. He disappeared."

She looked back at him, desperately holding on to what measure of self-control remained. "I want to believe in the reality you're talking about, but I don't have the luxury of exploring every mathematical possibility like the voidskin do. Women need assurances—stability. That's what a consort provides. If he isn't obedient, what good is he? Dead, alive, heretic, what does it matter? He's gone, and that's my reality."

He held up a hand to her protests. "Obedience to an ideology is not power unless the ideology itself is *true*. Truth is the real power. And the truth of your situation is that sometimes things are not always as they first present themselves. We wield our beliefs as if they are truth itself, but what are they really?

They're just an algorithm we apply over the obstacles in our lives. A decision tree. A set of rules. Now, just like with Taigan, you're stuck pondering more questions your algorithm doesn't seem to answer. If you aren't getting the answers you need with the truth you hold, you need to be open to other rubrics."

Timeon reached out and touched her arm to indicate they were now back in formal relations. "You are Vesni. Your powers of perception are the stuff of legend, so it's easy to rely on your training and instinct. Just don't let that perception become your only truth, Shay. We're all still human after all."

Ygger threw his dusty overcoat back on and tucked a pair of dark goggles into his pocket, patting them slightly as he did so. All that remained of him above the towering coat collar were the swooping locks of jet-black hair. He was dressed like everyone else on the street, but he carried himself differently—different enough to attract attention if anyone cared to notice. They were getting closer to the academy now, and Xard was becoming more tense about discovery.

"I did mention there's a wall and heavy security around the academy, didn't I?" Xard was almost embarrassed to mention it at this late stage.

Ygger scoffed. "Walls are for physical entry. Our only concerns are the firewalls." He stopped as they came within eye-shot of the tower that formed the center of the Vesni academy and started intermittently looking around at the street markers. He mumbled to himself momentarily before letting out a reassuring "a-ha." It was a small hatch nestled against the side of a building, almost completely obscured by the darkened environment.

Kharik bounded right up to it, inadvertently reminding Xard he couldn't see as well as he could in the dark. Ygger plugged a small wire into the code panel on the hatch until it cycled and made a short rusty *screech*. He pulled open the hatch and motioned for them to descend. As they made their way down a loosely attached ladder, a faint dampness began to fill the air. When Xard finally reached the bottom, he was greeted with the sounds of squishing mud and echoing darkness.

Ygger broke the silence as he ignited a mag-torch to better illuminate their surroundings. "This is one of the coolant flows we use to run the mine. When the academy was built, this flow was specifically diverted around it to form a kind of moat in case there was an underground ignition. It was built and forgotten. There's no direct access to the academy, but we can make our own if we can get close enough to where the wall is thin."

Xard finally started smiling. "Clever. I can almost guarantee the Vesni won't have accounted for an underground breach. Their noses are too high to be focused on anything beneath them. This could really work. But how do we access the network?"

Ygger smiled. "Patience, clean-shirt."

The three followed the mucky path until the adjoining coolant began to flow more briskly. "Okay, this should do." Ygger pulled a small inflatable raft from his pack and launched it into the flow. As the three of them climbed aboard, the faintly-glowing coolant flow pushed them quickly ahead. Ygger pulled out his grapple-gun as the speed began to increase and tethered himself to the side of the raft.

"Okay, you two. Hang on. It's going to be a sudden stop." Ygger looked up at the top of the cavern as it began to ascend higher above them.

"You've done this before, right?" Xard asked as he tightened the wet straps around his wrists.

Ygger didn't pause to look at Xard directly, but instead continued to focus intently on the cavern's ceiling. "Saw a holo once." Suddenly a small opening emerged in the ceiling above them. It was an unmarked opening to the ground above covered in a simple mesh grate. It was too high to climb out from, but it was immediately clear that climbing wasn't Ygger's plan.

"That's our mark." Ygger stopped gazing at the ceiling and took aim at the rocky wall along the passage and fired. The grappler wedged into the rock as the raft suddenly jerked beneath them. As Ygger began to reel them in, he finally turned to them both. "Welcome to academy central!"

Ygger pulled the raft up on a narrow shore in the cavern and started scanning the wall immediately. "The wall is too thick to dig through here, but it's structurally weak. No life forms registering or movement on the other side. I think we're safe to enter from here. Any idea what kind of security they might have?"

Xard grimaced as if to say he should have asked this sooner. "No one really knows for sure. They put it here on Urm to keep what happens here private. The only thing I know for certain is that the Urmian environment is supposed to keep the students on edge, so expect people to freak out if they see us. Worst we'll see is a few students with ceremonial weapons. If we're lucky, they'll be too focused on academics and lore to even notice us."

"Good," Ygger replied, "because I found us a breach. See this? It's a dual-power conduit. They normally don't run so close together on Urm. It violates code because it's a safety hazard. Looks like the Vesni greased some palms when they had this built. If I can cycle the power differently in each conduit, the interference should trigger fracturing in the wall when it resonates with this frequency."

The three of them stared at the blank wall as he linked to the power conduits with his scanner. "Annnnnd, jackpot." The wall began to vibrate in front of them. Kharik reached out to touch the wall momentarily before Xard swatted his hand away.

He looked nervously at Ygger as the humming grew louder. "Do we uhm, need to move?"

"Nah. It should just crumble right down."

Xard pulled his own goggles back over his eyes just in case. A small series of *pops* emerged from the wall as the stony surface began to splinter and fall away leaving only the sparking conduits in their path. "You did it!" Xard gasped before realizing he should avoid any further exclamations. Once the power had been cycled back to normal, the way in was finally clear.

Ygger headed in first, hoping to follow the power lines directly to an access node. "Bah, it's just an electrical closet of some kind. Oh well, at least it means we can cover our tracks a little better. You're up, clean-shirt. Find me somewhere to jack in."

Xard now led the way, wincing as the closet door slowly creaked open into what appeared to be a decorative chamber. Unlike the rough-hewn cavern walls they'd just breached, this room was meticulously constructed—a perfect circle with a domed ceiling of fitted stone blocks. The walls were adorned with intricate tapestries depicting the history of the Vesni order, each panel illuminated by natural light funneled through cleverly positioned mirrored shafts in the ceiling.

At the center of the room stood a circular stone dais, its surface worn smooth by generations of use. Seven white marble pillars surrounded it, each engraved with one of the Vesni virtues in an ancient script that seemed to shimmer as they moved past. The room smelled of cedar and rare oils, but beneath it lingered an unmistakable acrid scent.

"Meditation chamber?" Ygger asked softly, taking in the circular layout and ceremonial fixtures.

Xard shook his head, wrinkling his nose. "No. By the smell, it's some kind of training area. Don't let the fancy oils fool you, that's definitely urine."

"So, someone got the piss scared out of them?" Ygger joked.

"More likely someone ruptured a bladder with an abdominal punch." Xard stopped in his tracks and became more serious for a moment. "Actually, abdominal punches are not a Vesni maneuver. They go straight for chest fractures. This seems more about humiliation—something they train voithos in."

Xard paused a moment to think. "Some teenager got the piss beat out of him here alright. If this *is* a voithos training area, that means we're probably in the right place to find what we're looking for. They're always positioned near the archives. We still need to be careful though. Even young voithos can be deadly given the right situation."

Kharik whispered as loud as he could. "Got it, general!"

Ygger simply threw up his hands. "Hey, this is your show, but I can't work the magic unless you find me the rabbit hole. Just try and lead us somewhere that isn't going to be swarming with zealots or whatever."

Xard nodded as they snuck out of the tiny chamber and into the corridor beyond—their muddy footprints already betraying their presence. He had no idea which way he should be headed, but he assumed the direction opposite the sounds of chanting was his best bet. He led them down a long corridor lined with ornately carved alcoves, each containing a life-sized statue of a historical Vesni figure. At the base of each alcove, fresh offerings—small tokens, dried flowers, handwritten notes—had been carefully arranged by students seeking the favor of their predecessors.

They passed several smaller meditation rooms and what appeared to be voithos quarters—sparse chambers with simple pallets, writing desks, and personal shrines. Xard's confidence surged. The corridor gradually widened as it curved, eventually opening into a dramatic three-story atrium.

Unlike the meditation spaces, this area buzzed with quiet activity. Young men in simple gray tunics moved purposefully between levels, carrying scrolls and ancient-looking texts. The walls were lined with row upon row of wooden shelves, each laden with books, manuscripts, and sealed document tubes. A magnificent mosaic dominated the far wall—a stylized depiction of a feminine figure holding aloft what appeared to be a relic of some kind, her face obscured by its radiance.

Balconies ringed the upper levels, connected by a spiraling staircase that wound around a central column of stacked stone basins. Water flowed continuously from the highest basin to the lowest, creating a gentle ambient sound that masked their footsteps.

"This must be the archives," Xard whispered, his eyes wide. "Every piece of knowledge the Vesni have collected over centuries. Histories, prophecies, military tactics, theological debates—it's all here."

"Where's their network access?" Ygger asked impatiently.

Xard pointed toward a secluded area of desks on the ground floor that seemed devoid of students. "There. The scriptorium."

They skirted the edge of the atrium, keeping to the shadows cast by the massive support columns. Each column was carved to resemble a tree, its "branches" extending across portions of the ceiling in delicate stone lacework.

"Wait," Xard suddenly froze. "Change of plan." He gestured toward a narrow corridor branching off from the main atrium. Unlike the rest of the academy's harmonious design, this passage seemed almost hidden—its entrance partially obscured by a shelf that appeared to have been deliberately positioned to draw attention away from it.

"The Vesni are too pretentious to hide anything." Xard squinted. *"Even their toilets are meant to be on display. This shouldn't be here."*

"You might be on to something. Everyone knows the best tricks start backstage," Ygger muttered. *"Come on."*

The hidden door led to a staircase descending steeply beneath the main level. As they followed it down, the atmosphere changed dramatically. The temperature dropped several degrees, and the air took on an antiseptic quality. The ornate stonework and wooden elements of the archives gave way to smoother, more sterile surfaces. The staircase eventually opened into a clinical corridor—stark white and brightly lit, completely at odds with the architectural style above.

"This doesn't match the rest of the place," Ygger murmured.

"No, it doesn't," Xard agreed, peering down the unusual corridor. "This seems more... medical."

"Good. Good. This is good," Ygger smirked. "Medical means records. Find me a place to jack in." The sound of footsteps and conversation suddenly cut their excitement short. The three of them ducked into the first room they could find. It was cold and dark, but they waited it out until the voices trailed off again. Kharik made a sudden crinkling noise as he leaned up against something in the dark which earned him a sudden shushing.

Ygger's face was suddenly cast in a pale blue light as he started to let the scanner run its cycle looking for network access points. "We're close actually. I might even be able to access from here. Get me some light."

Xard went back toward the door and hit the lights. Kharik let out a stifled scream before covering his mouth with his hand as he stared around the room. Children, stacked three-deep along each wall, lay dead in clear, crinkly, packages.

Ygger stopped his scanning for a moment and moved from package to package to assess the faces of the dead. "Hey, clean-shirt, how old do you have to be to train at this academy?"

Xard sighed, annoyed at the inconvenient quizzing as he searched for an access port. "For voithos, it's sixteen. For Vesni it's twenty."

"Then why do all these dead kids look like they're about 9 or 10?"

Kharik continued to cower in the corner unable to speak but managed to point out the small tag at the corner of each bag. "S-S-S-Sentia."

Xard turned in surprise as he grabbed one of the tags off the sealed funerary pouches. "It's a Sentia tag alright. What are these doing here? We're collecting dead kids now?"

"It's the mehdisticians," Kharik whimpered. "They killed them and dumped them here. Ygger, we need to go."

Xard looked more closely at the tag. "Wait. These are revival instructions: Remove from pouch and pull stasis wire behind left ear. Revivification capsule activation takes between 14 and 16.5 minutes. Caution: Revived persons may experience acute amnesia."

Ygger shook his head. "You religious types are freakier than I thought. Keeping dead kids on ice? Pretty sick. Are they stockpiling future followers? Because the way I heard it, the religion will probably be dead in twenty years."

"Faster than twenty if I have any say in the matter." Xard patted Ygger on his dusty shoulder before moving a small cart out of the way. Behind it was a partially hidden access node. Xard turned back toward Ygger and smiled broadly. "You're up!"

Ygger wasted no time. He plugged the small access wire into the node and brought up hordes of data. "Looks like schematics. Schedules. Rosters. Cameras. All kinds of goodies here for you.

There's just one problem. I can access whatever you like but the academy has a pretty impressive system to prevent recording and downloading. They must have developed it themselves because there's nothing like this even on the black market. This data's unsecured, but there's not a thing I can do to copy it."

"So, what does that mean? Can you get me the access or not?" Xard's face twisted at the unwelcome development.

"It means I have access for you, but you'll have to sit here with the dead kids to look through it all. We have no way to take it with us unless..." Ygger's fingers sang over the small scanner, lulling security protocols to sleep with every new verse.

"Got it. Best I can do with what we currently have. I just set up a remote mirror access. If we record anything in-system it will get flagged, but this way we can still access the live feeds and data without making any noise. You should be able to monitor what's happening from the mine if you like. Now. Can we please leave? This place is grossing me out."

Xard nodded his approval. "Fair trade, my friend. Fair trade. Let's go."

The three of them silently made their way back out the way they came until they reached the coolant flow. The water was calm now. Ygger dove in as he spat out instructions to the other two. "Reverse flow in three minutes. When the flow reverses, we can just ride it back to the access hatch. Until then we will have to paddle."

Xard's mind raced as they floated back. It was awash with possibility. The Vesni were lying about something, he just didn't know exactly about what yet. All he knew was that he was going to need to catch them in the act to bring them down, but for the first time in many days he felt hopeful that his plan might actually work.

By the time they had returned to the mine, he had lost all track of time. Shyne's voice finally stirred him from his distractedness. "I don't know what you are doing to my monitors, Ygger, but I still have a mine to run. You have taken up most of my screens now with... with... I don't even know what dis is."

Ygger swooped in and kissed his sister on the cheek. "Thanks for the screen time, Shyne. We won't be long. With as creepy as these religious freaks are I'm sure our new clean-shirt will find what he's looking for pretty quickly."

"Shhh! Quiet. Look. They are moving one of the bodies." Xard tried to adjust the signal to get a better view of the procedure.

"See? What did I tell you? Freaks."

The four of them watched as a small child of about 6 was pulled, leg-first, from the package. The ear wire was pulled out and the body twitched slightly before being placed on a small gurney. "Follow it!" Xard shouted. Ygger accessed the cameras from corridor to corridor as the small frame was moved into a room near the center of the academy and dressed. "What other rooms are near there? Can we check the cams?"

"Looks like a church or a large congregational area of some kind. See? Guess this is where everyone goes when they aren't wetting themselves." Ygger panned to the center vestibule. A Vesni-earia stood before a large group of students, both male and female, festooned in ceremonial garb. She stood waving her arms about, speaking emphatically to the congregants in attendance. "I can't get any sound. The cams must not be wired for it. Let me see if I can access someone's personal comms."

Xard continued to stare at the collection of trainees and mentors, studying their every tell, looking for an indication of what might be happening. "Here comes the dead kid. Look!" Xard watched as the small boy's body was wheeled into the chamber before the earia. Suddenly, the audio streamed across the speakers as Ygger punched into one of the security personnel's comms.

The earia's unfiltered voice was so loud that Kharik covered his ears out of reflex. "You are the chosen. You are the ones that have lived and suffered and lived again, reborn in the power of our Goddess. Many of you have struggled, as all do in these training days, to know whether or not your pain was worth it, whether your struggle was real.

Now, by the authority given me by the Mitera and the power vested in me by the Goddess herself, let us witness the living power she holds over all creation. In the name of the one who comes, I bid you rise!" A moment of silence gripped the room until someone gasped. A twitch, a small movement of a finger, then a toe. Excitement began to visibly grow in the room as the young boy began to stir.

Xard stood, mouth agape at the audacity of it. "This is ridiculous! It's all fake! We can prove it! Those idiots think it's real."

"Actually... We *can't* prove it. Only the four of us saw it, and no one cares what we think. Trust me."

"They are faking a resurrection and giving the Goddess credit for it! No wonder they're all such zealots. They think they wield supernatural power." Xard clenched his teeth as he struggled to find a way to take advantage of the situation unfolding before him. "I need to record it. I need full holo capability. Everyone on Kael needs to see this. How do I do it?"

Ygger laughed. "Well, you can't do it from here. You'd need to go back and set up an on-site immersion drive. It'll capture the whole scene in full color 3D. You can even zoom in if you have a large enough drive.

Sadly, they aren't cheap, and even if you passed me the money for one right now, it would take some time to procure one. Until then, you may want to keep your cover intact. Why don't you take a break from your mission for a bit, 'general?' The Vesni aren't going anywhere. Besides, the FLIPP matron is going to be studying your work metrics after today because we only allow for one training day. Until I can get you that drive, you're going to need to play cyptum miner if you want to keep people from asking too many questions."

Ygger's advice to return to the FLIPP pods was a sound one, even if it meant more delays. The adrenaline of the day's events had exhausted him, and for the moment, nothing sounded better than sleep. The gentle *chirp* of the day's assignments running on the 'chore' board barely roused him the following day. Not so for Kharik, who managed to bound out of his bunk and tug on Xard's arm almost before hitting the floor. "The jobs are up, general!"

Kharik ran to the board to scour the list looking for their names. "Ahh, bosca! I hate the fringe quarry."

Xard leaned up on one arm as he continued to lounge in his bunk. "Well, what did you expect? It's not like the regular mine is in any condition to be worked. Besides, the mining is all the same, right? Shave off the red ore. Keep the lights lit. Easy."

"No, it's not like that. The fringe stones are bigger and harder to move."

One of the other FLIPP pod-mates gave Kharik a gentle shove. "Stop your whinging! Wouldn't you rather just blow up from a big piece of ore? Beats burning to death from loose dust, cupa."

"Language, young sirs!" One of the false voidskin emerged from the hallway into the pod to check on everyone's progress. Xard shot him a snide smile, and he nodded back until he noticed Xard's pack had spilled open at the end of his bunk. "Young sir, I hope that isn't a mining instrument still in your pack. Mining equipment is meant to stay in the mine."

Xard had almost forgotten about the grapple gun. He scrambled to the end of his bunk to tuck it away. "Yes, of course. It won't happen again." The false voidskin nodded and left the room before Xard mumbled back to Kharik under his breath. "Won't happen again that *you* see anyway. How long do you think we'll need to keep up this mining charade before Ygger can get us what we need?"

Kharik beamed. "I dunno, general, but he's always been quick with the things the other boys ask for. I guess it just depends on if he has to see Shyne's father or not, but usually he's quick. I'd guess a day or two at most."

Xard sighed. "Okay, I guess we better get back to it then. You lead. I don't know where this fringe quarry loads up at. What's the deal with Shyne's father anyway? Is he some stuck-up mining exec or what?"

Kharik barely slowed his scurrying toward the shuttles to answer the question. "It's his face. Ygger's dad used to own the mine, but he died a while back. After his mom took control of it, she married Shyne's dad to help out. I guess their dads never liked each other and he kind of took it out on Ygger on account of the fact that he looks just like him. Then when his mom died too, I guess it became a real problem. So now he basically lives in the mine just to get away from him."

"You sure know an awful lot about people, captain. You're a pretty handy little helper."

"That's why they send me to do the snooping, er, I mean, scouting." Kharik smiled a broad grin back at Xard. It pained him that this kid followed him around like a lost pet. He had a mission to accomplish, and Kharik was still just a tool. His face soured when he thought about how it would probably end in disappointment, but he shook the thoughts from his mind as they stepped onto the shuttle.

Kharik was finally quiet for a change owing to the growing darkness around them as they raced toward the day's work site. Kharik wasn't

228

lying—they had been dumped in a very dismal section of mine. It was quieter than he expected. No sound, save for the gentle vibration of the mining lathes and the quiet hum of the UV lights. The two of them found their way to a secluded area where they could work and talk in private. As they set to work, it wasn't long before the crimson ore began to fall from the rock face in tiny red grains.

Xard's thoughts were elsewhere as he scraped at the wall, barely focused on the monotonous work. His mind was still awash with all the new possibilities—like looking for the most severe way he could punish the Vesni with what he knew. A three-dimensional exposé of the Vesni lie would be almost too good to be true. If he could get it into the hands of the omyym in the plains and have it broadcast amongst the tribes, the embarrassment to the whole system would be profound. If they tried to send anyone after him, he could still leverage what he knew about the voithos-moro's hidden cache to blackmail him. Even so, he worried that the omyym were too simple to effectively use the information in the drive even if they had it.

He could always sell the information to someone else who had a grudge against the Vesni. That would all but ensure the lies would be exposed, and he could even make some money on the side. It began to dawn on him that in spite of his newly found gains, the battle wouldn't end with exposure. He needed to think about the long game, and what would happen when all the cards had been played. The assets tumbled around in his mind as he finally sat down to take a break.

Kharik sighed as a very large red crystalline formation began emerging from the rock. "See what I'm talking about? I hate these big ones. I can't even reach the top of it with the lathe! Why do they put little people out here? If I shave around it, it might fall out on top of me."

"Well, at least you won't blow up." Xard laughed.

229

"Big people are supposed to help little people. Didn't you know that?"

Xard became suddenly sullen. "Not all big people do. Sometimes big people just suddenly leave and don't tell you where or why." He was speaking from experience, but he used the words as a test to see how Kharik would react to his ultimate departure from Urm.

He stared intently at his grapple gun as he spoke. "These are sad, dark, worlds, captain. Hopefully we can bring some light into them by telling people the truth. Then they can stop sticking their heads in the dirt and make a difference."

Xard paused for a moment and pulled back the housing on his grapple gun. It was a simple device with a cold start battery mechanism. "Hmm. Rechargeable." As he fumbled with the lighting element inside, he noted that removing it left a small cylindrical hole in the front and smiled to himself. He scrambled to his feet in excitement as he slid the hidden selasin off the back of his hand and fished around inside of it for its quantum core.

"Kharik! Check this out! This fits perfectly inside the grappler. I think I can load my weapon core in here and no one would know this wasn't an ordinary mining gun."

"Until it was too late..." Kharik giggled with equal delight as he motioned with his hands like a gun pointing at random rocks.

"Wow. It's almost like it was made for this. Gallamar must make these mining tools as well. I wonder if they just make cores in standard sizes everywhere. They don't teach us about energy weapons, just martial skills." Xard frowned that this was probably another piece of useful information that had been hidden from him in his training. He sat back down abruptly, kicking up dust in his wake as he went back to securing the selasin core into its new home. He tucked it into the small holster on his leg and drew it out a few times before getting lost in his thoughts again.

230

"My father liked energy weapons, but he didn't share any of what he knew with me," Xard complained.

"You make him sound really mean. Did he beat you or something?"

"No. No, not really. If anything, it's him being gone that hurts me most. He left my mother, and that turned her into a raving skika—even more than the Vesni had already made her! But you wanna know the worst part? Everyone consoled my mom.

It was almost an afterthought that *I* might be hurting. It's like if someone died and at the last second someone said, 'oh who will take care of his pets?' No one cares on Kael, just like no one cares on Urm. Be glad you can't remember your past. You only have to deal with the future."

Xard shook his head at his own sulking and stood up with a sigh. "Come on, captain, we've done enough heavy lifting for one day. Time to show you the secret stuff." Xard pulled the modified selasin from its holster, hefting it in his hands. He panned it around him a few times before aiming it at the large red formation behind Kharik.

As Xard aimed the modified weapon at it, a subtle vibration passed through the crystalline structure. The air around them seemed to grow heavier, colder—the nearby UV lights flickering almost imperceptibly.

"Stop! You'll blow us all up! Please don't." Kharik waved his hands frantically in front of himself, his eyes darting nervously to the crystal and back.

"Relax, it's not an explosive. It's a quantum weapon. It makes little black holes that collapse in on themselves and evaporate. Besides, light is a by-product of the reaction, so the cyptum won't ignite anyway. It doesn't even make any noise. Makes a real mess out of people, bet it works on rocks too. Go on, move. Trust me, I've seen how they work plenty of times on the holos."

231

Kharik retreated behind Xard, but not before casting one more uncertain glance at the crystal. "Something doesn't feel right about this," he whispered, but Xard had already taken aim.

"At least it won't fall on you!" Xard laughed as he steadied his grip and focused on the rocks surrounding the crystal.

click

Time seemed to fracture around them as the energy struck the rock in a twisted beam. The large chunk of red crystal fell before them with a heavy *thud* that echoed strangely, as if within his own head. Inside the translucent crimson surface, something shifted—a darkness deeper than the absence of light.

Kharik's eyes began to widen as he stared past Xard and into the fallen crystal. "General? I-I-I can't see." The mining lights remained lit, but a strange darkness began to move across Xard's field of view as well.

Within the crystal, a shape assembled itself—not simply amorphous but geometrically wrong, like seeing too many dimensions folded into three. Angular shadows formed and reformed, crawling across the inner surface of the crystal with intelligent purpose. Thin tendrils of darkness reached the edges and pressed against them like fingers testing the strength of a cage.

The air soured, taking on a metallic taste that coated Xard's tongue. The temperature around them plummeted as frost began to form on nearby equipment.

Kharik began to whisper-shout, "It's one of them! One of the dead voidskin! It's here to haunt us!"

Xard fell back to the ground away from it as the entity inside the crystal began to spin and pulse with increasing violence. Each rotation seemed to tear at the fabric of reality, leaving faint

232

afterimages in the air. Something in his mind recognized this—a flash of memory from the tapestry, from stories of the ablation that had nearly wiped out an entire species.

Instinctively, he leveled the selasin at the crystal of cyptum itself.

click

Time began to move erratically now—stretching and compressing in nauseating waves. The fragment of red crystal expanded and collapsed in on itself with a silent concussion that Xard felt in his bones rather than heard. The shadowy entity scattered into countless geometric fragments—shattered obsidian mirrors reflecting only darkness before coalescing again into a singular presence.

Free from its prison, the entity moved with predatory intent—shifting between forms that reminded Xard of ancient stories he'd read in forbidden texts. For a moment, it hovered before him, and he suddenly felt a terrible recognition—not of what it was, but of what it seemed to know about him.

It surged forward, fragmenting around obstacles only to reform with unnatural precision. A kaleidoscope of only black, it tumbled in tiny fragments before finding itself again and charging at Xard in a steady stream. He couldn't tell if what he was seeing was even real until it struck his chest with enough force to nearly knock the wind out of him. The impact wasn't just physical—each blow also seemed to carry a psychic weight, as if it was trying to hammer through his very essence. With each strike, fragments of memory flashed behind his eyes—his father's departure, his mother's rage, his own darkest thoughts reflected back at him with terrible clarity.

Kharik started screaming almost unintelligibly before his voice faded from hearing. "General! Generaaaal! Generaaaaaaaaaal!"

Xard felt the entity beat the air from his lungs as it continued to hammer down on him. His sight slipped to darkness, consciousness spiraling inward. Every breath felt like it was the last, stuck in a constant loop where his final error just continued to replay itself over and over again. It was all happening too quickly to know if he was dreaming... or dying... or if he had set the whole planet ablaze.

The assault became more than physical—it was intimate, personal. The dark form wasn't just attacking his body; it was excavating his sins. Each impact resonated with a hatred so ancient and specific that Xard realized this wasn't random. It recognized him, or something about him, as if the quantum disturbance had awakened an old enemy.

His only perception became one of darkness and rage, and Xard became genuinely afraid. His life was passing before his eyes, but with only the worst of him on display. It seemed to hate him in ways he didn't even know a person could be hated. He just wanted it to end, but the experience continued to recycle again and again until he became lost in it and all the light finally went out.

In the moments before consciousness fully fled, Xard thought he heard a voice—not Kharik's, but something older, speaking in a language he shouldn't understand but somehow did: *You don't belong here.*

***

"Don't take this the wrong way, Shay, but if Xard dies I think you would be missing out on a unique opportunity."

Shay continued to stare out of the window of their stately shuttle compartment. The curvature of Kael had barely begun to fall away before the scarred surface of Urm descended into its place. "This should be informative. Perhaps the Vesni mind is being sufficiently formed in you after all. I wouldn't dare take issue with a well-thought-out plan, especially since it reflects on my training. Although, in fairness I can't really credit my training with all the interruptions we've had. So, let's hear it."

"If he dies, the best we can claim is that it was a fool's errand. He'll be hoisted up as a warning for future voithos, but you gain nothing other than ending the blue-hair's plan to discredit you. If we retrieve him ourselves and bring him to justice for his crimes it could backfire on her, solidifying your position rather than weakening it. You would be demonstrating 'supreme sacrifice'—a rite only practiced by earia and above."

"It's good to see you still checking all the boxes on my career." Shay laughed and turned to look at Drasha directly. "He's so close to becoming a voithos now it's just been easier to think of marrying him off. Problem solved. Once he's another woman's consort nothing reflects back on me. But regardless of his reasons for doing so, he's a leaver. Just like his father. Everyone will see it when this comes to light. The only thing I can really control is *how* he ends."

Shay returned to staring out through the viewport. "He's always pushed the limits. Maybe he did me a favor by finally crossing the line. I have so few options now. If he's dead, there's nothing to do but file a report and pick up the remains. If he's just a runaway thief, I can capture him and turn him in.

In that case, your plan has some merit. But, if he's somehow gotten himself entwined with the death cult, I'll have to kill him myself." Shay steeled herself into a cold silence for a time until the shuttle touched down on the academy grounds. The two of them fastened their rebreathers and stepped out into the courtyard to take in the dusty and darkened expanse before heading inside.

Drasha broke the prolonged silence. "Goddess! I forgot how depressing it is here. Have they never heard of sustainable lighting?" Drasha looked toward Shay and saw the momentary laugh line flex in the corner of her eye that indicated it was safe to continue with normal conversation. "If we can access the scriptorium, we should be able to run down where our smuggler hails from and where any of the remaining resources currently are. With any luck we may be able to recover the aurum the moro let slip away as well."

"You haven't worked many of these death cult cases, have you, Drash?" The sound of Shay's boots seemed to punctuate her words as they strode into the academy's darkened foyer. "These cases come up every so often, but they're loners. We're not really looking for a 'cult', we're looking for a 'cultist'. Each one's motives are as different as its own individually twisted interpretation of the scriptures. This is why we believe in one interpretation... and one interpreter."

"The Mitera, yes. Bless her coming."

"The problem is that there is no way to accurately interpret what a cultist may do. They have no established code with which to gauge their next action. It's a wild shoot. The odds of us recovering the aurum are just as good as us finding it lying around in our shuttle compartment when we return home. No. We have better chances of finding it if my son's managed to hang on to it."

***

"Hang on, Xard!"

The voices suddenly began to re-emerge in his senses. He felt withered—maimed. Thoughts of the three trampled flowers filled his mind. For a moment he longed to be one of them—to find more acceptance and hope in their cast-off blooms than in what the present experience had left him with. The ground felt as cold, wet, and unforgiving as those three once-brilliant flowers that lay in waste in the darkness.

"Xard!"

A gentle rain now. Light began to return to the scene. In his mind he could see his father again, searing his mind with more words that would never be fruitful. "The things that move away always come back around."

Ygger shouted to Kharik. "He's coming back around. Throw some more water on him."

236

Xard jerked suddenly as another splash of cold water hit his face. The faces of Kharik and Ygger were staring down at him. Shyne emerged to complete the triad of faces hovering over him, eventually eclipsing all the others as she came closer to him on the ground. When it occurred to him that her jowls hung more prominently in this position, he realized that he was snapping back into his normal train of thought. He barely refrained from commenting on it as the fleshy mass came closer to him and kissed him on the forehead.

"What happened?" Xard reached up and held his head as he lay there trying to make sense of it all.

Ygger sighed with relief. "The official version? You two had a light failure and ignited a cyptum pebble, causing an explosion that knocked you both unconscious. The miners that found you had a different story."

"How different?" Xard struggled to lift himself up slowly on his elbows.

"They saw the same black thing we did, general. They said it was hammering against you until it finally quit and flew away." Kharik held on to Xard's arm as he spoke in worried tones that bordered on tears. He tried laughing it away. "I told you I hate the fringe quarry!"

Xard continued to struggle with his awareness of time and place. "Wait. Where are we? The control room? How long have I been out?"

"Out long enough for you two to miss your call-back time at FLIPP. Don't worry, though, I put in an overtime notice to let them know you two were staying here for the time being. Besides, you two look like you need the rest. When you're up to it, it would be nice to know what really happened out there.

We can't have our miners spreading stories about 'phantoms in the fringe.' It's bad for business. They even named it already; can you believe that? They're calling it a *skeen*. We need to get ahead of this thing before people start claiming they're too ill to work."

"I... I don't really know what to believe right now." Xard's presence of mind began to return. "My grapple gun!"

"Psh. Look at this kid, Shyne, he gets the stuffing knocked out of him, and he's worried about losing our equipment. Wish they were all as loyal. Don't worry, we scooped it up with you and Kharik. You may want a new one though, it looks like your UV mount is loose."

Xard shot a glance toward Kharik whose nervous expression indicated that he hadn't said anything about the modifications.

Ygger continued almost as an afterthought. "When you get your bearings, come visit me in the living areas. Some good dirt is coming over the mirrored relay we set up at the academy."

Shyne interjected. "Yes, and it will explain why I help you now. These crazy womens are worse than de cultists! And Sentia? Oiy!! They are devils!"

"You two shout if you need anything. I'll be in my quarters when you get your feet back under you."

Kharik and Xard sat still for a moment before finally attempting to stand. Xard winced as he felt the bruising under his ribcage. The wounds were worse than he thought, but there seemed to be no permanent damage. Kharik, finally overwhelmed by the experience they had just shared, began to cry and stumbled toward Xard, arms outstretched. Xard began to wonder if he was back in his fugue state or whether it was really happening. Nevertheless, he tentatively returned the embrace.

Kharik mumbled through his tears, intermittently trying to wipe his face on Xard's shirt. "It was trying to kill you. I could feel it. It didn't talk. It just hated you. I thought it was gonna come after me next, but

238

it didn't. It only attacked you. What if it comes back? What do we do?"

Xard reluctantly patted his small companion on his back as he tried to minimize the whole event. "It'll be okay, captain. It's like you said. Probably just an old voidskin ghost looking to get back to the surface, but let's not think about that right now. In any case it's gone. Come on, let's see what all the fuss is in Ygger's quarters."

Xard held his arms around his chest as he nursed his wounded ribs. As much as he wanted to play it tough in front of Kharik, the event had left him in a state of derealization. *What was that thing? Was any of this real? Am I in a dream again?*

The questions all tumbled through his mind as he shambled down the hall. Kharik followed closely behind him like a grubby nursemaid. When they finally reached Ygger's makeshift living area, it was covered from floor to ceiling in holo-adverts from various brands and commodities he no doubt obsessed over: fizzing drinks, music artists, trikes, hair creams, and fashion. It was a different side of Ygger he hadn't expected. In spite of his officiousness on the job, his personal life showed him to still be a teenager after all.

Ygger spun around with his usual grace as they walked in, his long coat twirling around him as he greeted them. Xard continued to look at all of the unique adverts lining the walls as Ygger pulled up the live feed from the academy. "There aren't any tech stories up there if that's what you are looking for. I keep my tech interests to myself.

I don't need the 'deep well' knowing I have interests in anything that could be construed as hacking. Besides, there are plenty of adverts up here to keep my attention." After tossing a stack of clothes into the corner, Ygger dusted off a small bench for the two of them to sit on and observe the activity.

"I'm glad you came down right away. I wouldn't want you to miss anything. You were right about one thing. They are very overconfident about security there."

"The Vesni are overconfident about everything," Xard replied.

Ygger redirected Xard's gaze back to the live stream. "Okay, so it's quiet at the moment, but I did uncover a very interesting conversation earlier between one of the workers and a Sentia rep. Well, at least he looked like he was from Sentia. Hope you don't mind but I've been primarily focusing on him when he shows up because Sentia hardware is harder to crack.

Watching individual mannerisms sometimes gives me insight into how they code. The fact is, Sentia shouldn't even be here. They're scientists. You'd think they'd have nothing to do with religious groups, but..."

"But?"

Ygger pulled out a small scratch pad where he had been taking notes. "From the conversations I've seen so far, it appears that the Sentia mehdisticians have been trafficking children on Urm for quite some time. From what it sounded like, the abductions are purely scientific for them, but when they finish, they sell the used 'husks,' as they call them, to the Vesni for their training ceremonies. The husks are still alive, but they are in a chemical stasis, so they appear dead."

Xard began to grin from ear-to-ear. "So, the Vesni wake one of these husks every class cycle in the name of the Goddess to show her fake resurrection power. I knew it! Those damned liars!"

"Wait, there's more. When these little hamsters wake up, he said they don't usually have any memory of what happened, so they just get released into the streets. I haven't confirmed it yet, but my guess is that FLIPP picks them up and puts them to work mining. It's a win-win for Sentia because they can experiment on them, sell the husks, and probably get kickbacks from FLIPP afterward."

Xard began to clench his teeth as he pounded his fist into his hand. "Then we've got 'em!"

"Not so fast. We don't have anything yet. We know the truth, but we still can't prove it. We still need that immersion drive, but Shyne should be able to siphon off enough credits for us to make it happen. At least now we know how to catch them when we get one. All we need to know is when the next 'resurrection' will be. Come on, let's go check in with my sister and see if she has the creds yet."

22 – Payback

Shyne's corporate office was a surprisingly well-appointed stateroom designed for meeting high-end cyptum buyers. Some might even consider it opulent given its location in the bowels of Urm. But the only truly out-of-place item in the entire office was Shyne herself. Her voluminous teen-aged body conveyed neither health nor business acumen, yet there she sat—chief spokesperson for an impressively large cyptum mine, of all things.

Shyne's body poured over her chair's armrest as if she had been de-boned while tiny FLIPP runners continued to come in and out bringing her invoices to sign. For the life of him, he still couldn't understand the children's affection for her. Nevertheless, she had what he needed now, and it was time to play nice. Shyne turned to the two of them with a sigh as she saw them enter.

"I know why you two are here, but there is a problem." She paused for a moment to catch her breath. "I can't siphon off any more monies for your drive at de moment. Something has happened. There is a new player in de cyptum mining business. From nowhere. They bought up new mining rights and started undercutting our contracts almost immediately. I'm very sorry, but if I siphon off credits for your hardware faster, I will put us at risk. If that happens, our markets will go 'boom.'"

Ygger held out his hands to his side incredulously. "How much time are we talking here, Shyne? And, who is this new player? It's been the same nine mining businesses on Urm for a hundred years. No one appears overnight. Who are they a subsidiary of?"

Shyne pulled up a holo of the new cyptum licensee. "This is de man. I've never heard of him before. He just showed up. New man. Buying up all de mining field licenses. I'm sorry boys. It could be some time before I can get de resources you need."

Xard's eyes widened as he stared at the holo of the new buyer. "That's him! That's the noodle man. That's the guy that stole half my aurum!"

"What? Wait, are you sure it is de same man?" Shyne probed him intensely with a look of ferocity he hadn't seen in her before.

Xard nodded. It was unmistakable. "Yes. It's him. I recognize the head markings, the weird piercings, everything. He even has transmission implants when he rolls back his eyes. It's really gross."

Ygger and Shyne stared at one another silently for a long moment, the length of which began to make Xard feel uncomfortable. Shyne broke the silence as her eyes snapped back to Xard. "How much aurum did he take from you?"

"Over 100 half-ingots," Xard scowled. "111 to be exact."

Her eyes snapped back to Ygger. "You think what I am thinking, don't you oncha."

"It's almost too good to be true. No one could be this careless." Ygger ran his fingers through his hair in excitement and let out a long breath.

"Unless they aren't knowing we are aware of de aurums. Is de algorithm current?"

"Perfectly."

Xard finally interrupted. "What the hell is going on?"

The two of them turned and smiled at him. Ygger put his arm around Xard's shoulder as he spoke. "If he purchased the mining licenses with your aurum, then he had to do it back-channel without using the 7-layer encryption system. That means that if I know the exact amount, I can hack the account they were deposited into and run my algorithm to siphon the credits back out."

"Wait, are you saying you can get my credits back?"

Ygger smiled. "And then some. We could *own* this guy. You'd have to trust me though. To back-trace the account he stored the aurum in, I'll need to dissolve all the credits left in your K-rings. Each account the credits came from is coded in a way that requires all of the sequences to crack. If he loaded at least one of your rings from the same account as his own, we've got him."

Xard looked at them both incredulously. It was one more obstacle on what should have been an easy task. "I'm not 'dissolving' my credits until I have an immersion drive. Sorry."

Shyne chimed in. "No, no. You will not be doing dissolvings of them. You are *trading* them. You will be buying the cyptum mining credits with them, yes? They are like monies all over de system. But to work, you must eliminate de K-ring accounts entirely. If we don't, they will find you once de transfer and de algorithm is done."

Xard crossed his arms and looked back and forth at the two of them. He had few options now, but he wanted them to think it was still his idea. "Fine. As long as I still get to keep the same amount, I don't care what kind of money it is. I just want to see the Vesni burn, and I feel like we're running out of time before they discover your mirrored server."

Shyne smiled at him. "You don't understand, young one. When this is over, you could probably *buy* de Vesni academy. We have been waiting for an opportunity like this for a long time. So full of surprises, this one!" She let out a laugh that sent ripples over her body before turning to Ygger. "Make sure we set up a shell account to dump de chits into that de young one can access on his own." Shyne clapped her hands together and stared back at Xard. "I love crushing bad boys like dis tattoo man!"

Xard laughed at the sight. Her mix of ferocity and feebleness flew against everything he had learned from the Vesni. Yet, he found a deep satisfaction in knowing that someone like her would play a key role in their demise. Not only was she everything the Vesni were not, even her own name mocked them with its overwrought usage of the sacred sounds. Xard fished around in his pockets for his three K-rings and slid his fingers around the ring of each, releasing their biometric encryptions before reluctantly handing them over to Ygger.

Ygger hurried to the control console behind Shyne's desk and began transferring the credits off the K-rings and into a shell account. Xard suddenly felt naked without his resources close at hand, but it was too late now. If they burned him, he reasoned he could always just disintegrate them with the selasin. Shyne spun her chair around to watch Ygger work his magic.

He anticipated the questions that he knew were forming in Xard's head and started explaining the process. "Okay, the credits are loaded into the shell account. Now all I need to do is run the trace and..." He paused. "Got it. Wow. That tracked freakishly fast. Your noodle man did not cover his tracks well at all."

Ygger continued to interface with the terminal as he explained it to Xard through his dark locks. "See, when you mentioned his transmission implants, that's when I knew. I figured he had to be using Darkstar 80s. They're run-of-the-mill as far as comm implants go, but they're the only ones that have a proprietary software for money transfers. Problem is, they're not encrypted, so no one actually uses them for more than just comms."

Ygger shook his head and smirked back at Xard. "It's a magic trick. A shell game. Shuttling money this way is actually pretty clever...so long as no one's watching. Unlucky for him, we were."

"So, he's stupid. Right?" Xard asked, looking for reassurance.

"Just the opposite. Normally unencrypted transfers like that would be too risky. A man-in-the-middle attack could snatch the transfer as it moved. But aurum is physical currency; it has to be paid in person. It means he can input the aurum directly onto a ledger without risking it being snatched in transit. The plan is pretty smart unless..."

"...unless someone is specifically looking for it?"

"You got it, kiddo. Even then, it takes someone as brilliant as me to crack in and run the siphon. Don't worry, clean-shirt, I've been preparing for an opportunity like this for years." A warning notification began to flash on the monitor.

Ygger stopped for a moment and took a long breath before turning back to Xard. "Okay, it's ready. Want to do the honors?" Xard walked up to the console, took his own deep breath, and pressed the flashing 'commit' button.

Numbers began to flash across the screen as thousands of buy and sell trades began to happen simultaneously. Shyne's eyes widened as she began to instantly interpret what was happening in front of her. Then just as quickly as it started, the algorithm had finished. Ygger and Shyne sat staring at the screen silently.

"Wait. Is that it? Did it work?" Xard felt stupid asking a question he was sure the two of them already knew the answer to.

Ygger continued to stare at the screen as he put his arm around Xard's shoulder again. From this angle, Xard was almost certain he could see Ygger's eyes welling up under his long dark locks. "You, sir, are now a very, very rich young man. And this mine probably has enough mining credits to run on automation for the next five years if we wanted.

All your aurum that you sold and all the aurum that he stole have been converted to cyptum mining chits. They spend like currency pretty much anywhere but Kael. You can convert it back anywhere at any time, but honestly, it's safer in this format. The algorithm I ran was a single-use buy-sell multiplier that leveraged the aurum on the account 500 to 1.

This *never* would have worked without your aurum connection. It's like you were the perfect combination of resources meeting my perfect combination of programming and Shyne's perfect combination of, of, of..."

Shyne flipped her hair to one side as she smiled. "Brilliance."

Ygger laughed. "Yes, her brilliance."

"And you saved de lives of all de childrens that rely on this mine. I know you are only out to hurt de Vesni peoples, but I want you to know that this means so much to all of us." Shyne leaned in and gave him a warm hug as he stood there trying to understand what they were telling him. "You make us so happy, rich boy! You can buy all de immersion drives you want! Ygger, contact de friends of yours and have them deliver one right away. I know this is very important to him."

"Already on it." Ygger slapped Xard on the back harder than he planned to causing him to lurch forward. "We did it, buddy! Cleeeeean money!"

***

"Dirty money leaves dirty trails, Drasha." Shay gently strummed her fingers across one of the academy's massive interfaces as she began to access the scriptorium's data core with her upgraded credentials. "I'm going to guess that the trails leading into and out of those stolen K-rings are quite dirty indeed. See this? These sequences all indicate transactions which occurred on the stolen K-rings, now we just need to sort out which ones match any known criminal activities. Start with the largest transactions."

Drasha's porcelain face began to bathe in the blue light from the console as she peered over Shay's shoulder. Shay paused for a moment, struck by the unique beauty of her protege's sudden visage. A conflicting sense of both loss and hopefulness washed over her as she considered her own wasted beauty and the possibilities that still lay before her trainee. In this light, she looked every bit the fragile doll, but there was nothing at all fragile about Drasha. She'd made sure of that. All she needed was experience and she would be atop the Vesni ladder in short order.

A sudden chime from the console snapped Shay back to the matters at hand. Drasha leaned in and pointed to the new stream of data that had emerged. "Okay, look there. Hundreds of transfers into these K-rings from hundreds of separate accounts, but only one expense location. That's going to be our birthing operation crew on Kael, correct?"

Shay nodded in agreement.

"Then it looks like three of the K-rings were reactivated with this large amount just recently. It could be your son, but that amount doesn't match the amounts for the lost aurum, so is it something else?"

Shay leaned back in her seat and laughed. "Unless."

"Unless what?"

"Well, the fact that the K-rings are here at all is indication enough that he came here. He either loaded half his aurum on K-rings and kept the other half in physical currency or—more likely—he simply got robbed."

Drasha crossed her arms in front of herself. "Of course, there is also the possibility that your son has neither the K-rings nor the aurum and is lying in a trash heap somewhere."

Shay reluctantly agreed and turned back to the console. "True. But since these are hot, active K-rings, they'll either lead us to my son, or the aurum, or the perp. Any or all of those help our efforts here. I just wish there was a way to trace the transactions from before the birthing operation—the encryption is very complex. Whoever did this was a professional with good financial backing. I doubt we're dealing with just a few small-time thugs looking to make a buck."

"You think this was Sentia?"

"They certainly have the resources, but they don't seem to have the motivation. Gharsa could do it, but it's not their style and would mean they have a new financial backer." Shay studied the console more intently. "Hmm. It looks like they've recently been emptied again into a new corporate account using some kind of hyper-mesh subroutine.

This is getting uglier by the moment. Someone recently tried to launder these credits." Shay's stomach suddenly began to turn, but she played it off as best as she could. "That doesn't bode well for my son being involved. He's smart, but not that smart.

In any case, we have what we need. Let's find out where this mining operation is and pay them a visit. Maybe we can put this whole sordid business behind us before the blue-hair has a chance to adapt her plan."

***

Shyne continued her day with a broad smile while half-sized runners continued their flurry of activity. It was the best financial report the mine had seen since it had been in her hands. She reflexively seized one of the FLIPPrs at random as they passed through her work area and pulled them in close for a hug. "This is a good day, young one!" The young child made a twisted face and nodded as if he knew what she was talking about and then ran off with the next batch of orders.

Shyne then set her office status to 'private' with a swipe of the console and sat down to draft a message to her father in their native tongue. It was short, but went out of its way to highlight Ygger's role in saving the mine and improving their financial position. She fretted over every detail of it and recomposed it several times before settling on a description of events that shone him in the best light. It was the best news she had been able to pass along in quite some time and a satisfied smirk curled up the corner of her mouth as she added the finishing touches.

A flashing hailing light on the console brought her quickly back to the common language as she responded. "I'm sorry. I am not accepting clients at de moment. If you like to make de appointments, I can have someone—"

"You'll see us right now." A man—several men perhaps—crowded around a small camera outside her office. She paused for a moment to mentally assess the situation, but the men gave her little time to process. "You'll see us now or we will set every speck of red dust in this mine on fire."

Shyne quickly swiped her hand over the console again to trigger the alert, but there was no response.

The voices turned sarcastic as they continued to eclipse the camera's field of view. "There's no point in keeping us out here waiting. No one is coming. Now please, won't you be so kind as to allow us a moment of your time?"

Shyne was used to dealing with troublesome clients, but she was at a loss without backup. She quickly fell into her professional demeanor out of habit and squeezed a small bauble in a specific sequence that she kept in one of her many pockets. Then she stood, adjusted her attire, and pressed the door release. Her initial reaction was one of relief as the loud-mouthed man that first entered her office was actually not much larger than a child. Her ease, however, quickly gave way as five much taller ones followed in behind him.

They tried to look the part. All of them were armed with mining gear of different types, with the exception of the tallest one who carried a large maul on his back and a carbine on his hip. Custom gear. Probably a mix of miners and mercs, she thought. She'd seen this kind of display before. It was a kind of show-of-force, and it only served to steel her resentment at the intrusion.

"Gentlemens. How can I help you today?"

The short, loud one mirrored her with false airs. "We're here to see the proprietor, young lady. We have a business matter we need to address. So perhaps you could point us in his direction. You are his secretary, correct?"

Shyne clasped her hands together and squeezed until the knuckles audibly cracked. "I am de on-site manager here. I can answer any questions you may have, thank you. But if you would get to de questions quickly, it would be helpful as we have a very busy schedule today."

The loud one's mouth fell into an open-mouthed smile as he continued to taunt her. He pointed at her and looked back at the men incredulously. "You're the on-site manager?" It was pure theater, but Shyne held her ground waiting for some kind of brief explanation for the intrusion.

"Well then, Madam Manager, it appears we have a problem that only you can help us with. You see, I represent a Mr. Attrus Henche, a mining proprietor here on Urm, uh, much like yourself only..." He paused to gesture to her figure. "...not like you at all. He's become concerned that maybe there is a problem with your mine. It seems that a large quantity of buy-sell trades occurred recently that he

252

didn't authorize, and we have reason to believe you may know something about it."

"I have enough to do managing my own mine. Why would we bother trying to manage yours? Perhaps you need a better manager. I could maybe look at your paperworks and help them figure it out, but I do charge de fees. Are you hiring?"

Shyne continued to turn the screws back on him. "If you have some kinds of evidences that someone from de mines *here* was involved in accessing your systems, we take such things very seriously. Why don't we just take de matter to de authorities to sort out, yes? I'm knowing they will have de answers for us."

The loud one finally dropped the charade. "Fine. You like games. Here's one. It's a mystery game. Except, that all the competing mines in this sector all pointed to you as the likely culprit.

They say you steal power for your lights. If someone steals power, they likely steal other things as well. See, this thief didn't just steal cyptum out of the ground like a common thief, no. This thief stole mining futures.

This person knows that cyptum has to be slowly harvested to avoid explosions. Only a mining op could take advantage of that long term. So, either you, or someone on your team was a party to this. So, let's just stop all this before one of my friends here feels cheated and wants to flip the table over, so-to-speak."

Shyne simply stood there stoically for a moment.

"Don't hurry on our account, but if you are waiting for the constables to suddenly come barging in, I'm afraid you're in for some disappointment. You see, we called them already and explained that you were going to be running security drills here. So, sadly they already know that any emergency calls coming in are for...training purposes."

"That means no one will be coming to *your* aid either." Xard's voice emerged from the darkened corridor behind Shyne as she let out a gasp of relief. She turned to see her brother and Xard standing with his mining grappler drawn on the loud-mouth. "Tell Mr. Henche he should've stuck to selling noodles."

One of the men instinctively lunged for Shyne and grabbed her by the arm in an effort to use her as a shield. Xard's reflexes took over instantly. He aimed at the man's outstretched arm and fired.

click

A silent flash of twisted light emerged from the end of Xard's modified grappler and struck the man in the shoulder. A fine spray of carbon, oxygen, and hydrogen appeared where a shoulder had once been as the rest of the man's arm fell to the ground.

Ygger used the moment to grab Shyne and hold her against the back wall while he triggered a backup security measure. "Xard! Back wall!" Xard threw himself back against the office wall as Ygger tripped the directional UV lights, temporarily blinding the men and simultaneously releasing a red aerosol of powdery cyptum into the room. Ygger dragged Shyne and Xard into the corridor and killed the lights behind them. A bright white ignition lit the room behind them as the men were flash-burned by the destabilized red dust.

"Come on. That dose wasn't strong enough to kill them, just slow them down. We need to get you out of here."

"You got my message!" Shyne struggled to breathe as she shuffled down the corridor with them.

"You know it! Told you that old bauble would come in handy. Head for the rubble cat. We've got a better chance of ditching them if we go surface-side. I'll grab Kharik."

23 – CHASE

Shyne's chest was already heaving when Ygger and Xard caught up with her at the cavernous launch bay. She wheezed plaintively, "Help me with de hoses."

Ygger rushed to the side of the open-air rubble cat and dropped Kharik—who had been rousted from sleep—off of his shoulder and into the back seat with an unceremonious *thud*. It was the shiniest thing Xard had seen on the dusty planet. It had a smooth, silvery bottom and hovered about waist high. Posh seats, rich interiors, Shyne certainly moved in style. Then, all at once the illusion of finery was gone as Ygger hard-pulled a lever to extend a tangled mass of dusty hoses from the back—the glamour of what-could-have-been suddenly doused by the realities of safety on Urm.

"One more pulls oncha or we won't be able to keep enough dusts away!"

"I know how it works, Shyne. Just get in. In fact, you drive!" Ygger pulled with one more determined tug, extending the dangling cords of black tubing from the rear of the rubble cat even further.

Voices began to emerge from the corridor behind them—angry voices. Ygger ran back to the dock's entrance and pushed a large pallet of barrels in front of the entrance and deactivated its lev-sled leaving it firmly in place. He ran full speed back toward the rubble cat, eyes wide as if he knew what was coming up behind him. He dove into the back seat on top of Kharik and simply yelled, "Go!"

255

Shyne hit the accelerator, and the cat lurched off of its dock and out towards the tunnels to the surface. Behind them on the dock they watched as barrels flew from the opening. The bald man with the sturdy maul had knocked them off of the palette with one clean stroke.

Xard turned to Shyne. "We're gonna need a lot more of that 'go' I think."

Shyne sped through the widening mine corridors in a race to the surface, dodging slow-moving mining haulers dragging rocks toward the sluices. Despite her size, she was quick on the stick, deftly moving between jutting rocks and slower-moving vehicles in the channel. Ygger continued watching over the back, constantly assessing whether or not their escape had been successful. "Shyne! Take the firewinds egress! We can double-back once we're on the surface."

Shyne nodded and pulled the rubble cat around a sharp turn into a corridor leading topside. Xard's face erupted in a wide, toothy grin as the two merc vehicles flew past in the wrong direction. "We ditched 'em!" Xard grabbed Ygger around the neck and giggled with relief. "Yes! Smart plan. Very smart. Now let's get out of here!"

Kharik suddenly screamed, eyes-wide as he looked at Xard. It scared him to see the full green brightness of his eyes, but it was a look he had seen before and it needed no explanation. Xard instinctively looked around them for what he knew must be there, and there it was. The dark miasma of pure chaos Xard had unleashed in the mine now tumbled from an adjacent tunnel and began to follow them at great speed. Kharik screamed "Skeen!"

Ygger's face turned pale as he caught his first glimpse of it. It was an oily, elongated shadow that seemed to coil and uncoil with every movement, stretching out in all directions as it gave chase where the mercs had left off. Xard climbed over Kharik and leaned against the back seat with his selasin pistol.

click

A ball of distorted light appeared a short distance behind them, but the skeen moved just out of range. "Come on you bahki thing... come a little closer." Xard tried to get a steadier aim on it, but Shyne's maneuvering continued to throw his shots.

It finally moved within range as it sped up effortlessly—raging as it charged them. Xard was certain he could feel its intent as it drew closer. Its very presence spoke great hatred into the air around it.

Shyne never turned to look. The palpable sense of anger in the atmosphere around them told her all she needed to know. She boosted the reserve power. "Almost to top now!" Xard took aim one more time.

click

The ball of distorted light formed right at its core, but the skeen simply reacted by forming into a torus around the distortion before reforming again into a long, dark tail. It was gaining now, and Xard was starting to panic when suddenly they became enveloped in a brilliant light. Shyne's rubble cat finally exploded out of the mining tunnel and back over the sun-drenched surface of Urm. The skeen was nowhere to be seen. "Where did it go?" Ygger asked. "Maybe it hates light."

Kharik finally began to recover from his half-awakened, paralytic shock and slowly began to sit upright. "I don't feel it. I think it's gone."

"I'm with you on this one, captain. I don't feel it either. Still, I don't want to hang around to find out. Where can we go now? Is there anywhere on this bahki planet that won't try to kill us?"

Shyne pulled the rubble cat into a low hover over the brilliant red and black surface. "These are de fire winds. De dust blows from here to de dark side and burns. Very small dusts. Burning as they lose de light. We don't want to do crossings there. We needs to go back to de light plains."

Spectacular chasms of cyptum ore now appeared in great fissures along the planet's surface just below them. As the crimson dust from the windy surface began to rise up to meet them, the dangling hoses began to vibrate underneath them. "We needs to go see papa now, oncha. De dust filters won't last out here. Besides, he needs to know what happened."

"You should have left me in the tunnel with that, that thing, whatever it was. I'd be better off," he groused. Ygger cut his protest short as he looked back toward one of the planet's open wounds that lead to the mines below. "Uhm, sis. We might need to rethink that strategy. I think our merc friends are back."

"Wait, are you sure?" Xard squinted in the bright light but couldn't make out any more than a speck behind them.

"Yep. I'm sure. Mining carts go painfully slow here, for obvious reasons. These two are gaining on us. Time to put that quantum weapon you have back into service. Oh, and remind me to have a talk with you about wielding X-Class weaponry in a damned cyptum mine if we manage to survive this thing."

Xard smirked at him with a devious grin as he pulled the modified grappler out of its holster again. Ygger just shook his head and laughed at his expression. "You are full of surprises clean-shirt. I think I'm just gonna duck." Ygger began to slide down into the back seat with Kharik. "Shyne, hand me the hose filter controls. Maybe we can keep them at a distance if we can kick up some dust."

The two mining carts were closing now at a pace that indicated some extensive modifications. They had come prepared. They counted four people. Two in each cart. "I'm not that good at math but I think that means we lost at least one" Xard blurted out. "Too bad we didn't lose the big one with the mining sledge."

Ygger looked back at Xard. His signature suave style suddenly re-appeared on his face. "I got this. Just tell me when you can see all of their eyes."

Xard peeked over the back side as they raced across the surface. "Now!"

Ygger mashed the hose controller and a deep vibrating *flarp* emerged from under them as a cloud of red dust was ejected off of the hoses and toward one of the mining carts. As soon as the dust hit the drivers' eyes, he reflexively blinked, inadvertently blocking the light from the dust that had just accumulated on them. His eyes immediately burst into flames. The subsequent screaming only compounded the problem by forcing more of the crimson dust into his lungs. As soon as the cyptum passed down into his darkened windpipe, it too ignited. The burning man's flame was so intense that it became too hot for the passenger to grasp the controls, and the cart careened into the ground.

Ygger looked at Xard. "I'm guessing that worked?"

Xard shot a wide-eyed look back at the slouched Ygger.

"Heh. Now we know they aren't from Urm. Urmians wouldn't have fallen for that. Two left?" Ygger looked to Xard for updates.

"Yep. I got this one." He quickly threw his arms over the back end and took aim before ducking back down again.

click

Xard's shot nicked the stabilizer on one side of the mining cart sending it into a lurch as it attempted to regain control. Xard peeked back at the cart to see the giant man removing his mask and his shirt slowly without taking his eyes off of Xard. He could see more clearly

259

now that he was a mountain of a man; covered in intricate tattoos from his beard down. The bald man looked toward Xard and pointed at him now.

It was a challenge. Even Xard's inexperienced mind understood that it had somehow become personal. He watched in a kind of mild terror as the man jumped recklessly onto the front of his cart as his cohort slunk down to drive.

"Did you get him?" Ygger asked, not wanting to look for himself.

"Uhm. I think he's got mods."

"Wait. What? How do you know that?"

Xard yelled back at him in frustration. "He's free-walking a 45-degree angle over a cyptum field with no protective gear, so I'm guessing he's had some work done!"

"Point made. We don't have enough hose build-up yet to fire another cloud. Can you hit him?"

"I just wanna make sure he doesn't hit me either."

Shyne yelled back to them. "We are almost at de automated defenses. Just hold de mens off a bit more!"

Xard braved another peek over the back end. The bald man had retrieved the carbine from his thigh and was bearing down on them with one-hand. Xard ducked back down behind the seat. "A little more 'go' Shyne. He's aiming at us!"

"Heads down boys! De defenses are coming online!"

As Shyne raced the rubble cat over the outer marker of their father's command center, defense towers began to activate behind them, and their pursuers peeled away. Both Shyne and the three boys began to whoop and yell out of the pounding adrenaline coursing through them. "We ditched 'em!" Xard exclaimed as he sank back into his seat smiling.

Ygger's excitement visibly waned off of his face as they approached the central tower. "Well, let's just hope the pain of parental disappointment doesn't throw too much water on our successes, eh Shyne?

24 – Deputized

"Sluice six is the one we're after. Attrus Henche. Proprietor of the newly formed Dark Cloud Mining." Drasha continued to study the holographic details on her bracer as they rode one of the local trams.

Shay spoke plainly, "This is definitely our guy. No one just starts a cyptum mine without inheriting it, and no one steals one without the whole planet knowing about it. Hmm. Here we are. Ass-end of City 87."

The two of them found the entrance to Dark Cloud Mining to be little more than a makeshift squatter's residence. Nothing in the way of equipment or mining of any kind graced the interior. It was dark and unsettling, but they used the darkness to their advantage as they moved through the interior.

Drasha was the first to speak again. "Are we sure this is the right place? Seems like a front? Not much in the way of resources out here."

"Or witnesses." The heavy clank of mining boots emerged from a darkened corner and stood under the room's solitary canister light. "You girls ought to be more careful roaming about this part of Urm."

Shay appeared behind the man in the darkness and flicked out the hooked wrist-blade from her right bracer and held it against his rib-cage. "No armor, that's brave. But I had you pegged the moment we walked in. My partner over there played the perfect little mouse to draw you out, didn't she? I can assure you that mouse bites even harder than I do."

The man laughed as he felt the blade's sharp edge scratch slowly over each rib. "Well met. You must be Shayameen. And I'm guessing that since your blade's not at my neck, you know who I am."

Shay released her blade and stepped back. "Only by the smell. What are they pumping you Sentia boys with these days? Your skin reeks of it."

"Grade-C dermal gel." The man continued to laugh under his breath in the dark.

"You should know that even 'sterile' has a smell in places like Urm." Shay walked around toward the front of him to stand alongside Drasha, lowering their threat posture. "So, Sentia's follow-up on the pod issue led here too. I guess that's reassuring."

"Lights." A series of lights now illuminated the space where the three of them stood. The bald and bearded man stood there wearing only a pair of black combat pants and heavy, metal mining boots. He casually reached into one of his cargo pockets and retrieved a long cigar which he lit and drew a long drag off of before speaking.

"Name's Fasaan, but they probably put that in my file. Nice of you girls to show up now that the work is done." The tattoos that covered his skin slowly faded from view as he stood there.

"Sorry about the smell. I've been running these damned cult tattoos on my skin for a good week. In any case, I don't need them now." Fasaan reached down behind one of the counters and dragged out what was left of the former noodle man, Attrus Henche, for them to view.

Shay dropped her normal poise and let out a sarcastic laugh. "Where's his face?"

"Oh, yeah. Sorry about that. The maul swings a bit easier here on Urm. I'm still getting used to it. Anyway, I tracked this character trying to get a hold of a big wad of cyptum. Probably just another

264

wanna-be death cultist." Fasaan gave the corpse a swift kick. "This one didn't even have any family. Makes it pretty easy to figure out which one has the 'explosive' personality when there's only one person in your death cult."

Shay stood there taking it all in as Fasaan continued to regale them with his exploits. It frustrated her that he had killed their one lead, and now he was their only means of tracking down the aurum. A side comment about "damned rich kids" brought Fasaan back into focus.

"Wait. What was that last bit?" Shay inquired.

"Yeah. Apparently this Henche guy was planning on using the money from this mine to restart the pod-farm you two found on Kael. Then a bunch of rich kids in another mine siphoned off his stash." Fasaan laughed as he took another drag off his stogie.

"Damned cultists can't be that smart if they got bested by a bunch of runts. He had us go out and try and put some muscle on them, but they ended up wasting pretty much everyone that went out there. 'Cept for me of course. Made a damned mess of the mine though. Look for yourself."

Fasaan pulled the holo from his waist-band. "I doubled back to their mine after they gave us the slip up top. I jacked this from their office console on my way back. Helps me remember faces."

Shay snatched the holo from his hand and triggered it. The blue-green light of the projection filled the space in front of them as Drasha moved in for a closer look.

"Pfft. Don't thank me all at once." Fasaan slung his heavy maul back over his back and clipped the carbine to his thigh. "My work is done here so you girls have fun. My contact info is in there in case either of you want to get a closer look at my dermal upgrades later."

Then he paused and turned back around to look at them before leaving. "Oh, and make sure you don't lose your head like some of these other guys. It was the damnedest thing. Apparently, someone showed up with a quantum weapon. I wonder where something like that could have come from?" Fasaan shot them both a knowing glance and then turned toward the exit.

Drasha bristled and whispered to Shay as he walked out. "Should I kill him?"

Shay immediately turned back to study the holo recording more deliberately now as she spoke. "No. Not just yet. He's an idiot, but a useful one at the moment. When he's outlived that role, be sure to ask me that question again."

Drasha was dismissive of his taunt. "Poor sod's probably never even seen a quantum discharge. I swear, these idiot mercs get a taste of life outside the plains and they think *everything* is exotic."

Shay laughed as she pored over the holo feed. "You're right. Probably a cyptum flash. Not even the omyym would be stupid enough to use a quantum weapon so recklessly here. Besides, it would attract too much attention.

They're all strictly accounted for, even the unregistered ones. I damn near buried mine. Haven't carried in years. Even Xard doesn't know I was issued one, unless..." Shay's eyes suddenly snapped up to meet Drasha's in a flash of horror. "...unless someone told him." An immediate uneasiness welled up inside Shay at the thought of having been played so flawlessly again by one of her competing sisters. She pounded her fists against the small table that held the slowly advancing holo. "That bahki skika!"

Drasha attempted to keep Shay focused as her expression shifted from panic to rage and back again. "Shay, even if that's the play, it doesn't matter right now. Whatever this weapon turns out to be, we'll find it. No one in the Order is even looking for missing weaponry right now—they're looking for the aurum.

That buys us time. But, for the record, I don't like the idea that some Sentia merc might have info about a quantum weapon that could be traced back to us. It's damning information if the wrong person gets it, even *if* we get the weapon back."

Shay began to regain her composure as she thought it through more deliberately. "No. If it's true, he won't talk. He's just toying with us. Sentia might call him an agent, but he's still just a merc. He'll try to get his hands on the weapon for himself first.

If that fails, *then* he'll want to sell the news of its existence to someone else. He's more likely to hold that info close to his chest for now. Besides, if he's after it, he's certainly not going to tell Sentia about it. That makes him our asset for now. We just need to let him sniff it out, and when he does..."

Drasha smiled cautiously, "...we'll retrieve it."

Shay and Drasha finally reached the recording of the encounter from Shyne's office and played it back slowly. Shay paused the recording as Xard and Ygger entered the room. "Well, I'll be." Shay zoomed the visual render in closer to take a look at Xard's face. "Still alive."

Drasha laughed somewhat in relief, "I don't know, Shay; he looks more than just 'alive.' I expected him to be soiling himself in some back alley, not taking on a room full of goons. Isn't he the runt of his cohort?"

"Mmm." Shay nodded in agreement as she studied his face closely. Drasha was right on this one. He looked confident, and that in and of itself was telling. She was almost impressed, but she tried not to show it in her expression.

"I'd say it meant he was desperate, but the look on his face says 'retribution' more than anything else. He has his 'blame' face on. Trust me, I've seen that one more than once. He looks smugly self-righteous, almost indignant at these intruders."

267

"So, you think this new mining outfit is the one that stole the aurum?"

Shay sighed. "Whether they did or not, his expression tells me he *thinks* they did. Only one way to find out. Now that we know the players, we should be able to backtrack its final sale from the library and recover it."

Drasha probed further. "What is that thing he's holding?"

Shay examined the holo more closely. "I'm not sure. It looks like a mining laser of some kind, but that emission... that's definitely quantum."

An unexpected look of relief washed over Shay's face. "This is good. If it *is* my selasin, he's disguised it somehow. Maybe he's pulled the core from an old one and rigged it to fire from that clumsy pistol. It's crude, but efficient, so long as it doesn't explode back on him. Either way, it doesn't *look* like an official selasin, so our exposure to sanction is still limited for now."

Drasha turned to her with an astonished face. "Then this could be a complete success! If he *does* have a selasin and he's managed to keep it, we can retrieve the aurum and make this whole thing vanish. The death cult gets the blame for the illicit birthing farm, and you get the credit for the bust. It's almost too perfect."

"You're right. But we need to hurry. By the looks of it, he seems hellbent on turning all of Urm into molecular vapor with whatever that monstrosity is he's loaded the core into. Its presence won't stay a secret for long if he keeps firing it."

"Too bad that Sentia thug is still alive to talk about it. Without him in the picture we might've been able to keep its disappearance a secret indefinitely."

Shay's eyes squinted as an idea washed over her. "Exactly. We need his silence. Killing him will only make Sentia look deeper into it. So, we'll buy his silence."

"With what resources? Any finances we procure will trigger an audit that the blue-hair will use against you."

Shay ignored Drasha's protests and triggered a call to Fasaan.

His face and voice crackled over the poor reception. "You know, I'm used to ladies being desperate, but I at least expected to get back to my room before the two of you were calling to go for a ride."

Shay smirked. She usually loved the sexual banter that came just before she emasculated someone with her words, but this time she had other plans in mind. "I have a different kind of proposition for you. Since your work for Sentia has now dried up, I thought you might be interested in another assignment. I have a loose end that needs tightening."

Fasaan let out a broad smile on the other end of the screen. "And what's in it for me?"

"By virtue of my rank and position as a Vesni-sentinel, I have the authority to deputize you as a veneras in the Order. The title is non-transferable, but it's also permanent unless I decide to revoke it for failure to perform. There's no monetary attachment to the job, but the title will almost certainly open doors for future contracts with the Vesni should you find yourself in need of additional employment.

It also authorizes the use of force or restraint against any voithos without legal repercussion. However, it binds you to confidentiality. Since you're from Kael, I can't imagine you wouldn't see the inherent value in this."

Fasaan stroked his beard as she spoke. It was obvious that the bait was working. "Permanent restraint rights against any Vesni?"

"No. The voithos and vikos only. Women can only be apprehended or restrained by other women, though I doubt you could restrain a fully-trained Vesni in any case. So, are you interested in the job or not?"

"Yeah, okay, fine. But don't go thinking I'll be playing the sub later just because you two are paying the tab. Who or what is the target?"

"The young man with the dark hair and the flashy pistol. I need him restrained and returned to me. He's no good to me dead unless I kill him myself. You know the one I am referring to?"

Fasaan smiled again. "Oh yeah. I know the one. Lucky for you I fired a tracker on that mining shuttle they scampered off in. I can track him, but I can't get to him yet. Once he's on the move, it shouldn't take more than half a day to snag him, even *with* that flashy pistol. Which reminds me... the pistol. Since it's clearly *not* a Vesni weapon, I'm sure neither of you will mind if I keep the pistol as a small souvenir, right? Or, am I mistaken about its origin?"

"The boy is our priority; the weapon is nothing. If you manage to retrieve it and hang on to it, consider it part of the spoils. Contact me when it's finished." Shay dropped the connection and turned to look at a stunned Drasha.

"Brilliant maneuvering, but the selasin? It defeats the whole purpose of having everything working in our favor if a quantum weapon is lost."

Shay smiled back at her as she pulled on a pair of gloves from her thigh pocket. "Men with sticky fingers have a habit of losing them. Do you really believe he'll be able to keep it once he's gained it? Not to worry Drash, success is right around the corner."

Shyne pulled the rubble cat into a tight ascending turn and made several passes around the central tower before coming in for a landing on one of the elevated landing platforms. At this height, the brightness of Ayu's sunlight had partially blanched the dark central structure, giving it a somewhat softer appearance than its foundations below. Ygger, however, maintained a guarded rigidity as they touched down.

"They are not mades for de rubble cats but Mama Shyne makes it work." It was clear from her forced smile at Kharik that she was only speaking for her own reassurance. The platform itself seemed empty and no one had come to greet them upon landing. It seemed an ominous sign.

Ygger shook out his jacket and twirled it back on over his shoulders. "I have to applaud you, sis. You managed to land without us being shot at. He's not going to be happy you brought me here. You realize that, right?"

Shyne simply waved her hand at him as they crossed the narrow, grated walkway toward the central tower. Kharik made the mistake of looking down momentarily before grabbing Shyne's hand and caging his eyes onto the more solid landing just ahead. A small seating area was just outside the main entrance and Xard collapsed into it.

Ygger plopped down next to him and signaled to Shyne. "You got this, sis. I'll wait here until you call me. We both know you'll have better success if I'm out of view."

271

Ygger nudged Xard and pulled a slender, black object from his coat pocket. He whispered as the others went inside ahead of him. "I didn't get a chance to pass this to you at the mine, but I gotta say, you more than earned this, clean-shirt." He slipped the smooth black cylinder into Xard's hand.

"It's pressure activated too. So, no voice commands needed. You just squeeze and drop it. It will record in three dimensions for three full planetary hours. If you don't get what you need, you'll have to come back and reset it, but I think we both know you won't have any trouble finding something incriminating in that time."

The adrenaline of the chase and the shock of having just killed someone had made him almost completely forget about the immersion drive. "Oh. Thanks," was all Xard could muster at the moment.

"You know, besides making us all rich, you kicked some serious bunta back there. If we hadn't ditched those mercs, we wouldn't even be talking now, not that the old man will care." Ygger nodded toward the door. "Her father's a spiteful bahk, but at least I don't have to worry about getting tossed out of the mine anymore. I have options again, thanks to you."

He turned his attention back to the somber Xard. "Listen, I don't know what your mission is supposed to be exactly, but I'm betting you're gonna feel some serious heat if you actually decide to use that drive. I just want you to know, if you find yourself in over your head, you can always come find me, clean-shirt. You've earned that much." Then he mussed up Xard's hair to try and cheer him up.

Moments later Shyne emerged from inside. Her cold, pale face was now even more washed out in the bright surface light. Ygger stood up and sighed before Xard had a chance to thank him. "Okay, clean-shirt. Back in a flash!" Shyne held the door for her brother as they both disappeared into the central tower.

Xard sat alone now with his thoughts as he waited for them to resolve their familial issues. He looked down at the slender black drive in his hand; fidgeting with it like a mnemonic device for a few moments as he collected his thoughts. He had everything he needed now to bring down the Vesni charade. All that remained was to execute the recording back in the academy.

He tucked the immersion drive into a small cargo pocket in his pants and double-checked the fastener's security before fishing out one of his new credit chits. He struggled for a moment as he worked out how to activate his new currency. A small holo emerged from it with different data sets. The only one Xard cared about was the total. It was a phenomenal sum and perfectly untraceable now. He mused for a moment about how it might have helped him become a better voithos candidate, but any chance he had with them was about to end once he revealed them for who they were.

A sudden wave of isolation gripped him as he realized he was truly on his own now. He stood and began to pace in front of the reflective door to the central building. Ygger, Shyne, Kharik, the other FLIPP kids—they were all temporary figures. He had used them well.

It's what he had been trained to do. He caught his reflection in the door and paused to think about how much he had changed in scarcely a week. And yet, this time he felt no need to pose; no need to play the hero. He was about to win his gambit, but the cost to his countenance was already noticeable.

The image of the man he'd just killed continued to force its way into his mind. He placed his hand on his makeshift selasin pistol there at his thigh, but it gave him no sense of security. He still felt alone, naked, and powerless. He was a killer now; the guilt and fear of that first kill now intruded powerfully into his mind.

He was still fairly certain no one would come for him, but his positive self-talk did nothing to assuage the pit in his stomach. He had scarcely finished the turn in his anxious pacing again before he was interrupted by Ygger bursting out of the reflective doors next to him. "Time's up, clean-shirt! We're out of here."

Shyne and Kharik were close behind him as they headed back out over the walkway toward the landing platform. "Wait! What happened?" Xard chased after them with questions no one seemed in a hurry to answer.

Ygger continued to walk directly toward the hovering rubble cat and hopped in the passenger seat. "I swear, Shyne, if he says one more thing about my face, I'll cut it off and hand it to him! I've got enough creds now to buy a new one from Sentia."

"Oncha." Shyne's voice was subdued. She slowly heaved herself into the driver's seat and powered up the rubble cat. "It doesn't matters now. I will use de funds to automate the mine and hire other workers. There is no need for either of us to come here anymore. We both needs time away, I think. I will just spend time with the FLIPP childrens and enjoy next few years until it pass. You should do de same. Take times."

Xard climbed in the back with Kharik behind Ygger and leaned into his ear. "That bad, huh?"

"Yep. Ask me about it some other time. At least the bastard smoothed out the legal wrinkles, so the mining purchases we leveraged are all locked in to the shell company. In any case, we won't have any more problems from the other miners, so it's safe for us to go back now. Apparently, someone else nicked the new mining op's boss too."

"Wait, the noodle man is dead?" Xard slumped back in his seat with a half-satisfied smile. He was exhilarated by the elimination of another threat, but troubled by another death being added to his tally.

Ygger turned around to look at him as Shyne pulled the rubble cat off the elevated platform and dove down toward the planet surface. "He's gone, clean-shirt. Someone smashed his face in. Probably a rival mining outfit. New startups only thin the profits for everyone else, so it doesn't surprise me really."

Xard simply looked out over the landscape as they began to speed along the surface. "So, what now?"

"Well, we're headed back to the mine to get the automation ordered and probably spend some time planning our next move. It'd be great if you wanted to stick around here for a while, but I'm guessing you have your mission or whatever to get on with. Did you want us to drop you by the academy access point on our way back?"

Xard simply nodded at him, and he turned back to Shyne. "Take us back to the old Vesni moat, Shyne. We need to make a delivery. Hopefully someone else gets what's coming to them today."

***

The sudden wave of blackness was jarring as the rubble cat veered back into the mining caverns from the bright surface light. By the time Xard's eyes had grown accustomed to it again, Shyne had already pulled the hovering vehicle into one of the elevated docks nearest to the academy. Ygger turned around to look at Xard one last time. "This is it. You know the way from here, right? Come find us when you're done. We'll celebrate or something."

As Xard hopped out of the back seat, Kharik attempted to follow him. "I've got it from here, captain. Besides, you're gonna be safer with Shyne and the FLIPP matron than you would be going back into the academy. Your job is to scout, remember?"

"Oh, that reminds me!" Kharik began to bounce on his toes again. "Before Ygger grabbed me and started running out of the mines, I saw two women in black flight suits on your academy cameras. They looked like police walking around. I thought you should know."

Xard's face turned grim. "Wait, sentinels? Are you *sure* they were wearing black?"

Kharik simply pulled up his goggles and pointed to his brilliant green eyes. "I can see black in the dark, general."

Xard's heart sank as he tried to force an approving smile. "Good scouting again, captain." Xard patted him on the back as he looked out over the city just below. "They don't usually come here for anything once they have their rank."

Xard turned and continued mumbling to himself. "It doesn't make sense unless they're onto me, which means I'm running out of time." Xard stopped again and turned back to the three of them. "If they sent Vesni-sentinels here, it's definitely better if you all go back to the mine and forget about having seen me. You don't want them connecting me with anything you have down there in the mine. It will just be more trouble for you."

"If we don't hears back from you by de time de recording times out, do you want us to come lookings for you?"

"If I'm not back by then, there's probably not going to be anything to find."

Ygger and Shyne both looked anxious about leaving him alone after all he'd done for them, but they honored his request to finish it alone. Ygger reached out one last time to muss up Xard's hair before hoisting Kharik back into the seat. "You're welcome back at the mine when you finish, but if you really think you'd put us in danger, we can always meet up again at the club. Just... take care of yourself, clean-shirt."

Xard nodded nervously as the rubble cat pulled away. Kharik's forlorn face hung over the back seat watching him as they departed, but Xard steeled himself as best as he could. *Okay,* he thought to himself. *Time to do this.*

26 – Flow

As the small lift brought Xard back down to the streets below, the darkness seemed to swallow him whole. This part of City 87 was nearly uninhabited, but the added solitude of being alone almost seemed like an invitation for shadows to feast on him. He didn't enjoy clinging to the unlit alleyways as he made his way forward, but he didn't need any sentinels finding him now—he was too close.

He slunk down the darkened streets towards the hatch that led to the moat below, but quickly found himself lost in the darkness. He doubled back. Depression began to weigh heavily on him. Until now, there was no indication he hadn't had a clean getaway. Now he knew someone was onto him, and he couldn't find the access point for the moat.

No time to go back. Too risky to light a mag-torch. He was starting to regret leaving Kharik behind—or at least his eyesight. He passed the hatch a third time, unable to find it again in the dark, before realizing there was another option—the grate. He'd have to jump, but at least he knew where to find it.

He moved silently through the dark now, trying to steel himself with his thoughts. *I'm a killer now*, he told himself. He tried it on like a mantle to cover the deep shame he felt, mumbling affirmations about how he was going to kill the Order in the same way. Yet, with every step, the self-lauding only felt hollower.

He had come here to prove he could make it on his own and tear down the Vesni's empire of lies. Yet, for all his successes, he could no longer feel the joy in it. He was on the cusp of achieving everything he had set out to do, but the damage to his soul in making it happen had become an unforeseen side effect.

He suddenly longed for his simpler childhood—a time when a parent's embrace held everything in place. Now everything and everyone were slowly drifting away from him. But his father's departure had been abrupt and without closure, not some gentle farewell. "What goes away always comes back around..." *But you didn't just go away. You vanished without a trace.*

He hated his father for leaving him. Yet on some level, he needed him now more than ever—even if it was only to be held once more before he stepped out on his own as a man. He cursed his name under his breath as he walked, angry that he felt the weight of what seemed like empty promises. "You went away and left me—but you never came back around. Worse, you left me with *her*. Well...I'm about to prove I don't need you—don't need *either* of you."

A dark sense of foreboding suddenly washed over him. He recognized the feeling. The skeen was nearby. In his hurry to get on with his mission, he had nearly forgotten about it, but he could feel it now. Out amidst the shifting darkness, its vague shape could be discerned, coalescing and dissipating in a manner that suggested the creature was constantly changing form. Its movements were fluid and serpentine, as if it were simultaneously everywhere and nowhere at once.

Xard began to shake uncontrollably. He stopped for a moment to collect himself and sat against one of the darkened walls under a solitary street light. He cried and shook as the overwhelming sense of loss poured over him. For a moment, he secretly longed for the skeen to just come and take him and end the sudden onset of emotional pain, but his stubbornness would not allow it.

It was so close now, clawing at the back of his mind, following him just out of sight. It seemed to chide his thoughts about needing his 'daddy.' He was tired of being afraid, of being weak. The skeen had overplayed its hand now, and it only made him angrier. He stared straight back into the darkness and scowled at it before hoisting himself back up and marching toward the grate. Fear and anger fueled him now. If he was going to die, he was going to take the Vesni with him.

In his fervor, he almost missed it. It was a simple coolant vent in the ground, glowing faintly from the enriched fluid far below. He had seen it from below when they had rafted through the cavern, so he knew it was a long drop from street-level. No one even noticed when he released the grate and it splashed into the coolant below.

Xard still shook as he stood there. He wanted to die and just start over again. He didn't like who he had made himself into, but neither did he like who he was before. His thoughts of his father suddenly clawed and dug into the deepest recesses of his mind again. The tumorous pain of his loss now suddenly metastasized, leaving pain in every muscle as he started to shake again.

"I don't even know who I am anymore!" he yelled at the open grate below. His emotions began to overwhelm his ability to control them. Fear now mingled with the pain of his parents' rejection until he finally became numb. All that remained was to fall back onto his training and keep moving forward.

Being resolved to finish it or die trying, he jumped through the open grate, flailing in the air as he fell. He didn't know the exact distance, but it was long enough for him to shout fully half the curse words he knew before hitting the coolant below with a loud splash. Muscles seizing. Arteries closing. He forced himself to the surface of the freezing liquid.

The glowing blue current was faster than he remembered. At this rate, the opening would appear quickly. He hurried to reach for his grappler. Stuck. He tugged harder. Still nothing. The opening was just ahead, but the wet leather holster continued to stymie his efforts.

281

He was drifting dangerously wide now. When the opening was finally in view, it was too far and too fast to swim. He was going to miss his chance. His eyes widened when he noticed the current dragging him into a return grating just ahead. When it was clear that he was going to be pinned against it, he braced. The vest hardened instantly as he struck it, protecting his vital organs from the impact.

The current was stronger than he ever imagined it would be, but the sudden reality of imminent drowning shocked him out of his panic. He was past his opening, but not so far that he couldn't get back if he could get a secure shot. The current, however, was relentless. It held his arms and legs fast against the grate.

His head was above water for now, but he knew he needed to free himself quickly before the current swelled. "Okay," he gasped, "at least I'm not drifting. I can make it. I can make it."

Is this the embrace you longed for? A thick sludge of words mired his thinking, but he knew they were not his own. They taunted him as he wrestled in vain to free himself. He began to cry again in self-hate as he struggled against the current's icy grasp. He was so close to finishing his mission, but so impossibly far from success. He hated his weakness, but his angst and rage were powerless against the flow.

He looked around for an exit, a latch, anything, but nothing was there. He was trapped and alone, and the coolant had now risen to just above his chin. He shouted profanity loudly into the chasm, but there was no one to hear. With his options slowly dwindling, he stopped trying to fight for a moment and instead reached for the immersion drive in his pocket. He triggered it, and it began recording all around him in high definition.

The sudden realization that he might still fulfill his mission without freeing himself calmed his nerves and pulled him out of his panic. He began to speak plainly into the air as the drive began recording. "Okay. This drive has a pretty large range, so hopefully whoever finds this will be able to learn the same truth I learned... that the Vesni religion is a hoax. I'd hoped to plant this a little closer, but as you can see, I'm a little preoccupied. In any case, I can still finish my mission even if I end up drowning here, which..." Coolant began to splash him in the face as it rose. "...is honestly not really optimal, but at least you'll all know the truth.

Mother, just so you know, I wasted a lot of creds to make this stupid recording, but I wanted you to be able to remember just how much I hate you before I die. With any luck, you won't find my body until it's badly decomposed. In any case, you'll get to watch my dying face in pretty good detail for a few hours. Maybe you can replay it at one of your Vesni get-togethers. That would be fun. You can all enjoy it over a glass of wine as you watch your whole damned religion burn to the ground."

He continued to hurl sarcastic venom at her as he began to explain all the lies that he'd uncovered in both the academy and the voithos-moro's secret stash. When it began to degrade into yelling about petty indignities and other lies she'd told him throughout the years, he finally stopped. Yet as the flow of coolant began to grip him tighter, a memory surfaced unbidden—one of his father gripping him tightly and kissing his head as his mother applied a salve to his scraped knee, her voice as gentle as the morning light through his bedroom window.

"And remember when," he started, his voice softening. "When I was seven and you put that goop on my knee? That stung! You never warned me about prickle bushes. How was I supposed to know I would get sick? You stayed up with me for three nights straight..." He trailed off, blinking rapidly as the coolant splashed his face. "No, that doesn't matter now. You probably only did it because it would make you look bad if I died."

But even as he spat the words, they tasted false on his tongue. He began to wrestle inside as well as out as both the coolant and his memory began to spar over which would drown him first. "Maybe you thought the lies would protect me," he said more quietly. "Maybe you really believed them yourself."

For a moment, grief overtook rage, a grief for the mother he thought he had, for the relationship that could have been. "If you loved me, I might have been..." His throat tightened. He swallowed hard against the sudden ache. "No. You chose your precious religion over me. Every. Single. Time. You'll probably throw this away before you even watch it when you figure out who recorded it. My father was the only one who showed any interest, and even *he* left me!"

A sudden realization swept over him even as the words flowed from his lips. "Unless you lied about that too. What really happened to him? Did you drive him away like you drove me away? Or did you kill him off yourself?"

Xard inadvertently aspirated a large gulp of coolant as the level continued to rise. The shock triggered his over-sized vest to momentarily harden again, causing him to suddenly sink down into it. The unexpected slouch inside his vest allowed his knees to slightly bend, giving him new leverage against the grate. With one solid push, he found himself above the waterline again. He coughed and sputtered as his small body tried to push the coolant out of his lungs as he inched his way slowly higher.

Once his arm broke the plane of the water, he reached for the grappler again and fired its lone shot into the wall near the opening. The retracting cable instantly jerked him out of the coolant, skipping his body over the surface as it pulled him back to the small shore near the makeshift academy entrance. He lay there for a moment to catch his breath, trying to take in what had just happened. It didn't make sense. He should be dead.

The vest his father had made for him had now saved him a second time. He shook his head, refusing the implication. "Just a coincidence," he muttered through chattering teeth. But as his fingers traced the contours of the oversized vest, understanding came reluctantly.

Timeon was wrong. It wasn't made for him to wear when he was older. It was too big on purpose. If it had been snug, he would have drowned. It was meant to save him *now*.

"He *knew*," Xard whispered, his voice small against the vastness of the chasm. "He *knew* I'd be here." The realization fractured something inside him. Someone had planned for his safety. Someone had cared enough to protect him even after they were gone.

If his father had planned for even this, what else might he be wrong about? For a terrifying moment, he allowed himself to consider that his mother's deceptions might not all have been malicious. What if some truths were too dangerous? What if some lies were meant to shield? What was she protecting him from?

The revelation caused Xard to scramble to his feet again. He didn't know if it was the coolant's evaporative effects on his skin or the fact that he had just unloaded years of pent-up rage into the drive, but he felt decidedly lighter now—cleaner, yet somehow less certain about his parental animus. He gripped the immersion drive tightly in his hand. "Still lots of time left," he whispered. His brief brush with death had left him feeling resolute and new, and it was time to find out who the 'new' Xard really was. "Let's finish this."

27 – Processional

The grand hall inside the academy's central structure was a cathedral-like thoroughfare that led from the exterior of the complex toward the ceremonial chamber at the center. Along its peak, a series of enormous, circular skylights piped in reflected light from the surface while ornate sconces and chandeliers lit the areas below. Mid-way up, Shay and Drasha walked along a wide mezzanine that ran along either side as they made their way back toward the scriptorium.

Drasha queried her mistress playfully as they walked. "Ever wonder why they put us through all that sensory deprivation in the dorms only to make it so homey in here?"

Shay cast a confused glance at her. "Homey?"

"Well, I mean it's not homey like Kael, but I've always wondered why they went through the trouble of having skylights when the whole goal of putting the training center on Urm was to get us out of our comfort zone. I mean, I realize they are just simulations, but you can tell they took great pains to make the light track along the ground as if we were still on Kael."

A small smile curled up in the corner of Shay's mouth as they walked, but she held her tongue.

Drasha persisted. "Think about it. Urm doesn't rotate, so having the light track along the ground must have been a deliberate choice. I think they wanted us to connect the ceremonial elements with Kael and Kael alone. What, you disagree?"

"Are you sure we went to the same training academy?" Shay teased. "The light is just another ruse they play here to build stress in the attendees. It's an illusion. The timing of the skylight here is actually much slower than on Kael. They do it to make the days seem longer than they actually are."

Drasha squinted at the revelation. "You're joking? Another stress technique? Really? How did I miss that?"

"It's subtle. It's only four hours longer than a normal day, so don't feel bad. You'd have had to be in here for an extended period to have even noticed." The words were barely off her lips when her expression suddenly changed.

"What is it?" Drasha instinctively began to scan the mezzanine around them.

"Something's off," Shay whispered as she moved to peer over the railing. "I can't explain it. The air's wrong. It suddenly breathes heavier."

"A new stress technique maybe? I don't sense it. Maybe there's a processional today. If it's Illumination Day, they may have prepared new incense."

"It would explain the empty corridors. Come on, the aurum search can wait. My gut says we're being watched. Keep scanning the alcoves while we walk. We need to find a crowd. If it *is* Illumination Day, the biggest crowd will be in the apse."

***

A new sense of purpose and confidence now pulsed through Xard. With the immersion drive now running, he didn't have time to wait for the perfect moment. He needed to move swiftly to capture the data. Following the same path they'd taken before, he moved deliberately toward the central promenade. As he snuck past the small storage room where they'd made their first discoveries, it occurred to him that the camera hack was probably still in place.

He smiled for a moment and waved into the air on the off-chance that Kharik and Ygger might actually still be watching. He was close to where the sentinels had been spotted, but he couldn't afford to be overly cautious. Time was running out. As he began slinking quietly toward his goal, the sound of chanting could be heard in the distance. A processional was starting.

Xard moved quickly down the corridors, counting on the fact that almost everyone would be at such a formal assembly. He approached the apse of the academy's ceremonial grounds from the side through a small antechamber. He was close enough now that he could hear the shuffle of feet in ceremonial gear just beyond. Xard held his breath for a moment and whispered to himself, "*close enough.*" He placed the immersion drive in a small niche behind a statuette of the Goddess with her arms upraised. Then he looked around for a place to hide until the recording was done.

***

Shay and Drasha filtered quietly through the sacristy and back into the mezzanine closer to the apse. The large semi-circular end cap of the grand hallway held a large statue of the Goddess in an inviting pose. Throngs of Vesni adherents in formal regalia processed in tight formation down the center. A look of surprise flashed across Drasha's face. "Goddess, I didn't realize the cohorts were so large now."

About a hundred new Vesni graduates in clean white gowns formed the front of the long processional. Behind them were the Vesni officers, dressed in golden microplate which shimmered in the torchlight from the end of their long staves. Then came the voithos trainees dressed in simple black pants with a matching black ephod. Finally, the voithos officers brought up the rear with their dark microplate and golden pikes.

It was a river of monochromatic flesh, and it moved and swayed in perfect formation. Dulcet tunes by voice and flute filled the air as the chasm between mezzanine levels swelled with glittering formality. "Keep your wits about you," Shay replied. "Something's still not right. It's like a worm in the back of my mind. Someone's here."

"You think it's the blue-hair? She couldn't have gotten here unnoticed. Maybe she sent someone else to do her dirty work." Drasha continued to offer up possibilities, but none of them seemed to align with Shay's intuition.

"No. It's something else." She tried to shake off the oppressive feeling. "Whatever it is, we should hold here. This is a good vantage point. If someone makes a move on us, they'll have no choice but to come to us if we stay put. Besides, everyone's focused on the illumination rites. Just keep scanning the crowd for anything out of place."

***

With the drive in place, Xard scrambled around the antechamber looking for a place to hide. It was a small room, but it happened to be stacked with boxes of sacramental food and drink. As he shoved the boxes to one side to create a hiding space, he noticed a large white chest that sat near the door. It didn't have a label of any kind, but he recognized the design—Sentia.

He walked over to the cool white chest and opened it. Inside, the small, refrigerated body of a young blonde girl, no older than about 10 years, lay wrapped in a package. It was the same setup. The reanimation tag and instructions were still in place. A determined smile crossed his lips as he realized he was really going to capture it all on the drive.

He began to talk quietly for posterity, knowing that the immersion drive had high enough fidelity to record everyone's conversations, including his own. "As you can see, Sentia is involved with the Vesni in making this little charade possible. This girl will be presented as 'dead' by those lying skikas out there in a few moments. Then they'll pull this tag behind her ear, and she'll wake up. Then all you idiot Vesni and voithos will be convinced of the Goddess' miraculous power."

Xard scoffed for a moment before looking more closely at the girl's face. She was pretty, and it infuriated Xard that because of her beauty she'd probably eventually be recruited into the same hell-cycle he'd been in. "They would have eaten you alive, the whole damned lot of them. But I promise you this, you'll never have to grow up in that world of lies. After today, the market for dead kids is over, just like the Order. Who knows? Maybe you can even have a normal life and live it with someone who actually loves you someday."

The sudden sound of slow, condescending claps startled him. "Touching." Fasaan stood there leaning against the wall behind him, clad in the black microplate of the voithos officers. "Is that what this was all about? You're pissed 'cuz these Vesni skikas are stealing all the tender cuts of flesh? Ha! Sorry to have to tell you this but, if you want to get your rocks off on that one, you'll have to reheat it first."

Xard scowled at the imposter. "I almost didn't recognize you without your hammer. What happened? Did you drop it when I almost ghosted your face back on the surface?" Xard snapped the modified selasin from its holster and aimed it squarely at Fasaan's chest, but he remained un-fazed.

Fasaan simply twirled the long, golden pike in one hand as he spoke. "Cute. I'm betting that mouth is what got you into this mess in the first place. Explains why those Vesni tramps paid me so much to come find you." He paused to study the black plate on his arm as he spoke. "No, I just thought swinging a hammer through a stained-glass church was kind of problematic when you want to fit in. Besides, this gear is actually a lot more comfortable than it looks."

Xard kept the weapon leveled on him as he stalled him for time. Neither of them belonged there, but if they were discovered, it would be Fasaan they focused on first. He was very clearly *not* a voithos under plain light. He just needed to keep him talking about himself. He'd seen his kind of predator before, all bravado. "It's microplate. It's lightweight and durable. Joints are stretchy, but it tends to tear if it's not properly sized. Probably explains why your bunta crack is showing."

Fasaan laughed out loud. "You really are a cheeky little bahk. If I wasn't being paid to turn you over to those two, I'd probably offer you a job on my rig."

Xard shot back. "What makes you think you wouldn't be working for me on *my* rig?"

Fasaan simply stared at the glint coming off of the slender gold pike as he spoke. "Well, for starters, I might take you up on that offer if you had the money and training to back it up, but since you have neither, I guess I just need to continue with my original plan."

"I have money," Xard protested. His eyes stayed fixed on Fasaan as he continued to creep slowly along the wall toward the curtain that emptied into the elevated chorister. "More than enough to buy your services."

"Well, then you only have half of what you'd need." Without another word, or even looking at Xard, he swept the boy's feet right out from under him with the long end of his pike, sending him straight onto his back.

click

A shot of light burst from the end of the pistol, vaporizing a small head-sized hole in the ceiling above. Fasaan grabbed the pistol with his hand and leveraged it away from him before grabbing him by the neck and pinning him to the ground.

"Looks like you need to go back to class, boy. Even I understand the reason they mount these weapons on the back of their hands. It's so they can't be so easily disarmed!" Fasaan squeezed the boy's neck even tighter, incensed that he'd even tried to take a shot at him. "Don't worry, though, I have to bring you back alive. So as soon as you pass out, I'll get you where you need to go."

Xard tried in vain to pull Fasaan's massive hand from his neck as his senses began to dim. Hearing the procession draw closer, he squeezed tighter in an effort to knock him out more quickly, but it was too late. Two voithos assistants walked from behind the curtain to prepare the girl for the ceremony. Xard used the distraction to swing his feet around against Fasaan's pelvis and give it a hard kick with his mining cleat before scrambling away and out through the curtain. Fasaan stood and barked commands at the two men as if he was still in charge. "Veneras business, get back to work!" Then he chased Xard back out through the curtain into the chamber just beyond.

Even the upper chorister had now filled to capacity by the time Fasaan was able to scramble after his prey. Instinctively, he resumed his guise as a voithos officer by donning his helmet and moving slowly through the balcony crowd as he hunted for Xard. On the other side of the room, on the opposite mezzanine, Xard caught his first glimpse of his mother. Instead of running, he froze and leaned against the railing, staring at her.

Fasaan tried to close the distance, but with the entrance of the academy's prelate into the apse, movement quickly became impossible. Hushed tones and the murmur of anticipation replaced the sounds of singing as the crowds increasingly turned their attention front and center. The glares from the surrounding sycophants around him told him that any further movement would jeopardize his cover. He needed to hold and track.

Shay's gaze scoured the crowds below until slowly scanning up to the mezzanine across from her. The ferocity of the eyes that stared back

293

at her startled her momentarily. "Drasha. Our little bird has returned home."

Drasha immediately tracked onto Xard. "*Heh. That's bold,*" she muttered. "Shall I go around behind him, or will you?"

"No. Wait. See his eyes? He's daring us. Whatever his move is, it's already in play. Keep scanning the crowd. He'd expect me to follow."

"You're going to have to teach me that trick before you release me, you know. You sensed he was here. What cued you into him?"

Shay intermittently turned her eyes back and forth from Xard to the crowd as she spoke. "*I... I didn't. I mean, I see him there, but whatever I'm sensing isn't him. Something else is happening. Keep your eyes open.*"

Drasha nodded toward the crowd across from them in the opposite mezzanine. "Does that voithos seem painfully out of place to you?"

Shay looked and simply rolled her eyes. "Fasaan, you fool. He could have taken a better position if he hadn't just chased him out there. Goddess, these omyym rejects are so stupid even *with* enhancements. Keep an eye on him. If things go bad, he's liable to make it worse. Just neutralize him if he does anything...unnatural."

Drasha kept her eyes locked onto Fasaan. "Say no more."

With the processional finally in place, the prelate walked onto the center dais in the academy's apse and turned toward the throngs of adherents around him. He was an elderly man, but as a voithos-ka, he was second only to the Vesni-earia at the academy and the default spiritual leader of the day's event. Dressed in an all-white flowing garment and a simple white cap, he began the ceremony by welcoming all those in the spaces around him. He cleared his throat and raised his hands for silence.

"Vesni and voithos alike, both students and veterans, we welcome you to this illumination rite. It is unusual for us to have two illumination rites so close together, but the Goddess has shone her blessing on us once again. As I look out among you who are about to take on new roles within the Order, I can say with absolute certainty that the Order—and indeed the entire future of our system—is in very skilled hands."

He coughed again and turned toward the statue of the Goddess with outstretched hands. "Since the earliest times, Goddess, you have revealed yourself as the giver of life. From your holy womb come the blessings of ages past and ages to come. Every cohort, you do for us what is impossible for us to do on our own by revealing yourself as the Great Mother. Show your favor again to these who are new to your love, by demonstrating your power in a very real way."

The prelate turned and nodded toward two voithos standing at the sides of the curtain nearest him. They exited the room momentarily before emerging again with the lifeless body of the young blonde girl on a simple golden cart. They wheeled it to the center of the room, just under the statue's open arms.

"Here lies a poor waif from Urm, plucked from the trash heaps of this forsaken planet. Unwanted. Unloved. Left as refuse on the rubbish piles of this unholy society we find ourselves in. Dead some days now, she was lost, searching for the sweet milk of our Mother."

Shay's stomach began to turn as she stared back at Xard. His face was less anger and more pain now, but he held his place and gaze. She nudged Drasha again. "Something is definitely wrong, and I think our young man over there feels it as well. I don't think he's who we're looking for, but I suspect he knows who it is. He's trying to communicate something. Keep looking."

The prelate continued rambling until the revivification time had passed before concluding. "Now my fellow sisters and brothers in the faith, I ask you to demonstrate your trust in the unfailing power of the Goddess. Trust in her great love for all the poor lost souls on all the worlds of Ayu. If her love can extend to these degenerates of Urm, then it can extend anywhere. Let this demonstration fill you with a lifetime of memory. Great Goddess! Show us your loving embrace!"

The prelate had scarcely finished his proclamation before a dark, swirling mass shot from one end of the long corridor. Tumbling in on itself as it came, the kaleidoscope of dark energy flew headlong down the center path, knocking unaware adherents to the ground on either side. It went straight for the tiny husk that lay on the simple golden cart, throwing it with such force that the girl's body hit the statue behind it with a series of nauseating *cracks* and *pops*. For a moment, there was complete silence. Then the crowd began to audibly gasp and murmur as the small child slowly emerged from under the overturned cart at the foot of the Goddess.

She walked, slowly at first, toward the crowd in front of her. It was disjointed and broken, with eyes now blackened with blood. Her ribs jutted out on one side and made an obscene crunching sound as she walked closer to the gathering crowd. One of the new Vesni candidates whispered quietly to her classmate as the macabre child shambled by. "*It's a miracle.*" The child stopped. Then it screamed in such a way that scarcely seemed human. It reached for the woman that spoke and began to force her head into the dark marble floors, striking it again and again until the woman's face collapsed.

Several of the Vesni officers jumped in to intervene as the rest of the procession went scurrying for the exits in terror. Shay and Drasha watched in horror as the small child seemed to be able to anticipate their every move—quickly dodging and launching them effortlessly. Fireworks of golden metal showered down on the congregants as the officers began to be thrown great distances into the darkened columns. Shay and Drasha struggled to get down to the action.

"Get behind the chorister and sneak around from behind! I'll take it from the front!" Shay's commands were clipped and battle-ready. Drasha asked no questions but went straight into action. They were a flawless team, but Shay felt something within her opponent that she hadn't seen or experienced before—a familiarity. It *knew* her, though she couldn't say how.

Immediately, its black gaze turned to Shay in the upper mezzanine the instant she locked onto the feeling. Shay could wait no longer; she had to act. She leapt from the balcony and rolled into a tactical dismount onto the processional floor below before picking up one of the long, golden pikes. The young girl stopped now, and slowly tottered toward Shay. It struggled to speak through its shattered windpipe, but when it spoke her name, all ambient sound seemed to leave the room.

"*Shayameeeeeeen.*" It whispered her name with contempt. The room seemed to spin for a moment as she began to lose her sense of space. She knew she was in the academy, but the atmosphere had become suffocating as the little girl began muttering heresies in long-dead

297

languages. Another Vesni officer attempted to grab the child but it turned and ripped the skin from the woman's arm in one clean piece.

The distraction was enough for Shay to momentarily regain her sense of distance. She hurled the pike at the young girl who simply caught it and used it to vault back at Shay before knocking her to the ground. It never stopped speaking in guttural intonations, though no one seemed to understand what it was saying. It simply started clawing and scratching at Shay in slow deep furrows as if to prolong the pain.

Drasha finally circled around until she came to Fasaan. "Give me the selasin!"

Fasaan just scoffed at her. "You'd better step back, girlie; this was part of my payment."

"There isn't time for this! Besides, it's not yours until you finish the contract. Now hand it over!"

"Hey. This isn't my fight, remember? You said the Vesni have the womenfolk all under control. Looks like this little situation's your arena."

Drasha leaned back with a sarcastic look. It was tough to muster given the current crisis, but her training told her sarcasm would be better than force in this instance. "Oh, right. I forget bio-enhancements are inferior to pure cybernetics. If you can't make the shot, you can't make the shot."

Drasha didn't wait for a response. She turned toward the stairs as if to walk away when Fasaan grabbed her by the elbow. "You just wait right there." Fasaan drew the selasin from his chest pouch and took easy aim at the girl. One 'holey' child coming right up. Fasaan's bio-augmentations kicked in as he tracked the little girl's jerking movements with relative ease.

click

A brief flash of light spiraled from the end of the pistol. It seemed to strike the girl, and slowed her momentarily, but her body simply reorganized the broken molecular bonds back into human tissue. Then it turned back on Fasaan and Drasha and galloped on all fours toward the stairs leading up to them. The two of them tried to move away from the stairwell landing, but it was too late. The child grabbed them both by their collars and flung them over the mezzanine railing before jumping down on top of them.

She kicked Fasaan in his side with her bare foot, causing an indentation in his microplate and sending him skittering back across the room. As his body bent back around one of the columns, the selasin spun out of his hand and into a corner as he lay unconscious. Drasha attempted to get up and run to Shay's aid, but it was of no use. The little girl grabbed Drasha by one arm and flung her with one swift movement toward the dais, knocking over a table full of sacramental elements.

The girl's black eyes returned to Shay as it began to taunt her. It pounced on her again pinning her to the ground as it sat heavily on her chest. This time it spoke its sickly words in a language she could understand. "It belongs to me. It's mine by right, you filthy whore. None of you will live to take it. When I am all that remains, then he'll see. Then he'll see."

As Xard watched the skeen infested girl continue to bloody his mother, he ached with an overwhelming sense of loss. He'd already lost his father, and now his mother was about to be torn apart before his very eyes. He hated her, but for the briefest of moments, he saw her as human. His thoughts drew him back to his childhood, of remembrances about how much his father had loved him—had loved her.

He didn't know why his father had left, but he knew that even if he hated his mother, his father did not. What separated them was something else. He knew it somehow, though he couldn't understand why. He saw her differently, without the bravado, without the false confidence. She was only human after all, and for the first time he could see her in a way he never had before—through his father's eyes.

As he watched the relentless scratching of claws and pelting of fists, for the first time in his life he understood that she needed him. In that moment he forgot about the wasted years—the time and love he'd lost because of her. He had wanted her to die, but now she was his only link to what was left of his father's memory. Like it or not, he needed her, and she needed him.

Without any thought to himself at all, Xard leapt from the balcony and landed with a *thud* behind the jittering husk. A long smear of blood from Shay painted the floor between them. It turned back toward him, expecting another piece of meat for its broken nails to sink into. The little girl's expression mirrored the one he'd felt in the mine. Rage. Unbridled rage.

Xard had no way to stop the skeen he knew was inside her. He had no weapon. He had little strength. All he had was abandon, and the longing of a boy for his father. The expression on the husk's face changed from anger to terror and back again to rage. Time seemed to move so slowly in that moment. The husk began to gallop toward him in stages, jittering as it came.

But Xard didn't care anymore. He'd lost too much already. If he was going to lose any more, it was no longer worth the fight. Even as the beast charged him, all he could think of was the week of years now lost to time. Seven planetary circuits. The empty prison his life had become with his mother. The empty existence his life had turned into without his father.

The trauma of wasted years glued him firmly in place. It was close now, even in the seeming slowness of time. Xard was defenseless, but pain had become his armor, and sorrow his shield. He could no longer feel his lips as his face ran pale, but he managed to resign himself to a final thought. "If this is where my father's choices have led me. So be it."

As it reached for him, Xard's overwhelming sense of abandonment peaked, and he surrendered himself to whatever came next.

Then it stopped.

The broken child that had been chasing him began to freeze in place. Though he didn't bother to look about, the sudden silence told him that time had somehow stopped. The husk of the little girl and the beast that polluted it now stood frozen before him. He saw it differently now. It was a pathetic creature. Powerful, but still just a shell of what it could have been. The atmosphere continued to change around him until light began to flood the darkened corridor behind him.

"Son."

The word nearly severed him in two. The pain it brought him was immediate and searing.

"Son."

There it was again. He tried to be angry at it for a moment, but its very utterance stripped him bare of all pretense and left his emotions raw and exposed. He could do nothing, not even look to where the voice had come from. He simply fell to the ground in a heap and began to sob.

"*Son.*"

The words were louder now and more emphatic. This time a strong pair of arms hoisted his limp frame up from behind and held onto him tightly, kissing the top of his head again and again. It was the desperate embrace of someone who had lost something valuable and feared losing it again if he lessened his grip. That moment seemed an eternity to Xard as memories of what once was flooded his mind.

He wasn't sure how much time had passed before the man finally let go of him long enough to turn and face him. The smooth beard and wavy locks were unmistakable.

"You're taller," he said with a tear-stained smile as he looked him up and down.

Xard's eyes welled up as he continued to stare back at the man, knowing full well who he was but not daring to hope. "Am I dead?"

He pulled Xard into a tight embrace as he spoke into his ear. "No, son. You aren't dead. In fact, this is the only version of you that *isn't* dead. But I need you to listen to me now because we don't have much time. I know you have questions, but the signal here will not hold very long."

Xard cut him off and pulled away slightly before he could continue. "Why did you leave me? Just tell me. I don't care about anything else." He made a valiant effort at retaining his composure as he spoke, but the weight of his question and the sight of his father proved too much for his child-like mind. They were all the words he could muster before sobbing again into his father's chest.

"Son, I've been here all along, right next to you. We're in the same time and place, but in different dimensions. Trust me, when this is fixed, you'll forget all about the pain you're feeling right now. But for that to happen, I need you to listen to me, so you understand what's coming next."

He nodded at the skeen as he held his son. "This creature that's hunting you, it's hidden your mother across countless planes of existence. I searched for so long... but once I was sure I'd finally

302

found her, we brought you into this world. I promised your mother that you would be what anchored us together, and you will be the reason we're all together again. But for that to happen, I need to open the portal home.

Another cataclysm is coming. Soon every world in Ayu will die. So, for us to be together again, I've had to find a way to get you both out of here before that happens. That's why I had to leave for a while. I've learned that the signal that first drew men to Ayu is a living thing. What they thought was just a message from a long dead race was the actual being they'd come to find.

That same helix signal is what allowed me to find you again now, and it will bring us home as well. Xard, do you remember what I said? What goes away, always comes back around?" Xard nodded, but all he could process was that his father had said his name properly, sacred sounds and all.

"The spiral is a metaphor for this. The path we are on makes us seem like we are very far away from each other, but we are in the same place, on different planes. Trust me, I never wanted to leave you, but the destiny of this particular Ayu made it so. I left *because* I loved you. It was the only way to save you both."

Xard listened as his father spoke, but he did little more than stare at the words coming off his lips. He could scarcely understand what his father was saying about danger and calamities. All he wanted was his father's embrace and approval. It was then that he remembered he was still in danger of being shredded by the husk. He turned to look back at it for a moment, just to reassure himself that it was still frozen in time and space.

Taigan followed his gaze. "This creature is the one who stole your mother from me. A jealous, hateful thing, it's totally consumed with power. There are others like it, but this one is their leader. Now that it knows I've found you, things will only get more dangerous for you.

With your birth, I've anchored the plane you are on. Once I anchor the other end, we can all be together again. Until then, I'm going to move some relics into your path that will offer you some protection and help you to better understand the nature of the universe.

Study them closely. They'll help you understand the signal and follow what I'm doing if you get discouraged. Just be patient. Remember the moro's tapestry? Many will speak to you in ways they don't speak to others."

A sudden sense of slipping time washed over Xard as his father began to stare back at the creature. "I wish we had longer. I know you have more questions, but trust me, those answers will come." He pulled him close once more and whispered in his ear as the slow creep of time began to pick up pace again.

Xard let out a muffled cry as he buried his face into his father's chest to hide the embarrassment of tears. "Don't leave me here. I don't want to be alone."

Taigan held him tightly as he whispered into his ear. "If you hear one thing I'm saying, Xard, it's that I love you and you're not alone. Listen to the signal. It will remind you of me until I return for you. When this is all over, I promise that every moment that's been stolen from us will be restored. Now go. Your mother needs you now, whether she knows it or not." Then he kissed him on the cheek and he was gone.

Then it began to move.

The husk's blood-blackened eyes spoke terror again, but this time Xard didn't care about the beast. He'd held his father for the briefest of moments in an ecstasy of childhood regained, only to have it slip away again before his eyes. The pain of his jarring departure tore a

304

new and angry void inside of him, and he vented the rage and loss of it right back at the husk. The power of that tremendous vacuum suddenly burst out of him as his scream sent a shock wave of unseen power from his lungs, sending the broken girl tumbling backward through the air.

His tormented scream carried his pain in supernatural echoes throughout the room, compelling all who heard it into a spontaneous weeping. His empty arms had become a vacuous testament to a child's loss at the hands of another. Only this time, Xard knew where to place the blame. He saw the husk now for what it was. It was a thief and he despised it.

The husk stood and began speaking again. Though he couldn't understand the dark tongue, he knew the words were malevolent. When he heard his father's own name tumble off its lips, he became incensed. Courage began to course through his veins again as he spit his own words back at her. "That name belongs to *me*! You're not even fit to speak it, you jealous little girl!"

It screeched back at his words and ran at him one more time, but he'd become enraged now at its very presence. His thoughts turned again to his father, hoping against hope that this new attack would yield another few moments with him. Instead, his body began to tingle, from the top of his head and down into his hands as if they had fallen asleep. The tingling quickly grew stronger and formed en masse around his arms as it approached. Xard threw up his hands toward the beast's face and felt the energy in his arms suddenly leap off of him.

Two broad beams of sea green energy spiraled out of Xard's hands and hit the husk full force in its chest. The young girl vaporized immediately into a puff of carbon dust leaving only the skeen in its wake. It remained frozen in space under the beam's immense energy as the light began to bend around the formless creature. Xard kept his thoughts on his father as he watched the dark energy writhe under the molecular furnace of quantum energy. Xard could sense the shredding skeen trying to reknit itself, but with no matter to reconstitute it, it began to dissolve under the continuous blast until it was no more.

Then, just as quickly as the energy had started, it ended. The girl, the skeen, and even his pain were now gone. In the surreal moments between his imminent death and his present victory, he'd shed the painful skin of regret, and replaced it somehow with hope for something better. For a moment, light seemed to distort and warp around where the skeen had once been, but it slowly returned to normal as he hurried to be at his mother's side.

29 – REVELATIONS

Shay, who had been thrown onto her back, now scurried away from him on her elbows for a second as he approached. The power of the preceding moment still vibrated over him as he reached down to help her sit up before kneeling next to her. "Are you alright?"

The words washed over Shay with a familiar resonance, as if Tai's own voice had rumbled out of him for a moment. The unexpected sound instantly put her at ease. She half-laughed as she spoke. "I'm a pretty sturdy skika, in case you didn't know that already. I should ask the same of you. I knew you were up to something, but this is nothing like I expected."

He helped her to her feet as she leaned on him to avoid putting too much pressure on one of her ankles as she walked. It was eerily silent now, with only the faint rustling of the injured making any sound. "Son, why are you here? What have you done?" Shay caught her own words before proceeding. "I-I don't mean that in an accusing way. I mean how did you do what you just did? What did you even do? Is it gone?"

"Yes, mother, it's gone. Come on. I need you to see something." He helped his mother hobble past the scattered processional debris toward where Drasha had been thrown. She too, sat up and collected herself, unaware of what had just transpired. Shay motioned for her to give her a moment and then continued to lean on Xard until they reached the small annex where he'd hidden the immersion drive. Shay sat down on one of the unbroken crates of sacramental wine as she nursed her wounded ribs.

307

He plucked the immersion drive from behind the small statue and checked the readings. It had worked. "Mom, I've known since before I left that the Order's built on lies. The voithos-moro himself proved it to me when they sent me to him. He has an entire cache of relics hidden there in the sanctuary.

The only reason he didn't discipline me was because he wanted me to help him recover more relics for his private collection... same as my father did. There was no way to win. If I refused, I would have been disciplined. If I stayed, I would've ended up digging up relics in the high plains the same as my father and you'd have hated me even more."

"Son." She paused for a moment in exasperation. "My goal was never to hurt you. If anything, it was *him* I meant to hurt. When I see you, I see him. I feel him. Goddess, sometimes just being in the same house as you makes me feel like he is in the next room. Don't you see, boy? When your father left, you brought the pain of it right to my face every day. I could never heal while you were with me."

"But that's not my fault!"

Shay raised her hands to stay his protests. "I know that, but it was my job to prepare you to move on when you reached the age. When I couldn't manage the emotional toll, I just turned it all off. I realize that becoming cold only served me, but I did what I had to. The Vesni are strong, not imperfect. I hope you can learn to forgive that weakness in time."

"Do you forgive my father?"

Shay became exasperated again and sighed in protest to his question. "Son. The man *left* me. He left *us*. He fell in love with the work and out of love with me. There's no one left alive to forgive."

Xard stepped back away from her. "You're wrong. I saw him. Just now. He talked to me. He never left us. He said he's been trying to get back to us, or get us back to him or something. Something about there being hundreds or thousands of us and he's been trying to find the real ones. I can't really remember. It all happened so fast." Xard fumbled with the immersion drive by scrolling it to where the event took place and brought up a small 3D image of it.

Shay studied the boy's face as he did. He became frustrated as he scrolled back and forth at the point where the husk had charged him, but other than a brief flash of light, there was nothing but Xard's scream and the beams of energy coming from his hands on the recording. "It was right here! This is where it happened, I swear!"

Shay managed to reach out and put her arm on his shoulder. "Son. I can't even begin to understand what's happened here. No one could. Sometimes things happen that defy our explanation. You say you talked to your father. I have no reason to doubt that you actually believe what you say, given what happened afterward. Nothing like this has ever happened at an illumination rite. It defies any explanation that isn't divine."

"Divine? You still think this is the Goddess? Oh, trust me, I *know* what happened." Xard closed the drive and shook it at his mother. The Vesni goons here have been harvesting half-dead kids off the street from Sentia and faking it like your Goddess is bringing them back from the dead! Who knows how long it's been happening? It's all fake, mother, and I've got it all right here."

She shot back at him. "And yet, here you are wielding 'divine' powers, claiming to have seen visions from beyond, and talking to those long departed. Does that not seem unusual to you?" She calmed her voice after the strain on her ribs made her flinch. "Son! You just fired some kind of, of, quantum energy from your bare hands! No selasin. No weapon of any kind. You *became* a living weapon just now!

Nothing like this has been seen or heard of in a thousand years. Does that seem like a false religion to you? You want to call it a fraud. Fine.

But first, you should consider whether or not the Goddess allowed this abomination to appear just so she could demonstrate her love to us through you. How else could you have done it? It defies explanation, and yours leaves even more questions than answers. If anything, you just proved the Goddess' reality to everyone who saw it."

Xard paused to consider the one question he hadn't yet asked himself: What if the Order was actually based in some truth that they just didn't fully understand? What if destroying it outright only served to kill the divinity it held at its core? "I-I don't know. I didn't do anything really. I just needed my dad." He paused and stared at the drive for a moment before flopping his weight against a wall.

"The selasin is meant to be a symbol of the Goddess' own quantum power. It's why the weapon is only given to those who are elite among the Vesni. But you? You *as a male*, somehow physically harnessed it to defeat a quantum foe." Shay was incredulous. "There isn't even a precedent for this. It will take the Order decades to pick this apart to try and understand it." A sudden look of concern washed over her face.

"When word of this gets out, the Order will probably come looking for you in earnest. If you're lucky, they'll just want to study you indefinitely. If you're not..." Shay paused to consider the implications. "Let's just say, heretical objects tend to get swept away pretty quickly. I'll do what I can to get this incident covered over for a time, but the damage here is pretty extensive."

"Wait. Why do you care? Why cover it?"

"Son, if what you say is true, then more's happening here than we have time to process. It won't be safe for us to be found together until we figure out what the outcome of this will be. Without any recording of the event, the Order will be forced to accept whatever the witnesses saw. I know you won't like it, but I can convince them that you died trying to defend the Order. If nothing else, it'll buy us some time."

Xard held the slender black immersion drive out in his palm. "I planned to just expose the Vesni for being liars. If I release this to the omyym like I wanted to, you're saying everyone will know I survived and come after me to experiment on me?"

"I'm saying it's a possibility. Look, son, I'm just as lost as you are right now about what the hell just happened. All I'm saying is that maybe we need some time to figure out what's really going on before you go about destroying the foundation we're all standing on."

Shay took his hand in hers and slowly closed his fingers around the slender drive. "I wanted something different for us. This didn't turn out at all like I'd planned," she sighed. "What I'm about to say, I don't say lightly. This may not be the path I would have chosen, but it's a path that's clearly choosing us, and in supernatural ways. If this *is* your father's work, then I also need time to process what's going on before the Vesni think to come looking for you.

Look, you're strong. A lot stronger than most give you credit for. If any viko was ready to become a voithos, it's you. I've seen it—many have. But I've also seen how big your head can get. A man's pride can destroy him, which is why I've worked *so hard* to keep you in your place. When the time is right, we can meet again, but I won't force you. You've earned that much today. Until then, hang onto this, and don't let it out of your sight."

Xard's eyes widened as she gently pushed the immersion drive back toward him. "You need to take this and run. If anyone discovers you have this, you'll become a very large target. What you've done, what you've achieved here? It's indescribable. That's why I'm trusting you for now. When the time comes, if there's a path forward for us, I'll find a way to reach out to you, agreed?"

Xard's eyes welled up at the long overdue praise from his mother. He smiled and nodded at her, unsure of what he should do next.

Just then, Drasha stumbled into the room nursing her own wounds. The move startled Shay, and she immediately donned the role of Xard's interrogator. "Now tell me where you put the aurum before I have to flay it out of you!" Shay tapped her foot and looked menacingly at him. "Don't look at Drasha! I'm the one asking the questions right now."

Xard instantly understood that it was a game, and he played it to the hilt. "I-I-I'm sorry! I had it, and then I lost it. I mean. I didn't spend it. It's for the Mitera! I was going to make a headdress and I heard they have good forges here for cyptum, and, uhm, I thought a headdress that symbolized the union of Kael and Urm would be something unique."

"Oh please, boy. You expect us to believe that?" Shay continued peppering him with her fake rage until Drasha stole her attention.

"Mistress, you may want to ask him about this as well. I'd love to hear how this fits into the story." Drasha passed the modified grappler to Shay.

Shay smirked as she studied it. "It seems our veneras friend wasn't able to keep his grip on it after all. Perfect. Which leaves the question of how my quantum weapon core ended up on Urm, lodged in this, this, I don't even know what this is. A mining gun? With a grapple hook? It's the most ridiculous thing I've ever seen."

Xard continued with the charade. "Mom. I knew I wasn't allowed to handle a Vesni weapon, so I read through the ancient laws before I did it. It clearly said voithos are forbidden from using a 'Vesni selasin', so I retrofitted the core into something new, so I wouldn't be breaking the law. I was trying to do right, but I figured since the project was expensive and I had all that aurum, I just wanted a way to keep it safe."

Shay laughed sarcastically. "You little kata. You have an answer for everything. Drasha, would you mind leaving us for a moment while I show this little whelp what 'quibbling the law' means?"

Drasha nodded. "I'll go check on the survivors and see if anyone else knows what's going on."

After Drasha had left the room, Shay continued her tirade as she unloaded the quantum cartridge from the weapon. Once she was certain Drasha was out of earshot, she pulled him close before speaking again and tucked the quantum core into Xard's front pocket.

"You're going to need this wherever you end up now. Everyone knows I don't carry mine anymore, so no one will come looking for it. Even if they do, I'll just tell them the core was destroyed before I had a chance to retrieve it. Now you need to go."

Her words came out like ice.

Xard leaned in to give her a hug, but she pushed him away. His face fell white at being rebuffed, but she persisted. "No. I need you to hate me right now. You need a reason to run, because if you ever come back to me before we have this figured out, your life will be as good as spent."

Rage flashed across his face again as he tried to force his arms around her, but she simply swept his feet and sent him onto the wine-soaked ground. "Go. If you want love, find your father, and when you do, send him to me. If what you say is true, you won't find him by clinging to my neck. Until then, I'll be waiting." Then she picked him up from the ground by his collar and shoved him out through the back door.

30 – Decisions

Xard found himself alone again as he wandered back out the way he'd come in. He paused for a moment and spoke into the air around him before making his way back to the moat. "If you guys are still watching, I sure could use a ride about now." Xard walked out through the closet opening and into the moat only to find Ygger and Kharik already waiting there in a raft.

"General!" Kharik whisper-shouted to him from the raft. A sense of relief washed over Xard as he saw the two slowly bring the raft in closer, but Xard couldn't wait that long. He jumped into the flowing coolant and swam to meet them before being dragged into the raft.

"We saw the whole thing! We were gonna just see how you did, but when all that fighting started it was the best holo we'd ever watched! Shyne is still watching it right now, general. So, did you do it? Did you finish the mission?"

Xard flopped back into the raft as Ygger triggered the engines to move them back to the egress point. "Yes, captain, I got it." Xard patted the pocket which held both the drive and the quantum core. "But now they gave me more work to do, so I need to think about what to do next. Do you mind if I stay with you at the mine for a while until I figure it out?"

"That sounds like a terrible idea clean-shirt. None of us are staying in the mines, at least not now that we have the money to automate it. I've convinced Shyne we might do better out on Carcinia. I told her they have issues with wandering orphans there, and she got all excited about it. As for me, what's not to like about living in a capitalist kingdom rife with electronics to hack?

***

Shay returned to find Drasha excoriating Fasaan. He simply held his hands over his ears as he tried to block her out. "Enough already! Can't a man even wake up without a bunch of hens clucking in his ears." He paused to survey the scene. "Damn. You girls really know how to throw a party. What a mess." He paused as he saw that Shay was holding the makeshift grappler. "Hey, that belongs to me."

Shay simply smirked at him. "The deal was you got to keep the quantum weapon *if* you could hold onto it. Apparently sleeping on the job was more important."

"Bosca! I earned that weapon," he retorted.

"Well, considering you didn't actually retrieve the boy, you're lucky we haven't killed you ourselves. We did that part. He's bound up in that antechamber over there. As for you, well, your efforts were at least... memorable.

We'll let you keep that veneras title for now. You might be useful again in the future. Until then, take care of that back, you may find yourself on it a lot. Come on, Drasha, let's check on the prelate before we head back. Maybe he can tell us how some little girl managed to wreck an illumination rite."

***

Shyne greeted Xard with a warm embrace. He held onto her for a moment, lost in the comfort it suddenly brought him. It was at that moment that he began to understand the orphans' affection for her. Her love was truly unconditional and welcoming regardless of status or skill.

316

She loved them all, and they loved her. "I watched it all, young one, and Mama Shyne knows how to fix things. Don't you have any worries now. I know hows to make things right with the Vesni girls. I made some calls. I sends them something special, yes? Come, we have much to plan! Lots to discuss."

***

Shay had no sooner finished talking with the prelate than one of the Vesni officers approached her. "The young viko you said was restrained in the antechamber? He's gone. There's no sign of him." Shay feigned her disgust well this time. "Damn! One more thing to chase after before we can get off this miserable rock. He'll never survive with that wound! Idiot!"

Drasha took the bait. "Hold on, Shay. Was he injured?"

"Yes, the damned thing ripped his side wide open, didn't you see all that blood? Come on, he can't have gotten very far if he's bleeding out. If we hurry, we can recapture him and seal that wound."

Drasha took Shay aside. "Wait, Shay," she whispered. "This could work out exactly right for you. It doesn't matter how convoluted his story sounded, it's believable childhood foolishness. Think about it. A young viko goes to Urm to craft a unique headdress for the Mitera only to find himself in the middle of some kind of terrorist attack on a Vesni ceremony?"

Shay followed along with her line of reasoning. "But what about the weapon?"

"That's just it. We use his silly story about misinterpreting the scriptures. It removes intent. In the end he stops the terrorist but is killed in the process. No one has to deal with the untidy breach in the law if the lawbreaker is dead. It clears your name!"

"Hmm. It could work. With the illegal birthing op shut down and the death cultist eliminated, maybe we've done all we can actually do

317

here. Come on, I need time to think this through more thoroughly. We can discuss it on the way back to the shuttle. We'll need an air-tight story before setting down. The academy's probably capable of cleaning up what's left of the mess here."

Shay and Drasha paid their farewells to the prelate and arrived back at their shuttle only to find that the hatch had been left ajar. Drasha drew her sidearm as they entered the darkened interior. As soon as they triggered the lights, they saw it—a small lev-sled resting in one corner. Drasha walked over and cautiously popped the top hatch to reveal that it was filled to the brim with aurum half ingots. Drasha's eyes widened like saucers. "Shay, the Goddess herself has done this! This, this is impossible. Is that?" Drasha struggled for words.

Shay herself wondered about the meaning of it all. They had recovered everything. Every evidence of failure had now been removed from her life. With the aurum now mysteriously back in hand, they would go back as heroes. Of that, there was no doubt. Drasha continued to ramble and stumble over herself in elation and wonder at how it could've come to pass. Shay simply looked on and smiled, for the briefest of moments, wondering if Xard had somehow made this possible.

***

Xard spent the rest of his day nursing his wounds with his friends. He smiled knowing that somehow, his course had changed for the better. He'd shed the ugliness of who he had been, and who he was becoming, by that one moment with his father. It was empowering. He still didn't understand the depth of who he was yet, but he knew who he *wasn't*, and for now, that was enough.

He stared for a moment at his empty palms, remembering briefly what had happened. If he knew anything about the Vesni, it was that they had an innate gift for lies. By now, he reasoned, they'd already found a way to ignore what really happened and made up a story about it. It wouldn't surprise him at all if it was never even brought up again. But he knew the truth, at least in part.

He reasoned that religion was just humanity's attempt at explaining something supernatural. They had built whole philosophies around it. The Vesni, the kosonor, the gharsa, it didn't matter. They were all trying to stick their hands into the same mysterious box and attempt to explain what was inside by touch alone.

But this time was different. Xard had seen something with his own eyes—something supernatural—something *personal*. He knew that his experience contained some measure of truth, but he still couldn't fully understand it or figure out how it applied to him. Nevertheless, it gave him focus and purpose, if only for the mystery of it. The vacant space in his heart had been swept clean by the experience, but it was still empty nonetheless. If his father *was* somehow a part of it all, he needed to find him again if only to briefly refill it just one more time.

Ygger interrupted his thoughts with another attempt to muss up his hair. "You're missing the party. You look like you need a refill on your sweet drink. Come on, live a little! You're the reason we're even able to have this little shindig. Or has the Vesni spy game made you a boring chorma already?"

"I'm not a chorma," Xard protested with a laugh.

"Well then come on!" Ygger grabbed Xard by the arm and dragged him out into the main equipment hall which had been turned into an impromptu hall of festivities. It was an unusual choice to Xard owing to the fact that it had a wide window overlooking the mine's recent accident site. "Look. It was obvious to anyone watching you on the live feed that if your mission was to really just 'bypass security', you did all that and then some. Since the last shuttle to Kael left hours ago without you on it, I'm guessing it's the 'then some' that probably has you here mingling with us useful idiots." Ygger slapped him on the back with a laugh.

Xard forced a smile and tried to play it off. "Yeah. I need to set up a new operation somewhere a little further away from the Vesni. There are more to the relics than they let on about. I need to find a place where I can do my own research and stop relying on what the Order spoon-feeds everyone. If I can get my hands on some of the new relics before the Order has a chance to hide them, I might actually find what I'm looking for."

Ygger toasted Xard silently, took a long gulp of his sweet-drink, and motioned toward the stars through the now blasted-out ceiling of the mine. "If it's relics you want, the unclaimed ones are still floating out there in the reach. Come with us to Carcinia. Lots of black-market reliquary trading happens there. Might be a good chance to get your hands on some if you can keep a low profile."

Xard nodded but didn't say much else as the party continued around him. He just kept staring out into space through the massive opening above. He didn't like the idea of leaving, but his new world was already moving away from him. "What goes away always comes back around."

The words never made sense to him before, but now they brought him a strange new comfort. If he was ever to find his place again, or discover who he was really meant to be, it meant leaving again. How far, he didn't know. How soon, he would soon find out.